CONTEMPORARY AMERICAN FICTION

AN EVENING PERFORMANCE

George Garrett is Henry Hoyas Professor of Creative
Writing at the University of Virginia. He is the author of
twenty-three books, six of which are collections of
short stories.

AN EVENING PERFORMANCE

George Garrett

PENGUIN BOOKS

PENGUIN BOOKS
Viking Penguin Inc., 40 West 23rd Street,
New York, New York 10010, U.S.A.
Penguin Books Ltd, Harmondsworth,
Middlesex, England
Penguin Books Australia Ltd, Ringwood,
Victoria, Australia
Penguin Books Canada Limited, 2801 John Street,
Markham, Ontario, Canada L3R 1B4
Penguin Books (N.Z.) Ltd, 182–190 Wairau Road,
Auckland 10, New Zealand

First published in the United States of America
by Doubleday & Company, Inc. 1985
Published in Penguin Books 1986
Reprinted by arrangement with
Doubleday & Company, Inc.
Copyright © George Garrett, 1985
All rights reserved

LIBRARY OF CONGRESS CATALOGING IN PUBLICATION DATA
Garrett, George P., 1929–
An evening performance.
(Contemporary American fiction)
I. Title. II. Series.
PS3557.A72E9   1986   813′.54   86-12357
ISBN 0 14 00.9208 0

Printed in the United States of America by
R. R. Donnelley & Sons Company, Harrisonburg, Virginia
Set in Caslon

This book, representing work done during all of my adult life, is dedicated, first of all, to my wife, Susan, who has fully shared that life with me. And to our children—William, George, and Alice. And to my farflung blood kin and true friends, in praise and thanksgiving for those among them who are alive, in honor and memory of those who are dead.

> What child is this
> wounded and smiling
> armed with a new shiny knife
> and flowers for an early grave
> who wears my face for his own?
>
> "Familiar Riddle"

Trouth is put doun, resoun is holden fable;
Vertu hath now no dominacioun;
Pitee exiled, no man is merciable.
Thrugh coveitise is blent discrecioun
The world hath mad a permutacion
Fro right to wrong, fro truth to fikilnesse,
That al is lost for lak of stedfastnesse.

CHAUCER
–"Lak of Stedfastnesse"

CONTENTS

III. From COLD GROUND WAS MY BED LAST NIGHT

IV. From A WREATH FOR GARIBALDI

V. NEW AND UNCOLLECTED

PREFACE

This gathering is meant to be a representative selection (no more and no less) of short stories, old and new, previously published in book form or so far uncollected, covering roughly thirty years of time during which, among other things, I have been writing and publishing short fiction. It does not claim to be collected or even close to complete. Without counting, I would guess that a little less than half of my published stories are here. I have hopes that there will be newer and maybe better ones before I am done.

By and large I have left these stories alone, just as they were and are, with only a lick and a promise of revision where I felt that something, large or small, did the story an injustice and needed to be fixed. I probably wouldn't write some of them nowadays. And, as I have changed and the world has changed all around me, I might not be able to write some of them anymore. Stories, like poems I think, even the slightest and most lighthearted of them, are gifts. I took them gratefully at the time and I stand by them one and all now, though with a full awareness that many are less than they might be, and none, not one, is as good as it ought to be. But all are as good as they can be or, anyway, the best that I can make them. I know their flaws and limits well enough, and I hope to do better and differently in the future. Meantime, this is what I have and who I am.

Although a few of these stories first found a place in national, commercial magazines, most of them were at home in literary magazines and quarterlies. That seems appropriate to me; for, as writer, I, too, have mostly been at home in literary magazines and quarterlies. No apologies for that. It was and is my pride to have played the game in that league. Not many people know these stories, so I am pleased that they are here granted a sort of a second chance, a replay not quite instant, but soon enough in a lifetime. Still, all pride and arrogance to the contrary, I have to confess (gladly) that there are a few readers and writers who have been faithful and encouraging to me from first to now; and I thank them kindly and deeply for that. We are never nearly as alone and lonesome as we sometimes like to imagine that we are. "We are," as John Berryman wrote in *Homage to Mistress Bradstreet*, "on each other's hands who care."

Sir Robert Carey, a cousin to Queen Elizabeth and a wonderfully vital man whom I came to know a little while writing two novels set in his own times, wrote one of the very few autobiographies of that period. He began it, as was the ancient custom, with a short prayer. From which I would like to borrow a line to end this prefatory note; for in a sense this gathering of stories is a different kind of autobiography. Here is what he, a very old man rehearsing his own story, wrote: "Though my weakness be such and my memory so short, as I have not the abilities to express them as I ought to do, yet, Lord, be pleased to accept of this sacrifice of praise and thanksgiving. . . ."

George Garrett
Charlottesville, Virginia

Prologue

AN EVENING
PERFORMANCE

Let brotherly love continue.
Be not forgetful to entertain strangers; for
thereby some have entertained angels unawares.

HEBREWS 13: 1–2

AN EVENING
PERFORMANCE

FOR SEVERAL WEEKS, maybe a month or so, there she stood, a plump woman in a sequined one-piece bathing suit, poised on a stylized tower which rose into the very clouds, like Jacob's dreamy ladder, with here and there around it a few birds in tense swift V's, and below, far, far below, there was a tub, flaming and terrible, into which she was surely going to plunge. Beneath in fiery letters was printed: ONE OF THE FABULOUS WONDERS OF MODERN TIMES/STELLA THE HIGH DIVER/SHE DIVES ONE HUNDRED FEET/INTO A FLAMING CAULDRON.

These posters had appeared mysteriously one Monday morning, and they were everywhere, on store windows, on the sides of buildings, on telephone and light poles, tacked to green trees; and you can believe they caused a stir. The children on the way to school (for it was just the beginning of the school year) bunched around them in excited clusters—staring at her buxom magnificence, wondering at her daring—and buzzed about it all day long like a hive of disturbed bees. By midmorning grumbling adults were ripping the posters down from windows and buildings, and a couple of policemen went up and down the main street and some of the side streets, taking them off telephone and light poles. But there were so many! And it was such a mystery. Lurid and unsettling as a blast of trumpets, they had come nevertheless in the night as silently as snow.

It would be later, much later, that the night counterman at the Paradise Diner on the outskirts of town, beyond the last glare of filling stations and the winking motels and the brilliant inanity of used-car lots—where, no matter how carnival-colorful with flags and whirligigs, no matter how brightly lit, the rows of cars stood lonesome like sad wooden horses from some carousel set out to graze—it would be later when he would remember that the man, the angry little man with the limp, had stopped there for coffee that same night that the posters had appeared.

In spite of all effort, a few of the posters remained, tantalizing in their vague promise of a future marvel, teased by the wind and the weather, faded by the still summer-savage sun and the first needling rains of autumn, the red letters blurring and dribbling away, fuzzy now as if they had been written by a shaking finger in something perishable like blood. Talked about for a while—and there were those who swore they remembered seeing such a thing and certainly those who had heard of it, a subject of some debate and even a little sermonizing in certain of the more fundamentalist churches where amusement is, by definition, nearly equivalent to vice—the promise faded with the posters. There were few who hoped that Stella would ever dive there, fewer still who believed in her coming. It seemed, after all, only another joke of some kind, pointless, mirthless, and in a strange way deeply distressing.

Then one evening in late October with the weather now as cool and gray as wash water the truck came and parked in the field by the old Fairgrounds. At first it was nothing to take much notice of, merely a big, battered truck and pretty soon an Army surplus squad tent, sprouting (sagging in a most unmilitary, careless way) like a khaki mushroom beside it.

And there were people.

There were three of them. There was the man, gimpy (his left leg might have been wooden), his face puckered and fierce and jowly and quizzical like a Boston bulldog, his eyes glazed and almost lightless like the little button eyes of a doll; fierce and tired he seemed, spoke in mutters, showing from time to time a ruined mouth with teeth all awry and at all angles like an old fence; and sometimes around the town, shopping for groceries at the Supermarket, once taking a load of dirty clothes to the Washeteria, buying cigarettes and aspirins and comic books at the drugstore, and busily sorting out bolts and nuts and screws and clamps and brackets at the hardware store (for what?), he talked to himself, a harsh, steady, and indecipherable monotone. There was the little girl, a frail thing made entirely of glazed china with altogether unlikely eyes and hair as bright as new pennies, like a shower of money, richly brushed and shining and worn long to her waist. She wore white always, starched and ironed and fabulously clean; and the women had to wonder how her mother (?)—the woman anyhow—living in a sagging tent and a worn-out truck managed that. The little girl was heard to answer to the name of Angel and did not play with the other children who sometimes, after school, gathered in shrill clots around the tent and the truck to stare until the terrible man came out, limping, waving a pick handle, and chased them away.

The woman was an equal curiosity. She was short, broad-shouldered, wide-hipped, huge-handed, sturdy as a man. Her hair, dyed redder than you'd care to believe, was cut in a short bowl. She appeared to be in early middle age, though she might easily have been old—she wore such savage makeup, wild, accented, slanted eyes, a mouth of flame, and always two perfectly round spots of red like dying roses on her high cheekbones. Still, she had a smile that was a glory and she smiled often. She was not heard to speak to anyone and when she was talked to she smiled and stared, uncomprehending. It was not long before everyone knew she was a mute; it was proved when she was seen to communicate with the man, her hands as swift as wings and not a word.

The truth came out like a jack-in-the-box in a week or so. One fine morning the man had unloaded an enormous pile of boards and pipes beside the truck, and by noon he had erected in the center of the field what seemed to be the beginnings of a good-size drilling derrick.

"For oil?" That was the joke around town before a few promi-
nent men and a policeman went out there in cars, parked at the
edge of the field, and walked to where he was working. He paid
them no mind at all as they straggled toward him, and, as they
drew near, they could see that he was sweat-soaked and working
at his task with an unbecoming fury, all in hasty, jerky gestures
like a comedian in a silent movie. He did not stop his work until
they spoke to him.

"What are you trying to do here?" the policeman said.

The man spat and put his heavy wrench on the ground.

"What the hell does it look like I'm doing?" he said and someone giggled. "I'm putting up the tower."

"What kind of a tower?"

"The tower for Stella," the man said, sighing between his
teeth. "How can she dive without a tower? That's logic, ain't
it?"

"Oh," the policeman said. "You got to have a license to put on
any kind of a exhibition around here."

The lame man lowered his head, seemed to shrink and sag like
a slowly deflating balloon, and muttered to himself. Finally he
raised his head and looked at them, and they could see the tears
glisten in his eyes.

"How much do the license cost?" he said.

"Twenty-five dollars."

"We don't have to do the dive," the man said. "We got a lots of
tricks. I can put up just a little bit of a trapeze and Angel can do
things that would make your eyes pop out of your head. If worse
come to worst we don't have to build nothing at all. If I have to I
can stand on the back end of the truck and swallow swords and
fire and Angel and Stella can dance."

"Any kind of exhibition costs twenty-five dollars for the license."

The man shrugged and hung his head again.

"Don't you have the money?"

He shook his head, but still would not look at them.

"Well, what the hell?" the policeman said. "You better take
that tower down and get on out of town. We got a law—"

"Wait a minute," a merchant said. "You aim to sell tickets, don't you?"

The man nodded.

"If you put on the high dive, I reckon you may get as many as a thousand to see it, counting kids and all. What kind of a price do you charge?"

When the man looked up again, he had his ruined smile for them all. "Two bits a head," he said. "We got a roll of tickets printed up and everything."

The merchant made a hasty calculation. "All right," he said. "I'll tell you what I'll do. I'll get your license for you and you cut me in for half of what you take."

"*Half?*" the man said. "Half is too much. That's a dirty shame. It ain't hardly worth it for half. Besides, the high dive is dangerous."

"Take it or leave it."

"All right," the man said. "I can't do nothing but take it."

"Tell you what else I'll do," the merchant said. "I got a nigger boy helps me down to the store. I'll send him to help you put that tower up. How soon can you put on the show?"

"Tomorrow evening if the weather's good."

While they were standing there talking the woman had come across the field from the tent and stood holding the hand of the little girl, smiling her wonderful smile. She seemed to have not the least notion of what was going on, but as they walked away they saw that she had turned on the man, unsmiling, and as he shook and shook his head, her hands flashed at him like the wings of a wild bird in a cage.

All that day the tower grew and by noon of the next day it was finished. It stood not nearly so tall as the cloud- and bird-troubled structure on the posters, but menacingly high, a rickety skeleton that swayed a little in the light breeze. All the way to the top there was rope ladder and on the top a small platform with an extended plank for a diving board. At the foot of the tower the lame man had created a large wooden and canvas tank into which he and the woman and the Negro who worked for the merchant poured buckets of water, drawn from a public spigot, all afternoon, until it was filled about to the depth of a tall man. There was a large GI can of gasoline nearby. The lame man rigged up a string of colored lights and two large searchlights intended to focus on the diver at the top. He set up a card table at the corner where the main road turned into the Fairgrounds. He put up a few of the posters on the poles and the side of the truck, and by midafternoon everything was ready.

Then the weather turned. The wind came from the north, steady, and with it a thin rain like cold needles. The tower moved with the wind and shone with wet. The woman and the little girl stayed in the tent. The lame man stood at the card table, with a newspaper on his head to keep off the rain, waiting for the first customers to arrive.

Just at dark the merchant arrived. There was a good crowd, equal at least to their expectation, gathered in a ring around the tower, standing in raincoats and underneath umbrellas, silently waiting.

"Well," the merchant said, "it looks like we did all right irregardless of the weather."

"Yeah," the man replied. "Except she don't want to do it."

"What's that?"

"I mean it's too risky at a time like this."

"You should have thought of that before," the merchant said. "If you don't go through with it now, no telling what might happen."

"Oh, we'll give them a show," the man said. "I'll swallow swords if I have to. We'll do something."

"She's got to dive," the merchant said. "Or else you got a case of fraud on your hands."

After that the two of them went into the tent. Inside the woman was sitting on an Army cot, wrapped up in a man's bathrobe, and the little girl was beside her. It was cold and damp and foul in the tent. The merchant winced at the smell of it.

"Tell her she's got to do it."

The lame man waved his hands in deft code to her. She moved

her hands slowly in reply and, smiling, shook her head. Outside the people had started to clap their hands in unison.

"She says it's too dangerous. It's dangerous anyhow, but on a night like this—"

"Come on," the merchant said. "It can't be that bad. There must be a trick to it."

The lame man shook his head.

"No, sir," he said. "It ain't no trick to it. It's the most dangerous activity in the world. She don't like to do it one bit."

"That's a fine thing," the merchant said. "Just fine and dandy. If she don't like it, why the hell do you put up posters and build towers and sell tickets, that's what I'd like to know."

"Somebody's got to do it. If it wasn't us, it would just have to be somebody else."

"Oh my God!" the merchant said, throwing up his hands. "Now you listen here. If you don't get the show going in five minutes, I'll have you all slapped right in the jail. Five minutes."

He opened the flap of the tent and went out into the dark and the chill rain. He could hear the little girl crying and the lame man muttering to himself.

Almost at once the lame man followed him. He started up the truck and turned on all the lights. Then the woman appeared in her outsize bathrobe and wearing now a white bathing cap. She walked to the foot of the tower and leaned against it, one hand clutching a rung of the rope ladder, smiling.

"Ladies and gentlemen," the lame man said. "You are about to witness a performance that defies the laws of nature and science. This little lady you see before you is fixing to climb to the top of the tower. There, at that terrible altitude, she's going to stand and dive into a flaming tank of water that's barely six feet deep. You won't believe your eyes. It's a marvel of the modern world. 'How does she do it?' some of you will ask. Now some show people will give you all kinds of fancy reasons for how and why they do their work. They'll tell you they learned it from the wise men of the East. They'll tell you about magicians and dreams and the Secrets of the Ancient World. Not us. The way that Stella does this dive is skill, skill pure and simple. When

Stella climbs that tower and dives into the flames she's doing something anyone could do who has the heart and the skill and the nerve for it. That's what's different and special about our show. When Stella sails through the air and falls in the fire and comes up safe and smiling, she is the living and breathing proof of the boundless possibility of all mankind. It should make you happy. It should make you glad to be alive."

"Let's get on with it," someone shouted, and the crowd hollered and whistled.

"All right, we won't give you no special buildup," the lame man continued in an even voice. "We just say, there it is. See for yourself. And without further ado I give you Stella, the high diver."

He touched her. She removed the bathrobe and, opening her arms wide, showed herself, pale and stocky in the tight bathing suit with the winking sequins. Then she turned and began to climb the rope ladder. It was a perilous ascent and the ladder swung with the weight of her. When she reached the top, she rested, kneeling on the platform; then she stood up and unhitched the rope ladder and it fell away in a limp curve like a dead snake.

The crowd gasped.

"Do you see?" the lame man shouted. "Now there's no other way to get down except by diving!"

He hobbled over to the tank and sloshed gasoline on top of the water. He stood back and looked up at her. She stood on the diving plank and looked down. The tower rattled and moved in the wind and she seemed very small and far away. She stood on the end of the plank looking down, then she signaled to the man. He lit the gasoline and jumped back awkwardly as the flames shot up. Just at that instant she dived. Soaring and graceful, her arms wide apart, she seemed for a breathless time to hang at that great height in the wind, caught in the brilliant snare of the searchlights. Then she seemed to fold into herself like a fan and straight and swift as a thrown spear she descended, plummeting into the tank with a great and sparkling flash of fire and water.

There was a hushed moment while the crowd waited to see if

she was still alive, but then she emerged, climbed out of the tank smiling, and showed herself to them, damp and unscathed. She put on her bathrobe and hurried back to the tent. Some of the people began to leave, but many stood gazing at the tower and the vacant tank. The lame man switched off the lights and followed after her, disappearing into the tent.

The merchant entered the tent. The three of them, sitting in a row along the edge of the cot, were eating something out of a can. A red lantern glared at their feet.

"Is that all?" the merchant said. "I mean is that all there is to it?"

The man nodded.

"Kind of brief, don't you think, for two bits a head?"

"That's all there is to it," the man said. "She could have killed herself. Ain't that enough for one evening? They ought to be glad."

The merchant looked at her. She was eating from the can and seemed as happy as could be.

"Can't you swallow some swords or something? We want everybody to feel they got their money's worth."

"Goddamnit, they did!" the lame man said. "They got all they're going to."

The merchant tried to persuade him to do something more, but he continued to refuse. So the merchant took his share of the money and left them. Soon the rest of the people left too.

The next morning the three of them were gone. The tower was gone, the truck, the tent, and they might never have been there at all, for all the trace they left. Except for the dark spots on the grass where the flaming water had splashed, except for a few posters remaining (and they were not true to fact or life), there was no trace of them.

But if the evening performance had been brief, it remained with them, haunting, a long time afterwards. Some of the preachers continued to denounce it as the work of the devil himself. The drunkards and tellers of tall tales embroidered on it and exaggerated it and preserved it until the legend of that high dive was like a beautiful tapestry before which they might act out their lives, strangely dwarfed and shamed. The children pestered and fidgeted and wanted to know when the three would come again.

A wise man said it had been a terrible thing.

"It made us all sophisticated," he said. "We can't be pleased by any ordinary marvels anymore—tightrope walkers, fire-eaters, pretty girls being fired out of cannons. It's going to take a regular apocalypse to make us raise our eyebrows again."

He was almost right, as nearly correct as a man could hope to be. How could he even imagine that more than one aging, loveless woman slept better ever after, smiled as she dreamed herself gloriously descending for all the world to see from a topless tower into a lake of flame?

One

From
KING OF
THE MOUNTAIN

Non loquimur magna sed vivimus.
MINUCIUS FELIX
—*Octavius*

KING OF
THE MOUNTAIN

THE TIME IS the heart of the Depression and the place is Florida.
Not the one you know about with white beaches and palm trees,
orange-juice stands and motels, shuffleboards and striptease, amateur and professional, for young and old, all the neon glare and
gilt of a carnival. This is at the center of the state where you
might as well be a thousand miles from the unlikely ocean in
long hot summer days, where in those days truck farmers and
small-time ranchers grubbed for a living from the sandy earth or
maybe planted and tended orange trees and hoped and sweated
through the year for enough rain and, especially in winter, for
warm weather, no frost.

Ask me why I pick that time and I'll tell you. There's a whole
generation of us now, conceived in that anxious time, and if
we're fat now, flash wide advertisement grins at the cockeyed
careless world, we know still, deeply as you know the struggles
of blood on the long pilgrimage of flesh, the old feel and smell of
fear, the gray dimensions of despair, and, too, some of us, the
memory of the tug and gnaw of being hungry.

As for the place, it's a place I know. I know the weather, the
sights and smells. I have a child's view of it. I know what's
happening down at the roots of the grass among the worms and
crawlers and I know how a jaybird looks flying in a feathered

flash of blue and white like a swift piece of the sky. Thinking
about it, time and place, over years and miles, I can still wince
with being there. I can see the faces of people who are dead. I
know what some of them loved. And I love it still, that time and
place, believe it or not, because where you suffered first, acquired your first wounds and scars, is where you've hung your
heart once and for all and called it home. . . .

They beat the hell out of him. It was the Fourth of July and
the band was playing to the crowd in the heat-stricken park; so
loud and near it blared that it drowned out the fury of white
shirtsleeves around him. The boy's mother screamed, but he
could only see her mouth open and her whole face and lips
quivering tautly as if her flesh were elastic. He couldn't hear a
sound of her anguish. Some women held her back, but nobody
was holding the boy. He saw his father go down amid that flailing of white like a man thrashing in the surf and bobbing under.
He came up gasping for air, scattering them every which way,
his own white shirt shredded now and his crude, powerful body
tense with heavy muscles, using his fists like hammers, his great
bald head shining like a polished stone. He went down in the
middle of them again, surged up bloody and terrible, roaring
above the sound of the band. And, as if in a dance, they came in
closer around him, forcing him to earth by the sheer weight of
them. Then they kicked and beat him almost to death. When he
had stopped moving, twitching, they stepped back in a ragged
circle and looked at him silently like a ring of hunters around a
fallen beast. Then they scattered into the crowd and the band
still played march music.

The women released his mother, and she ran and bent over
his fallen father in the long bright curve of her summer holiday
dress, fanning him with one of those paper fans that undertak-
ers put out for the ladies on public occasions, for advertising.
She just bent over him fanning and nobody paid any attention.
He was too big a man for her to move out of the sun by herself.
After a little while a Negro came from across the street and
together they dragged him under a shade tree. The Negro had a

tin cup in his lunch pail and he got some water from the old stone horse trough at the edge of the park and sloshed it over the boy's father. When the water hit him he shook his head and tried to sit up. He tried to say something through the bloody bubbles of his mouth, couldn't, laid his head back on the ground gently, slowly, like a man settling on a soft pillow to sleep. Then the woman saw her son. She called to the policeman who had been watching from a little distance.

"Take the boy home, Ernie," she said. "At least you can do that."

The policeman took the boy's hand in his own, as if the boy were a little child, and the boy felt the strange sweaty chill of it, but clung to his hand, wouldn't turn loose. He clung to the policeman and kept looking at his mother fanning the fallen man.

"You want a ice-cream cone?" the policeman said. "Sure you do, boy. And I'm going to buy you one."

That sounded like a fine idea, and they turned and walked away from the park together, hand in hand.

Those were bad times then with so little money and people having to claw and wrestle each other for the little there was. It was the time of the Ku Klux Klan in that place. Not those men in sheets, crackpot fanatics, you can joke about now or piously deplore, but a ruthless political machine, a club for the lost and lonely, the embittered and the discontented. They had the county and a lot of the state and they meant to keep what they had. They didn't hate the man. Nothing personal. They were afraid of him. They knew him. He was one of their own, a hard farm boy who had read the law and now was a lawyer in the town, and, being self-educated, he believed in some few things with an unsophisticated tenacity. He had said in public that they were going to have law and order in the county and that the Klan must be swept out of office and authority. He had said they are few and we are the many and we have the vote. So when he went to say it again in a formal speech on the Fourth of July, they met him at the edge of the park and they made a cripple of him. Always after that he had a limp and a cane and the hurt face of a prizefighter.

When he finally came home from the hospital, still bandaged, using his cane, the boy stood shy in the living room next to the upright piano his mother played and watched his father move awkwardly among familiar objects like a stranger.

"What's this?" his father hollered. He was bent over the desk, looking through the drawers.

"What is it?" his mother said from the kitchen.

"I say what's this you've got in the desk drawer?"

And he pulled out of the drawer a shiny pistol and held it loosely in his left hand like a dead thing. His mother came from the kitchen wiping her hands on her apron. As soon as she saw his father standing there with the pistol in his hand she started to cry.

"They almost killed you," she said. "They're liable to kill you next time."

He started to stamp out of the room past her but she snatched at the gun. He pushed her away.

"It's mine," she said. "Let the blame fall on me. I bought it with my own money. I have the right. They might try to do something to me or the boy."

"You know I don't allow no firearms in this house," his father said. "If it wasn't for the boy I'd beat you with my cane."

His mother turned away, hiding her face in the crook of her arm, and he heard his father stamping through the kitchen and, slowly, down the back steps and he heard the banging lid of the garbage can. After that it was very quiet for a moment, so quiet the boy could hear a mockingbird in the backyard, probably in the mulberry tree, making a sound like a cat, and even behind that sound, the hum, not much louder than the sound of a bumblebee, of the colored washwoman in the house next door who always sang and hummed when she ironed. He heard his father then begin to mount the back stairs like a clumsy creature on three legs. When his father spoke in the kitchen his voice was so soft and controlled he might have been the Episcopal minister giving the benediction.

"You don't have to worry," he said. "I'm home now and you don't have to be afraid anymore."

And she saying, "It's too much to ask. I can't go through it again. The women held me and I could have scratched my eyes out of my head rather than to watch anymore."

"And what am I supposed to do? What am I supposed to be? God knows I am not a little boy anymore."

"They hurt you," she said. "My God, how they hurt you."

"They only *confirmed* me," he said. "You could call it the laying on of hands."

"We can go," she said. "Let's move up to Jacksonville. You can practice law there. You can make a good living in Jacksonville and we'll be safe there."

"We're not going anywhere," he said. "I'm going upstairs and lie down for a few days and get a hold of myself. Then I'm going back out on the street and hold up my head."

"I believe in you," she said. "I know you have the strength. But it's so futile, like Samson pulling the roof down on the Philistines."

"If I have to I'll pull the house down on their heads," he answered, laughing the big outdoor laugh that sounded like a wild animal in the dark. "Whoever heard," he said, still laughing, "whoever heard of a baldheaded Samson?"

After his father went up to the bedroom, climbed the flight of stairs painfully, his mother came in from the kitchen and sat down at the piano. She played a couple of little waltz tunes. He knew them, but he liked "The Washington and Lee March" better. She was in the mood for little waltz tunes. She had never liked it in this raw town. She was a lady and her people were different. They had been to Waycross, Georgia, to visit; and he remembered his grandfather, a kind man with a soft voice who always smelled warmly of whiskey and cigars. He stayed in the house, padding about as light-footed as a cat in his bedroom slippers, and he had opened his leather-bound history books and showed the pictures to the boy. He knew how ashamed his mother must feel in this town, remembering the big house and the people there, especially his grandfather.

"All right," he remembered his father shouting at her one night after they had returned. "Make a hero out of him. But just remember this. They would all be in the poorhouse if it wasn't for me. There wouldn't be any big house for you to go and visit and show off to the boy. Oh, he's a fine old gentleman and I do dearly love him, but bear in mind sometimes when he's sitting in his armchair by the fire and talking so well behind the smoke of a twenty-five-cent cigar, so gracefully, that it's my cigar he's smoking. He's a fine old gentleman by grace of me."

"What's the matter, honey?" his mother said, looking away from the bright slick piano keys, stopping in the middle of a tune. "You look so sad, honey boy. Don't you be sad. Everything is going to be all right."

Then she lay her face on the piano keys and started to cry, noiselessly, only her body shaking as if she had fever and chills, and the tears rolling down her cheeks. The boy went outside in the backyard and picked up a stone to make that mockingbird be quiet, but the mockingbird was gone. He climbed up into the mulberry tree and looked all around, as high and proud and lonely as the king of the mountain, and nobody, nobody would dare to come and pull him from his perch.

They had a little dog in those days, a Boston bull, as cute as he was ugly, and smart. He could do all the ordinary tricks like begging, rolling over, and playing dead, but they had taught him a very special one. In the afternoon they'd turn him loose and he'd run all the way downtown to the post office. The clerk would put the mail in his mouth and he'd run straight home to stand at the screen door scratching with his paw until somebody let him in. He never messed up one of the letters. It was called a mighty fine trick and the people around town knew all about it and talked about it. You might find it hard to believe a dog could learn a trick like that. Don't doubt it; I know myself of a dog that a grocer uses to deliver packages in a dogcart.

It hadn't been long after his father came home from the hospital, on a Friday afternoon, when the boy noticed that the dog didn't come back from the post office. He took it for a sign and kept quiet about it. Around suppertime the clerk from the post office came and brought the mail to the house. His father limped out on the front step and took it from him.

"Thanks for the special delivery," his father said. "Did you see my little old dog today?"

"No, sir," the clerk said. "It's the first time I can remember that dog didn't show up."

"That's a remarkable thing," his father said. "How would you account for it?"

The boy stood inside the door, his face pressed against the screen, watching. He could see that the clerk was embarrassed. He wanted to do right but he was scared. And the boy could also tell that his father knew this and he would get the truth out of the man easy. He would have the truth even if the man went down on his knees and begged not to tell.

"I don't know, sir. I don't have any idea. Maybe he just run off."

"Ha! Ha!" his father laughed like a big wind in the man's face. "Oh! Ho! That's funny. After five years all of sudden the dog gets sick and tired and runs off."

"Well," the man said, "it could have happened."

The boy watched the bulked muscles in his father's body tighten under his shirt and saw him jut his neck forward, thrust his bald, battered head so close to the man's face they could have kissed. When he spoke now, the boy knew, he would be staring into the depths of the man's eyes, so deep the man would feel naked, and when he spoke it would be hardly more than a whisper, but with the tone of a growl in it, like a dog guarding a bone.

"Now you listen to me," his father said. "I know what happened. They killed him. I know that much. Now what I want out of you is the truth. That's what I'm going to get. I'll have the truth from you if I have to gut you like a catfish from your jaw to your crotch. You understand me?"

"Yes, sir," the man said. "They killed him. Chief of Police shot him right outside the post office."

"They had a big laugh? That produced a great big laugh?"

"Yes, sir. Chief of Police said he don't allow no mad dogs running loose in this town. . . ."

"He's a real good shot? He can shoot that pistol like a marksman?"

"Yes, sir."

"Will they give him the distinguished dog-killing medal? Will he cut a big notch in that .38 and strut his fat ass up and down the sidewalk like a bad man?"

"I don't know, sir. I really don't know what he's going to do."

All of a sudden his father broke into a wide bright smile and slapped the clerk on the back. The clerk jumped as if he thought he was going to be struck down, but when he felt the hand soft on his back and the arm around his shoulders he relaxed. He leaned back on that arm and let it hold him up, like a girl in a man's arm.

"Well," his father said, "you done right to come here and tell me. It took some doing what with people waving pistols around and shooting dogs and things. Come on in and have a cup of coffee. You want a cup of coffee, don't you?"

"Yes, sir," the clerk said. "That would be very nice."

In the morning, Saturday morning, his father was up early, singing in the bathroom while he shaved. It had been a long time since he had been singing in the morning. The boy went into the bathroom and stood beside his naked father watching him shave. Keeping his eyes on the mirror, his father popped a white-lather beard on the boy's chin with the shaving brush. His father laughed while the boy wiped his chin with the back of his hand.

"You better watch. You better study," his father said. "One of these days you'll have a beard to shave. You want to know how to do it right."

"How come you still got hair growing on your face and none on the top of your head?"

"That, boy, is a mystery," his father said, tipping himself a wink in the mirror. "If I knew the answer to that question I'd be a millionaire."

"Would you like to be a millionaire?"

"Well, I don't know. I don't have any idea what it's like to be a millionaire. You might just as well ask me if I'd like to be a jaybird."

"I know what it's like to be a jaybird."

"You do?"

"You got to be mean to be a jaybird."

"But maybe the jaybird don't think he's mean. Maybe he don't know what mean is."

"I never thought of that," the boy said. "A jaybird is smart, though."

"Oh, you can be smart, real smart, and you still can't tell how you're doing something. You can tell most of the time *what* you're doing, but you can't always tell *how* you're doing it or why."

"I always know why I'm doing something."

"You're lucky," his father said.

"It's not so lucky," the boy said. "Sometimes it worries me so much I don't feel like doing anything."

His father laughed and splashed himself with water, rubbed his face hard with a towel until it flushed pink, and then patted some sweet-smelling lotion on his cheeks.

"Looka there, boy," his father said. "I'm as pink as a baby."

The boy went with him into the bedroom to watch his father dress. He dressed as if he were going to the courthouse or the church, the Episcopal church of his mother where people dressed better and walked more softly than the Baptist church where his father's family had always gone. His father put on a dark suit and a white shirt with a gleaming starched collar and a necktie. He wore his best shoes, black ones shined up like patent leather. When he had finished and inspected himself in the mirror, the two of them went downstairs to breakfast.

"Where in the world are you going?" the boy's mother said.

"I thought the boy and I would take a stroll down to the post office and pick up the mail. It comes in the morning on Saturday."

His mother stood by the table like a statue of a woman with a coffeepot in her hand.

"Don't take the boy," she said. "You don't want to do that."

"We're just going to stroll downtown."

"You know what I mean," she said. "Keep the boy out of it."

"No, I don't know what you mean. I just got an idea I'd like to go down and get the mail."

"He don't have to go along. If you have to go downtown, just looking for trouble, let him stay here."

"Ask the boy. Ask him if he want to go or not. You want to go with me?"

He thought about it before he said yes. His mother looked angry but she must have known there was nothing to say, so she poured the coffee and sat down. When they had finished, the boy's father rose from the table and picked up his cane.

"It might be a waste of time," his mother said at the door. "There might not be any mail."

"We'll see about that."

Saturday was the day for county people to come to town, the farmers, the ranchers, the citrus growers, the hired hands and the Negroes from the sawmills and turpentine camps. They came, clogging the highway with trucks and wagons, on foot, the women to pass their time window-shopping and gossiping, the men to lounge in knots and clusters at public places. They leaned against the walls and posts, squatted on their heels, smoked and chewed and spat and studied each other, friends and enemies. Saturday used to be a strutting day, but now there wasn't much to buy in town and no money to buy it with anyway. His father could not have been more conspicuous that day, his shaved face shining in the light, his Sunday clothes vividly crisp. They had started to mount the stairs to the post office.

"Hey, lawyer!"

His father stopped and turned slowly, glanced along the line of farmers who were sitting on the fence by the walk until he found the face that went with the voice, a tall thin long-legged farmer, his clean khaki trousers flapping loosely above high-topped mail-order shoes, his eyes keen and uncommitted.

"What you going to do now, lawyer?"

"Nothing," his father said. "It's up to them. They got to think up something else to do. They tried to kill me with their hands and they couldn't. The best they could do was to cripple me up a little bit."

He let his voice rise as the man swung down from his perch and came forward to the edge of the steps. Others came, one by one, from the fence and the curb and the sidewalk and grouped close to listen. The boy stood in his father's shadow and listened, noticing as he assumed the old pattern of the country speech, the rhythm and tone of it.

"Why, a whole army of them jumped me and tried to kill me but they couldn't. Know why? They forgot something you and I know. They forgot I was a man, a farmer's boy raised here, a real cracker. They thought maybe reading a lawbook had changed my flesh and bones and blood to something soft. You can't kill a man that easy. You can stomp and beat and make a cripple out of him. You can cut and shred him in little pieces and scatter the parts of him like the chaff in the wind, but when you turn your back and wipe your hands all those parts come together and he's standing there ready for a fight."

"Tell them about it!" somebody yelled. "Tell them about it!"

"That's what I'm doing. I'm telling them all about it. Those boys forgot that a man in truth has got nine lives like a cat. I got eight more coming to me. Oh my! Oh my! They found out though. Oh my, didn't they find out?"

"Didn't they?"

"They know now I got blood like turpentine in my veins and two big fists like knotty pine, like cypress knees, and I got a head like a cannon ball. Oh, they found out. They know about it now. And what do you think they done? They was so mad I wouldn't just lay down and curl up and die for them. They was as mad, as all around frustrated as the preacher comes for Sunday dinner and don't get nothing on his plate but the tough old neck of the chicken. They wanted breast and soft meat."

"Keep talking. Tell 'em about it!"

"Why, they just didn't know what to do with theirselves.

They didn't know whether to shit or get off the pot. And then, and then, and then an idea come to one of them. They got a plan. Down come the Chief of Po-lice and hid hisself behind that oak tree over there, laying for my dog. There he is trying to hide his fat ass behind a tree and along comes my little old Boston bulldog to pick up the mail, and out pops the Chief of Po-lice. A bang! bang! Shooting at a little old dog. It made him feel good. It made him feel so much better. Oh, yes, none of them could kill a man, but they was brave enough to rise up in righteous indignation and shoot down a puppy dog. Well now, my friends, I'll tell you the honest truth, when I got over being mad about it, I was glad they done it. It showed them up for what they are. What do you think a dog is?"

He leveled his cane and jabbed out with it at the crowd.

"Know what that dog was? He wasn't nothing but a poor little old son of a bitch. And any man that would shoot a dog is lower than a son of a bitch. He's lower than anything in all of God's whole wide creation except a diamondback rattler. And I got my doubts about that. I'll let a diamondback come a-wiggling on his belly in the dust of my backyard before I'll let their Chief of Po-lice come a-hanging around."

The boy stood tense beside his father, looking out into the crowd of faces. It was a big crowd now, out into the street, and his father was shouting out to them. They were bunched together and they swayed with his voice, were moved by the rhythm of his waving cane, as if they were dancing to a tune.

"Man back here says we're blocking the street," a voice called from the street.

"Tell the man to go and get a policeman. I'm going to stay right here. I'm disturbing the peace and I'm going to keep right on disturbing the so-called peace."

His father flung off his hat. It sailed in a wild arc, fell in a flutter like a wounded bird into the crowd. He tore the coat off his shoulders and his white shirt shone in the sunlight when he spread his arms wide.

"I'm bigger than a dog," he yelled. "Ask the policeman can he hit me from the street. Let them kill me now if they're going to because if they don't they must reckon with me. I'll come on and I'll be tearing flesh off of bones and I'll be scattering brains and innards from here to kingdom come!"

"Tell 'em! Tell 'em about it!"

"Ain't nobody going to shoot at you. Keep talking."

"I'm going to tell you all about your Ku Klux Klan. Oh they're a brave bunch, they are, noble shooters of dogs. They come out at night, like thieves in the night, dressed in white sheets like children on Halloween and they spend their time harassing the poor niggers and the poor folks. Poor folks . . . that's all of us, ain't it?"

"Amen. Amen."

"Oh, they're waxing fat and sassy on taxes and who's paying for it? Your sweat, brothers, and mine put every hole in the Chief of Po-lice's belt. And, brothers, that's a mighty big piece of leather goods."

(Laughter)

"You could rope a calf with it!"

(Laughter)

"You could hang a man with it!"

"Let him be careful he don't trip up and hang hisself," a voice hollered.

"Now when they go out in their costumes they burn the fiery cross. Burn it! That's what they do with the holy cross of our Almighty Lord and Savior, Jesus Christ!"

"Amen! Amen!"

"Let them take heed! Let them heed my words. We're not going to pluck them out and run them out of town. We ain't going to run them out of the state or the United States of America. Let them take heed lest we purge the last trace of them off the face of the earth. They can't hurt us. We ain't afraid. We ain't dogs, by God!"

His father kept talking, shouting at them, and the boy saw that he was leading the crowd now like a bandmaster. When he wanted to he had them growling and snarling like animals in the zoo. His father put his arm around the boy and leaned over close to his ear.

"Let's quiet them down a little," he said.

Then he began to talk softly, so soft they had to strain to hear. He told them what the law was and he told them what he had been planning to say on the Fourth of July about the vote and the elections in the fall. They yelled at him to run for county judge, but he shook his head and smiled. That seemed to rile them up and they kept yelling for him to run for office until at last he held his hands wide apart and they got quiet. He told them if that's what they wanted he guessed he would have to do it and if he lived to take office he would throw the whole bunch of public enemies in the jail and throw the key away.

"Now I've said my piece," he said. "I'm going across the street and celebrate our victory, going to buy my little boy a bottle of soda pop and smoke myself a rich man's ten-cent cigar."

The crowd fell back in front of them, making a path. They walked all the way across the street through the dense Saturday crowd, his father dripping sweat, smiling at everyone and calling out to people he knew. Afterwards, as they strolled home, people, friends and strangers, stepped up and shook his father's hand and looked into his eyes. And now the boy knew for the first time how close is violence to love. If you rubbed the lamp and said the right words you could call up a giant.

When they entered the house, his mother was playing the piano.

"Was there any mail?" she asked. "Did you get a letter?"

"Isn't that remarkable?" his father said. "I got to talking to some fellows and completely forgot about the mail."

After that the conclusion was foregone; everything was quiet. His father went back to work every day at the law office, the summer ended, and the boy started school again. It might never have happened. He might have dreamed it all in the long, breathless, heat-humming days of midsummer, except that there was a car parked right across the street from the house night and day, and always a man in it, sitting on the front seat with a high-powered deer rifle sticking out of the window.

In November they held the elections and then one midnight the telephone rang and they woke the boy. As they walked to the courthouse the band was playing in the street and there were fireworks and men fired rifles and pistols in the air. They climbed the flight of steps in front of the courthouse and stood there while the people cheered and hollered, his father laughing, tears of joy running down his cheeks, shaking his big cane at the people while they cheered him. His mother smiled and smiled, looking right through the swirl of faces, smiling and not seeing any of them, like a queen from another country. . . .

I know the place and I know the time, the rich, sweaty, bootleg liquor smell of that night, the brass band sound of it, the once-in-a-blue-moon flavor of the celebration that follows the slaying of a dragon.

I could tell you the rest of the story about the man, how he became a public man, a senator, a governor. I know the anecdotes of his terrible temper and his inconsistencies. Years later I saw him beat a man to his knees with his cane for talking sassy to him on the street; yet I've also seen him have an Air Force officer jailed for browbeating the Negro bootblack in the barbershop. I know the rest of the story, how the boy grew up and went away to college and, as he grew and changed, came to see those days in a different and a sadder light.

"It's a pity," he told me once, "that it took a narrow-minded, petty demagogue with a wild desire to be a martyr to stand up for law and order at that time."

"Somebody had to do it," I said. "Your old families with their fine names and fine silver wouldn't lift a finger to do it. Who was going to take responsibility if he didn't?"

"You may be right," he said. "But it's a pity."

"Why do you hate him?"

"Wouldn't you?" he said quickly.

"I don't know," I said.

"I'll tell you the truth," he said, smiling. "I don't know either."

WHAT'S THE PURPOSE
OF THE BAYONET?

I. Hooray for the Old Nth Field

WE WERE THE BUMS of the Army. There was no other unit like ours. We were the losers, the scum, flotsam and jetsam, the scrubs, the dregs, the lees, blacksheep, Falstaffs, n'er-do-well uncles, and country cousins. Our outfit was formed up overseas, ostensibly composed of men from the regimental infantry companies who had an artillery MOS. What really happened in this case is as follows. They sent a letter down to all the infantry Company Commanders, letting them know about the new outfit and asking them if they had any men to spare who happened to have an artillery MOS. The Company Commander, sitting behind his polished and dusted, almost virginal desk, would puzzle out the letter and, as its contents dawned on him, a great big grin would light up his face and he'd holler for the First Sergeant and the Company Clerk. It's amazing how all the misfits, deadbeats, eightballs, VD cases, alcoholics, and walleyed, knock-kneed, slewfooted stockade-bait suddenly turned out to be trained artillerymen. Then an officer was flown over from the States to take charge of this pirate crew. Picture him the first time he realized what had happened. He's the man who sat down on the Whoopee Cushion. He's the Original who was sent out in search of a left-handed monkeywrench and a bucket of polka-dot paint. He's scheduled to be nailed to the cross in the company of thieves and tramps.

We were lucky. The CO they sent us was a bum himself. Somebody in the Pentagon had a nice sense of decorum. He was potbellied and middle-aged. All his contemporaries were Bird Colonels or Onestar Generals. He was still a Captain. He chewed on an enormous two-bit stogie all day long and most of the time he forgot all about having it in his mouth. He didn't even take it out of his mouth when he saluted. No matter how clean his uniform was when he put it on, in fifteen minutes he looked like he'd slept in it on the ground. He had been through some hellish times in the War and he had come out the same man who went in. He was one of those men who valued the accident of living so highly they will never betray themselves for anything. Least of all ambition. He didn't seem to be the slightest bit sorry for being exactly what he was, and he didn't seem to be gnawed by the furtive wish to be anything or anybody else.

The first time the battery fell out for his inspection we looked like the early American cartoons of the Continental Militia.

"I'll be a sonofabitch," were his first words to the assembled troops. The rest of his speech was short and to the point. "F——— you guys!" he said. "You are without a doubt the crummiest collection of decayed humankind I ever laid eyes on, so help me God. We deserve each other. If you want to be soldiers, try it. See if I care. First Sergeant, take charge of this so-called battery. I'm going to get drunk." The entire battery cheered him. We threw our helmet liners in the air. He just shrugged his shoulders and walked off the paradeground, slumped over, chewing on his cigar stub, feeling maybe the way Francis Drake and Henry Morgan sometimes used to feel.

It was the best outfit I was ever with in every way. You might not think so, but I'll tell you why. We were insideout men. All our vices were apparent. Our virtues were disguised. Talk all you want about your *camaraderie*, your *esprit de corps*. We had something better than that. We clung together hand in hand like men overboard. We found out that with sleight of hand we could soldier when we wanted to or if we had to. We found out that when we felt like it we could outmarch the infantry, outrun the airborne, and outdrive the armored. Most of the time we were worthless, a crown of thorns to the Commanding General, a severe drain on the Taxpayer. Between inspections the billets we lived in were a pigsty. Off duty we drank and fought and whored. We always had beer and vino cooling in the breechrings of our howitzers. Combat ready. Rust and dust were our constant companions, shooed out of sight only on very special occasions.

Needless to say the Army was ashamed to have us around. They stuck us up near the Yugoslav border in what used to be the Free Territory of Trieste, miles from anywhere, in a village called Padricano. Look it up in an atlas sometime. See if you can find it. We were supposed to guard the border. Before we came up there it had been pretty tense, but we soon discovered that the Yugoslav soldiers—called Jugs—were almost as notorious tramps as we were. We used to drink together and the border almost vanished. One time the Lady who used to be the Ambassadress to Italy came up and inspected us. They were so afraid they notified us a month ahead of time. After she left the CO called for the Battery Clerk, who was a college boy. "Say, son," he said, "who in the hell *was* that Clara Bell Lou we fell out for?"

Once a week they'd let a truckload of us go down to the city of Trieste to get civilized for an evening. We played hide and seek with the MP's all over town. Even though we didn't get down there often, we knew every whore in the city by her first name, which was a lot more than the Vice Squad was ever able to accomplish. Once, during the riots, this paid off. They alerted the Nth Field and made us put on the full combat costume— steel helmets, field packs, gasmasks, fixed bayonets, the works. We were taken down in trucks to the main square in Trieste. Thousands of people were milling around, shouting and screaming about something. Some of them had clubs and knives and rocks, and some of them, I guess, had small arms. When we dismounted and formed up and they saw our guidon and saw what outfit we were, they started laughing and cheering. The whores were calling out to us by name. So we started laughing and yelling back to them. The whole riot was over in minutes. The only real trouble the Army had was rounding us up again to go back to Padricano. It took a couple of hours to smoke out all our guys who had headed for the first bar or trattoria they could find. A couple of them were dead drunk, and the local people carried them and all their gear and loaded them gently on the waiting trucks.

Eventually the Army just gave up on us. They broke up the outfit and sent us far and wide. They sent me up to Linz, Austria. The Army thought we were barbarians and maybe we were, but if you ever have to die with combat boots on, you could do worse than to do it with the Nth Field. Save me, good Lord, from companies and battalions of well-adjusted, dead-serious, cleancut, boyscout, post-office-recruiting-poster soldiers. Deliver me from mine enemies, West Point officers with spit-shined boots and a tentpole jammed up their rectums, and their immortal souls all wrapped up cutely like a birthday present containing at its secret heart something about as insipid as a shelled peanut. Save me from good people, on a piece of graphpaper, percentagewise. Give me the bottom of the barrel, men who still have themselves to laugh at and something real to cry about, who, having nothing to lose and being victims of the absurd dignity of the human condition, can live with bravado at least, and, if they have to die, can die with grace like a wounded animal.

2. Guts

PEOPLE TAKE UP BOXING for a variety of reasons, none of them very sound. Show me a fighter, amateur or pro, and I'll show you a man who's got some impelling obsession, hidden maybe, that makes him want to destroy and be destroyed. I suppose with the pros, they get over it with experience. They reach a point where they don't care much anymore; the original motivations have been lost, disguised, or maybe even satisfied. By that time there isn't much else they can do and it's just another dirty business.

The obvious reason I boxed in the Army was to get out of work. If you made the team you got to sleep through reveille and you didn't have to march or stand any inspections. Officers didn't harass you. You just went down to the Post Gym twice a day and worked out. The true reason why I took up boxing, way back in public school, is more complex. The easiest way to explain it without going into much detail is my size. I'm a natural welterweight. All the lacerations of flesh and spirit that go along with being small are partially compensated for by being given the opportunity to face another small man and try to heap some of the stinking weight of your own anguish on him.

Joe was just about my size. He had fought some professionally around Philadelphia. He started fighting in self-defense at the state prison where if a little man couldn't fight he was as good as gone. He was really good, he had class. He could make the light bag dance to any rhythm he set his fists to. He had a hundred different ways to skip rope. He could bob and weave like a machine when he was shadow boxing and when he hit the heavy bag it seemed to groan under his punches. He used to take it easy on me when we sparred and I learned a lot from Joe. I wasn't trying to be any competition for him. I just wanted to stay on the team as a substitute.

Often I'd go on pass with Joe. He had a shack—he was living off Post with what you'd probably call a whore, a big blonde about twice his size named, believe it or not, Hilda. He paid the rent, bought the groceries and some clothes for her, and now and then he'd bring her a present from the PX. In return she had to do his laundry, cook dinner for him, and make love like an eager rabbit. It wasn't a bad deal for some of those girls because jobs were scarce and a lot of them might have been hungry otherwise. And it was a definite cut higher on the local social scale then being a regular prostitute. There were two big dangers: pregnancy and rotation. Sooner or later every soldier had to rotate home to the States. Once their man was gone they either had to find another one or become prostitutes. Pregnancy was something else. Either they took their chances with quack abortionists or they had a baby. The whole place was full of little GI bastards. Some of the girls had two or three.

Hilda and Joe seemed to have a happy shack. She always cooked up schnitzels with fried eggs on top, served with potatoes and Austrian beer. We weren't training so hard that we wouldn't drink beer. Not for three three-minute rounds.

"Hilda is the girl I used to think about in jail," Joe would say. "I didn't see a woman, not even a picture of one, for two years. I used to close my eyes and picture a big blonde, one with boobies the size of Florida grapefruit and a big soft ass as wide as an axhandle. I had to come all the way to Austria with the U.S. Army to find one along those lines."

Hilda used to laugh at that and she didn't seem to mind much when he compared her with his wife back home.

"Now you take my wife in Philly," he'd say. "Hilda is a pig along side of her, a slob. My wife is a real beauty. She even won a bathing-beauty contest when she was in high school. She could be in the movies if she wanted to I guess."

"Who do you love?" Hilda would say. "Tell him which one you love."

"That's easy. You, you big barrel of lard."

"Tell him which one is good in the bed."

"Well, hell now, Hilda, that ain't fair. Give the girl a chance. You've had a whole lot more experience."

I really admired Joe. I took everything he said for gospel and I studied his fighting movements and copied all the ones that I could. Some of the other guys on the team said he was a fake. Wait and see, they said. We know his kind. Notice he don't like to muss his hair. He's a liar. He never was no kind of a fighter. He might of been in jail, but even that don't seem likely. I didn't pay any attention to them. I figured they were just jealous. I noticed none of them wanted to get in the ring with him.

Finally, the night of our first match came around. The gym was packed with people—troops, officers and their wives, and civilian employees. It's surprising to me how so many nice people and nice girls would come to see a thing like that. The same people would be sick at their stomachs if they saw a dogfight. To tell you the truth I can't think of anything uglier than a couple of men beating each other bloody under the bright lights for the amusement of a lot of people.

It was almost time for his bout when Joe came up to me.

"I'm sick," he said. "I can't fight tonight." He was supposed to fight a sergeant from Salzburg, a little guy with heavy muscles like a weightlifter who looked like he could really hit.

"The hell you're sick, Joe," somebody said. "You're chicken."

"I'm sick," he kept saying. "I'm too sick to go in there."

"Okay, Joe," I said. "I'll fight him for you."

"Don't be a knucklehead," somebody told me. "Let him fight his own match."

"Go ahead if you want to," Joe said. "I couldn't care less."

I just had time to slip on my trunks and get the gloves on before the fight. I went in there and jabbed him and kept moving. He turned out to be one of those big hitters who have to get both feet set flat before they can punch. So I just kept moving around him and sticking the jab in his face. After the first round he got mad and started to run at me like a bull. All I had to do for two rounds was to keep my left hand out and he'd run right into it. He was dazing himself. The madder he got, the less chance he had to get set and tag me, and that's how come he lost the fight. We were both glad when it was over, him because it had been so frustrating and me because my luck would have run out in another round or so. As soon as it was over I ran back to tell Joe what had happened. He was sitting in the dressing room, crying.

"Joe," I said. "Joe, I won!"

"Think you're pretty good, don't you?"

"No," I said, "I was lucky."

"Listen," he said, "you'll never understand this, but tonight I just lost my heart for it. I was sitting here and it dawned on me that there wasn't no reason, none at all, to go in there and get beat around anymore. It made me sick."

"I can see how you'd feel."

"No you can't," he said. "You'll figure just like the rest of those guys that I was nothing but a big liar."

"No, I won't," I said. "I'm just glad I could win the fight."

"You rat," he said. "How do you think that makes me feel, you bastard?"

He put on his cap and left. The next day he quit the team and went back with his regular outfit. I heard he even quit Hilda. I felt bad about it, but what could I do?

3. The Art of Courtly Love

YOU CAN FOOL YOURSELF quicker in a dozen ways than it takes to tell about it. Then, if you discover the irony of your self-deception, you are liable to turn right around and cast your guilt on somebody else. That truism, I suppose, explains how it was with Inge and me. Inge lived in an apartment just across a little field from an off-limits *gasthaus* where a few of us used to go in the evenings or on Saturday afternoon and drink beer. One Saturday I looked through the window and saw her hanging out her washing. She was a small woman, curiously dainty and precise in her movements, with a pretty, troubled face. It was almost like watching a dance seeing her hanging out her washing in a brisk wind. For no good reason I said to myself I must have that woman. I'm not going to rest until I have that woman. I asked around about her and found out that she was a DP, a refugee from the old German part of Czechoslovakia. Nobody knew much about her except that she had shacked up with an officer for a while and that he had rotated to the States a year or so ago.

It took some doing. At first she didn't want to have anything to do with me.

"I don't like you," she said. "I don't even like your type. Little nervous men make me sick."

All right, I said to myself, we'll see. We'll see about that. I almost crawled for it. I tried everything I could think of. I kept coming around, bringing her food and gifts from the PX, spending my money like a drunk. One night I brought my portable record player and records and a bottle of wine. Once she heard the music playing I was home free.

"I hate you," she said. "All this time I have been living with so little, but you keep bringing things and now I start to want again. I want to eat good food and I want to wear good clothes again. I want to start to live good again."

That suited me fine. At the time it seemed like a big victory. I moved in and set up a shack. I felt like a rooster in the henyard. This is pretty hard to explain because it was easy enough to find a girl to shack with around Linz, but this had been a real quest. Inge did everything she was supposed to. She cooked and did my laundry and made love, but I could tell that she didn't like it at all. The truth is her barely concealed distaste added to my sense of pleasure. She used to be so ashamed she kept all the shades pulled down when I was in the apartment. She liked to make love in the dark, but I used to trick her by suddenly snapping on the bedside lamp to astonish her in the light.

Inge had been married in Czechoslovakia, but her husband had been killed in the War and she didn't know where her children were. She was at least ten years older than I was. The American officer had been very good to her, she said, and he had promised to marry her. After he went to the States she never heard from him again. Still, she kept a leather-framed picture of him on her bureau, overseeing everything, a lean, good-looking, smiling man. She had a vague notion that someday, any day, the postman was going to bring her a letter from him telling her to pack her things and come to the States. We used to play a game with his picture. When she undressed to go to bed, she used to turn his face to the wall, but as soon as she wasn't looking, I would turn him around again.

Inge kept the apartment neat and trim—everything had its exact place. If you moved a bottle of perfume an inch on the bureau from where she had put it, she sensed right away that something in the room was out of order. She had some cheap jewelry and some knickknacks that she cared for like a saint's relics. She was very fastidious about her clothes and she used to bathe every day even though this meant a lot of trouble. The only thing to bathe in was a big washtub and she had to bring the water by the bucketload from a pump in the yard. On the other hand I used to go for days without taking a shower out at camp just to infuriate her. She stood this and a hundred small humiliations as well or better than anyone could be expected to under the circumstances.

Oh, I was as happy and thoughtless as an apple on a tree until another girl told me that Inge had an Austrian boyfriend and that whenever I was on guard or had some other night duty he came and stayed in my apartment. I could hardly believe that, but I decided I had to to find out. I told her I was going to be on guard one night. After dark I came off Post and sneaked up close to the apartment. The shades were up and I looked in the window. She was all dressed up in the best clothes I had bought her, dancing with a young Austrian. They danced and she was laughing as I'd never seen her do before, and all the time my portable record player was playing my records. I went over to the *gasthaus* and watched from the window. I sat up all night, fuming and tormented, and at dawn I saw him leave, blowing a kiss to her. As soon as he was out of sight, I ran across the field to the apartment and opened the door. She sat up in the bed, clutching the sheet over her breasts.

"What are you doing here?" she said. "What are you going to do?"

"You bitch," I said, starting to take off my belt. "I'm going to beat the living hell out of you."

"Please don't," she said. "Please, please don't touch me. I never said I loved you. You've been good to me but I never said I loved you."

"So what about the kraut?"

"I love him," she said. "That boy doesn't have any money, but I love him. You've got to understand."

"Okay," I said. "You go ahead and love who you want to. I won't lay a finger on you. I've got a better idea. I'm going to tear this place apart."

"Don't!" she said. "Don't do that."

"I'm going to tear this place to pieces and if you say anything about it to anyone I'll turn your name in to the CID as a whore."

That frightened her because if she was even arrested under suspicion of being a prostitute she was done for. As a DP she could never hold a job or be legally married in Austria, and certainly with that on her record she would never get to the States. I was in a terrible rage, more at myself than anything else, I guess. She sat in the bed sobbing hopelessly while I broke everything to pieces. I even smashed my own records and the player. I took her clothes out of the bureau drawers and off the hangers and ripped them into shreds and ribbons. I tore that smiling photograph in half.

"You had no right," she said.

I slammed the door and ran to catch the bus back to camp. At first I felt almost good about it, but after a day or two I began to realize how much I had fooled myself and what a terrible thing I had done. I went to the PX and bought a lot of things to take to her, but when I got to the apartment the landlady told me that Inge had run away and left no address. I paid her the rent we owed and went back to camp. I don't know where she went or could have gone. Salzburg probably, where there are a lot of troops. I never heard from her or found any trace of her again.

4. What's the Purpose of the Bayonet?

I ALWAYS USED to hate pulling stockade duty. They had some regular personnel up there, but the actual guarding was detailed to individual units. When your name came up on the list you had to move up there and guard the prisoners. This meant hours in the towers around the barbwire compound or else being a chaser. I hated being a chaser. You had to pick up a little group of prisoners at the gate in the morning and take them to whatever job they were supposed to do. You weren't allowed to smoke or talk to the prisoners. You were just there to shoot them if they tried to run away or refused to obey an order. You had to be spic and span and pass inspection every morning. It was almost as bad as being a prisoner yourself. Not quite.

This time I was assigned to a different job—the cage. In the center of the compound they had a building they had converted into a kind of stronghold for very serious cases—men who were being sent back to the States for long terms. They had double doors with armed guards outside, and inside they had two rows of cages with bars all the way around. It was kind of like a zoo. They kept the men in the individual cages like wild beasts. They were afraid they would try to kill themselves rather than go back to the States and do time in Leavenworth. They wouldn't let them shave. Some of them grew long beards waiting for shipment. They wouldn't give them silverware with the chow. They had to eat it off the tray with their fingers. They were like savages. There weren't any windows but the room was always brightly lit. You could easily forget whether it was night or day. You couldn't hear a sound from the outside world. I had four hours on and eight hours off, sitting alone in the middle of the room at a big desk. I had a telephone and they called me every half hour to find out how everything was. If anything happened I was supposed to shoot the prisoners with a .45 pistol.

There were four men in the cages while I was there, two long-term AWOLS, a lifer who had killed his shack job while he was drunk, and a rapist. They said the rapist was going to hang when they got him back to the States. He seemed crazy as hell. He was filthy and obscene and he probably was guilty. He had been accused of raping a young Austrian girl and they threw the book at him. They gave him a big public trial and invited the local population to come and see the show. They had buses to pick them up, free lunch, and earphones for the trial so they could follow by interpreter what was going on. A real goodwill gesture.

This particular guy used to worry me more than all the rest. They had their moods, but all in all they seemed resigned. He didn't seem to know what was going on. I don't think he had the faintest notion he was going to hang. He used to talk to me all the time about what he was going to do when he got home. He received mail once in a while, but the people writing him didn't have any idea he was even in trouble. He either talked about home or else he paced up and down his cage silently and you could tell there was a big blowoff coming. After a while he'd start hollering at the top of his voice, crazy things. I remember he used to yell questions and answers like the ones from basic training, the one they yelled at you in bayonet drill. "What's the purpose of the bayonet?" they'd yell. And everybody was supposed to answer back, "Kill! Kill! Kill!" He'd carry on like that. The rest of the prisoners put up with it most of the time, but sometimes it got on their nerves and then a couple of the regular stockade people had to come in and hold him while the doctor gave him a shot that knocked him out cold.

The officer in charge at the stockade was a recent graduate of West Point and he was plenty mad to have a dirty little job like that. He used to come in the cage and take it out on the prisoners. He never touched them, he just teased and harassed them, hoping that one of them would give him an excuse to get tough. Helpless men like that seem to bring out the worst in some people. One day he was standing in front of the cage of one of the AWOL's, telling him terrible stories about Leavenworth and how rough they were going to treat him there for the next ten years. The guy finally got tired of just listening and walked over to the bars. He cleared his throat and spat in the Lieutenant's face. The Lieutenant didn't flinch or move a muscle, I'll say that for him. He just took a handkerchief out of his pocket and wiped his face clean.

"That's going to cost you," he said.

He was right. A day or so later they came in and shaved and cleaned the guy, put a uniform on him, and took him away to be court-martialed.

"It was worth it," he told me when they brought him back. "It was worth a little more time just to get a shave and a bath and a clean uniform on. I'll spit again if he gives me half a chance."

The Lieutenant must have been satisfied. He never bothered that particular prisoner again, except in little ways like taking chow off of his tray. Finally some MP's from Livorno showed up to take the prisoners to the ship.

"So long, old sport," the rapist told me. "I'll see you on Times Square."

"In a pig's eye you will," the MP guarding him said. "You're going to hang, buddy."

That was the last that I saw of any of them. I was put back outside as a chaser and I was glad to be back in the fresh air and in the open view of the world again. The first day one of my prisoners, a seventeen-year-old kid who was pulling sixty days for some minor infraction, started to act up. He asked me what I was going to do if he tried to run away.

"I'm going to kill you if you try and run, fatface," I told him. "Because if I don't kill you, they'll throw you in the cage and in a week you'll wish you were dead."

He shut up and went to work.

5. Torment

THERE ARE ALWAYS things going on out of sight. Creatures move in disguise and there's a vigorous invisible life everywhere. You have to poke around or have an accident to discover it. Trip over a decayed log or just roll it upside down and you'll find a swarm of white wormy life, or death if you want to call it that, lively death; and I know no matter how content your eyes are with the green sweetness and your nose with the winey odor of the woods, you'll turn away almost sick at your stomach. On the other hand, in innocence, in ignorance, you may be fascinated by the idea of corruption, just as leaning over a fence and watching a great-bellied sow wallow in the dungy mud you may have wished to be a lot less than human. Knowledge is always something else. If somebody rubs your face in the filth you may yearn for even two-legged dignity.

When I was a boy we had an old leather-bound set of books purporting to be the history of the world and even before I could read I used to rifle those pages for the illustrations of great events. Before I ever went to school I had an idea about the Pyramids and the Fall of Rome and the Storming of the Bastille. As a matter of fact that first experience of history, flipping pages and looking for pictures, ruined me for any of the conventional ways of looking at history. Your first impressions, like your first wounds, are deepest. So I've always had a kind of haphazard view of time. What difference does it make whether you begin or end with the Fall of Rome?

There's one picture I remember quite well from another period of my childhood. It was a favorite of mine during the nervous time of early puberty when a woman is only a sign or signal of desire and might as well be two-dimensional. Next to the rather vapid girls in underwear available in the Sears Roebuck Catalogue the best pornographic material I had access to in those days was in *The History of the World*. There was one especially titillating picture—"The Inquisition in Session." It showed a full-blown woman as naked as God made her, hiding her face. A huge executioner with a black mask on had just ripped away the last shreds of her clothes. In the background there was a raised bench with ecclesiastical dignitaries, bored or leering, and in one corner there were instruments of torture, whips, and irons heating red-hot on a fire. It was a perfect field day for undeveloped sexuality. An innocent's paradise.

The reality of torment is somewhat less appealing. I used to pull Courtesy Patrol downtown in Linz. We had an office in the main police station and whenever we were off duty we used to gather around the stove in that room. It seems to me it was always cold in Austria. The police station was a big gloomy building, cold and high-ceilinged, poorly lighted. In the rooms around us the local police carried on their daily jobs with a muted efficiency. You could hear their heavy boots sometimes in the hall and there was always the faint insect noise of a distant typewriter, but most of the time the place seemed as quiet and decorous as a tomb. We had a feeling of awe for those cops. They were all big, handsome men and they never seemed to relax from a dignified, unsmiling position of attention. Their high boots gleamed and their uniforms were immaculate. Next to them we felt like a bunch of civilians in costume.

Every once in a while the authorities would decide to crack down on prostitution in the town. Sometime around midnight they'd wheel out the trucks and be gone, and in an hour or so they'd start bringing in the night's catch. Then there was some excitement in the halls. The whores would be shepherded in, old ones and young ones, fat ones and skinny ones, in all stages of dress and undress, expensive ones as shiny and clean as a model in an advertisement, cheap ones with black ruined teeth and an itchy look. They all seemed dazed or numb. They were taken down our hall and through a door at the end. After that crowds of cops went down there, too, and pretty soon you could hear military band music being played on some kind of loudspeaker. Once I got curious about what was going on. I asked the interpreter they had assigned to our office about it. He just grinned and shrugged.

"See for yourself," he said. He was an easygoing guy who was happy just to sit around the office and smoke our cigarettes.

I went down the hall and opened the door into the blaring military band music. It was a hell of a sight. They had all the whores stripped and the cops were running around among them beating them with rubber truncheons. It was like a picture out of Dante's *Inferno*. The women were all crying and screaming and begging and praying. The cops were running around in circles like crazy sheepdogs. They'd beat at random and then spontaneously single out an individual and beat her down to the floor, the truncheons blurring with fury and speed. Some of the cops had their shirts off. They had wild faces like men hopped up on dope. One man sat on a table where the record player was, changing the records, smoking and just watching. When the whores were like this, naked, scared, and in pain, they all looked alike, just poor flesh and bones suffering. But the worst thing was the blood. Nobody ever talks about the blood of beatings. Their faces were swollen and bleeding from broken noses, cheeks and jaws, split lips. Their bodies were bleeding from dark bruises and cuts. The floor was slick with blood like the back of a butchershop. They were slipping and falling in it, cops and whores alike.

I shut the door and went back to the office.

"So?" the interpreter said. "Now you have seen our floor-show."

I felt so numb I didn't want to say anything.

"Why?" I said finally. "Why do they do it?"

He shrugged. "There is no severe penalty for prostitution," he said. "They try to scare them."

"Does it work?"

"No," he said. "It's the same ones all the time. They can't afford to be anything else."

"What's the sense of it then?"

"Maybe some of them leave town," he said. "Who knows?"

I went to the window and looked out at the soft, foggy winter's night and the old sleeping city. All those people sleeping safe and sound for the time being, having dreams, rooting among the wreckage of their absurd, forlorn desires. Down the street the Beautiful Blue Danube flowing. On the other side of the bridge, the Russian zone, the lonely Rusky guard stamping his boots, blowing on his hands, thinking about the big lost spaces back home. And me sick. I was sick thinking about the fine avenues and boulevards of this world where you walk with your head up, strut if you want to like a god, and meanwhile all the time there's an invisible world breeding and thriving. In back rooms, in hidden corners, behind blank smiles, all over the world people are suffering and making other people suffer. The things God has to see because He cannot shut His eyes! It's almost too much to think about. It's enough to turn your stomach against the whole inhuman race.

THE STRONG MAN

"CHEER UP," Harry said. "It isn't really a serious matter."

"You don't think so?"

He only smiled. It was a great gift, that smile, sudden, frank, wholly disarming, and, like a child's, shaped by secret mischief. It was impossible to talk seriously about anything in the face of such an abrupt and charming defense. She looked at him, studied him as she might have examined a perfect stranger—the close-cut, sandy hair, the small eyes, bland and sad as a dog's, the soft lips and the thrilling brightness of his smile. Harry was almost handsome, certainly, but, she thought, strangely unreal. There was a sense of the alien about him. You never quite thought of him in three dimensions.

"No," he went on, "we'll get over it. And anything you can get over isn't really serious—like the measles."

"Or smallpox."

Harry smiled again and poured some beer into her glass. They were sitting in a little trattoria beside the Arno. It was twilight, the long gold twilight of Tuscany in late summer, and all of the tables were taken. Along the sidewalks on both sides of the street the bright, close-pressed crowds flowed as slowly as the river. They had just arrived in Pisa that afternoon from Rome.

"We'll stay here a couple of days and rest," he said. "It's a restful place. We can sit by the window in the hotel room and have late breakfasts and see the river. In the morning I'll take you over to see the *campanile*. It really does lean, you know."

"Does it?" she said. "I'm not sure I'm going to stay with you. I'm not at all sure I ought to."

"Don't be silly," he said. "Of course you'll stay."

"You're so sure of me. Why are you always so sure?"

She was fumbling in her pocketbook for matches. She thought for a moment that she was going to cry and she didn't want that to happen. He leaned across the table and lit her cigarette with his lighter.

"Where would you go?"

"You bastard," she said.

"No, I'm serious," Harry said. "For once I'm being perfectly serious. Let's try and be rational about this whole thing. Where would you go?"

"Home. I think I'd like to go home."

"Out of the question," he said. "What would you do when you got there—get a divorce?"

"Stop it, Harry. I don't know what I'm going to do."

"I want to know," he said quickly. "Do you want a divorce or don't you? It's just that simple. Either—or."

"I don't know, Harry. I don't know what to do yet. I'm trying to work all this out in my mind. Will you please stop asking me dumb questions?"

"What about the baby? You ought to think about that. Did you ever stop to think about the baby?"

At last she began to cry. He gave her his handkerchief.

"Please," he said. "Even if these people can't understand English, they can't ignore a sobbing woman."

She stiffened a little.

"You care what they think, don't you?"

"There, you see, you've stopped now."

"I could say it in Italian," she said. "I could stand up and say it in very simple Italian. This is my husband who is making me cry. My husband is always making me cry. My husband is always sleeping with other women. When I find out about it we leave. We are always leaving places."

"You know what they'd say? They'd say, why don't you leave him? The logical answer."

"You'd like that, wouldn't you?"

"I don't know," Harry said. "I never really thought of it until just now."

"You can't even imagine it. After all this time, you can't even conceive of my leaving you. Now that I'm pregnant, you're certain."

"Do we have to go through all this?"

"You can't even imagine my leaving you, can you?"

"No," he said. "To tell you the truth I can't."

"All right," she said. "Suppose I don't. Suppose I just stay. Then what?"

"Everything," he said, smiling wonderfully. "Then everything. We'll begin again. No reason why not. We could go up to Paris. I know some people there."

"Why not home?"

"Why not?"

"Are you serious? Would you really go home?"

"I might even go to work," he said. "Idle hands . . ."

"The awful thing," she said, "is that I never know when you're telling the truth. I never know whether I can trust you."

He signaled for the waiter.

"I suppose you'll have to," he said, "I suppose you'll just have to take that chance."

They crossed the street and edged into the crowd walking along the bank of the river. It was getting dark now and the mountains to the north were only a bulk of heavy shadows. The mountains were disappearing and the river was dark. She could smell the river and she could hear it, but she could only see it where light fell. She felt dazed, as if not only Harry but the whole world was unreal, vanishing. It gets dark and the mountains go away.

"Where does everything go in the dark?" she had asked when she was a child.

"Things just goes to sleep," the colored nurse had said. "They just curl up and go to sleep."

They moved across the bridge with the crowd and then they were on a narrow cobbled street with cafes and restaurants and movie theaters. They heard a military band playing faintly somewhere and they heard the laughter and the rich syllables of the language all around them. Farther along the street they entered a small square. At the corner there was a tight circle of people around a single figure. The man was very pale under a light, powerfully built, in bathing trunks and sneakers. He stood relaxed, slump-shouldered, while a short fat man, his bald head shining in the lamplight, walked slowly around the circle of viewers displaying a placard with a picture of the man in bathing trunks.

"What is he?" she asked. "A magician?"

Harry laughed. "No," he said. "He's some kind of a strong man. Do you want to watch?"

"I don't know. I've never seen one."

"Let's."

There was a hush as the man began his performance. He lifted heavy weights over his head, straining, his pale muscles bulging and the sweat glistening all over his body. When he had finished, the short man passed through the crowd taking a few coins in his hat. The strong man leaned against the lamppost breathing heavily. She thought he looked so lonely out there in that zone of light, alone and almost naked. He did not seem to be looking at anyone or anything. He seemed unaware of the crowd. He only rested, breathing hard, tautly aloof like a beast in a cage. She took Harry's hand in hers.

"Let's go," Harry said. "This is a bore."

"Wait," she said. "He's going to do something with ropes."

Two men from the crowd carefully wrapped him in a net of knotted ropes. When they had finished, he could not move his hands or his feet, and they stepped back into the crowd. The strong man remained still for a moment. Then he closed his eyes and began to strain against the ropes. Sweat was slick on his forehead. The large veins in his neck showed blue and swollen against his skin. Very slowly, painfully it seemed, he began a shrugging motion with his shoulders. The ropes left raw red lines where they bit into his flesh. For a desperate moment it seemed to her that he would never be able to free himself, but then he twisted sharply and somehow freed one arm. The crowd clapped and the short man passed the hat again while the strong man finished wriggling free of the rest of the ropes.

"He's going to try chains next," she said. "Let's see him get out of chains."

"It's just a trick. Don't you see that? Come on."

"I want to see it."

"For Christ's sake!" Harry said. "Oh, all right."

This time he was wrapped tightly in chains. He stood looking blankly into the faces of the crowd while two men wrapped him in chains.

The strong man started with his whole body twisting against the chains. Abruptly he slipped and fell and there was a gasp and the brute sound of iron on stone. He lay as still as a fallen doll on the street.

"Let's go," Harry said.

"I want to watch," she said. "I want you to stay and see it."

"He'll never get loose now. They'll have to set him free."

"I don't think so."

"This is silly," Harry said. "I can't see any earthly reason why we should have to stand here and watch this."

"Look!" she said. "He's moving now."

The strong man began to writhe on the street. He moved along on his back, tense and fluttering like a fish out of water. He rolled over onto his stomach and now they could see blood on his lips and the glazed, fanatic concentration in his eyes.

"You don't have to look," she said. "Close your eyes if you don't want to look at it."

She watched the man in chains and she felt a strange exhilaration. She felt her own body move, tense with the subtle rhythm of his struggle. One arm free, then, slowly, very slowly, the other, and, at last sitting up, he twisted his hurt legs free. While his companion passed the hat, the strong man sat in the street and looked at his legs, smiling a little. She turned away and looked at Harry. Poor Harry would never understand. Whatever she finally decided to do, Harry would never understand.

"Let's go back to the hotel and have dinner," he said.

They walked back the way they had come, and as they crossed the bridge over the Arno she saw that there was a new moon and she could see the dark shape of the mountains. They were still there, and she could feel the strength and flow of the river, and she could feel her child, the secret life struggling in her womb.

SEPTEMBER MORN

When the new gardener came Lily couldn't resist calling her husband. She dialed his office at the library. He answered, brisk, abstracted, professional.

"Professor," she said. "This is Lady Chatterley."

"Hi," he said. "Anything wrong?"

"The new gardener arrived. Sexy and surly. Sort of a poor man's Marlon Brando."

"Can you protect yourself?"

"I don't know," she said laughing. "Maybe you'd better come home and take care of me."

"Oh you can take care of yourself all right."

"Play tennis this afternoon?" she asked casually, hopefully.

"Can't make it."

Lily had really hoped he would want to play. Neither of them could play well. But, dressed in crisp white, however clumsy they might be in the softly flaming arena of autumn, the maples extravagant around the courts and the air chill in the late afternoon, there was something significant about their playing together. She was better, more graceful and deft in driving long forehand shots to the back line. Each game began with this feminine aggression of hers, forcing him to respond. He'd become a little angry; not wishing to show it, he'd smile and take his time between serves, and this pleased her. Power was his next attempt. Savagely, even crudely, he'd slam the ball back to her, missing more often than not, the lines of anger becoming more explicit as he sweated and lunged to take command and she, teasing, exasperating, returned his shots. At last, crafty, taking control of the game, John would depend on soft shots, lightly arcing lobs and placed junk shots that made her run. Something would stir in her, thrive as he gained confidence, bloom as he mastered himself and then overpowered her. Of course he was unaware of all these things happening to her, though he would be pleased with himself, petulant and sly as a child.

"That was fun," she'd say as they walked back to the car, watching the other games. "We ought to do it more often."

"Yes," he'd invariably agree, "I don't get much exercise these days."

Lily finished the breakfast dishes and watered the plants in the dining room. She looked over their green confusion through the window and saw him raking leaves. He was sweating already and, she thought, a lazy young man. He reached far out with the rake and urged the leaves toward him with an easy stroke, moving himself as little as possible. She supposed she'd have to talk to him. He'd stopped working for a moment and leaned against an elm, smoking. The grapes in the far corner of the lawn were almost ripe. She might take a basket and see if they were ready.

"It's very warm for September, don't you think?" she said.

He grinned and wiped his hand across his face, whipping the sweat off.

"Why don't you take off your shirt and be comfortable?"

Without a word he unbuttoned his khaki shirt and hung it on a knot of the tree.

"I can't get used to this American weather," he said. "Hot days, cold nights."

He was dark-skinned and soft, his body rounded, indulgent, for she could easily discern the angled lines of his male power, the bulked shape of muscle beneath the puffed contours of his torso. It was the broad powerful body of a wrestler, perhaps, but indolently disguised. It offended her that he could be so careless with himself. Lily had been a fat girl. Rigor and severity kept her lean now, and only a certain stiffness, a woodenness about her movements, revealed that she lived in an attitude of constraint. He smoked and patted the fine hair on his stomach, his glance never diverted from her eyes. She looked down. She felt that he was laughing at her, as if he could see around her, or perhaps through her, the shape of the fat girl she had been. Women have spoiled him, she thought. He takes admiration for granted.

"My husband was in Italy during the war," she said.

"So?" he said, actually laughing now.

"He was there for two years."

"And you were alone? The war was a great pity."

She could look at him unflinching now. She met the arrogance of his look, the slight glow of irony in his eyes with perfect control.

"I was in the Navy," he said. "Not much war."

"Oh yes," she said, "the Italian Navy."

"That's true," he said. "It was not like the mountains and the winter. We were mostly in port."

He smiled widely. She pictured him doing the things she imagined sailors do, idly dripping paint, sunbathing on the hot deck with all around him the fantastic blue and the brightness of an ideal port. She pictured him swimming with a crowd of tanned equals, and in the evening in his tight-fitting uniform swaggering in the warm lights pooled into the street from dusky rooms where there might be laughter and music. Lily had a picture of her husband on the bureau, tall, thin, as ill-fitted in his fatigues and mud-stained boots as a recruit, posed against a barren hillside. Everything in the picture was splashed with gray.

"The Army is a bad life," he said. "I hate the cold."

"No," she said, "I suppose you wouldn't like the cold."

He looked at her, the tall American lady in her wool skirt and high-buttoned long-sleeved blouse, her hair severely knotted back, the whole an effect of restraint and simplicity, and he looked at himself, familiar, appraisingly as if he were looking at the body of an animal.

"My husband is a professor at the university," she said. She tried to speak simply as she might speak to a child. She wasn't sure how much English he knew. He raised his eyebrows.

"Then he must be wise."

She wasn't certain whether or not he meant that as a question.

"He can speak Italian very well."

"Good," he said, throwing the butt of his cigarette into the grass. "We can talk sometime."

He picked up the rake and began again to rake the leaves into a pile. She started across the lawn, past the flower garden, toward the tangle of grape vines where the careful lawn disappeared into the woods. She passed close by him.

"Signora," he said in a soft voice, not looking up from his task, "does the Signora have any children?"

"No," Lily said, as she walked briskly past him. "We have no children."

The grapes were not ripe yet and she was glad that there was nothing else to do outside. She walked back into the house and climbed the carpeted stairs. She wanted to be busy and she decided to change the sheets. She tore them off the bed and neatly, tightly tucked in the clean ones. All this time she knew that she wanted to look at herself in the mirror, but she knew that she shouldn't. She caught only glimpses of herself passing in the mirror on the bureau and the mirror on the closet door while she made the bed.

There were so many things to do. She could vacuum and there was shopping to do and there were letters to write and a few telephone calls, but she felt weary. She wanted to lie between the clean, cool sheets. She knew this was silly, but perhaps she did need a nap, and she threw a blanket over the bed and pulled the pillow over her face. Dozing, she heard the gardener whistling and she smelled the smoke of leaves burning.

She saw herself as a girl in the big drafty house, alone in her room in the afternoon. September afternoons were so lonely. The summer had ended and school—she felt a kind of dread remembering the press of bodies, the shrill hall, the monotone and the smell of the classrooms—school had not yet begun, and she wanted most of all to be alone in her room. The chill would be coming on and there would be a fire downstairs, but also her mother knitting, and teacups, and her sister, her older sister, the frail beautiful Margaret. She would be alone in her room, naked against the harsh wool blanket, and closing her eyes she became the Sleeping Beauty, milk-colored, long-limbed, half-dozing, waiting for the sound of hoofs and the heavy boots of the horseman on the stairs.

Suddenly the telephone was ringing. She rose up from her half-dream and snatched the receiver. She heard her husband's voice.

"Lily," he said, "I think I can make that tennis this afternoon."

"Can you?" she asked, eagerly.

"We haven't played for quite a while," he said.

"What time?"

"Oh, about three-thirty. I'll pick you up. I'll beat you," he said. "You better be ready."

She felt relieved, yet sad, somehow, inexplicably sadder than if he hadn't called. She got up and straightened her skirt and blouse. She washed her face and smiled at herself in the mirror. She was exactly the same as before. She went to the window and saw him squatting by the fire. The leaves were burning slowly, going up in pale smoke, and he was whistling a tune she didn't know.

THE RARER THING

HE SPRAWLED INDOLENTLY, propped on one elbow, spinning the earth around with his index finger. He'd put his finger on the white cap of the North Pole and spin the whole multicolored globe first one way and then the other. She hated that casual abandon. It was so like him, she quickly decided. She watched him smiling to himself like a shower of gold on his slovenly beauty. Beauty, yes, but slovenly was the right word for it. He had a corrupted athlete's body, flesh that had once been trained and trim, that had once been utterly possessed by energy and rhythm, the spring and dance of anxious blood. She could easily imagine how it had been, his face taut-skinned, his shoulders round and smooth and well-defined, his stomach flat from navel to lean loins and ridged with a delicate washboard pattern of muscle, and his legs knotted and angular as whittled wood, but lively, twitching with inner life like the glossed nervous body of a good racehorse. He had been a runner in college some years before, she knew that. But now, careless as a god, he seemed to flaunt his decay. She could see the softness of his torso rise and fall beneath the light summer sports shirt as he breathed. His face, coarsening, puffing at the jowls; his neck, once a clean thick sinewy line like rope, bulged now, overflowed at the open collar. Strangely, though, the whole impression was one of constriction

rather than self-indulgence. It was as if he had deliberately confined all the life in him, disguised his surplus of vigor in shapeless flesh, as if he wore a magic cape or shawl. As he looked up at
her, his eyes traveling the short pilgrimage of her body as if she
were no more than some vague object, sleepy-eyed, indifferent
as well to whatever she might be thinking of him, she despised
him for what he had done to and with himself. But more than
that she hated (or was it envy?) his male freedom to do whatever
he pleased with himself. That was what wounded her, the way
even now one could tell at a glance what he had been and could
be if he really wanted to and how he used that image of himself,
the imagined one that dogged his real presence like an attentive
shadow, with squandering ease to mock and make fun of the
world of appearances, to sneer especially at every kind of striving, burning, longing within that world, like her own. Unset-
tled by these thoughts, she decided to accept this more ratio-
nally as only another intolerable example of the crude vanity of
insensitive maleness.

Rozanne noticed these things. She was an artist, a sculptress,
and, without intellectualizing, without thinking a word, she
could feel the graceless self-satisfaction of him. What she felt
was as true to her, as much a fact, as if he had made some direct,
obscene gesture with his hands, as real and ineffaceable as a
dirty word scrawled on some public wall. She had never met
Roger before this. She had known Frances, who was now his
wife, for some years. They had both come originally from the
South, met in New York, and through some bleak years shared
an apartment in the Village. Just today, this Friday afternoon,
Rozanne had come from New York to visit Frances for the first
time since the wedding.

In one way it was a shame about Frances. Frances had been
studying the classical guitar before she married Roger, and she
had a fine talent, a very special gift; not so much of technique,
for she had to struggle to master each new piece technically, but
the rarer thing, an inner and immediate sense of the meaning of
music. The rigor of learning was a discipline simply, its sole
purpose to cultivate the music she already knew, heard, felt, into

life. It was a gift altogether different from Rozanne's, but she respected it. For herself technique was a keen weapon, creation a kind of conquest. Of course, Frances had given up all that when she married Roger.

"She's getting better all the time," Roger was saying, speaking of his wife's cooking.

Rozanne recalled the picture he had presented at the dinner table, amid candles, good silver, china, glass, all those middle-class symbols of security, hunched over his plate like a hungry dog, eating in huge mouthfuls, talking, while he chewed, of politics, of television, of his own insurance business, gesturing with an intense, gravy-dripping fork as if all these subjects were profoundly significant, taxing him to summon up all the subtlety and imagination he surely must have thought he was displaying (or did he care?), the stained fork winking light from its slender tines. Frances was sitting now in a high, antique rocking chair, bought at one of their auction excursions it was likely, smiling, too, modestly proud, it seemed, of her languid husband. Her rich dark hair and the smooth and even softness of her, which was explicit in a round pale face kindled by bluebright eyes, made her seem wholly alien to this man, to this time and place. There was something mythical about her. To Rozanne she had always seemed like a cameo figure or, perhaps, a graceful virgin in a tapestry with unicorns. She was one of the few, perhaps the only woman, that Rozanne had admired without the least shiver of envy.

"At first, right after we got married, I had to make do with hot dogs and baked beans," he said. "But things have taken a turn for the better."

"You seem to be thriving nicely," Rozanne said.

He grinned and stretched and she noticed his hands. They were large and strong, veined and possessed by a movement and rhythm of their own, something which did not seem to belong to him. She found herself wondering what in the world his mother had been like.

"You ought to plan to stay awhile with us this summer," he

said. "Some suburban air and a few regular meals would be good for you."

"Oh, *Roger,*" Frances said, apparently amused. "Rozanne's not too thin, really. She was always the center of attention in a bathing suit. I remember one summer half the lifeguards on the Cape—"

"Well, we'll see," Roger interrupted. "We'll all go for a swim tomorrow if the pool fills up in time."

The swimming pool had been empty when she arrived. There she had seen Roger for the first time, standing in the empty cavity, scrubbing with a long-handled brush, sweating in the late afternoon sun, pale and soft in his bathing trunks. He had looked up at them and laughed when she and Frances peered over the deep end of the pool from the mowed and green, bee- and bug-lively lawn. He said he was glad to meet her and that he had heard so much about her. He apologized for being practically naked at the moment, but thought, laughing again, that a sculptress must be familiar enough with the male form and physique to let it pass.

"I'd love to stay with you-all for a while," Rozanne said. "But I'm afraid I'd be completely unnerved by all the furious activity in a commuter's house."

"It's not as gruesome as it seems," he said. "Maybe you could do some work here, or just rest."

"I really *do* need a rest," she said. "It's a lovely idea. But what I'm really afraid of is that I'd get used to it. That would be terrible. I'm afraid if I stayed any longer than a weekend, I'd start to take all this comfort for granted. I'd become quite stout and complacent."

"You don't have to become complacent unless you want."

Without a doubt he was the most insensitive man she had ever known. She had known her share, oh more than her share, of sensitive men. She had drawn them to her, really in spite of herself, cradled them briefly and destructively, as a small flame captures for an instant the brief joy of the moth. From childhood there had always been sensitive men—her father, hen-pecked, browbeaten, ineffectual—her older brother, cruel then, pitiable now, in the state mental asylum. *This*, however, was rather amusing. It might have been genuinely funny if it hadn't involved poor Frances.

"I guess," he went on, "after the wild bohemian life, you find us terribly dull."

"On the contrary," she said. "Most of the men I know are so *energetic*, so *ambitious*, such *anxious* people. They're all trying to *do* so many different things at once. It's refreshing to discover that there's someone in this world who's relaxed and content with things just as they are."

"Really?"

Frances was still smiling, obviously not bothered, not in the least embarrassed by either of them. Roger rolled over onto his stomach and laughed, giving the globe a savage spin. Quite suddenly, as he was laughing, his face seemed to change. His eyes brimmed with light, an unexpected light like the occasional glimpse of wildness seen for an instant in the eyes of a family pet. There was, after all, something satirical about him that she hadn't observed before. It was as if he had really been hiding, just as her brother used to do when she was little, around some corner, behind a curtain or some piece of furniture, and had suddenly leapt out to frighten her. She was offended to realize that he was perhaps being not quite honest or straightforward in the guise which he had been presenting for her inspection.

"You must think we're awful," he said. "If you do, you're right. This is a naughty life we're leading, sort of like living in sin. I guess it is a kind of sin to be happy these days."

"It is a little new to me."

"Yes, it must be strange, almost exotic," he said. "There's a paradox for you—you people are fond of paradoxes. Given the right set of circumstances and even the commonplace becomes exotic."

He stood up, yawned and stretched, then returned the globe to its proper place on a table with reference books.

"Well, it's nice to meet you at last, " he said. "You've been kind of like a ghost in my life until now, but here you are in flesh and blood. I hope you'll plan to stay awhile."

Roger left the room and, soon after, she heard him outside in the darkness whistling for the dog.

Frances came to talk with her in her room before they went to bed. They sat on the bed, smoking and talking, trying to recover some of the ease and intimacy they had known before. They talked of names and places, but for Rozanne there was something elusive and strained about their reminiscences. Frances seemed now to possess an untroubled secret which she didn't wish to share. In those other days it had been Frances, in her innocence, her rare and literal virginity, seeking after the knowledge Rozanne owned. Rozanne, faced with wide-eyed wonder, able to parcel out the truth as she pleased, had discovered that her own life, sad and sordid enough, was transformed into something desirable, enviable. Seeing herself in Frances's eyes had made even the most ordinary aspects and events glow as from a Midas touch. Now, though they talked freely enough, Rozanne felt a little shabby, baffled, and insecure.

"You look wonderful," Rozanne said. "I think you must be very happy or very lucky. Maybe both."

"Do I? I hope you like Roger. He's so different from everyone else we know. I want you to like each other."

"You have my blessing," she said. "He's a very attractive husband."

"As husbands go," Frances said, and they both smiled.

Looking at Frances, Rozanne thought of a cat curled by a fire and the way that a cat's body at rest, in perfect purring contentment, still somehow conveys, suggests, implies all the beauty of wildness, the furred speed, stealth, and the satisfaction of realized dexterity.

"Do you ever find any time to play the guitar?"

"Only once in a while," Frances said. "There are so many different things to do. You'd be surprised how many things have to be done."

"I can imagine," she said. "Maybe you'll find time later on to pick it up again."

"Maybe," Frances said. "With children it will be difficult. It would be nice to play again. I miss it sometimes."

"Yes, I suppose you do."

After Frances said good night and left, Rozanne snapped off the bedside lamp, but instead of trying to sleep, she lay awake watching the red glow of her cigarette in the dark. She felt vaguely sad, listening to the muffled sounds from their bedroom. The radio was playing dance music and she could hear their voices above the music without being able to hear what they said. Their voices rose and fell and intermingled, softly, like a woodwind duet. After a moment she heard his bare feet lightly in the hall, and then a knock on the door.

"Are you still awake?"

"Yes."

"Frances tells me that you're a bird-watcher. Maybe you'd like to get up early and see our birds."

"That would be very nice."

"Okay. I'll wake you," he said. "But I warn you it will be early."

"All right."

"Well, good night."

"Good night, Roger."

She heard him going on tiptoe back to their room. That would be his own kind of instinctive delicacy, to tiptoe, even in innocence, from the bedroom of another woman back to his wife. After a little while they turned off the radio and then the light. There was not a sound. She was listening, like a household spy, for even the least sign of movement from their room. A voice, laughter, any sound would have been some solace to her at just this time while she lay still and uneasy and alone in the dark. Of course she had always been alone in the dark like this, even when her bed was anything but empty.

Rozanne sat up and turned on the light. She rose and stood looking at herself in the mirror. She hated him, oh yes, despised him completely. Still, she had an answer to his challenge and contempt. Compared to Frances, she was lean and hard-muscled, almost boyish, but she knew well the virtues of her singular attractiveness, as cruel as shears. Given the chance (and the whole weekend was still ahead) she would repay him in kind.

She would expose him after her own image. At the right time, in the right place, a gesture would reduce him to all fours. Sooner or later, like any other, he'd howl like a lost dog. It was wrong to think of doing this to Frances, but necessary. There was purity even in this feeling, this desire, a purity she intended to keep intact, inviolable. Her naked image stared back at her with solemn assurance she could not be wrong. She turned off the light again and lay down. As she dozed, eased into sleep, she felt her lips compose a tranquil smile.

THE SLEEPING BEAUTY

THE FISHERMEN STOOD at a long wooden table, heavy in black hip boots, each holding a knife in his hand, waiting. Boys carried heaped baskets of fish from the boats to them, staggering up the rock-strewn slope of the beach, and dumped them in a cascade of squirm and silver on the table. Then the knives flashed in the sun. They worked smoothly, swiftly, cutting off the heads at the gills with one stroke, then, with a deft scooping, gutting them clean. Yellow and blue and red, the guts fell on the table like a tangle of wilted flowers. In another moment, a quick scraping, they were scaled and each man dipped his cleaned fish in a barrel of salt water, tossed it into a waiting basket. The guts and fish heads were wiped into another barrel and they kept on working. At the lapping water's edge oil and grease floated in spreading rainbows. Overhead gulls screamed whitely.

"Can we go now?" Anne asked.

"Just a minute," her husband said. "I want to get a couple more pictures."

He crouched down on his plump thighs, squinting into the viewfinder of his camera. He was a handsome man, but, she thought, a little absurd juxtaposed against the rude scene in his American tourist clothes. Those brilliant sport shirts and the expensive slacks made any man look rather like a boy in a sunsuit. She glanced at the table, furtively intrigued by the laughter and the shouting in the curious French dialect among the fisher-men, the air of hectic festivity. In the elephantine hip boots they seemed like mythical beasts, the colossal legs and lower bodies merging with more fragile human shoulders and heads. Their faces were darkened, wrinkled by wind and sun like cured meat, and their eyes, vividly contrasting, were lively, satiric, cruel. The young boys, pale and straining under the weight of the baskets, hurried anxiously from the boats to the table, awkward on slime-slick rocks; like acolytes, she thought, like uninitiated novices. On the table with trained, impersonal hands the fisher-men were performing the sacrifice. She stared at the weathered hands, identically crude and functional as if whittled out of hard wood. She shuddered at the glory of the knives.

"Did you ever imagine anything like this?" her husband asked rhetorically. He was still crouched on his haunches, winding the film. "Of course," he went on, "when I show the slides, it will turn out looking scenic and pretty like the pictures in *National Geographic*. I wish I could get the excitement of it all, but you can't do that with a camera."

"No," she said. "I suppose you can't."

Anne could not look at the table anymore. She had a dizzy, empty feeling and she knew she couldn't trust her eyes. She was possessed by the vague fear that if she looked again, if she dared, she would be witness to some unspeakable barbarity. She looked out at the bay and high, higher than the savage acrobatics of the gulls, into pure blank depths of sky, so clear, so chill, she felt if she let go of herself for even an instant she would fall into that immense distance, go tumbling head over heels to drown in infi-nite brightness. It was the rare, faint sensation she had known as a girl during Mass, when her family was still in the Church. She could not bear it, kneeling on the cold stone, seeing the distant and symbolic sacrifice. She had always looked away, up into the loft where, amid the purest fractions of coined light from stained-glass windows, she could discern the starched whiteness of the nuns. Overhead, abstracted, they seemed to poise like white birds, gulls or swans, in a keener atmosphere than flesh can know.

"You ought to be in the movies," her husband said, and she turned to see him fixing her in the viewfinder. She saw his index finger tightening on the button and she smiled forever, for posterity, hearing the little click of the lens.

"Shall we head back to the hotel?"

"If you're ready," she said.

They walked along the beach in the direction of the hotel. Earlier that morning in their room they had been awakened by the noise and then from the windows seen the fishing boats coming in, multicolored pennants streaming in a light breeze, moving in slow formation into the bay, each boat comically dignified by a bristling white mustache of foam. "We don't want to miss this," Fred had said, and they had scrambled into clothes and, almost forgetting the camera, run down the wide stairway, dodged among startled guests in the lobby, raced out onto the beach, laughing, excited. "What will all those respectable people say?" she had cried. "Oh nothing," he said. "Just those crazy honeymooners, they don't know any better."

They had seen it all, arriving just as the fishermen came ashore. There had been the knot of women who stood at a little distance, in wooden, unsmiling attitudes, watching their men come laughing and shouting ashore. The men were busy, setting up the long tables on a row of sawhorses, arranging their gear, struggling into the great hip boots. Around them young boys fluttered like shrill birds. The men seemed self-contained, unconcerned, though from time to time one of them shouted to the women on the shore. As they began the job of cleaning the fish, the women turned silently away, following a path in single file that went through the dunes to the cluster of the village and the shacks where they lived.

That had been a warm feeling for her. She wished vaguely to be one among them, inconspicuous in rough clothing, wearing a plain apron like theirs, and she knew she would have felt a wincing joy, too deep, too simple for smiles or tears, seeing her own husband leap blithe from the sea to the land. "I wish," she had said, "we could have sneaked a picture of those women's faces. I'd like to remember that." "Those old biddies?" Fred had said, laughing. "A waste of colored film."

Now they walked in the soft sand and it was hard going. They saw a path in the dunes that led to the road behind and they turned away from the shore following it. She felt her husband's hand in hers, small-boned, frail, and tense, she thought, as a musician's must be and strangely incongruous with the well-being of his body. It was as if the hands belonged to someone else, another man, a creature of imperceptible delicacy, concealed within the flesh and blood of Fred's good health. Ahead of them was a cliff, a sharp jutting among lesser dunes. There was a path from the road to the top.

"Let's go up there," she said. "It might be a marvelous view of the whole bay."

"Don't you want to go back to the hotel and have breakfast? I'm hungry, myself. I don't know about you."

"Oh we can wait," she said. "Do let's climb up and see. It's such a lovely morning."

"All right," he said. "Follow me."

The path was steep and narrow. Anne followed him, watching the muscles in his legs and buttocks quiver with the effort of climbing as the sea breeze blew against his slacks and thin sport shirt, outlining the whole shape of his body as neatly as a glove conceives the shape of a hand. She hurried behind him, breathing hard, wholly conscious now of the rhythm of her own body in a subtle awareness she had not known before. Not, certainly not, on the wedding night, dazed and tired from the public splendor, when the hotel room had seemed so shabby and his hands on her flesh had seemed no more than the wind from the wings of a startled flight of birds. Nor the second night, which they spent in a motel driving to get there. Then, that night, she lay placid under the weight of him and felt only a kind of calisthenic monotony. She had felt, too, a caged animal within her, dark and supple as a panther, crying in terms too precious and remote for speech. She had burst into tears and he had been gentle, troubled, fumbling to comfort her. She pretended to sleep and when she heard him at last begin to breathe in sleep she opened her eyes and watched his boy's face on the pillow and cried silently. But now as they were climbing the cliff she abandoned herself to the thought of her flesh and his, a rich hazy thought in her blood, her breasts and loins, like a raw warm liquor. She wanted to be naked. She wanted to tear off her clothes and race to the top of the cliff.

They neared the top and were faced with a barbed-wire fence on which red rags were hanging.

"Danger, no trespassing," she said.

"Maybe we shouldn't go on," he said. "It might be dangerous up there."

"It looks all right to me. Come on."

"It might be against the law or something."

But she had stepped past him over the fence, leaving him no choice. She ran up the path and flung herself prone on the sand at the top with the pale sea wheat blowing around her. She saw his shoes beside her, the foolish suede shoes coated with sand.

"I feel like a spy," she said, cupping her hands over her eyes like binoculars. "I can see everything from here."

The whole blue semicircle of the bay with its tan shoreline was visible, broken only by the cheerful angularity of the hotel. Behind them the village was jumbled and colorful like a post-card. She could see the fishermen's shacks and a woman by one of them hanging out washing on the line. On the shore she saw the fountaining sea gulls and the table where the fishermen were still working. She rolled over on her back and looked straight up into the heart of the sky.

"This is pretty," Fred said. "I ought to be able to get some fine shots from here."

She nestled her head close to his feet and looked up at him, a towering triangle against the sky, his head cocked to sight the camera. She ran her hand along his leg.

"Hey!" he said. "You'll ruin the focus."

She sat up, hugging her knees, and watched him finish taking pictures. He put the camera carefully in its leather case and sat down beside her, facing her.

"What would you do," Anne said, "if I took the camera and threw it into the bay?"

"I don't know what I'd do," he said. "I'd be pretty mad I guess."

"Let's see."

She snatched the camera and started to crawl toward the edge of the cliff. He jumped after her, seizing her arm, but she tore free and he had a wrestle with her. They rolled in the sand and he tried to get the camera from her hands. She felt the animal strength of her body surge in response to his. His hands gripped hard on her shoulders, forcing her down and she twisted and tried to bite his arms, but his weight slowly forced her flat on her back. He put his knees on her shoulders to hold her down. He was wide-eyed, panting into her face and she saw the sweat glistening on his cheeks. His breath was warm in her face and she thought she could gasp suddenly and swallow up all the breath in his lungs as they said cats could do when you were asleep. When you were a little girl asleep. Remembering it, she laughed.

"What's the matter with you?" he said. "Are you crazy? We could have rolled off of here and been killed. What the hell is so funny?"

"You're so funny," she said. "I bet you haven't ever wrestled with a girl before."

He smiled. "No," he said, "I don't make a habit of it."

She felt the weight of his knees on her shoulders cutting harshly, but she didn't care, she felt relaxed, as if she were floating.

"Do you give up?"

She nodded.

"Give me the camera."

"Make me."

He gripped her wrist, bending it back, forcing the camera out of her hands. She spat at him.

"That's not fair," he said.

"Do you want to know a secret?" she said. "When we got up

this morning, I dressed in such a hurry that I forgot to put on my underwear. Did you notice?"

"What?"

"My pants, silly," she said, giggling. "I don't have any panties on."

"Jesus," he said, "you mean we've been walking all over the beach with all those people around? What if the breeze had blown your skirt up?"

"Wouldn't it have been awful?" she said. "Scandalous!"

"I swear," he said, shaking his head solemnly. "Sometimes I can't figure you out."

"Don't be so pompous," she said. "Half the women you see walking around don't have them on."

"Is that true?"

"Fred," she said. "Take off your clothes. Let's make love right now. Let's make love on top of a cliff."

He looked around, distractedly.

"Here?" he said. "Oh no, we couldn't do it here. Somebody might see us."

"I don't care if somebody sees us. I don't care."

"Be sensible," he said. "Let's go back to the hotel."

"I don't want to go back to the stupid hotel."

"Be reasonable, Anne. That's a crazy idea. We could come back here tonight."

"I don't want to come back here tonight. I want you to make love to me now, right here in broad daylight."

"Use your common sense, dear. Get a hold of yourself."

"Do you care?" she whispered fiercely. "Do you really care that much about somebody seeing us?"

"Yes."

He stood up slowly, brushed the sand off of his clothes, picked up the camera and slung it by its strap over his shoulder. He wouldn't look at her. He looked out to the bay. She felt abruptly ashamed, confused. It had been a strange thing, not at all like her, not at all like the nice well-groomed, well-brought-up girl he had married. It had seemed important. It had been joyous and important and she had not stopped to think how he must feel. Now she felt cheated but she knew that it was a childish feeling and it made her angry with herself. Now he was ashamed of himself. The old sad weight of complexity settled within her. She stood up and brushed the sand off her skirt and straightened her hair.

"Shall we go down?" he asked.

She followed him down the steep path heavily, full of bitter thoughts.

In the evening after dinner, he brought out the chess set. He had brought a little traveling set along with him. He was teaching her how to play in the evenings. They went into the writing room just off the lobby and cleared a desk. Fred puffed on a cigar and set up the chessmen on the board.

"I like you when you smoke a cigar," she said. "Daddy used to smoke a cigar once in a while and I always loved the smell of it."

"It makes me look like a fight promoter or a tycoon in the movies."

"I don't think so," she said. "It makes you kind of distinguished."

"That's nice," he said. "Somebody ought to tell the advertising men about it. Shall we play?"

She played badly. She had quickly grasped the idea of the game, but she could not force herself to think ahead or to plan moves in advance. She mistrusted systems of implacable logic. She felt as if she were denying herself if she concentrated a small, dry intellectual light on the checkered board and its strict wooden people with all their limitations and hierarchies. She played spontaneously, trusting an instinctive immediate judgment and vaguely hoping for a series of happy accidents. She had no reason to doubt this method. She had been lucky. She had even beaten him before. An observer would hardly have guessed that her mind was altogether elsewhere. While some part of her awareness, like a single lamp in a dark room, focused on the small area, the strict geometry of the game, while the clock on the wall solemnly, silently, performed its services, she was far and vague away. There had been saints. She remembered them from childhood. They knelt in the burning sands of remote desert places until, all torment and confusion vanishing, they knew a bright and lonely vacuum of contemplation. Still, there were shapes and contours from another way, another kind of pilgrimage. Rich and improbable, there was a kind of jungle like a landscape by Rousseau where, castled in the full glory of the flesh, she could find herself. There was a strange vocation of the blood. There were miracles of ripeness too. But she knew that she must choose one way or the other, or let it be chosen for her. To have neither, she thought, would be a kind of death.

"Well," Fred said. "You can't win them all. You're learning, though."

"Oh yes," she replied. "I'm learning all the time, but I have such a long way to go."

He looked up at the clock, its second hand whirling like a lean sword.

"Better turn in early," he said. "We've got a long drive ahead."

"All right," she said. "I think we both need a good night's sleep."

When she undressed and slipped into the cool sheets beside him, Anne felt overwhelmingly tired. She felt as if she were about to fall asleep for years and years. She'd lie there between the crisp sheets with her eyes closed and the light dust would settle on her face and cobwebs would form in the room; the flowers in the vase would wilt away and the drip, drip, drip of the faucet in the bathroom would go on forever and ever. She did not think anyone would ever arrive to kiss the dust off her lips.

The next night they were in the luxury hotel at Quebec. There were American tourists and the familiar bustle and rhythm of a great hotel. Fred had changed into a suit and tie for the city. Businesslike, he handled the arrangements efficiently, and, once they were alone in the commercial elegance and seclusion of their room, she felt, for the first time in days, secure. From the window she could see the famous lighted boardwalk where people strolled, and from somewhere not far she heard the music of a military band.

"Would you like to go out somewhere?"

"I feel a little tired," she said. "I don't feel much like going anywhere."

"Good," he said. "I feel the same way. Let's have them send dinner up to us."

"That's so extravagant."

While he telephoned and ordered the dinner, she went into the bathroom to bathe. She lay in the tub for a long time with the water so hot she could hardly stand it, drowsy, luxuriant. Already, she thought, her flesh was strange to her. She looked at her body with a critic's eye, with, she thought, the eyes of a good butcher, wondering how it would change and how her flesh would appear to her in years. She had an odd desire to be fat, grossly fat, almost immobile, to fill up the space of the tub with her flesh. She imagined herself so fat she would get stuck in the tub. She felt very sleepy. After a while there was a knock on the door.

"Hurry up," Fred called. "Dinner's getting cold."

She was extravagantly hungry. She couldn't remember ever being so hungry. She ate everything hurriedly until she felt almost stupefied with satiety. And there was champagne. She drank eagerly until the room began to reel and tilt.

"It's all gone," she said. "Isn't it a shame. Can't you order some more?"

"It's too expensive," Fred said. "I still have a bottle of bourbon in my suitcase."

"Let's drink it."

"Don't get sick, now."

She drank until she felt a marvelous numbness like a fever. Fred's face, apprehensive, curious, blurred and returned and blurred again.

"You're out of focus," she said. "You're all out of focus."

She fell on the bed. It tossed and turned under her like a boat in choppy water. She closed her eyes, listening to the sound of the military band, the steady rhythm of the bass drum, dreamy, contented, indifferent to Fred's awkward hands as he struggled with buttons and snaps, trying to undress her. Nothing bad could happen to her now. No matter what happened it could not be bad or good either, she felt so safe and sound.

In the morning they went on a guided tour of the city. Fred apologized for the idea; but after all, it was the easiest way to see the city and find out what they wanted to see later by themselves. She had a splitting headache and she didn't care what they did. They sat in the back and she pressed her face against the cool glass, barely aware of the city or the people on the bus or the tired jokes of the guide crackling on the loudspeaker. From time to time they stopped for pictures and Fred, excusing himself, went out with the crowd to photograph a monument, a building, a vista, from all angles. "We will want to have something to remember," he said.

At the last stop of the tour they had to get out. They were to be conducted through the convent of a missionary and teaching order of nuns.

"Can't I just stay on the bus?"

"No," he said. "This bus is going to leave. We may not end up on the same bus."

"Well, I'll meet you back at the hotel then."

"Come on," he said. "A hangover isn't that bad. Walking around will do you good."

They were taken through the convent and led to some large rooms containing objects from the distant outposts of the order, reasonably chaste African wood carvings, East Indian baskets and pottery and rich strange cloths. They were for sale. The rooms had a close antiseptic odor like an empty schoolroom. She looked at the things listlessly while the guide talked and made his jokes. So many sad things from so far away, tossed up here like driftwood on the beach.

"Do you see anything you want?"

"Don't buy anything," she said. "What would we ever do with it?"

The party moved on to the entrance of a little chapel.

"I can't go in," she said. "I haven't got a hat on."

"Anything will do. Use your scarf."

It took a moment for her eyes to become accustomed to the darkness. The chapel was dark and damply cool as a cave, though there were candles on the altar. Then she saw the two nuns in the white summer robes of the order kneeling motionless before the altar. They knelt on the stone floor in prayer, and the flames from the tall candles troubled their figures with swift light and shadow. She had never seen anything so white as the robes of those nuns. She thought of the cleanest, coldest surf, immaculate foam, tossed by the huge waves of the open ocean. She saw herself as a girl, kneeling, dreamy, during the long ritual.

"There are two of them here always, the guide says," Fred said. "They take turns."

She felt a light-headed total passivity, a chill languor, watching the fixed shapes of the kneeling nuns. She felt as if all her life she had been drowning and here in this cave was the bottom of the sea that she had feared and fought so much. In the dark looking at the tall candles and the breathless whiteness, she felt that she saw herself kneeling, not as a girl now, but as a woman, one chosen out of many, like Leda for whom there was the tumult of the swan. At least Leda had known the shudder of divinity, though the god came in disguise. Now she would be kneeling there forever in white and when she left the chapel she would be leaving herself behind and she would always be lost. She would never find herself again.

They walked out, and as they came into the sunlight she felt her eyes brimming. They walked toward the bus where the grinning guide beckoned and beckoned, and she could feel the tears rolling down her cheeks.

"What's the matter, Anne?" Fred was saying. "Is anything wrong?"

"It's nothing," she replied. "I'll be perfectly all right in a moment."

THE WITNESS
(A Cartoon Strip)

MISS A. THOUGHT she saw a crime committed, but she couldn't be sure. It happened when Miss A., who was a middle-aged trained nurse, was returning home from work in the early hours of the morning. She took the subway. The only other people on the car were three men, two who were sitting together and seemed to be arguing about something, and another at the other end of the car who was reading a newspaper. She didn't pay much attention to them. She whiled away the time reading advertising placards. Shortly before she got off at Ninety-sixth Street she noticed that one of the two men who had been talking crossed over and approached the man who was reading a newspaper. He seemed to be asking him a question. The man lowered the newspaper until just his eyes showed over the edge. His eyes were dark and perplexed and pained like the eyes of a man who has been caught telling a lie or in a shameful act. They were pitiable eyes, but they did not ask for pity, she thought. This may have been because all she could see were his forehead and eyes. She could not see the line of his lips, but she imagined that to fit the expression in his eyes they must be turned down and drawn in a tight line like the lips of a child not quite ready to take a dose of bad-tasting medicine.

She was naturally shy of making direct encounters with

strangers, especially men, and she stopped thinking about him and went back to looking at the advertisements. The man who had spoken to the man with the newspaper walked back and sat down beside his companion, but he didn't say anything to him. The two men sat very still, and she saw out of the corner of her eyes that they were looking at the bright-colored placards too. The other man was not reading the newspaper now, but he had slumped down in his seat with the newspaper lying across his face.

When she started to get off at Ninety-sixth Street, when she stood waiting at the sliding door and holding on tight to her pocketbook, she knew that the man had put aside his newspaper and was looking at her. She also knew without looking that the other two men were looking at him. She decided to risk returning his glance, and she saw that he was a round-faced, soft-jawed man with beautiful eyes like a girl's. He looked at her, she thought, imploringly, with the desperate resignation of someone about to be wheeled away to an operating room. He was asking for more than compassion, but he knew he would not get that much. Just then the subway stopped and she stepped off quickly. She didn't want to look back, but she thought she ought to. She waited until she heard the door close and then she turned around to look. The subway had begun to move, and in the noise it was like standing under a waterfall or within the center of a crashing wave. She saw the man who had been reading the newspaper standing at the door, beating against it with his fists and with his face pressed out of shape against the glass. His face was wet with tears and his lips were moving though she could not hear him. She saw as the subway flashed forward into the dark tunnel that the two men were standing beside him and looking at him. She could not see their faces but she could tell by the tight rigidity of their bodies that they were about to do something sudden. They managed while they were standing straight to look as if they were crouched to jump.

Afterwards she thought about it a good deal. She began by reading all the newspapers carefully for several days to find out if anything terrible had happened. She found out about a number of other terrible things but there wasn't anything which could answer her special questioning. She wanted to talk to someone about it, just to tell them exactly what had happened as you would tell someone about a bad dream that you had. She hoped that if she told someone exactly and completely what she had seen, that then she would feel better, lighter. She felt heavy, as if she were carrying around a large rock and she didn't know what to do with it. Miss A. tried to tell several people. She didn't want to tell her good friends because she knew that none of those few shy people, who were too much like herself, would really understand. She felt that she would only be adding her burden to their own.

So she tried out the story on several people with whom she had managed to keep a cordial but impersonal acquaintance. She tried to tell it to the grocer and to the superintendent of the apartment house and she even tried to tell it to another nurse who was having coffee with her one night at the hospital. She couldn't make sense out of it as it was and she knew she couldn't expect anyone else to unless she told it exactly as it was and in the right order. And she couldn't tell it that way because nobody had time to listen to all of it and in order to keep their interest she had to start at the end with the man crying and beating on the subway door and work backwards. That part was interesting because you don't often see people doing it. But that was all they were interested in. They didn't want to know why and if they did she couldn't tell them. She couldn't tell what happened afterwards either, so it didn't make much sense and it didn't seem very important.

It was important to her though. She stopped riding the subway and started riding the bus so that she wouldn't be reminded of it. She stopped trying to tell about it to anyone.

As she thought more about it she decided that there was more to it. Now that time had passed she could see it as if she had seen it all at one glance. She began to see herself as one of the actors and this led her to think she had had an active part in what happened. Reviewing it, she wished to tell herself what was going to happen. She began just at the point when she was about to step off the subway and meet the question in the man's eyes. She saw herself tightly holding on to her purse and she saw herself refusing to be involved until after the door was closed and there was glass between her and the man's need, whatever it was. She imagined many endings. At first she wanted violence. This seemed logical and was the most satisfactory because, no matter how guilty she might feel about not helping, violence put an end to it. She felt relaxed imagining that the two men had participated in some unspeakable violent act against the other and she knew that if that was what happened there wasn't much she could have done anyway. On the other hand she figured that maybe nothing like that had happened. And if nothing happened to stop the man from crying then it was left that way forever and she was stuck with the image of his face against the glass weeping and speaking words she could never hear. Whatever happened, the two men who saw the end of it were luckier than she was.

Besides this, her thinking gave her a new sense of being more than the middle-aged nurse on the subway. When she found that she could look at herself as if she were looking at another person and when she discovered that she didn't even have to have understanding or sympathy for herself, she was astonished. It meant so many things at once. Most of all it meant loss. She felt that she had been deprived of a personal possession. And as Miss A. thought about it more and more she saw that she could even think about herself thinking about the scene. And she saw that even the second self, an almost pure eye, was not blameless. She felt as if she had done something hectic and fierce like smashing a public mirror and now she saw herself in many ways as if her image were distributed among jagged fragments of glass. She could not trust herself anymore.

Her life before had been tranquil, a calm which was intense because of her close knowledge of physical suffering. Now she could not view physical suffering in the direct uncomplicated way that her vocation required. She found that she began to feel a contempt for the suffering of other people. She did not communicate this contempt directly though. Instead she found that she increased in her efforts, began to pamper patients and be more concerned about their comfort. Their response was invariably to be grateful and when she saw this and saw that she could not make them know that she hated them for their frailty, her contempt increased. With it increased her reputation and success as a nurse and now she knew more about the world. She believed that everyone lived fixed and sullen somewhere in a life like an invalid in a shabby room. She decided that everybody lived the life of a raging recluse while outside fantastic things were going on at great speed with unbelievable noise.

Miss A. had stopped trying to tell people the truth. Her talk was full of incidental and irrelevant slight things which made her a delight to listen to. She learned how to make a number of clever anecdotes out of nothing at all and because of this her patients were glad to have her around. She seemed to brighten everything. She was pleased to think of this image of herself. It was a bitter pleasing thought to have, knowing all the time that she possessed a knowledge which could shame and confound them. She felt as if she could see through people's clothes.

Here she stopped, fixing her life as she had fixed her thinking. She committed herself to the day-to-day discipline of falsely rendered service while knowing, curiously, that her life was a wheel on which she was tied and tortured with herself the impersonal tormentor. It was remarkable to think that as she sinned she was at the same time doing penance. The world flooded away and she was glad of it. By losing everything she found herself in control of everything again, and as soon as she was sure, she could reconstruct things to suit herself.

Time and again she saw herself going on beyond her destination and while the other two men held down the struggling weeping man, in the midst of all that roar of forward moving she felt an exhilaration, a new and tugging lightness like a gas balloon on a string. She saw herself wielding a knife she had not owned before.

DON'T TAKE NO
FOR AN ANSWER

"WOMEN!" Stitch said. "Haven't you guys got anything to talk
about?"

"What else?" somebody said. "Name something else."

"You want me to tell you a war story?"

Everybody laughed. It was a Saturday afternoon, the last long
Saturday before payday, and a bunch of us were sitting around
the orderly room playing cards. For nothing. Who's got money
the week before payday? Stitch was CQ. He had to stay there
over Saturday to answer the phone and put out the lights. You
can bet he would have signed the pass book and been gone,
money or no money, if he hadn't pulled CQ.

"This is no joke, Stitch. How come you pulling duty on Saturday?"

"First Sergeant dumped on me," Stitch said. "He figures to
shoot me out of the saddle and spend the weekend in my shack."

"What are you going to do if you catch that slob lying in your
bed with your fräulein when you get home tomorrow?"

Stitch spun around in the swivel chair he was sitting in next
to the phone. He just looked at the guy who'd said that and the
whole room got quiet. All of a sudden his big hand shot into his
pocket and in one motion came out again with a little click and
there was the glint of a switchblade in the light. It was funny.

The instant the blade flashed in the light Stitch grinned and leaned back easy in the chair, laughing to himself.

"Why, I'll kill him," Stitch said. "I'll cut that bastard in four pieces."

Everybody relaxed and the card game got going again. You never could tell about Stitch. Know what I mean?

"What about the Fräulein?"

"Who, Irma?"

"Who else?"

"What about her?"

"What would you do to her?"

"You guys don't know nothing," Stitch said. "Just nothing. Irma's worthless. She ain't good for nothing—except bedroom push-ups. But she's so good at that, I wouldn't have the heart to hurt her. I'd just whip her fanny good and she'd love it."

"Tell us a war story, Stitch."

"Listen," he said, "I'm trying to read this magazine."

"Tell us about Paris."

Stitch had just come back from furlough, ten days in Paris. He could always tell a good story if you hit him in the right mood. The thing about Stitch was he was moody. He seemed okay at the time, though.

"What about Frenchwomen, Stitch?"

"I couldn't tell you," he said. "I seen some but I never even talked to one."

"Go on. Don't give me that. You went all the way to Paris and you never even talked to a woman?"

"Maybe he didn't have to talk to one."

—You guys make me sick, Stitch said. You don't know nothing. I went to Paris and had nothing but one good time, believe me. But not with no French girls. If I was to do things that way, like you suckers, I'd end up broke with nothing to show for it. Now if you guys want to learn the facts of life—you got to plan, you got to figure your chances, you got to play the part. Once you see what you want to get, don't hesitate, don't wait, it's yours. Don't take no for an answer.

—Now this woman was American. She was plain, oh my God

she was plain as Missus Murphy's pig. I meet her on a sight-seeing bus. First thing I do when I hit town is get rid of this uniform, put on my civvies, grab my camera, and hop a sightseeing bus.

"I reckon you wanted to see all the sights."

—Didn't I? So I get me a seat in the back of the bus and I just wait. I'm sizing them up. I'm looking for one that's alone and not too sharp. Know what I mean? A woman that's sharp has got a notion about the value of her body. A sharp woman wears a price tag on her panties. What I'm looking for is one that not only ain't sharp, she's got to know it too.

"Are you kidding?"

—Don't interrupt. Stick around and learn something.

—So, sure as the world, last one on the bus, there's this pig. She's alone—that's good. She's kind of shy, keeps looking around for somebody to give her ticket to and then she kind of sneaks up the aisle—excuse me for living—looking for a seat all by herself or at least by some nice old lady. I just sit back and light a cigarette. I say to myself, little lady, give your soul to God, because your ass is mine.

"What does she look like? Is she awful?"

—Awful. She's thirty or thirty-five if she's a day, dressed like she was fifty. Got a spread, some gray hair and a stupid hat.

"False teeth?"

—How the hell do I know, yet. I only just seen her get on the bus.

—I wait till we get off the bus in front of a church to take pictures.

—I wonder, I say, if you'd mind posing for a picture in front of the church.

—Why, she says, surprised, all shook up, I don't know. . . .

—I only want to show how big it is, I say. I want to send a picture to my mama and I want her to see how big the church is with somebody standing in front of it.

—All right, she says, I'll be glad to.

—Thanks a lot.

—So she stands there like a GI sack of spuds in front of this church and I fiddle with the gadgets on my camera— Just a minute, I say, I've got to get it in focus. I leave her stand there a minute or two. I can see she's trying to smooth the wrinkles out of her skirt and fix her hair so the gray won't show. Then I say, quick, how about a big smile? Boy! she gives me the pearly whites. You'd think she was a movie star.

—Would you like me to take a picture of you? she says.

—Oh no, I say. It's just a waste of film.

—Come on, she says. Stand over there. Wait. You'll have to show me how to work it.

—I come around behind her and show her how the camera works. I don't touch nothing but the camera but I can see her hands shaking. Come on, smile a little bit, she says. So I give her a smile and we climb back on the bus.

—Would you mind, I say, if I sat with you? It's so good to talk to an American.

—Yes, she says, it's nice to talk to somebody from home.

—We sit down together.

—What am I going to tell my mama about the picture? I say.

—Who will I say the pretty girl is? —She just blushes and clams up.

—I'm Pete Brown, I say.

—Oh, she says, oh. I'm Ellen Cook.

—From then on it's life-story time. I want her to feel easy with me so I tell mine first. This Pete Brown he's in the paratroops, a jumper. He's had an awful sad life. I tell her I like it all right overseas but I miss the old hometown and my poor old mama too.

"Get off it, Stitch. You couldn't say that with a straight face."

—Couldn't I? Now this Ellen, she's a schoolteacher from Kansas. She teaches the third grade. —Do you like it? —Oh yes, she says, only it does get trying sometimes. —Married? —And honest to God she blushes, like a kid. —No, she says, not yet. —Me either. Well, Ellen, you're wise. No use being hasty in a serious step like that. Are you traveling alone? —She nods. —I had a girlfriend, she's the gym teacher at the school where I teach, who was planning to come with me. But at the last minute she

got this job as life guard at the country club. —That's too bad, I
say. It's always more fun to travel with a friend. —Yes. —And
safer too. —She blushes again. —Now's the time, Stitch, you
start moving in. —I wonder, I say, if you'd mind seeing me
again while you're here. I've got ten days furlough and I don't
know a living soul. We could have fun seeing things together.
You could tell me all about everything. I don't have much education. If you wouldn't mind, I mean. —I wouldn't mind, she says.
Really, I wouldn't mind at all. —Just like the movies.

Stitch lit a cigarette and blew a couple of smoke rings.

"So what happens?"

—Cool it. Take your time. Rush things and you ruin them.

—Okay. I take it slow. For two whole days I never lay a hand
on her. We go everywhere. We see all the buildings and muse-
ums and pictures. We sit in the parks and in the sidewalk cafes.
The second night we go walking by the river. It's a real nice
night for that kind of thing. I just feed her the questions and she
talks. She talks so much about herself you'd think she never had
a chance to talk to anybody in her whole life. She tells me about
being a kid in Kansas, about going to school and Sunday school
and all about her Daddy. He's a big Bible-thumping son of a
bitch, straight as a shotgun six days of a week and drunk as a
lord on Saturday night. Raises hell around the house. Runs
around buck nekked hollering "I am the Emperor of the Island"
or some crap like that. Gives Ellen and her mama a bad time.
Well, the old slob killed himself in a car wreck. She loved him
but she hated him too. She knows she shouldn't hate him at all,
but she can't help hating the awful things he used to do when he
was drunk.

"Sounds like your old man, Stitch."

"Stitch never had no daddy. He was born in a cathouse."

—This ain't my life story.

—I understand, Ellen, I say. I know just what you mean.

—I believe you do, she says. I believe you do understand. I can
talk to you. I can tell you about things.

—I hope so, I say. I hope you feel easy with me. And I give
her hand a little pat.

"Her hand?"

—One thing at a time. One thing at a time.

—Why did you come to Paris?

—I wanted to, she says.

—You must have some reason.

—Well, she says, yes. Not exactly reasons. I just have feelings. You'll laugh at me.

—No, I say. I'm just a big, dumb guy without much education but I'll never laugh at you.

—I believe you, she says. You see, Paris was always in the back of my mind since I was a little girl. It was everything in one word to someone who never saw anything in the world except in her geography book. I loved geography. And Paris was elegance and splendor and beauty, all in a kind of music in my mind. There wasn't anything, except space, but that was big in my town, nothing cool and gray like the pictures of Paris.

—Then there was the wickedness, too, she says.

—Wickedness?

—You know what I mean. I mean ever since I was a kid I had heard things about the American Legionnaires in our town. I used to see them when they had a parade. I'd see them snicker and pinch the grown girls. I've seen them laughing at jokes I couldn't hear and looking at pictures with their hands cupped around them.

—That was Paris too?

—You've got to try to understand. These things were just feelings, they weren't ideas.

—I understand how it was.

—And then there is another thing. I don't know if I should tell you this. You wouldn't mind if I tell you this? You won't misunderstand?

—You can tell me anything, Ellen.

"Stitch, I believe you could sweet-talk the devil."

"He'll get a chance in hell."

—You guys got it all wrong. I'm not bad. I just play the part. You got to play the part.

—Well, she says, there was this boy. I loved him. I was crazy about him. Of course he never knew it because I was too shy and he was a class ahead of me in high school and it was silly. But he was very different from the others. He was gentle and different. He was beautiful, I thought. I loved him so much I wanted to be him. I wanted to be inside his body. This is awful to say, but in those days I used to stay awake in the dark in my room to watch him undress. He lived next door. Wasn't that scandalous?

—No, I say. Not if you loved him.

"Do you think she was telling the truth?"

—I figure she made up the last part, but what the hell, she talked like she believed it. Stitch, I say to myself, just keep your buttons on. You've got it made.

—Well, she says. The war came along and he was killed in it, just before the liberation of Paris. I was in college then and I cried and cried thinking about that beautiful boy dead.

—And that's the other reason you're here.

—Yes, she says, if you put it that way.

—I'm glad you're here, I say. I'm glad.

—Why? she says.

—If you weren't here, how would I know you?

—But you don't know me.

—Yes I do, I feel I do.

"What were you feeling, Stitch?"

—Quit interrupting.

—You don't really know me, she says. You don't know me at all. And she starts to cry.

—Maybe I don't, I say. Maybe not. But I want to. And I give her a nice quiet Hollywood kiss.

"For Christ's sake, Stitch, is that all?"

—Slow down, soldier. I have to look at the river and the buildings and the lights.

—This is the music you used to think about, I say.

—Yes, she says, it's so beautiful.

—You want to see the wickedness too?

—All right, she says. I guess it would be all right with you along.

—So I take her to this clip joint in Pig Alley. Cheap cham-

pagne, nekked women, and dirty jokes. She acts shocked. —I
don't see how they can walk around like that with no clothes on
in front of men. —They get used to it, I say. It don't bother
them. —I could never get used to it, she says. I'd be so embarrassed. —Yes you could, I say. You've got a nice figure. Nothing
to be ashamed of. —Then I concentrate on getting her drunk
which is no big problem. When she's drunk out of her mind, I
take her to a cheap hotel. She don't say nothing until we get in
the room.

—Where are we?

—Take off your clothes.

—No, she says. No.

—Okay, I say, I'll do it for you.

—She fights me like a bitch, scratching and biting, but she
don't holler. She don't make a sound. She just fights.

—All right, I say, when I get her stripped down. You see. You
got a nice body.

—Don't touch me.

—You look better than any of them girls.

—No, she says, no, I'm ugly and old and flabby and nobody
loves me.

—I love you.

"Tell her, Stitch!"

—I love you.

—No you don't, she says.

—Yes I do, I keep saying. And all this time I'm playing the old
tune on her just like you play a guitar.

—I'm a virgin, she says. Please, I'm a virgin.

—Yeah? I say. Well, so am I.

"So what happens?"

—What do you think, soldier?

"Was it any good?"

—It's always good. I just close my eyes and she's a movie star.
When she finally turned loose of herself she's like a rabbit.
Crazy! She was carrying on so I thought they was going to
throw us out of the hotel. You see, nobody was ever good to her
before I guess. Nobody ever treated her like she was somebody.

—The next morning, first thing, before she has a chance to start feeling sorry for herself, I ask her to marry me. I tell her I love her and I want it to be proper and all. I tell her that just as soon as my furlough is over I'm going back and get the chaplain's permission and we'll get married.

"Did she fall for that?"

—Didn't she? It's all like a dream come true, she says. And she runs out and buys a whole lot of clothes. I got to admit they made an improvement. You keep telling a pig she's wonderful and they start believing it. Hell, I almost believed it. By the end of the time I almost started to like the bitch.

"That's too much for the heart."

—I even started to feel bad about spending all her money. She even bought me a suit of clothes. I felt kind of bad, not real bad.

"Stitch, you're just too softhearted."

—Yeah. She even come down to the station to see me off on the train.

—Don't leave me, Pete, she says.

—I'll be back in two or three days.

"Maybe she's pregnant."

—Maybe.

"What would Irma say if she found out what you was doing on your furlough?"

—You guys! That's the first thing I done when I got back, was to tell Irma.

"What did she do?"

—She cried for the poor woman. Irma's always sorry for the women. She said I was terrible. She said I ought to be killed and she hated me. She said she was going to find that girl and make me marry her. She said everything. Then we hopped in the sack and she was all over me like a tiger.

"That don't make any sense, Stitch. That's crazy. It don't make a damn bit of sense."

"The trouble with you," Stitch said, "is you don't know nothing about women. If you don't know nothing about the subject, the best thing is to shut up."

Stitch looked so damn mean for a minute nobody moved. One

guy held a card in midair. Everything was frozen like a photograph. Then Stitch started laughing and cleaning his fingernails with his switchblade.

"You poor simple bastards," he said, and he kept on laughing.

He was crazy that way. As long as he was happy, we decided to go ahead and play cards.

THE RIVALS

THEY PADDLED ACROSS THE BAY, the boy in the cockpit behind, studying the man, watching the twitch across his shoulders as he leaned forward and the quick smooth action of his arms, the deft, almost rippleless stroke of the paddle. He tried to time his own motions exactly with his father's. The paddles rose and fell together in bright synchronization as the little canvas boat, delicate as a kite on its slight frame, moved swiftly on the still water. The boy saw beads of sweat thick on his father's neck and, as he paddled, he could feel the cool crawling on his own skin of sweat drying in the breeze. Up ahead, across a mile of water, he could see the white line of the outer beach, a frail sandspit humped with irregular dunes, protecting the bay from the Atlantic. Though he couldn't see the waves breaking on the other side yet, he heard the noise of them like vague thunder.

"Hold it," his father shouted over his shoulder. "I'm pooped."

The boy checked the swing of the paddle in midair, leaned forward in the cockpit, and relaxed. The boat bobbed idly with them like a fishing cork.

"They sound big," his father said. "They sound like real rollers to me."

His father had twisted around in the forward cockpit to look at him and grinned. He wants to get out of it, the boy thought. I guess he doesn't want to go through with it.

"They sound the same as they always do to me."

"Well," his father said, "let's see when we get there."

That's exactly like him, the boy thought. He would go that far, all the way to the edge of the ocean and then turn back. He wants to go back now, but he knows, he can feel it, that I think he won't keep his promise. So now he'll go that far and then seem to make up his mind that it's too rough today. He'll look at the surf and shake his head and say it's too bad we'll have to wait till next summer. Next summer will be too late.

"You know something?" his father said. "I had the oddest notion just when we could first hear the waves. I remembered something out of a clear blue sky that I had forgotten for years. I remembered riding up to the line as a replacement in Normandy, during the war. I was sitting in the cab of the truck because I was the only officer in the group. We turned a curve in the road and for the first time I could hear the sound of artillery firing up ahead of us. It was the strangest feeling because right up until I heard that sound, I hadn't made up my mind that I was really there or that there was a real war on."

"I bet you were scared, weren't you?"

"Well, yes, you might say so," he said. "But it was more than just being scared. I don't know how to explain it. You can be scared and it's only a physical thing, like being tired or sick at your stomach. This was different. It was that all of a sudden I knew it was me in the cab of the truck, nobody else but me, me alone and nobody there to see me, just me."

"It sounds like you were pretty scared to me."

"I can't explain it," his father said. "If you don't understand, I can't explain it to you. You'll have to find out for yourself someday."

He's been drinking, the boy thought. I can smell it. He gets to talking like that when he's been drinking. When he's drunk he starts to tell all about the war. And it's been like that most of the summer. He's going to treat this day just like any other day. He don't care. He don't care that it's the last day before we go home and maybe we'll never have another chance to try the boat in the waves. On top of that he's scared.

"Ready to go?" the boy asked.

"Okay," his father said. "Anytime."

They sat up straight in the cockpits and the boy poised, waiting, caught the least sign of movement from his father's back and bent forward. The two paddles flashed and knifed in the water and he could feel in his hands the keen surge of the boat. He could hear the sound of the waves louder now, and looking ahead, squinting against the midmorning sun, he saw first the far horizon where white clouds jutted like a rock coast. He followed the blue below them until he saw and felt the enormous bulk of the ocean, huge and slow, and then, abruptly at the far line of the outer beach a splatter and a flash of pure whiteness.

"I see them!" he shouted. "I see them breaking!"

"Yes sir," his father answered. "They're still there all right."

When they were at last in shallow water the boy eased himself out of the cockpit, careful to keep from rocking the boat, and, once his legs were free, leapt aside into the waist-deep water. He hurried, thrashing around in front of his father, and grabbed the short line they used to tie it to the dock, and he pulled the boat up to the edge of the sand. He stood on the beach, feeling the coarse sand that stuck to his wet feet, and watched his father climb awkwardly out of the forward cockpit. His father stretched luxuriantly and smiled.

"That little old boat is hard on you when you've got long legs," he said. "Sometimes it's tough to be tall. They don't seem to make anything the right size."

The boy, slightly built, small for his age, merely nodded.

"Well," his father said, "maybe you won't have to worry about it. You take after your mother more."

"I haven't stopped growing yet."

"You never can tell," his father said. "I knew a fellow that grew almost a foot after he was your age. It's the exception, though."

"All set?"

"I guess so."

They picked up the boat and balanced it on their shoulders, his father in front to lead the way across the dunes. It was heavier than you thought. It seemed so light and frail in the water, but the weight of the boat, slanting from his father's shoulders to his own, dug harshly into the boy's flesh. I won't quit, the boy thought. I'll go all the way to the far beach without stopping if that's what he wants to do.

"Okay?"

"Sure," the boy said. "Let's go."

They struggled forward, slipping in soft sand, the long unwieldy boat troubling their arms. The boy, with his face pressed against the canvas, couldn't see where they were going. He watched his father's feet in the sand ahead and kept in step. They began to climb a dune and he felt the weight settling on his shoulders as they climbed. His arms ached from the strain and the sharp keel cut into his shoulders until he wanted to cry out. But he wouldn't. Then he felt that they were on level sand again and suddenly he could feel the wild chill of the full sea breeze, the top of a dune.

"Want to set her down and take a breather?"

"Not unless you do," the boy said.

"Well, I'm tired," his father said. "I'm not as young as I used to be. Let's set it down. Watch your feet."

They lowered the boat and the boy smiled to himself. The taste of sweat on his tongue was like the light salty taste of blood after a fist fight, the clean taste of a minor victory.

"That's a real nice ground swell," his father said, scanning the surf. "Those waves are rugged."

"How come we came up this dune?" the boy asked. "It would have been easier if we'd gone around."

"It's the same distance any way you go. It doesn't make any difference."

The boy looked out at the surf. It was perfect. Farther out the ocean was calm, but bulging with a ground swell which, as it neared the shore, was broken into huge comers. They started as ragged lines, swelled and surged, rising, rising, until it seemed that the whole sea was rising behind them and would sweep over the entire sandspit. Just at that moment with a brilliance that made him gasp the waves broke into an explosion of white, followed by the deep resounding sound of the tide.

"It's still coming in," the boy said. "It's still high tide."

"That's a blessing."

From the tone of voice the boy detected irony, the last inscrutable mask of the adult world. It seemed to him that whenever his father was forced into some corner of truth, just at the moment when you might face the real flesh and blood of him, he simply turned aside, donning a kind of false face behind which he felt wholly secure. It was an odd perception. He seemed to glimpse his father in a Halloween mask, pathetically cocksure of himself, like the emperor in the fairy tale, strutting in his expensive, fine-spun, invisible new clothes.

Without a word they picked up the boat and went down the dune, through a blond patch of sea wheat and onto the coarse, rock-strewn outer beach. They set the boat down facing the sea and sat down beside it. His father, looking into the extravagant surf, lit a cigarette.

"You want one?"

"No thanks," the boy said.

"You can have one if you want it," his father said. "I know you smoke now. It doesn't take Sherlock Holmes to figure it out. If you want a smoke just ask me. I don't care."

"I just don't feel like smoking now."

"I've forgotten about being your age," his father said. "I guess half the pleasure was in the secrecy."

"I just don't feel like smoking now."

It had popped into his head to say, *They say it stunts your growth*, but the words wouldn't come. It seemed like when you thought of something smart to answer back, your tongue just wouldn't form the words for you. And he had an idea that if he once, only once, let loose and spoke the truth from his anger and envy, the words would come like a great flood, like vomiting. How could he ever make his father understand then, drowning, overwhelmed in all that rage? The boy felt ashamed, wishing and wishing and not knowing what to do. He sat woodenly and looked into the surf.

"I could use a little pick-me-up," his father said. He stood up, fumbled in the cockpit for the rucksack they used to carry dry towels and sometimes sandwiches. His father opened the rucksack on the sand and took out a pint bottle. He grinned and took a long pull.

"Better be careful," the boy said. "You might get a cramp."

"You can't imagine how this beach was during the first year of the war," his father said. "Between the storms and the submarines it was a regular graveyard. I remember coming out here one day and finding the whole beach just covered with bunches of green bananas. It was such an odd sight I wanted to laugh."

One drink, the boy thought, and he starts to talk about the war. It's funny that he thinks anybody cares. Mother doesn't care, that's for sure. How many times does she have to tell him that's all over now, that's ancient history, why don't you talk about something somebody cares about?

"What do you think?" his father said. "Think we can make it all right?"

"If we're careful," the boy said. "Once we get out beyond the surf the only thing we have to worry about is keeping up with a wave when we're riding it in."

"I don't know," his father said. "This boat is pretty flimsy. A good wave might break it to pieces."

"We could fix it easy enough."

"It's pretty rough out there. I don't think you know how hard it is to handle a boat in the surf."

"We can try it. How can you tell something before you've even tried?"

"I don't know," his father said. "It's tricky. I wouldn't want anything to happen to you. Your mother would never forgive me if I let something happen to you."

"What could happen? I can swim."

"Most anything could happen if we capsized."

"What's the matter? Are you scared?"

Now at last he had said it. It had come out in the open, not, as

he had feared, in a tirade or childish tantrum, but in the form of
a simple question, as definite and keen as the cutting blade of a
jackknife. His father put out his cigarette in the sand and looked
away. After a moment he looked back at the boy, grinning.

"That seems like a funny thing to say," his father said. "I was
worrying about you."

"You don't have to worry about me."

"It seems kind of silly to me to make such a big issue out of
nothing. Try and be reasonable."

"Okay," the boy said. "I *dare* you to do it. That's all there is to
it. Just a dare."

"In that case, I guess we have to do it. I'll take your dare."

They seized the boat, raised it, and half-running, staggering,
hurried to the water's edge.

"Leave one paddle behind," his father said loudly above the
noise of the waves. They would have to shout now to be heard.
Until the trial of the boat and themselves was finished they
would have the noise of the waves all around them. The boy
looked at his paddle. The two paddles were heavy, hand-carved
Indian ones his father had bought out West, richly whittled.

"Don't want to lose both," his father said.

The boy threw his paddle up the beach. His father was already in his cockpit, so the boy shoved the boat out until it
floated well in the shallow water; then he settled, empty-handed,
in the cockpit behind. He watched his father lean forward and
briskly begin stroking with the paddle. The boat was headed at a
slight angle into the surf and the first wave broke over them,
only a little one, almost spent, but the boy could feel the wildness as the boat bounced and shivered from the impact and
water splashed into the cockpit. He gripped tightly and leaned
over as his father paddled into the surf, jockeying the boat amid
the uproar and the chill spray. He could feel now the power of
the waves as they were slammed, spun around, whirled and
dashed in a white fury, and he could see his father working,
paddling, the muscles in his arms taut and pulsing. It was like a
dream of falling downstairs. The shapes of the waves, like huge
blue animals stampeding, were all around them, and the boy

closed his eyes, partly from the fierce sting of the salt. When he opened them it was calm again. They were outside the breakers, and his father, laughing above the noise, paddled in a wide circle. The cockpit was full of water and the boat was heavy. The boy fumbled at his feet and found the tin can and began to bail as fast as he could while his father continued to paddle aimlessly around.

"We made it!" his father shouted. "I never thought we would without capsizing, but we made it."

"Here we are!" the boy shouted.

"How about that!"

While the boy bailed, he looked at his father. The big man, stripped to his trunks, his chest heaving from his effort, his head spray-drenched and glistening in the sun, seemed strangely different. It hadn't been as the boy imagined it would be. Thinking about taking the boat in the surf, talking about it all summer long, until finally wheedling his father's promise, he had only pictured how it would be coming in with the waves, the glory and hectic joy of it. He looked back into the turbulence they had come through and he felt something close to fear, for he knew now. And he felt a curious admiration for his father. They had done this thing together. He passed the bailing can to his father and hunched down, breathing deeply.

"Ready?" his father said when he had finished bailing.

"All set."

His father headed the boat straight for the shore and began to paddle. They caught the crest of a wave and the boy felt it seize the boat, carrying them in a high rush forward. He could feel the wave mounting slowly under them as they sped along, and then they poised almost motionless for a breathless instant on the brink, shot forward in a dazzling flash of foam; it seemed they were falling, falling until they shuddered to a stop as the keel dug into the sand in shallow water. They leapt from the boat and dragged it ashore, fell exhausted on the soft sand. The boy lay on his back looking into the dizzy brightness of the sky and thought he could feel the earth turning under him.

"That wasn't so bad," his father said. "That wasn't so bad at all."

"That was good," the boy said. "Did you ever have a ride like that?"

"Better than a roller coaster."

He lay there beside his father with the sun and the breeze drying his body and he felt marvelously light as if he were floating on his back in calm water and nothing, not even the percussion of the surf, could interrupt his spent tranquillity. The air seemed full of tunes his blood could dance to.

"All right," his father said. "I had mine. Now it's your turn."

The boy felt his guts knot and tighten like a fist.

"I don't know if I can do it," he said. "I might wreck the boat."

"I'll take that chance," his father said. "You ought to try it once. After all, it was your idea."

The boy tested the weight of the paddle in his hand. It felt heavy. The trouble was you could never finish anything and just leave it that way. His father was giving him the chance to prove himself and he knew he must take it, that was vital, whether he failed or not. He settled himself into the cockpit when they were afloat and paddled. As he fought the boat forward into the surf he knew now what it had been like for his father because now he only had time to act, neither to think nor plan ahead, only to feel what the waves were doing and move instantly in response. The waves rolled over them and he fought in a happy fury until one caught them, smashed over them, and sent the boat reeling back to the shore.

"Bail it out and try again."

"I don't know if I can do it."

"There's no harm in trying."

The boy seized the tin can and bailed. It was an awful thing, he thought, to be about to do something that he knew he couldn't. It was different when you didn't know. He was thinking, as he bailed, that maybe being a man would be like that, going ahead with something and doing it because you had to even when you knew what the outcome would be. After you once knew, there was no outside mystery anymore. There was only the secret of yourself to worry with. He felt suddenly as frail and fragile as a china doll.

He tried again, pointing into the surf, paddling as fast as he could. He fought, his body tensed against the cold and the power, his eyes squinted against the spray. He could see his father, sitting, leaning forward, completely relaxed, and he felt urgently alone. They made a little progress; he could see the calm area behind the waves he was striving for, and he struggled for it. Then it was like a shape from a dream: in a timeless moment a wave bulked high above them directly ahead and he could feel the boat slipping back under him in the trough and see his father turning in the cockpit shouting words he couldn't hear as the wave broke over them, turning and turning, and he jumped free of the cockpit, crashed against the sand and rolled in a shower of bright lights, came up gasping for air, hurt, tasting blood in his mouth. He saw the boat dashed empty on the sand and then he saw his father come up out of the foam still shouting, his face twisting in pain. He moved to where his father was, grasped him under the arms, strained to pull him up. A wave broke over them and he heard his father scream. Somehow, dragging and pulling, he managed to get his father to the beach. His father lay still with only his head on dry land, breathing hard, white-faced.

"It's my leg," he said finally. "I think I broke my leg."

The boy looked quickly, furtively at his father's legs stretched limp in the water. They had never seemed so long and thin. He had never really imagined his father as possessing flesh that could be injured or bones that could break.

"Which one?" he heard himself asking. "Which leg is broken?"

"The right one," his father said. "Run up and get the bottle. I need a drink."

The boy raced up the beach to the rucksack, fished the bottle out, and returned with it. He stood tensely watching while his father drank.

"Just what the old doctor ordered," his father said. "Go and see about the boat."

He ran down the beach to where the boat had been dashed ashore. The frame was broken in several places, but the canvas wasn't ripped. It would float all right. He got under it and, gradually, slipping in the wet sand, using all the strength he had, he tipped it over and the water poured out of the cockpits. With most of the water out, the boat was lighter and he was able to pull it farther ashore, high and dry. When he came back, his father was propped up on his elbows looking at his leg.

"It's a nice clean break," his father said. "Not bad, but we have got some trouble."

The boy began to shake and he could feel tears in his eyes and the taste of tears in his mouth. He didn't want to cry but the tears came. He tried to speak but he couldn't.

"Take it easy," his father said.

"It's my fault," the boy said. "I dared you to do it and it's my fault."

"The hell it's your fault. I took the dare didn't I?"

"I didn't mean for anything like this to happen," the boy said, still crying. "I didn't mean for anything to happen. I just wanted to show you. I didn't want you to get hurt."

"What did you want?"

"I can't explain it."

"Try it," his father said roughly. "This one time tell me what you wanted."

"I can't put it in words."

"Try, dammit! It's important to me, believe it or not. Dammit, try and put it in words."

The boy stopped crying and squatted down on his haunches. He looked at the sand, thinking.

"I just wanted to show you I was a man," he whispered. "I wanted to prove it."

His father laughed. He leaned his head back and laughed above the roar of the surf.

"In that case," his father said, "it was worth it. Because now you've got the chance."

The boy looked at him, wondering, and waited.

"Now listen to me," his father said. "You've got to go back without me. Tell your mother to call a doctor and get Joe Soens to come out with his motorboat and pick me up. Tell him to bring somebody. It will take two."

"All right."

"You're going to have to drag the boat over the dunes by yourself. That'll take maybe an hour if you work steady at it. The tide will be running out and it will be hard work paddling across the bay. Can you do it?"

"I think so."

His father's hand seized his arm and the boy could feel the strong fingers digging deep in his muscles, but it didn't hurt. He felt numb.

"Can you do it?" his father asked fiercely.

"Yes," the boy said.

"All right," his father said. "That's all I have to know."

The boy ran down the beach and started to drag the boat toward the dunes, inching it along the sand. He looked up for a moment and saw his father wriggling on his back, getting clear of the water. He saw the tall man in his lonely effort and he felt a new and troubled joy, a joy too deep for guilt or tears or any of the knowledge of childhood. It was a strange and precious feeling, as small as the first moment of a catching flame, but hard too, and brimming with an inner glow like a jewel. He kept dragging the boat, pacing himself, measuring his strength because he had a long way to go.

Two

From
IN THE
BRIAR PATCH

We roar all like bears and mourn sore like
doves; we look for judgment, but there is none;
for salvation, but it is far off from us.

ISAIAH 59:11

A GAME OF CATCH

ON THE WAY to the beach the brothers began to argue. Naomi sat between them in the front seat of the convertible, Tee Jay's car, and ate candy bars. Naomi didn't drink or smoke, but when she was away from the girls' college where she was the basketball coach, when she was away from it all on a day like this, going to the beach without a worry in the world, she would stuff candy. Sometimes she ate so much she got sick. Tee Jay knew all about it. He was the one who brought a whole box of Baby Ruths along just for the trip. Courtney, the crazy one, brought her a flower. When they tooted the horn for her in the alley behind the gymnasium and she came running out of the back door smiling at them, it was Tee Jay who handed her a box of Baby Ruths. He knew about her sweet tooth. Courtney got out of the car to let her in and gave her the gardenia, one fifty-cent gardenia.

"What's this for?" Naomi said. "Are we going to a dance or something?"

"I don't know," Courtney said to Tee Jay. "Are we?"

Tee Jay ignored him. Half-smiling, he kept staring into Naomi's eyes, until she looked down at her flat shoes.

"Don't look at me," Tee Jay said. "It's his idea."

"I'll tell you what," Courtney said. "Why don't you eat it? For dessert, after you finish the candy, I mean."

Naomi laughed and clapped him on the back, hearty, comradely. What else could she do? That Courtney was something, you never knew what he might think of next. You never knew how to take anything he said. Besides, he was just out of the State Asylum. He had been in and out a couple of times. They said he was cured now, but you wouldn't know it. You couldn't be sure about a thing like that.

They drove along the highway to the east coast, and the brothers were arguing as usual. Naomi chewed candy and let the warm air trouble her hair. It was dark and cut close, but with the breeze fingering it, combing it, she imagined it was long and blowing in a dark cloud like smoke behind her, long and mysterious as Lady Godiva's. Floating on her skirt between the firm bulge of her thighs, the gardenia was already turning brown at the edges, but it was sweet.

"I don't care where you read it," Tee Jay was saying. "It sounds like crap to me."

"I'm telling you that something like that, a murder, is just love in disguise. He might have just kissed them. It would be the same thing."

"Books! Books! That's all I get from you. Do you believe everything you read in a book?"

"He's got a thing about books, you know," Courtney said to Naomi. "Do you know the only book Tee Jay ever read? I mean *read*, all the way, every word from the beginning to the end."

"Don't try and involve me in the discussion," Naomi said, her mouth rich with chocolate.

She had been listening vaguely to their words, but it was all so morbid. They were arguing about some old man who had gathered his whole family together for a photograph, sat them down in a tight group on his front steps, his wife, his grown children, even his grandchildren. When he had them all ready and posed for the picture, he excused himself for just one moment and went back in the house. He returned with a shotgun, and before any of them could even move, he fired both barrels into them point-blank. He was reloading the gun to shoot himself when the next-door neighbor came running over and knocked him out with a shovel. The papers were full of it. They were always full of things like that. And Naomi couldn't care less. Trust old Courtney to bring up the subject. Trust him, too, to try and get her in the argument.

"I'll tell you the only book Tee Jay ever read all the way through. It was called *The Bitter Tea of General Yen.*"

"So what," Tee Jay said. "It wasn't a bad book."

"How would you know? What have you got to compare it with?"

"Look," Tee Jay said. "You're the one with the college education. I'm the one that went to work. I don't have time to read a lot of books. All I do is pay for the books you read."

"It doesn't take a lot of time to read a book," Courtney said.

"It takes too much time for me."

Naomi licked the candy off her fingers and reached forward and turned on the radio. When it warmed up, she twisted the dial until she found some music playing, then she turned it up as loud as it would go. It roared over and around them like a storm, scattering music to the four winds. She saw their mouths still moving furiously, but they couldn't hear each other if she couldn't, sitting between them. Courtney leaned close and whispered in her ear.

"Flaming Youth," he said.

"What?" she mouthed.

"Flaming Youth," he whispered again. "It's a sort of a joke."

Then he stuck out his wet tongue and fluttered it in her ear, and she jerked away from him. If it had been anyone else in the world but poor Courtney, she would have slapped his fresh face. Tee Jay, who was turning down the radio, missed the whole thing.

"Reach in the glove compartment," he said. "Hand me my cigarettes."

"I'd prefer if you didn't smoke," Naomi said. "You know how I feel about it."

"Who cares how you feel?" Tee Jay snapped at her, taking the pack from Courtney. "Maybe I don't like candy. Maybe it makes me sick to watch people who eat candy. I don't have the right to object, do I?"

"Candy is altogether different," Naomi said. "If God had intended for you to smoke, He would have made you a chimney."

"Yeah? Yeah?" Tee Jay said, lighting his cigarette. "Maybe you'd like to walk to the beach. If God had intended for you to ride, He would have put wheels on your ass."

Naomi glared straight ahead.

"It makes me sad to be the only one who isn't indulging in something, some lonely, stupid, solitary, ineffable private vice."

And with that curious remark Courtney simply put his hand in her lap and took the gardenia. He held it under his nose, sniffed it, and then began to chew the white bitter petals.

"Don't *swallow* it!" Naomi cried. "What's the matter, are you crazy?"

She blushed then, realizing that it had just slipped out like that.

"Oh no," Courtney said, his mouth white and full of flower. "I used to be, but I'm not anymore. I'm just as sane as everyone."

Inexplicably, Tee Jay laughed.

"How does it taste, boy?" he said.

"Not too bad," Courtney said. "On the other hand, don't feel that you're missing out on anything."

"You better be careful," Naomi said. "I've heard they're poison."

"You'll never know for sure until somebody tries one," Courtney said. "That's science for you."

After that they rode without talking, just listening to the music on the radio. Naomi felt a lot better now that they had stopped arguing. The only trouble was still Courtney. He kept putting his hand on her leg. That would be all right, just resting there, but he wouldn't leave well enough alone. After a while, all of a sudden, he'd stiffen all his fingers at once and start edging up her thigh like a spider, sort of on tiptoes or tipfingers. When his hand got too close for comfort, sneaking toward the ultimate destination which Naomi, in spite of all, to her dying day, would call her privates, plural, she would have to take his hand firmly in hers and remove it. Then the whole process would begin all over again. Courtney kept looking straight up the road, and so did she. She didn't want to make a scene, and she knew if Tee Jay noticed anything, he'd stop the car and beat Courtney up.

When they got to the beach it seemed like a perfect day. The sun was bright, the water was blue and scaled with the white-caps of a brisk east wind. The tide was down, but rising, so they could still drive up and down the beach in Tee Jay's good-look-ing car. Far out along the horizon clouds like dark bruises were massing and swelling, but they were a long way away. They drove up and down the beach a few times, slowly, just looking at the people, the children running and jumping and splashing and throwing sand, as shrill and swift as gulls, the muscular young men, bronzed and cocky, the girls in their bright bathing suits, and, too, the old people, the fat and the thin, misshapen and grotesque, sprawled under beach umbrellas, or burning lurid shades of pink in the sun. The men with mountainous stomachs and the little jiggly breasts like girls at puberty, and bandy, veined legs, and the women, thin and wrinkled as old, cracked leather, or enormous, all rippling, shaking bellies and buttocks, and great breasts sagging like overripe fruit, disgusted Naomi. She could not stand to look at them. They had a nerve, exposing themselves like that! Still, she was irresistibly fascinated; she couldn't help studying them and wondering, with an inner chill as if her blood had turned to quicksilver, if she would ever be like that.

After they had driven up and down awhile, Tee Jay turned south and drove past the last of the cottages, clinging to the dunes precariously like driftwood on the swelling sea, past the last of the swimmers, the last lifeguard, dozing and golden on his stilted perch, to the open beach.

"Where are we going now?" Naomi asked.

"Swimming," Tee Jay said.

"Well," she said, "I'd like to go to the bathhouse and put on my bathing suit."

"The bathhouse? Christ, what for?"

"Turn the car around, please," she said.

"That's the craziest thing I ever heard of," Tee Jay said. "The bathhouse costs fifty cents apiece. We can dress in the dunes for free."

"I'd prefer to dress in the bathhouse."

"What's the matter with you? Courtney won't mind."

"Can't you see the girl is moved by natural modesty?" Courtney said. "Take her to the bathhouse."

"Natural modesty, my ass! Fifty cents is a whole lot of money to fork over all of a sudden just because for the first time in her life Naomi decides she's modest."

"Women are that way," Courtney said. "Full of little surprises."

He only said that, Naomi knew, because of the way his own wife had done him. After three years of married life and two children, she simply left one day, drove off with Billy Towne, who was a salesman of fishing tackle up and down both coasts, from Fernandina to Coral Gables, from Pensacola to Key West. Yes, Billy Towne could take Maxine all over the whole state. She could go to the beaches while he was working, and at night they could go to all the bars and nightclubs. It was a good life for her. The thing was how hard it hit Courtney. He worshiped Maxine, like a fool, because anybody could have told him how she was born a bitch and would die a bitch, no matter how pretty she was. So away went Maxine, with the two little girls, living in open unashamed sin with that Billy Towne. And *poof!* Courtney was in the State Asylum. Oh yes, he would make all of those nasty cracks about women in general, but the world knew that if Maxine crooked her little finger at him, he'd go back to her on his hands and knees. Tee Jay, of course, had never married anybody. He hadn't even mentioned marriage in all this time. Still, there was always the chance that he would someday.

"I'm sorry," Naomi said, "but I really would rather dress at the bathhouse. I'll pay for it myself."

"In that case . . ." Tee Jay said.

And he turned the car around in a wild, wide, sand-scattering circle and sped back toward the main beach. He hunched over the wheel, close to the windshield like a racing driver, and put the gas pedal to the floor. That was Tee Jay for you!

Once inside the small unpainted cubicle in the bathhouse, standing on the wet, strutted slats, Naomi undressed and hung her clothes on a nail. She was a tall ungainly girl. Her face, though cast in large, coarse features, had a uniformity that made her seem conventionally pretty. But her body was oddly proportioned. Her thick, heavy-muscled legs, her hard high large buttocks, and her flat stomach seemed to belong to someone much larger, perhaps even, except for the curve of her hips, to a powerful man. ("My fullback," Tee Jay called her.) Her upper body was slight and frail-boned, flat-chested like a young girl's. In her clothes, wearing full skirts, loose blouses, and flat shoes, she achieved a kind of equilibrium, but at moments like this, alone and naked, she felt such a shame and self-revulsion that it nearly brought her to tears. She struggled into her black, one-piece suit, too tight at the hips, padded at the breasts, put on her white bathing cap, and placed the elastic-banded key around her wrist. She pulled the door of the cubicle to, sharply, behind her.

The two of them were waiting for her in the car. They turned their heads together and stared at her as she came across the boardwalk and down the wooden steps and across the powdery sand near the dunes. She began running toward them.

"Look," Courtney cried, "a female centaur. Whatever that may be."

"Let's get the show on the road," Tee Jay said.

Then, still staring at her as she got into the car, Courtney said, "Cough drops."

When Tee Jay found a place that suited him, out of sight of the main beach, the two of them took their swimming trunks and went up into the dunes to change. Naomi spread out a beach blanket and covered her exposed skin with suntan oil. She had a little plaid beach bag from which she took a pair of dark glasses and a confession magazine. Just then, settling comfortably in the sunlight, she heard the thunder and felt the breeze coming stronger and cooler off the ocean, saw lightning far off

in the clouds and whitecaps flickering across the whole expanse
of the visible sea.

"It's going to squall," she called.

"So what?" Tee Jay replied from the dunes.

And she looked and saw the two of them, the twins, standing
side by side on top of a dune, perfectly identical except that
Courtney was pale and soft beside Tee Jay. They came charging
down in a little whirlwind of sand and legs, leapt right over her
and past with flashing heels and flanks, raced into the water.
Soon they were splashing each other and shouting, but she
couldn't hear what they were saying to each other. She went
back to the car and got the box of Baby Ruths. She returned and,
opening her magazine, began to read the sad thrilling tale of an
innocent girl who was seduced by a state policeman.

By the time the two came back from their swim, they were
arguing again, and about the same old thing. Tee Jay opened the
glove compartment and produced a pint of whiskey. They both
had a drink. A lot they cared about her approval! Then Tee Jay
went around and opened the trunk. He fumbled around until he
found a softball and two gloves. It was a brand-new softball,
white, hard, and shiny.

"You want to play catch?"

"No," she said. "I don't feel much like it right now."

"Well, how do you like that?"

"I'll throw a few with you," Courtney said.

They moved out in front of the car and began to lob the ball
easily, back and forth. Tee Jay was the athlete. He played third
base for Morrison's Department Store Softball Team. Naomi
loved to go and watch him play on a spring or summer evening
under the lights, in his red and green and gold uniform. He was
so quick, so deft, so dandy around the bag. He was the only man
she had ever seen, except in newsreels and such, that she could
really *admire* when he was playing a game. The others, even the
good ones, were so sloppy and careless, like they didn't care, like
it was so easy for them, running and throwing and just being
men, like they didn't give two hoots what anybody thought. She
hated them. Tee Jay was nervous and quick and delicate; every

move he made seemed to have its reason. Naomi's heart leapt for him when she saw him move swiftly to snag a hard-hit ball, or when he came running full speed, but like a dancer on points, to scoop up a bunt, whirl, and in the same motion burn it down to first base. Courtney, on the other hand, had never been much at sports. That was a funny thing. The first time he was at the State Asylum he got the notion somehow that he was going to play shortstop for the New York Yankees. It was terrible. Tee Jay would have to drive up there and spend whole weekends batting him flies and grounders and playing catch with him. At least, Naomi noticed, he had improved from all the practice. She returned to her magazine story.

The storm moved in on them. Drops of rain began to fall, and, looking up, Naomi saw that the black clouds were overhead and all around them. They seemed to be shaggy and running like buffaloes in the movies. The waves were much bigger now and broke on the sand with huge crashes and bursts of foam like breaking glass. She bundled her things together and ran to the car. She pulled the lever that controlled the mechanism, and the gray top began to creak forward into place.

"Who told you to do that?" Tee Jay yelled at her.

He ran over, his face pinched and flushed with anger, and let the top down again. The rain was falling harder now, in thick drops. The trouble was that they had started the argument again.

"Cut off your nose to spite your face," she said. But a lance of lightning and a barrage of thunder drowned out her voice.

"What was that? What did you say?"

"Never mind," she replied.

She crouched in the front seat and the cold rain fell on her. The two of them, heedless of rain, thunder, and lightning, stood there shouting at each other and throwing the ball as hard as they could. They had tossed their gloves aside. They shouted and threw the ball so hard she didn't see how they could catch it bare-handed. It was very very dangerous for all of them, she knew. She'd heard so many stories about people being struck by lightning on the beach. Besides, the tide was rising; pretty soon they wouldn't be able to drive back along the beach. She got out of the car and ran to Tee Jay.

"Let's go," she said. "Let's go home."

Tee Jay threw the ball to Courtney. He threw it gently.

"Let's quit," Tee Jay said. "This is crazy."

"Are you *afraid?*" Courtney yelled.

The full strength of the squall was on them now. With the rain pelting, the high wind and the lightning and thunder, they had to scream at each other. Courtney fired the ball back to Tee Jay and he threw it back just as hard. Naomi could see the red round shape of the ball printed on Tee Jay's palm and fingers.

"You catch it," Courtney screamed at her. "You're the coach."

She caught it and threw it to Tee Jay. Then it was a three-cornered game. For a few minutes she was glad to be shielding Tee Jay, catching that wet, hot, skin-wincing ball and throwing it, easy, to him. But it hurt and Tee Jay seemed impatient to throw again. He didn't seem to appreciate what she was doing at all. So she threw it to him as hard as she could.

"Damn you!" he said.

Her hands were bruised and aching, and she was afraid of the thunder and lightning, but still they kept throwing the ball so fast that she didn't know what to do. Finally Courtney dropped one and it rolled away down the beach. He chased after it, and she was running behind him. When he seized it and spun around, wild-eyed, to throw it to her, she was close enough to kiss him if she had wanted to. Surprised, he started back. The tears started streaming from her eyes.

"Please, please, let's stop now and go home."

"No," he said. "No, we aren't going to stop."

"Please," she said. "Please!"

He squeezed the ball in both hands.

"All right," he said. "I'll tell you what. You take off your bathing suit, and we'll go home."

"Throw the god-damn ball!" Tee Jay yelled.

Courtney waved at him to wait a minute. Tee Jay stamped his feet angrily, but waited.

"Go on, take it off," Courtney said to her.

"Will we go home then?"

He nodded.

She undid her shoulder straps and slipped and wriggled out of the rain-soaked suit. It lay like a small wrinkled shadow at her feet.

"Now dance."

"What?"

"When I brought you the flower, you made a dumb joke about going to a dance. Well, this is it. Dance for me."

Clumsily, cold, shivering in the wind, and still crying, she began to dance. Courtney laughed at her. He reached out and touched her small, brown, shrunken nipples with his fingers.

"See what I mean about cough drops?" he said. Then he cupped his hands and yelled into the wind to Tee Jay, "See what I mean? See what I mean about love? I love her!"

"Never mind all that crap," Tee Jay replied. "Just keep throwing the god-damn ball and we'll see who's afraid around here."

Naomi knelt down then, beside her bathing suit, and hid her face. She huddled on her self like a child asleep, and the two men continued to throw the ball back and forth with unrelenting fury.

THE GUN AND THE HAT

IT WAS SATURDAY AFTERNOON and so when the dusty pickup truck came too fast down the street, heedless of streetlights and stop signs, and shrieked to a trembling stop like a dog on a yanked leash in front of Estes Hardware Store, not even anywhere near the curb, there were plenty of people, loafers and loungers, shoppers and spenders, all kinds, to look up and wonder what in the world it could be that brought Red Leland to town in such a reckless fury. One thing you could say for Red, poor boy, he was nothing if not a careful man, an unhurried man. Hard times and bad luck can teach a man patience. The weather, the years, and more than his share of tribulation had worn him, tanned and seamed his face, pursed his lips so he always looked ready to spit or kiss, and all but swallowed up the rich baritone voice you could hear fully, clear and true as a fine bell, only on a Sunday morning, coming from up in the choir stall of the First Baptist Church.

He swung out of the cab, long-legged and grim, came around to the other side and literally dragged the fat boy from his seat, lifted him with one hand over a space of pure air with the boy's feet dancing like a marionette's. The door on that side of the truck remained open, awkward on its hinges, like a broken wing. Red had three grown daughters to worry over and a sickly wife, and only one son, the fat boy, enormous for his age really, so burdened with flesh you could hardly call him a boy at all; and he surely couldn't be counted on to grow into a manhood that would ease Red's hard years on the farm. They said it was something wrong with the glands, something that couldn't be cured.

The tall man in neat and faded work clothes stepped over the curb and moved across the sidewalk, pulling the fat boy behind him, the boy crying silently, thick gleaming tears filling his squinty eyes and running down a face as sad and featureless as a moon by day, streaking his cheeks with long rivulets. On the sidewalk people gave way, stepped back to make a path for them. Somehow ashamed, they turned away and wouldn't look. Inside the store they felt the silence as swiftly as if someone had switched off the sound of their voices with a flick of the thumb. They moved back away from the long counter and stared at the shelves along the wall. Red Leland stopped then and stood with the boy beside him, both of them limp and relaxed now, just standing there holding hands side by side at the counter waiting until Wayne Estes came to them and grinned.

"Something for you, Red?"

"I want a gun."

That stiffened them all so suddenly they might have turned to stone on the spot. They knew, too, everyone around did, about Red's thing. It came from the Bible. Years before, young and gangling then, clutching a cheap black Bible to him like a bouquet, he used to stop them on the street and pester them about it. "The Bible says *Thou shalt not kill*," he said over and over again to anyone who wanted to or couldn't help having to stand still long enough to listen to him. "Now it don't say what thou shalt not kill. It just say you ain't supposed to kill, period! And what that means is everything in God's whole creation, everything living, growing, breathing, every kind of creature under the sun." He wouldn't, not in those days, hunt or fish or even eat meat. But that was when he was a young man, still a boy, before he married and before he had to go to the War. Nowadays he didn't talk about it anymore. He fished the lakes in the county because he had to, ate whatever he could get and afford just like everybody else does, when he could get it for himself and his family. But still to this day he wouldn't hunt, though the truth is the hunting is good out around his farm. He wouldn't allow anyone else to hunt his land either, and some said they had actually seen the small brown white-tailed deer come dainty-footed, printing their neat small hoofs in the soft dirt of his cleared field, to eat out of his hands. It was for sure he'd never allow a weapon of any kind in his house. Some said he wouldn't kill a snake to save his own skin.

Wayne Estes's immemorial, impersonal storekeeper's smile flickered, but retained its essential constancy.

"What kind of a gun would you have in mind?"

"Any kind, so long as it works and don't cost much. A cheap one."

"You want a rifle or a pistol? Or maybe a shotgun?"

Red Leland hunched forward, bowing his head to think about it, until his face nearly touched the smoky waxed finish of the counter. He shut his eyes and, freeing the boy's hand, pressed his own huge hands into the wood. It wouldn't have surprised a soul if, when he stood up tall again, the image of his two hands had remained fixed forever in the glossy wood, like prints left in soft cement. He straightened up and his arms fell loose and slack at his sides.

"A pistol will suit me just fine so long as it's cheap."

"I got a secondhand Police .38 Special here. It's pretty old and wore out, and I'll let you have it for ten dollars."

"Is that the best you can do?"

"Oh, I got better pistols than that."

"I mean the cheapest."

"Afraid so."

"All right, I'll take it," Red Leland said. "Give it to me."

Wayne Estes turned around, bent his clean, white-shirted sweaty back, and opened a drawer. It was bulging with old pistols—an Army .45, a snub-nosed Banker's Special, some long-barreled target pistols, even a little lady's pistol, shiny and nickel-plated—all with tags on them. He found the .38 and put it on the counter. Red Leland made no movement to reach for it, to touch it, to examine it, so Wayne Estes picked it up again, untied the string around the grip, and let the tag flutter away out of sight behind the counter.

"You want some shells for it?"

"Just give me a load," Red Leland said. "I ain't planning to use it but one time."

Very slowly, taking his own time about it, Wayne Estes walked the length of the aisle behind the counter, opened another drawer, rummaged there, and returned carrying a small squat box, heavy in his hand for the size of it. He counted out six shiny bullets and put them in a straight row next to the pistol on the counter.

"They cost thirty cents each."

"That's a lot for such little things."

"That's the price."

"Okay," Red said. "Load it up for me."

He broke open the barrel and placed the shells one by one in the cylinder. When all six were neatly, cleanly in place, he snapped it shut again and put the gun back on the counter. Red Leland fished deep in his pockets, and then his hand appeared clutching a soiled crumple of bills. He counted out twelve one-dollar bills and smoothed them, put them in a pile. Wayne Estes handed him the pistol, and his whole hand closed over the shape of it, loose and easy, as if he'd just picked up a rock to throw. The two men stood staring at each other, unblinking, and Wayne Estes's smile slowly waned, grew faint, vanished at last like a forlorn ghost.

"Well . . . ?" he said finally.

"I still got twenty cents change coming."

Wayne Estes chuckled, shook his head, and tilted back for a wide-mouthed laugh.

"I'll be damn," he said. "I'll just be damn. I clean forgot about your change. How about that!"

He hit the cash register, and the little bell that tolled for all his sales, rung over this whole county's needs, desires, and sometimes luxuries, chimed liquid and clear like birdsong in the hushed room. He gave Red Leland two dimes, and then the man and the fat boy, hand in hand again, walked slowly out of the store. Just at the door the boy snatched for his freedom, failed, and started to scream as the man took up the whole weight of him, arms and legs flailing vainly like a beetle on its back, carried him to the truck, sat him on the seat, and slammed the door to.

"Well, now," Wayne Estes began, but ceased there as Red Leland loomed again in the doorway, framed now by the brilliance of the Saturday afternoon outside, his shadow spreading in a wide quick stain on the floor.

"Where does he live?" Red Leland said.

"Who? Where does who live?"

"The teacher."

"What teacher? Who are you talking about? Which one?"

"Never mind," he said. "Let it be. I'll find him all right."

This time they waited until they heard the growl of the pick-up's engine and then the soprano noise of its tires as it rounded the next corner down the block much too fast before they all began to talk at once with a sudden inexplicable rising like the sound of a field of insects at twilight.

John Pengry sat cross-legged in a bathtub of cool water reading a book. There was an old-fashioned electric fan, big, black, strutted like an early airplane, standing on the toilet and it stirred the lukewarm air around him, each turning troubling the pages of the book. John Pengry was a small, slight man with the pinched, bony face and darkly shining eyes sometimes seen in pictures of desert fathers or the fakirs from the East, ascetics, hermits, some of them saints, those few who have been for a long time alone in some naked landscape, companioned by a cruel sun, the chill darkness, wild beasts and voices, utterly comfortless, yet strangely tempted beyond all telling or believing.

He lived alone in a rambling frame house at the edge of the town. He was alone now since his mother had died and his sister Louise had left—God alone knows why, at her age—to live in New York City.

That was a strange thing. They had come straight home, just the two of them, from the funeral, and they were standing together, still dressed for it, still wearing their hats, in the living room. The light there was dusky and submarine, filtering through the drawn blinds and the green shield of potted plants on the windowsills. And at that moment it was as if neither of them possessed any substance, any flesh or blood or bone, as if they existed only by virtue of the vague light, as if they were floating, bodiless, amid the crowd and clutter of her furniture and her things. He felt as if the light was passing through them both like an X ray and as if for once they were entirely composed of it, of sourceless broken light and tiny dancing dust motes. He imagined that if he shut his eyes and held his breath, he'd vanish, leaving the room with all its things and all the plants—so many of them, so huge and ungainly, hedging the windows—forever as it was, sealed like a tomb. It was so quiet that he fancied he could hear those plants breathing.

"You better see to getting yourself a maid," Louise said. "Someone who can keep things clean and do a little cooking for you."

"If we get a maid, whatever will you find to do with yourself?"

"I won't be here anymore," she said. "I'll be leaving tomorrow for New York City. Of course you'll want to stay."

How long she might have harbored such a notion, even secretly saved for it, it seemed, for she had never asked him for money, not for the trip and not once since she had gone, he could only guess. That she was in good health and working he knew from the crisp, formal letters he received from time to time, on holidays and private occasions. He replied always with long letters full of nothing but the news of the state of things in the house. There was so little for him to write her about. Whether or not she was happy now where she was, he did not know. The only thing he was certain of was that she had been right, that it was she, not he, who had been freed by that death. It had not occurred to him then or since to protest that he, too,

had done his share of service and ought to be entitled to a life of
his own as well.

So he stayed on, custodian to his mother's distant trophies of
an imagined (for him, anyway) past life, a random accumulation
of odd things like the shells, broken or whole, the starfish, the
strange growths and creatures left on a beach as a mute signature by the retreating tide. He remained in the rude country
town that they (his mother, Louise, and himself) had never even
belonged to or acknowledged. Though his father had been born
there, he died before John Pengry had more of him to remember
than the rough skin of a large face that loomed over him like a
hairy full moon, grinning, the harsh laugh, the strong warm
hands in which his own child's bones felt frail and small as a
bird's, and the mysterious rich odor of his breath which John
Pengry was to learn years later was only the smell of strong
cigars.

Forsaken by all his blood, living and dead, John Pengry remained. He hired a colored woman to come from time to time,
to clean and dust, to take the white covers off the furniture in
unused rooms, to throw open windows and let in light and air
enough to sustain the house until her next visit. He watered the
plants, which grew enormous and unkempt, a jungle of them
now. He wound and tended the grandfather's clock—his great-
grandfather's in fact—and he kept the solemn, familiar pictures
of his ancestors in place, straight on the wall. Soon the cleaning
woman was lost too. When, by an accumulation of chips and
cracks, by the misplacing and rearranging of objects, it was apparent that she could not humanly perform her duties without a
careless disinterest, he took over all the functions of maintaining
the house, at least the interior. He didn't care how it looked
from the outside. From then on he lived completely alone.

Of course he could be seen twice a day during the school year
coming and going from the Seminole Grammar School, where
he was the teacher of the fourth-grade boys, neat and clean, but
clearly eccentric, dressed in an old-fashioned way with a high
shining starched-stiff collar and, too, just a little absurd, with
one of his father's suits luffing around his skinny frame like a

sail in the wind. And on Sunday mornings he went to early
service at the Episcopal Chapel (for this was not an Episcopal
town), taking his place always in the same back pew, to kneel, to
rise, to sing with the others, and to walk forward, like a man in a
dream, to partake of the Holy Communion.

John Pengry was not insulted, injured, or offended by anything that happened out there, beyond the walls and windows of
the house. He taught, well enough, a whole generation of inter-
changeable little boys, aware of them chiefly as faces which
shone and wavered in front of him like a field of wildflowers in
the wind. Annually he introduced them to the mysteries of long
division and to some of the secret things of this earth—how coal
comes to be, and where lies in dark splendor the Caspian Sea.
He dealt out to them the necessary, conventional, two-dimensional figures from history like a hand of cards. He encouraged
them in penmanship and led them in singing. Teaching to earn
a living, to maintain himself and the house, troubled him very
little. Afterwards it always seemed that he had only dreamed it.
He thought of it as wholly unreal. He was a ghost teaching
ghosts.

Here in this house, where he sat in the tub enduring the hot
still Saturday afternoon, was as much of reality as he could bear.
And it was with real ghosts, the ghosts of his great-grandfather,
that he wrestled. It was with them that he argued or conversed.
They were his only friends and enemies.

He stood up, tossing the book aside, and he took a towel off
the hook and dried himself. He put on his mother's silk dressing
gown, a fragile thing of pale pink, furred at the neck and the
cuffs, and he walked out of the bathroom leaving the tub still
filled with cool water over which the fan, still running, cast a
regular, rippling breeze. In the living room there was a round
miniature of his great-grandfather done in pastels. It showed,
crudely, a face like his own, the same nose, the same pinched
cheeks and high cheekbones, thin sandy hair, the same dark
shining eyes. But for the careful pointed beard, it might as well
have been a portrait of himself. Except for the difference, the
enormous difference. John Pengry stood looking at it for a

while, then he went across the living room to the yellow china humidor where he kept his cigars. He took one of them, twirled it in his palm, bit off the end, and lit it with a kitchen match, deeply inhaling.

The thing on his mind was his great-grandfather's hat. It was not that his great-grandfather had been a man of great success as a planter, so successful, indeed, that a portion of his riches somehow survived the War and the Reconstruction, endured even the careless bravado of his grandfather and the reckless spending of his mother's older brothers, so that now a small part of that original still rested in the bank untouched; for he would no more take it or draw from it than he would sell the house and auction its contents. It was not exactly, either, that his great-grandfather had been modestly celebrated as a man of action, one of those around whom legends and stories circle like a magic ring of doves; nor that all of John Pengry's life his great-grandfather, in reality a small man like himself, had towered so tall over all of them, casting a shadow like some smiling giant in a children's tale. What troubled John Pengry was his great-grandfather's hat. And, too, the manner of his death, not the facts, but the manner of it. The hat, one that rested, sacrosanct in a glass case in the living room, one that he had been as a child forbidden to touch, had been the cause of his death. It was a gray, wide-brimmed Confederate officer's hat, but it had been greatly altered by women and it bore a burst of ribbons and tassels (they were faded now, pinned around the crown like a dim rainbow); and it was plumed with a high, foolish shock of feather, the feathers, he had been told, of rare, exotic birds. That plume, once bright, still stood up high and straight. In the crown of the hat there was a hole the size of a quarter where the bullet that had killed him entered. Inside it still had dark stains from his blood. The hat had come back to the family after he had fallen, had been brushed and cared for and kept safe under glass. But, John Pengry wondered, what kind of abandon or buffoonery had possessed the man to wear a hat like that in a war? How had he lived as long as he did wearing it? And what, after all, did it mean, that kind of rashness, except that he must have known that the hat would remain long after his bones were powder, to be attended to, to trouble and perplex his seed like a kind of curse or spell until the last of them were gone from the light to dust too?

John Pengry, puffing on his cigar, standing there in his mother's pink silk dressing gown, carefully opened the forbidden case and removed the hat. He placed it on his head and, catching sight of his image in a mirror, cocked his head this way and that, like a child at a costume party.

Red Leland stopped the pickup truck in front of a sprawling, sagging frame house, so weathered it seemed paintless, set back a way from the street on a lawn as shaggy and wild as a bearskin. Azaleas along the edge of the front porch grew in a crazy tangle of green, and there was a large swing on the porch, hanging by only one of its chains, lopsided. He climbed out of the cab and walked part way up the lawn. The fat boy sat in the cab looking straight ahead. Red Leland began to call softly. He called in a steady, singing monotone, and getting no answer, seeing no sign of anyone, he moved closer and called louder. After a little while the front door opened a crack and around it appeared a thin face, intent and curious like a squirrel's, and above the face perched the most amazing hat that Red Leland had ever seen.

"Come on out. I want to talk to you," he said.

"Oh I can't," the face replied. "I'm not dressed to come outside."

"Come outside now or I'm coming in."

"In that case . . ."

John Pengry walked out the door and stood at the edge of his porch looking at the tall, wild-eyed country man. The tall man, blinking, looked back at him, studied him for a moment, then he walked briskly back to the parked pickup truck.

"Is *that* the man?" he said. "Are you sure that's the man?"

A boy looked at John Pengry and nodded. The tall man came

back toward the house. John Pengry watched all this and wondered.

"I'm going to kill you," the man said.

Dazed by this, John Pengry merely nodded.

"You know why? You know why, don't you?"

"I don't believe I've ever laid eyes on you before," John Pengry said at last. "I'm afraid I don't know you."

The tall man whirled and ran back to the truck this time. He snatched the fat little boy from his seat and ran back, dragging him along behind at arm's length.

"You know the boy, don't you? You recognize him?"

"No, I'm sorry, but I'm afraid I don't. Little boys all look alike to me."

"*You teach him. He's my son.*"

"Oh, I see."

"Well, now you understand why I'm here."

"I'm trying to, but really—"

The tall man seized the boy and pushed him forward to the edge of the porch. He seemed to be a very fat little boy.

"Look at him."

"I'm sorry," John Pengry said. "I seem to know them when I'm in class, at the schoolhouse. I can remember them there. But here, out of the right context, so to speak—"

"You mean you don't even recognize him?"

"Please be patient with me," John Pengry said. "I'm doing the best I can."

"You made a joke about my boy," the tall man shouted. "You made some kind of a joke about him in front of the whole class. He come home so choked up and ashamed he couldn't even talk. I've taken about enough in this world. I've followed the paths of righteousness as near as I could, and the Lord has chosen me for my share of tribulation. But the Lord couldn't have meant for my seed, my own flesh and blood, to be laughed at. He give me affliction. He give me troubles. He give me this little fat boy for my only son. But this last, this making jokes, is more than a man can bear."

"I'm sorry," John Pengry said again. "I don't recall doing

such a thing. But if I said or did anything foolish or wrong, you'll have to forgive me."

"You don't even recall it?"

The tall man raised the pistol that he had been carrying in his right hand and pointed it. It was curious, John Pengry thought, that he felt so light-headed that he wasn't even afraid.

"I say I apologize for anything. I apologize for everything I've done and left undone," he said. "It could have happened. Sometimes I'm not really responsible."

"Take off that hat."

John Pengry shook his head, feeling the weight of the feathers.

"Take off that hat. I've stood for more than enough from you."

"Go ahead and shoot if you want to, but I won't take off this hat."

"Great God Almighty!" the tall man yelled. "I ask you for a sacrificial lamb and you send me a lunatic."

Then the tears began streaming down his face. He closed his eyes and pointed the gun straight into the blue heart of the sky and fired it six times, wincing at each shattering report. When he had finished firing, he threw the gun away. It soared brightly into the maze of azaleas and disappeared.

"I might have known I wouldn't do it when the time came," he said. "The hand of the Lord is on me still."

He took up the little fat boy in his arms like a baby and carried him to the pickup truck. He didn't look back. He climbed in the truck and drove away.

John Pengry locked the front door behind him. He tiptoed into the living room and peered through the camouflage of plants, holding the venetian blind aside, watching the pickup truck dwindle away down the long dirt road to the country, a furious roll of dust pursuing it. He thought he'd better wait until after dark to go out and hunt for the gun. It certainly was curious. He would mention it the next time he wrote a letter to Louise. In the meantime he might just as well climb back in the tub and cool off. In any event he would not put the hat back in its glass case. He'd want to have it handy in case those two came back.

After his father had stopped crying and slowed down a little, the boy reached over and patted him on the leg with his small soft white hand.

"Never mind, Daddy," he said. "It don't make no difference to me."

And then for some reason his father threw back his head and laughed.

"Sure, boy," he said. "By God it was worth the price of a gun to see a sight like that. What a sight to behold! Come on, let's us go on home."

THUS THE EARLY GODS

"DECENT PEOPLE just don't act like that," her mother-in-law said.

Jane's mother-in-law Mrs. Grim. How aptly named! Jane was amused by the thought until she reminded herself that it was her name too.

Jane's husband mumbled assent and held up his highball glass and looked through it to change the sky from blue to amber. Lately everything was being so changed.

Jane wasn't paying much attention to Mrs. Grim's desultory monologue. She sat with the other two on the front porch and looked on beyond the path that crawled like a lazy snake from the cottage through the dunes to the beach, beyond the glare and dance of light on the white sand of the beach and beyond the flourish of the breaking waves, perfectly ironed creases that became immaculate explosions into the dizzying blue of the sky, cloudless and pure today. There was a line of pelicans, a slightly lopsided V with one arm stretched out longer than the other, and they flew by with a brown sturdy grace like a crew of oarsmen in a racing shell. They followed the leader at the point. He (she guessed it would have to be a male) would spread his wings to soar, and all soared likewise, rising and hovering with delicate balance on invisible currents of air, maintaining always the shape and direction of the formation though, like a single, trained, instantaneous muscular action, like part of a dance. When he pumped his wide wings with a smooth strong motion, the others followed in quick succession. She liked to see them fishing and alone: the twisty, angled high dive followed by a small flash of white, and then up bobbed the pelican to float contented awhile before flying again. She had seen them up close, too, perched like silly newel posts on the pilings near the Fish Market, long-beaked, drab-feathered clowns. They seemed grotesquely comic. But now as formations of them passed by the front porch, at home in their native element of air, they seemed to be made of it, to partake of all the wild, wide-flung, dazzling substance and mystery and marvel of the sky. They were creatures of skill and grace and beauty, and she wished she could paint them.

But, of course, her paints were still packed tight in the wooden box underneath the double bed. She wouldn't dream of bringing them out.

"But they're so beautiful!" she exclaimed.

"Who?" the gray-haired woman, firmly in the rocking chair beside her, asked. "Who? Those Quiglys?"

"No, no," Jane said, laughing. "I was thinking about the pelicans."

Her mother-in-law snorted.

"I was speaking of the Quiglys."

Harper, Jane's husband, merely chuckled and sipped his drink.

Mrs. Grim had been talking about the Quigly family steadily ever since they had arrived and opened the beach cottage a few days (how many has it been already?) before. She noticed right away that they had been using her outside shower. ("Lord knows what kind of a staggering water bill I'll have!") She observed that they let their children run wild and free and naked as four little jaybirds all over the dunes and on the beach. And she complained that all of them, the gaunt, grinning scarecrow of a father included, used her path to the beach as if they had a perfect right to, instead of going the longer way around to the public approach. It was clear, too, at the outset, that they had no pride.

The Grims hadn't been in the cottage five minutes before the man was standing at the back door, beating on it with his bony knuckles, grinning and asking if he could borrow a quarter pound of butter and an electric iron; not explaining why, or, indeed, even making some kind of mannerable small talk about the casual incongruity of the two requests. He didn't introduce himself. He didn't bother to ask who they might be. He just asked for butter and the iron and then stood there waiting until he was given what he wanted.

Mrs. Grim had been fuming about the Quiglys ever since.

"Oh, Mother," Jane had said, mildly amused at first. "What's wrong with them? I mean really. They seem pleasant enough."

Her mother-in-law had stiffened.

"You're not from these parts," she had answered flatly. "So you wouldn't be expected to know or make distinctions. They're trash, honey, that's all. Trash, pure and simple."

The element that added insult to injury for Mrs. Grim was the occupation of Joe Quigly, whom she insisted on calling The Man, never by name. It turned out that he was a bulldozer operator. Farther south, more than a mile down the beach, he was daily engaged in leveling the pristine dunes for something or other. A new subdivision of cracker-box houses maybe. Perhaps even a motel. She wouldn't condescend to inquire.

"It really shouldn't bother you," Jane had said. "There's so much space down there, and there's a whole mile between here and there."

"When we first built this place, my late husband and I," Mrs. Grim told her, "there wasn't another cottage for miles. It was so peaceful. Now houses are popping up everywhere like the heat rash. Like pimples. They're tearing the dunes down, and new people—not the kind of people you'd care to have around if you had any say so about the matter—are coming here by the hordes to live. They're ruining the place. They're like a lot of weeds choking us out.

"You'd have to know how everything was in the beginning to appreciate what I mean," she added.

Of course, she never failed to remind Jane that she was an outsider, from the North, and wouldn't be expected to offer her opinions on subjects she couldn't possibly know anything about, among them the Quiglys. Jane never failed to resent this either.

At first, their very first night in the cottage, Harper, too, had been amused.

"Oh, you'll come to love her when you know her and understand her better," he said. "Everyone does. It's just that she was born out of her time or, anyway, that she had to live on beyond it. She's a lady living in a time when that word doesn't mean anything. And all she sees around her is change, change, change. Change and decay. The good, happy, comfortable world she grew up in turned inside out, turned into something else after the Depression and the War. She's just a minor, eccentric victim of the great social revolution. A bewildered mastodon wandering around in the postglacial age."

But by the next night he was past that kind of fancy speechmaking.

"Quit getting in a stew about nothing," he said. "Don't pay it no nevermind."

Which was both strange grammar and an unfamiliar accent coming from him. Jane's husband was a lawyer now in Philadelphia. It had taken him a day and a night to pick up the accent and the idiom of a speech he couldn't have used at all since he was a child, if he had used it then. It had taken another full day for him to lose the half irony that made his new guise acceptable. It had taken another day and a very bad night (But she was so nervous visiting here for the first time. Didn't he even understand that?) for him to start in drinking. And now he wasn't shaving anymore or brushing his teeth or changing his clothes or bothering to go down to the beach. And now he was always taking his mother's side.

They did look something alike. Strangely. For wasn't it always the daughter who was supposed to end up looking more and more like the mother? Sitting together side by side on the front porch, she with her empty hands folded, he with his clasping the almost empty glass, short, square-bodied, long-torsoed, they were clearly cut from the same pattern. Sometimes Harper's lips turned tight and down in precisely the same expression of unspoken disapproval. Sometimes, now, his small, quick, pale blue eyes reminded her of Mrs. Grim's. And Jane, slender ("Honey, you'll have to eat plenty while you're down here and put some meat on those bones. Harp, boy, you ought to be ashamed to let your wife get so frail and wispy."), milk-skinned, and long-limbed, was beginning to feel made out of another substance, a member of another race.

At this moment, inspired by the sight of the flying pelicans, images to her at once of rigor and beauty and harmony and freedom, she felt like arguing.

"Now that you mention it, the Quigly children are beautiful."

Mrs. Grim grunted at that.

"Well, if you think naked savages are beautiful, you might say so. Each one to her own taste, as the old lady said."

"As a matter of fact, I have seen photographs of naked savages which I thought were beautiful, the savages that is," Jane persisted.

Harper stood up, sighed, and stretched.

"Tell you what," he said. "You want to see some savages around here? You just drop over to Black Bottom about ten o'clock on a Saturday night."

"That would cure her of notions," Mrs. Grim said, chuckling. She said the word *notions* as if it signified some kind of physical disease, barely mentionable in polite company. "That surely would cure her."

"You'd get yourself a bellyful of beautiful savages," Harper said.

"Where are you going?" Jane said.

"To pour myself another little drink. If you don't mind."

"Suit yourself," she said. "It's your vacation."

"Did you say vocation?"

"I did not."

"Much obliged."

Harper's mother rocked busily and steadily, looking straight ahead. Jane turned again to watch the fine line of the waves rising, hovering, exploding on the sand in snowy profusion. She heard Harper stumble over something in the kitchen and curse. Well, there was nothing to be done about it.

A whoop and a holler! A shrill pandemonium of treble cries and then a burst of sun-bronzed flesh as four blond naked Quigly children shot around the corner of the porch, scattered like a flushed covey of quail down the path, and vanished into the dunes. Mrs. Grim was half out of her rocking chair, rigid, her face etched in lines of anger. Harper leaned on the door-frame shaking his head.

"They won't never learn," he said.

"I tried to speak to the mother—if she is the mother—yesterday. And do you know she was drunk? Stone drunk in the middle of the day. I mean staggering around inside of that trailer blind drunk. No wonder those poor little children have to run around wild without a soul to look after them."

"They seem to be getting along all right, considering," Jane said.

"It's a wonder to me they don't all drown in the ocean," Mrs. Grim said. "I'd feel kind of sorry for The Man, if he wasn't so common and worthless himself. They tell me when he gets home from work the two of them start drinking together and just keep on until they pass out cold. The children just have to fend for themselves."

"Who told you that?"

"A perfectly legitimate source. Someone who ought to know," Mrs. Grim said indignantly.

"She didn't mean it to sound that way, Mother," Harper said. "She was just wondering."

Not even Jane now. Just *she*.

"I did mean it to sound that way," Jane said. "Gossip makes me sick."

"Well!" Mrs. Grim said.

"What in hell got into you?" Harper said.

"I don't know. I'm sorry. I just don't know."

Jane brushed past him running back toward the bedroom, fighting the impulse to tears. She flung herself on the bed and pulled a pillow over her head. It was a silly, childish gesture. He wasn't going to come running behind her and try to comfort her. He and his mother would talk about it in low voices, and after a while he'd come back to the bedroom and talk to her. He wouldn't offer any sympathy. And she was perfectly furious with herself that what she wanted was his sympathy.

It wasn't just the usual battle, the immemorial tug of war between mother-in-law and daughter-in-law. It was that all right, intensified by the inescapable fact that Harper was an only child. But it was other things as well. She was seeing her husband for the first time in his native environment, without the well-mannered, gentle, acquired protective coloration he wore in her world, a world of strangers to him. (What camouflage was there for her here?) He was different. He seemed to sense it, too, to succumb in helpless fury to old pressures and forces. She felt that as long as they stayed here they were lost to each other. The man she had married and lived with was a ghost. The one in her bed at night now was not a very attractive stranger. In that sense Mrs. Grim had become in her eyes the evil enchantress of a child's fairy tale. But then, after all, the whole business was so childish!

Then there were the Quiglys, the Battleground. They lived, the whole tribe of them, in a small trailer behind the cottage and across a dirt road, just at the edge of a palmetto jungle. It was a sagging, worn-out trailer, set up on cinder blocks. And the yard, if you could call the littered and trampled space between the trailer and the road a yard, was a perfect mess. In the center of that space there was the cross-eyed wreck of an old Buick convertible. It never moved. Sun baked it and the sudden summer showers soaked it. Every day Joe Quigly came home from work and washed and sponged it down, apparently to protect the paint and chrome from the salt air that corroded everything under the sun before long. After he'd finished, he'd climb in the driver's seat and just sit there. It looked (from the distance of the bedroom window where she always watched him) as if he pretended to be driving it. Maybe he had wrecked it and it wouldn't run anymore. Maybe he had bought it as is from a junkyard and it didn't even have an engine. Maybe he simply didn't have the money for gas. (Which would be an odd thing for a bulldozer operator. She had heard they made lots of money. Unless . . . unless, maybe, alas, Mrs. Grim was quite right, and both Joe Quigly and his poor, frazzle-haired slattern of a wife—who usually appeared once a day anyway wrapped in an oversize dressing gown and wearing sneakers, blinking in the hard sunlight and stumbling over to the topless garbage can by the road to dispose of a bundle of . . . empty bottles?—*were alcoholics.*) In any case, Joe Quigly seemed to love that automobile and to be very possessive about it. If he found his children playing in it when he came trudging up the dirt road home, he ran and chased them out and away with kicks and blows and curses. They didn't seem to mind. They laughed and ran away and left him his car.

The strange thing to Jane was that neither did she mind. She should have cared. A man who mistreats his children! Of course he didn't really mistreat them. He had a tantrum and they had to flee, but it didn't seem to mean anything to them or, seriously, to him. It seemed to be a kind of game. It made her uneasy to think that she might have tolerated such a blow or kick or curse coming from him in just that spirit, though she was sure that if Harper ever struck her she would be badly hurt. Quigly was a curious one. Long, lean, shaggy-haired, his face high-boned, deeply tanned and lined, he moved around with a clumsy grace like an animal trying to walk on its hind legs. He grinned a snaggle- and yellow-tooth grin at her if they happened to pass, and he ran a hand through his thick, unruly blond hair. He was a kind of caricature of the country bumpkin. But—and this was what touched and troubled her—there was something else, indefinable, about him that was utterly alien, yet intriguing. It was as if the clothes, the flesh and bones, the face he wore were all composite parts of a disguise, donned by choice and for some reason. Somehow he communicated a sense of elemental shiftlessness, of sly, supple, and insinuative and irresponsible endurance. Thus the early gods, she thought, must have taken on their guise of mortal flesh and moved among us.

She had tried unsuccessfully to express this complex thing to Harper after she'd seen Joe Quigly standing at the back door waiting for his quarter pound of butter and the electric iron. Harper had laughed at her.

"You artists! Him? He's a typical cracker boy. That's the way they all are. God-like, my ass! Not worth a damn. Crooked as a bunch of snakes."

Since the bad night and the others following it when Harper tumbled into his side of the bed, dead drunk, and snored as soon as his face touched the pillow, she had discovered that she was increasingly fascinated by the myth she had made up for Joe Quigly. Oh, not in the ordinary way, to be sure. Not that way. But as one might be attracted by some wonderful new beast on display at the zoo. There was nothing to it, she assured herself, beyond that feeling of curiosity and delight.

Then yesterday something had happened. With Harper drinking and Mrs. Grim deep in a historical novel and Jane restless and bored, she had gone for a long, lonely walk down the beach. She passed the last of the houses and the few bathers splashing in the surf, and she walked on, following the straight and narrow ribbon of soft sand that seemed to stretch, like some ultimate desert, to infinity. The sun felt warm and good. After a while, alone and happy, she sat down at the foot of a high dune to enjoy it, soon lay back and closed her eyes, dozing in the light. It seemed to penetrate her and fill her veins, and she imagined all her blood, streams, rivers, networks, and canals as becoming a choir of pure molten gold. As she lay there in a complete blank pleasure, she heard at first dimly, then near and loud, a roaring sound, and she sat up just in time to avoid being buried alive by a falling mountain of sand. Choking and spluttering, she struggled to her feet with vague gestures like a drowning person and tried to brush away the sand which covered her. She looked around and then up above her. On top of the dune, poised perilously at the very edge of it, was the flat blade of the bulldozer, and standing above and behind the blade, tall against the whirling sky, straddle-legged, with the afternoon sun glaring behind him, was Joe Quigly, his wild hair tousled by sea breeze, his head tossed back laughing. Jane was furious. Though she was fully and modestly dressed in shorts and a T-shirt, she felt as if he'd been spying on her naked. And then to be covered up, nearly killed in fact, was no joke. Joe Quigly obviously felt differently about it, and, even if he guessed how she must feel, he didn't care. He was content to laugh at her, and she had to laugh too. She stood there looking up at him and laughing, and she shyly raised her hand to wave at him. He waved back, vanished, backed the bulldozer away from the edge and went to work again.

Neither of them had said a word. Yet she was as pleased as if he had tossed her a bouquet of flowers.

She kept that story to herself, not daring to mention it to Harper now.

Jane heard the bedroom door close behind her. She turned her head and saw Harper standing over her.

"I don't know what gets into you sometimes."

"I don't either," she said. "I'm sorry."

"You ought to be. That was pretty rude."

"I know it and I really am sorry."

He dropped down on his hands and knees on the floor and crawled under the bed. She heard him fumbling among the luggage they had stored there.

"What are you doing?"

"Looking for your box of paints," he said.

"What on earth for?"

"I got to paint me a sign."

"With those? That's too expensive."

"I'd be glad to use some other paint," he said. "But it happens we ain't got none. We've told these folks for the last time. Now I'm putting up a 'Keep Off' sign."

"That's silly, Harper. You've been drinking and that's a silly idea."

He backed out and raised his head to the level of the bed.

"You don't understand. Not at all," he said. "There happens to be a serious legal problem involved. If they keep on using the path and we don't put up a sign, then it becomes a common pathway. We don't want that, do we?"

"I guess not."

"Want to help me?" he said. "You can letter a whole lot better than I can."

"No," she said. "Just help yourself. The paints are right there somewhere."

"Where are you going?"

"Just for a walk," she said, shutting the door behind her.

She took the public approach to the beach and avoided the path to save herself from having to pass under the gray scrutiny of Mrs. Grim. She set off south at a good pace, feeling the warm sand between her toes. The tide was coming in now. Jane liked high tide best, though it was hard to explain why, even to herself. Somehow when the tide was high you felt you knew, were familiar with the things the water covered and concealed. At low tide shallow sloughs were mysteries. If you waded you were apt to step on something hidden there, some submarine creature, a quick, brittle, scuttling crab, a jellyfish. (She remembered with a shiver the story of someone stepping on a corpse in the surf.) High tide, though, seemed to be a blessing, the blue waves breaking over and finally covering the beach. The natural impulse of water. It seemed like a fine idea for water to want to cover the land. Perhaps that's how old Noah looked at it, she thought.

She almost tripped over a dead pelican and started back a step in surprise. It lay on the sand, a crumpled mass of wet feathers, a beak slack as a drunk's jaw, as an idiot's, bloody peepholes for eyes (the little birds had already plucked them like grapes), and crawling with black flies and small bugs. She had to hold her nose as she stepped by.

After the last houses and the last bather—a great fat baldheaded man bobbing and splashing like a happy hippo—she felt liberated at last. The sun glared on the empty sand ahead of her. She imagined herself as a pilgrim lost in a far land. It was almost blinding it was so bright, and the breeze had died down so that she could feel the heat of the sun. She started to run. She ran along the beach at the foot of the dunes, ran breathless until she heard the bulldozer working nearby above her.

She was panting and dripping with sweat, for it had been a long run. With nervous, clumsy fingers she took off her clothes. She looked back once to where the last houses were like small toys and saw not a soul now on the beach. She threw her clothes aside and didn't care, was suddenly drunk with sea and sun and sky and her lonely freedom. She lay back and closed her eyes and let the sun bathe her. Her brain was blank and heat-struck, and her flesh crawled with rivulets of sweat. Would he come to the edge of the dune and stand tall and see her now? Would he laugh then, or be struck blind? Would he bury her alive under mountains of sand? It was a strange sweet dream. . . .

She must have been dozing literally, for when she came to herself, the sun had gone behind the dunes and she was in shadow. A breeze had sprung up cool. She was goose-pimpled. The sand was uncomfortable and she felt cold and ashamed. She covered herself quickly with her hands and arms and looked around. Still no one on the beach. No one, thank God, had seen her there. No one, she was sure. What in the world had possessed her to do something like that? Crouching over, she slipped into her clothing and noticed, dismayed, that in her distraction, in her fierce haste, she had ripped off half the buttons of her shorts. She must have been insane.

When she was dressed again and had brushed the sand off her arms and legs, she was ready to start the long walk back. It was then that she heard the laughter, soft and mocking, heard as if at a great distance of time and space, like the light laughter of a ghost, like the memory of laughter. She looked up just in time to see four small blond faces, haloed by light, the Quigly children peering over the edge of the dune, disappear into the camouflage of even blonder, blown sea wheat. Stiff and ashamed, she walked briskly away, following now in reverse the path her bare feet had made in the sand.

When she had to pass the dead pelican again, lapped at, tumbled, and turned by the incoming tide, she was afraid she was going to be sick.

It was nearly dark when she came up the back way to the cottage. He was in the red shell of a car, hands gripping the steering wheel, mouth wide open, driving in some furious daydream, and he didn't see her pass by. Her feet were hurting and she limped a little, but he had nothing, not even pity, to offer her. Just at the edge of the path, facing the trailer, was a sign, crudely lettered with great smears of her good paint (half-empty tubes lay by the path), multicolored, the squandered paint dripping away from the letters as if they had been written in blood:

KEEP OFF THIS HERE PATH
This means you

And beneath this was drawn a skull and crossbones.

Jane opened the back door and went into the kitchen. She poured herself a drink of Harper's whiskey and tossed it off.

"Is that you?" he called.

"Yes," she said. "It's me. I mean it is I."

She walked through the house to the front porch. Harper was sitting in his mother's rocker with a double-barrel shotgun in his lap. He was vigorously cleaning it with an oily rag. Jane leaned against the doorframe behind him in weariness and slack despair and watched him work. He jerked his head around and grinned at her.

"Did you see my sign? Did you see the sign I put up?"

"Yes," she said. "I saw it."

"I found Daddy's old shotgun in the closet," he went on. "Next time I'm going to shoot. They've been warned aplenty. The next time one of them sets a foot on this land, I'm going to get me some tail feathers."

Just then Mrs. Grim came bustling through the living room. She brushed past Jane as if she didn't see her, and her eyes, her small, pale blue eyes, were bright with triumph. She put a box at the feet of her son.

"Honey boy," she cried. "I found the shells for the gun. I knew they were around here somewhere and I found them."

LION

In the morning they came back, two of them anyway, just as he knew they would.

With the first gray hints of light, when all the earth's as ghostly as a moon and the smell of the new day is as keen and sweet as mint, Jojo was up out of bed and stealthily crept to the window. Quick as a monkey he jumped from the windowsill across breathless space to catch, in his fall, the limber branch of the oak tree that grew nearest to the house. For an instant, waiting for his breath to come again, letting his heart fall back into its place, he hung on to the limb trembling from the shock, then swung high and easy, skinning the cat until he was safely on the limb. The rest was simple. He straddled the limb and slid down. Where it joined the trunk he swung free once again and dropped lightly to the ground. Then he heard the roosters start to crow all over town.

The rest of them, his family, would still be sound asleep. And at breakfast time who would miss him with so much going on, Raymond and Stony and Daddy all yelling for their breakfast at the same time in one loud voice, all of them going to be late for work; Marcia lingering ("loitering" Sue calls it) in the bathroom, taking her sweet time while Sue stands just outside the door, leaning thin and weary against it, beating on it and yelling bloody murder about what *difference* does it make how a *telephone operator* looks, she, Sue, being the receptionist for Dr. Trout, the chiropractor, has got to look pretty; and Marcia shouting back at her in her bright voice, cruel as a new knife, that Sue can spend all day and all night too in the bathroom if she wants to and she'll never look pretty to anybody; then come the tears and more loud beating on the door, and Marcia flushes the pot so she won't have to listen; while down in the kitchen Mama and Dalmatia, the colored maid, both of them huge and identically awkward as a couple of trained bears dancing on their hind legs, both so alike they might as well be the same person in two different shades, like dolls, both sleepy-eyed, both sloppy, stumbling and blundering into each other and nodding their *excuse-me-please's* as the bacon and eggs and toast burn to a crisp and the coffee boils over on the stove; neither of them will speak a word to anyone or to each other until the others have all spilled out of the front door in a simultaneous rush to leave, such a rush to the sidewalk they must seem like a handful of pennies hurled from the house; then the two of them will sit down at the kitchen table, enormous, bulging over their chairs on both sides, and over their own coffee will at last come to life, begin to talk and laugh together; in the midst of all that, who would even notice the presence or absence of Jojo, figuring him small and safe at school or somewhere, even though it's midsummer already and school's been out a long time; he whom his mother calls, always with a great belly laugh, her little P.S.?

So Jojo slipped away, quick and quiet as a shadow, and went straight downtown.

There, just as he had known, there were two of them anyway, sitting in the beat-up clay- and mud- and dust-covered ghost of a car with the cross-eyed headlights, parked directly in front of the Sheriff's brick, one-story office. The one behind the wheel was bald as a rock and short, too, pretty nearly some kind of a midget or a dwarf, wearing a sweat-soaked white shirt with the sleeves rolled up to the shoulder around arms like sausages, mopping at his bald head with a handkerchief gray as a dust rag, peering out at the empty street through glasses as thick as the bottom of a pop bottle behind which his large pale eyes glistened and swam like fish in a bowl.

"Jesus, Jesus," he kept saying. "We drive half the night to get here and then the bastard's still asleep."

The other grunted and stayed where he was, hunched over on the other side of the front seat with his face pressed against the rolled-up window glass. He was thin-faced as a hawk and very dark, and his black hair shone so and was cut so neat you wouldn't believe it could be real. He had a little mustache the same way, thin and straight like it was painted on, and the eyebrows, too, so black, so trim, so emphatic, they weren't to be believed. His eyes were weary and bored and unseeing. His lips, to Jojo's surprise, looked painted on with lipstick. He wore a dark coat and a bright shirt and a yellow necktie pulled all the way to the top just like it wasn't summer, and he didn't seem to be sweating at all. He could do whatever he pleased. He was Alonzo the Lion Tamer. Jojo knew his face, the tired blind eyes, red lips, slick black hair, from the yellow posters and from what had happened last evening as well. The other one with him was the owner or the manager, whoever is the boss of The Grand Clark Brothers' Traveling Circus.

While Jojo stood staring, the Lion Tamer rolled down the window on his side and extended, lazy, his hand with a coin in it.

"Little boy," he said. "Run and get us some coffee."

Jojo snatched the fifty-cent piece from that pale palm, cool as a flower, and he started running up the sidewalk to the French Cafe, hearing over his shoulder the other one saying "Jesus, you'd think he'd be here waiting for us at a time like this."

Last evening at dusk, just on the shores of darkness, with the last of the sun like a great splash of blood on the sky and already the first stars floating in the waning blue like lights reflected in water, Jojo had seen how it all happened. It began when out of nowhere, as if by magic, first came the car, the same one with the cross-eyed headlights, then the big trucks, so worn and dusty, so solemn and slow in line they seemed like a parade of shambling prehistoric beasts out of a picture book blindly following one behind the other. And he knew at once because of the yellow posters which had popped up brightly on walls and telephone poles a week or so before that this had to be The Grand Clark Brothers' Traveling Circus. He knew, too, from listening around to what everybody said when the posters first appeared, that the circus would not be stopping here, only passing through on the way to the city. He left one of his secret hiding places, one of his tree places where he could see everything that went on and not be seen, and he followed after, joined the wild herd of children, black and white, and, it seemed, all the yapping mongrel dogs in creation, wishing as he ran along that he was a little bit older, that like the big high school boys he could have his own bike to join in the procession, to wheel precariously, dangerously, in and out of the coughing, ambling trucks, shouting, shrill as birds, and with sometimes no hands at all on the handlebars.

He followed them all the way through town and to the place just beyond the last of the houses where they pulled off the road and parked in a line. The Bald Man was there then, running up and down the line of trucks, shouting at the drivers, pointing, waving his hands, but always only shrugging when any of them leaned out of the high cabs to ask him a question. Jojo wandered under and around the trucks, smelling all the strangeness, staring at the people who climbed out stiff-legged, stretching, to look with indifferent eyes at the town they had just passed through and the darkening land. The Bald Man got one of them to open a fire hydrant, the last one in town, placed out there in the field in a dream of expansion, and the men came with buckets. It didn't take long, either, for the Fire Chief in his red car and the Sheriff in his black one to come too. They came whizzing, sirens whining, and walked ponderously over and began to yell at the Bald Man above the noise of the running water and the catcalls of the men carrying buckets to and fro. They yelled, both at once, at the Bald Man, and he in turn yelled back at them, waved his little arms, shrugged, and mopped his brow. By the time Jojo got there to stand close by with the rest of the children, they had stopped shouting, though they were still talking.

"We got to have some water for the animals," the Bald Man said. "That's all I'm asking for. Just a little water."

"Seems to me you might have asked first," the Sheriff said, putting his hands inside the black leather belt that creaked with the bulk of him, that winked with a row of shiny bullets and from which, sacrosanct, a pearl-handled revolver sagged in its polished holster.

"We didn't think you folks would begrudge us a little water."

"You're supposed to get permission," the Fire Chief said. "You got to have permission first."

"How long do you plan to be here?" the Sheriff said.

"Just a little while, captain," the Bald Man said. "It won't take long."

"Make sure it don't."

Jojo left them all standing around the fire hydrant where the water flowed and spread on the ground and the men with buckets came and went, slipping and staggering in the fresh mud. He ignored the people who had come out of the trucks and huddled together in groups nearby. None of them were freaks or had costumes or anything. He sneaked among the trucks, sniffing for dry hay and the dungy, rich odors of animals, wishing that there was some way he could get to see them. He could smell them in some of the trucks, hear them moving about inside, but it was going to be hard to get a real look at them. He came to the end of the line.

Disappointed then, waiting for a sign or a glimpse of something strange, hiding under the last truck in the line, leaning against a pair of perfectly smooth tires taller than he was, he saw and recognized at once from the posters Alonzo the Lion Tamer. He came and stood so close that Jojo could have reached out and touched him. He leaned back against the side of the truck. He was wearing riding britches and a high-necked sweater, and he was smoking a little cigar. But Jojo smelled above the familiar odor of leather boots and a cigar something sweet like roses, like Sue's perfume.

A woman in a red T-shirt and red trousers, so tight around her legs and hips they looked to have been painted on her, came there and talked to the Lion Tamer in a low voice.

"You smell like a French cathouse," she said and her teeth showed very white in the increasing darkness.

"You ought to know," he said. "I wouldn't."

"Can't you take a joke? Can't you tell when I'm joking?"

"Sure," he said. "You got some rich sense of humor. You slay me."

"What's the matter with you? What am I supposed to do, draw pictures for you?"

"That I'd like to see. I'd like to see the kind of pictures you'd draw."

"You should hear what the others say about you."

"Who cares about them? What do they know, anyway?"

"Isn't it a big laugh?"

"Here we go again," he said. "More jokes."

"For the first time in my life I'm with a man I could really like and he turns out to be a cheap ungrateful bastard."

"*Like?*" the Lion Tamer said. "Who wants *like?*"

"You can't really love somebody unless they will give you half a chance."

"You don't know anything about love. Nobody knows anything about love. It's a mystery."

The Lion Tamer cleared his throat and spat on the ground by his boots.

"I guess it just serves me right," she said.

"Truth," he said. "You want to know the truth. Sometimes you make me sick. You make me so sick I could puke."

He threw his cigar away and turned his back on her, stalking up the line of trucks in giant steps, his high boots squeaking, that faint sweet odor receding with him.

She remained where she was, her hands pressed over her face and her body shaking all over. When she took her hands away, Jojo could see that she was crying silently, and the tears seemed to cause the features of her face to melt and soften like hot wax. She smelled like soap. She slumped over and looked much older than at first. Jojo heard the men up ahead begin shouting and he listened to their calls being passed back along the line and to the engines of the trucks as they, one by one, began to growl. He wondered if he'd better move out from under the truck and let her see that he had been there the whole time, but before he could decide what he ought to do, she moved. She straightened up, posed tensely, looking left and right like somebody getting ready to dash across a busy street, then she ran around behind the truck. He heard her fumbling with what must be a heavy chain. He heard the door open on rusty hinges.

First there was a strange odor, an animal smell for sure, but like wild dry grass and dust and dung. Then the lion came swiftly out on soft feet. He stood by the truck, great-maned, big-chested, head up high, sniffing the air. Jojo watched the lion go running off into the dark across the field and disappear. He heard the woman shut the door, trouble with the chain, and then she came walking right past him, smelling now of heavy sweat like somebody with a fever, and breathing deep and hard as if she had been running a long way. Next, all the lights of the trucks came on at once, and as they started to move forward he jumped out of the way. He saw the huge tires roll over his footprints, and he stared after as the bright parade of vehicles picked up speed and vanished down the highway.

When the last red taillights were swallowed by the dark, he ran across the field, sniffing as he went, following the way the lion had gone.

When Jojo came back with two paper cups of hot coffee the Sheriff was there, his black car parked at a jaunty angle, the way he was allowed to do, and the three of them were standing on the sidewalk. The Sheriff had his hands under his belt again and he was grinning.

"What is all this about anyway?" the Sheriff said. "What are you two trying to prove?"

"I told you on the phone," the Bald Man said. "Jesus, I thought you'd have a big bunch of men here to help us find him."

"I had one little talk with you yesterday evening," the Sheriff said. "Maybe you didn't quite get the point."

"Ask him," the Bald Man said pointing to the Lion Tamer. "See what he says."

Though the Lion Tamer was standing with them, he was aloof, not really looking at either of them. Now that the Lion Tamer was out of the car Jojo could see that he was wearing the same trim riding britches and high glossy boots. He also had yellow gloves on and carried a short riding crop. He still looked tired, weary and indifferent beyond telling, but in the plain daylight his color, his slick black hair, his razored mustache, his painted lips made him look like an undertaker's corpse. In fact he looked exactly the way he did on the posters, curiously two-dimensional. There was about him the faint sweetness of the night before. He simply stood there, gripping the riding crop behind his back with both gloved hands and looking through the two of them and the whole town, too, as if everything in the world had been made out of cellophane and as if, like some funny-book character with superhuman powers, he could see through everything under the sun.

"I wouldn't ask him anything," the Sheriff said. "I wouldn't ask that one the time of day."

"All right," the Bald Man said. "All right now. Let's don't everybody get excited. Let's try and keep our wits about us."

He dabbed at the sweat on his shiny head, his jowled face, and his neck. He was sweating so much that his white shirt stuck to him. His upper body was big as a barrel, but his legs were terribly thin and short, and Jojo was amazed at how small his feet were, tiny points in yellow and black shoes, just like a little girl's. On such delicate legs he looked something like a robin.

"Here, boy," the Lion Tamer said. And he took the cups of coffee and the three dimes change.

"You can have mine," the Bald Man said to the Sheriff. "I don't think I can keep it down now."

"Keep it," the Sheriff said. "I've had my breakfast."

So the two of them drank their coffee and the Sheriff watched them. When they finished the Lion Tamer lit up one of his little cigars and Jojo took the empty cups and put them in a trash can.

"Here's the way I look at it," the Sheriff said. "You claim you lost a lion last evening when you stopped here. You say you must have lost it then, but you don't know how—"

"I got a good idea how," the Lion Tamer said.

The Sheriff glared at him.

"We'll have plenty of time for your good ideas later."

"Okay," the Lion Tamer said. "Okay."

"Now take it easy," the Bald Man said.

"I said okay, didn't I?"

"Anyhow," the Sheriff said. "You want me to round up a whole bunch of men and hunt for this lion for you."

"Not just for us," the Bald Man said. "You don't want a wild beast prowling around town either."

The Sheriff just smiled.

"I want King back," the Lion Tamer said. "Give me a little help and I'll get him."

"King, that's his name?" the Sheriff said, giggling now.

The Lion Tamer flicked the ash off his cigar.

"That's logical," he said. "I call him King, so his name must be King."

"Don't you sass me, boy."

"Everybody calm down now," the Bald Man said, wringing out his handkerchief.

"All right," the Sheriff said. "There's two ways to look at this situation. Either you lost a lion or you didn't. Now my suspicion is you didn't lose no lion here. It don't figure. So, if you're trying some kind of a publicity stunt—"

"Publicity stunt!" the Bald Man said. "Jesus! You got to believe us, man."

At that point the Lion Tamer only smiled, showing his bright perfect teeth.

"If you are trying a stunt, I'll lock you both up," the Sheriff said. "I told you once to keep moving on and I meant it. We don't want no fly-by-night two-bit carnie around here. Period. Now let's look at it the other way. Suppose it's for real. Then it strikes me you folks are getting mighty careless with your wild animals."

"The bitch did it," the Lion Tamer said. "She don't care for King."

"That's against the law too," the Sheriff said, "turning lions loose and such. I could lock you up for that too."

"I don't know how it happened," the Bald Man said. "We got steel doors on those trucks and chains."

"Tell you what I'll do," the Sheriff said. "When the Deputy shows up, we'll take a little drive around and see what we can see. We'll take a look."

"We got to find him!" the Bald Man said. "What if we don't find him?"

"Well, if he is here," the Sheriff said, "it looks like we got us the beginnings of a pretty good zoo."

"You could never keep King in no hick zoo," the Lion Tamer said.

After a while the Deputy came. The Sheriff went inside his office and got a rifle and a length of rope, and the Lion Tamer exchanged his riding crop for a big whip and buckled on his pistol belt. The four of them climbed into the Sheriff's car, the two from the circus sitting in the back. Just as they were pulling away the Lion Tamer rolled down the window and threw Jojo a dime. It rang like a little bell on the sidewalk.

"Thanks, boy."

Jojo pocketed the dime and walked around to the side of the office where the first shade was forming a pool and squatted, leaning his back against the brick wall. To be a Lion Tamer would be very, very special. You likely had to have a call for it, like preaching. He closed his eyes to be able to picture how it would be, Alonzo the Lion Tamer caught in a net of golden lights alone in a cage with all those lions and tigers while outside all around the hushed dark tent every burning eye would be fixed on him. That would be a lonely wonderful thing to be there in a bright fancy costume and prove to the world that one man all by himself can crack a whip and make even the wildest animals dance and stand as still as statues or jump through flaming hoops. Talk about jubilation! Then they would have to notice you and love you for what you proved to them could be done, how brave somebody could be. But it would be kind of sad too. How could you ever tell anybody how it was? What could you ever say to them after you came out of the terrible cage and bowed to them and they clapped for you? "It's only some kind of a trick," they would say. No wonder you would be so sick and tired of everything.

And picturing all this Jojo dozed in the shade waiting for them to come back.

Maybe an hour or so passed, and then the Sheriff's car returned, cruising slowly up the street which was lively now with morning's first business. The rifle was poking through the right front window where the Deputy cradled it. They all got out of the car and stood on the sidewalk.

"I'll give you two rare birds about twenty minutes to be outside of the county," the Sheriff said.

"Listen," the Bald Man said. "You got to warn people to be on the lookout—"

"Man, are you crazy? We got people worked up enough already wondering what we're doing driving around town with a loaded rifle in the middle of the morning," the Deputy said.

"Time's wasting," the Sheriff said, looking at his watch.

"All right, all right," the Bald Man said. "We're going."

The Lion Tamer spat on the sidewalk.

"Be careful," he said. "That King's a mean one."

Then for all the world to see he started crying right there on the sidewalk like a little child. The Bald Man took his arm and led him to the cross-eyed car.

"Wait a minute," the Sheriff said. "Just in case we do find him, what does he like to eat?"

"Meat. Raw meat," the Lion Tamer said, still sobbing.

The Sheriff and the Deputy laughed as the beat-up crazy car made a big illegal U-turn and disappeared swiftly the way it had come.

"Don't that beat the world?" the Deputy said.

"You know how come that fellow there wears perfume?"

"No. Not unless he's queer or something."

"I'll tell you," the Sheriff said. "It's because he's really deep down a nigger. He may look like a white man, but I can tell every time. Let him try and hide the smell. You can always tell by the hair."

They both laughed as they strolled up the walk to the office.

That evening, just as he knew it would, all hell broke loose at home. There they were, all sitting around the dining-room table, Raymond and Stony and Daddy, tired out from a hard day's work, banging their silverware on their empty plates and hollering for supper. His mama and Dalmatia were staggering around the kitchen (they'd been drinking whiskey together, Jojo could smell that) looking everywhere for the missing steak.

"Come on," Raymond was yelling. "I ain't got all night."

Then his mama came as far as the kitchen door but not too close to the table. She leaned back against the doorframe and smiled a little smile.

"We had a steak," she said. "But it's gone now. I mean we really had one, but I don't know what came of it."

"No meat?" Stony cried.

She shook her head slowly, still smiling.

"Great God Almighty!" his daddy shouted. "Come on, boys. Let's us go down to the French Cafe and get something to eat."

They shoved back their chairs and all at the same time threw their china plates against the wall, his mama's pretty white china ones, and the plates shattered beautifully in many pieces and fell like a noisy kind of snow on the floor. As the three men stomped out of the room his mama started to cry and Dalmatia came from the kitchen and put her arm around her. Jojo got down from his chair and tiptoed upstairs. It was pretty bad up there, too, with Sue, a big pair of scissors in her hand, chasing Marcia around, both of them running up and down the hall as loud as runaway horses and in and out of all the rooms. Sue had only her slip on and Marcia wasn't wearing stitch one. Jojo stood in the hall and they ran all around him, as if he was a post or something. Sometimes you'd think the people didn't know he was alive around there. Then Jojo saw the water slowly spreading into the hall from under the bathroom door. The tub was overflowing. He went into the bathroom—the door was on one hinge like a broken arm because Sue had knocked it open—and turned off the water and pulled the plug. Just outside the open door Marcia and Sue stopped running and, panting, glared at each other.

"Oh, Miss Priss," Sue said. "Trying to play innocent!"

"I haven't the slightest idea—"

"For once I'm the one with a date in the middle of the week and what do you do? You're so green-eyed with jealousy, you up and take all my perfume."

"Hah!" Marcia said. "I wouldn't use your stinking perfume. And don't you act so holier than thou. Where's my new lipstick?"

"I'm sure I wouldn't know."

They continued to stare into each other's eyes, then Sue slapped Marcia, and Marcia, unblinking, slapped her back, and Sue dropped the scissors and went running back to her room crying, and she slammed the door so hard the whole house shook. Marcia whirled, smiling, and came into the bathroom.

"Oh," she said. "Oh, it's just you. Shut the door behind you. I'm trying to take a bath."

Jojo tiptoed to his room, shut the door, and lay on the bed with his eyes closed waiting for the dark to come.

As soon as it was good and dark, the stars all out and the subtle odors of the evening and the soft noises of insects rich and mysterious in the air, Jojo stirred. He rummaged in a great pile of his dirty clothes in the closet until he found his Royal Canadian Mounted Police costume that he got for last Christmas. It was already getting too tight, but he managed to get into it, though he couldn't button the scarlet jacket all the way. He reached under his mattress and found the paper sack all right. He threw it out of the window. Then he hopped up on the windowsill and squinted into the dark. Though he had done it so many times, in the dark it was always hard to see the limb.

There was always one rushing moment when he couldn't be sure that he had judged the distance right. He crouched and jumped into vacant air, holding his breath, his heart pounding until he felt the rough curve of the limb under his hands and he shivered from the shock. He climbed down the tree and picked up his bundle.

A good mile away, at the edge of town, there was a curious three-story frame house. It had belonged to a banker who shot himself when the Boom ended; and an old woman, his widow, crazy as a bat everyone said, lived there all alone. And it sagged from the careless weight of her loneliness and misery. The front yard, the front porch, were covered with junk—old shoes, umbrellas, newspapers, faded hats, broken toys, magazines, tires and inner tubes, even garbage; for that was all that she did for herself now. Late at night she would leave her lightless house and prowl the town, searching in trash heaps and garbage cans, poking among the smoldering things at the dump, searching for something, dragging a child's red wagon behind her until it was heaped, loaded with the wrecked, the broken, the thrown-away, forsaken things of the town. What these actions meant, nobody pretended to know. They left her to herself. After all, her husband had been a respectable man in those years before the Depression, and who could blame her now, seeing she did no real harm?

Jojo circled around the house to the backyard, picking the way through the litter and wreckage of a garden. The smell of it was terrible to him, but no one lived near enough to complain, and the dogs loved it. Back farther there was a ramshackle barn, left over from the horse and buggy days. Outside of this barn he stopped and opened the paper bag. First he anointed himself with Sue's perfume. He painted his lips with Marcia's lipstick, then, carrying the paper sack with him, he pulled back the bolt on the door, cracked it, and slipped inside. It was dark and foul in the barn, but he could smell that the lion was still in there all right. There had always been the chance that someone, even the old woman herself, might find out before now. He was glad they hadn't.

Then he could see the eyes in the dark. They seemed green and glowing from an inner light like jewels. He opened the bag and took out the steak. Holding it in front of him, he began to walk slowly toward the burning eyes.

TIME OF BITTER CHILDREN

THE TRUCK SLOWED to a hissing stop on the shoulder of the highway. The driver left the engine running. He pushed back away from the wheel, yawned and stretched, and, seeing that the man next to him in the cab was still sound asleep, hunched up in a small round ball of himself like a sleeping animal, he reached across and touched him lightly on the shoulder to wake him. At his touch the man uncoiled and sat up straight—alert, tense, red-eyed, and suspicious.

"This is far as I go," the driver said. "I'm turning north."

"You just going to dump me out here right in the middle of nowhere?"

"You suit yourself," the driver said. "Stay with me if you want to end up in Knoxville."

"I ain't bound for Knoxville. I'm headed south."

"That's what I thought you said," the driver said, grinning, easy. He was a big man, gentle in the knowledge of his own great strength and power. "You already told me you was going south."

The small man squinted at him, and his sharp rodent's face worked itself into a mask of fine wrinkles, sly and dangerous.

"Why do I have to get out then? It's cold and lonesome up

here in the mountains. Ain't nobody else on the road. What are you trying to do to me?"

The very idea made the driver laugh.

"Like I say, you can ride all the way to Knoxville if you want to. Suit yourself."

"You'll be going the wrong direction."

"From here on I will."

"Goddamnit!" the little man said. "Don't that beat all?"

The driver was still more tickled than anything else, but he looked at his watch to see how much time he was wasting. It was past midnight already. He was going to have to put down a heavy foot on the gas as it was.

"Would you just turn a man loose in open country? There's probably wild animals and Lord knows what else up here. You'd just stop your truck and make a fellow get out and shiver in the cold?"

"I didn't tell you to get out yet, but I'm fixing to."

"See there? See what I'm talking about? You don't give a hoot. What happened to all the charity in the world?"

"My charity, such as it is, goes as far as this turnoff. I guess I'm through talking. Time to get off."

The driver shoved a long arm around behind the little man, who had backed himself up against the cab door like a cornered animal. The man twitched and winced away from the arm as if he were dodging a blow, but the driver merely flicked the door handle and pushed it open. Then he had to be quick. The little man, with all his weight against the door, would have pitched out of the high cab if the driver hadn't seized him in a tight grip. For an instant they were locked there in a reluctant embrace.

"I guess somebody will be coming along pretty soon," the driver said.

"Who would stop and give me a ride?"

"What are you complaining about? I give you a ride, didn't I? You're just as bad as an old woman."

The driver shook his head, dismay now added to his natural curiosity. He refused to let himself be moved or troubled by the tears silently falling from the red-rimmed, bloodshot, phlegm-colored eyes, making jagged streaks along his dusty face.

"I see you've made up your mind," he said to the driver at last. "Invincible ignorance, I call it. Well, could you do me one thing?"

"What's that?"

"Lemme have a couple of cigarettes and a pack of matches."

The driver sighed with relief. He hadn't been able to guess what was coming next, and anyway this was going to make it simple and final. He took the half-empty pack from his pocket and fumbled for matches.

"Here," he said. "Keep the pack. I got another one."

The little man took them with his left hand, still keeping the other one out of sight as he had all along, jammed in his pants pockets. No "thank you," nothing. Just took the pack of cigarettes and the matches in his free left hand, slipped sidewise off the seat, and dropped down to the ground. The driver had to reach all the way across and pull the door to. He shifted into low and pulled the big truck off the shoulder and back onto the road, shifted again, made his turn, and drove north.

For a moment he thought about it. Then he laughed out loud to himself.

"It does beat all," he said, "the way some people you run into these days act."

Then, with all that over and down with, he started thinking about the diner up the road, up near Knoxville, where he would treat himself to a great big breakfast. There were a couple of cute little waitresses who worked there, and you could joke with them if you felt like it. Driving a truck on long hauls wasn't such a lonesome job as a man might think.

The small man left behind stood in the middle of the road, stamping his feet in a fierce little dance, partly against the sudden chill of the night after the close warmth of the cab, but equally out of an excess of puzzled frustration. He watched the red taillights of the truck and trailer vanish into the dark, swallowed whole. He spat on the road and cursed the driver and the truck and all of Creation. Clenching his fist, he felt the crackle of the cellophane on the half-empty pack of cigarettes and relaxed, feeling in the privacy of the dark a slow, sly grin forming itself on his lips.

He moved off the road, hopped lightly over a yawning ditch, sat down on the other side, and dangled his legs. Expertly with his left hand he opened the pack of paper matches, folded one match back, struck it and lit a cigarette, staring into the blue heart of the little flame, letting his cupped palm feel the warmth of it until the match was burned almost down to the end. He puffed and blinked and let his eyes become accustomed to the dark again. Gradually the stars grew bright and the bulked shapes of the mountains loomed like huge, crouching beasts around him. He hunched down as small as he could, as if to draw in against the dark and the cold, as if somehow to conserve and protect, like the cupped match flame he had stared at, the invisible heat of his body and soul. He was like a drab little sparrow there. He smoked and chuckled to himself.

"Well," he said, "if worse comes to worse, you could always get yourself a job as a scarecrow."

The picture of himself in a lonely field, arms outstretched, scaring the crows away, tickled him no end.

Then, more sober, shouting into the dark: "You foxed him! You foxed that fool out of half a pack of ready-made cigarettes!"

Lee Southgate was already on the road at that time. He was driving fast because he had some business in eastern Tennessee in the morning, and he wasn't sleeping well in hotels and motels anyway. He had stopped once, east of Ashville, and had an order of bacon and eggs and toast and coffee, even though he hadn't been the least bit hungry. A traveling man just had to stop every so often to get the feel of solid ground under his feet again, the earth he spent so much of his waking time and energy lightly skimming and scorning. Like a dainty-legged water bug swift across the surface of a pond, he thought. Sometimes, for no special need or reason, you had to light somewhere and take a look around.

So he stopped at the roadside diner, knowing the long, winding, lonely drive through the mountains lay in dark ambush ahead of him. He had eaten, played the jukebox, talked a while with the waitress and shown her the snapshots in his wallet, pictures of his wife, his two young children, his dog, and his new ranch-style house in the Tall Oaks subdivision. It had been a nice time. The waitress was big, plain, and sympathetic, motherly. He always got along easy with big, plain women.

Lee Southgate was a salesman for a sporting-goods firm. He made a good living at it, but his territory in this part of the country had to be large. He was on the road a lot of the time and it was hard on him, wore him down. He was a natural salesman, much the same as some are natural actors; selling came easy to him; but the trips alone, the vague gaps of time between meeting people and performing, for every sale was a performance, troubled him.

Even though he had promised his wife to be careful about picking up hitchhikers, for terrible things happened these days, he usually ended up keeping his eyes peeled for figures by the side of the road. They almost always turned out to be college students or young men going in search of some adventure. He was reminded of himself and his own youth in the drab days of the Depression.

By now it was almost dawn with the sky already gray and lightened. Lee Southgate's headlights leapt to discover and reveal a small shape, like a boy's, standing by the side of the road. Surprised, then relieved, he slowed down and stopped, opened the door.

When the man climbed in, a small man, almost a kind of dwarf, old and dirty, his right hand jammed in his pocket, and without a word, just climbed in, pulled the door to and looked straight ahead waiting to get going, Lee Southgate wished that he had passed by.

He just might have a knife in that pocket, Lee Southgate was thinking. *A crazy, twisted, little old man like that might do most anything.*

He drove on.

"Been waiting long?"

The man twisted to look at him, to look him over, scornful, surprised, and maybe even outraged at being asked a direct question. He did not reply for a while. He waited so long to answer that Lee Southgate wondered if he had really heard him at all.

"Long enough," he said. "I like to have froze down to the bones waiting for you to get here."

"Well, well! Well, then. Let me just turn the heater on and see if we can't take the chill off."

The man grunted at that and looked away again, staring at the dark nothing out of the window. As if to say it would take more than a heater and a few kind, impersonal words to get rid of his chill. Lee Southgate stifled a belch. He was beginning to suffer from indigestion. He almost always did have indigestion after he had eaten without really being hungry and when he was very tired. A man could change all that, lose the slump of sheer fatigue and the growl in his stomach, once he found a motel, took himself a good hot shower, and changed his clothes.

Furtively he sized up his passenger. One thing was for sure, he hadn't been near a bath or a basin of water for quite a while. He had noticed his clothes in the quick, impersonal, complete manner of a salesman when the door opened for him to get in and the overhead light briefly bathed the car in a yellow glow. Now without even looking he could see the separate parts. The shoes, worn, run down flat at the heels, scuffed and paper-thin. The pants dirty, ragged, and stained. Then the strange thing was the jacket, an expensive one, suede, a genuine luxury item. It had looked to be fairly clean too and didn't come close to fitting him. The sleeve almost hid his thumb. Maybe somebody down the road had given it to him. Then again maybe he stole it. If he had a knife in his pocket he might have just taken it off somebody. It would be a big man too.

"Where are you headed, old-timer?"

"South, if it's anybody's business but my own."

"You don't say," Lee Southgate said, for the moment too pleased with the sound of another voice to care what was said.

"And another thing."

"What's that?"

"My name is not old-timer."

"No offense meant," he said, smiling. "My name's Lee Southgate."

"Okay. Pleased to meet you. But just never mind who I am."

"Is it supposed to be a secret?"

"A secret? What do you mean making a crack like that?"

The old man turned again to stare at him with that same leathery crinkled expression of suspicion, curiosity, outrage, and incredulity. A mad look. Small as a boy or a jockey he was all right. Lee Southgate was drawn irresistibly, as to a kind of magnetic appeal, to think about that hidden right hand in its pocket. *Who knows? He might even have some kind of a little zip gun. Or maybe an old-fashioned set of brass knuckles. Most likely a knife though, one with an edge like a straight razor.*

He reached over and punched on the radio. If he wasn't going to be able to share a decent conversation, he could at least listen to something. They could listen together. That would be sharing something. Lee Southgate fiddled with the dial until he picked up, faint and static-clouded, an all-night disc-jockey show. He hummed along with the music and watched the road ahead swimming in the glare of his headlights. He felt better.

After a while he realized that his companion was still staring at him, waiting for something, maybe for the answer to the question he'd asked that Lee Southgate had already forgotten. Lee Southgate looked at him and flashed an amiable smile.

"It ain't a secret. You'd know it. You'd know it in a minute if I was to tell you."

"Is that a fact?" Lee Southgate began. Then, as if on second thought: "Sure now, I guess I would."

That seemed to satisfy the old man. He nodded solemnly, looked away, and eased back in the seat again. Lee Southgate shrugged and kept his mind on the driving. When the old man decided to speak again, it was so soft, almost a whisper against the noise of the radio, that Lee Southgate wasn't sure whether he had heard him say something or not.

"What's that? Excuse me, did you say something?"

"You could hear fine if it wasn't for that damn noise on the radio."

"Oh, I'm sorry." He twisted a knob on the radio and then the only noise was the slight whisper of the heater and its whirring fan.

"Thibault, I said. Battling Bill Thibault from New Orleans."

"Is that a fact?"

"Battling Bill Thibault, that's who I am."

There was a kind of patronizing smile about the way he said it though his fierce expression did not change.

"You don't say. What's your line of work, Mr. Thibault."

"My what?"

"Line of work. Occupation."

The old man gasped in simple amazement.

"You don't know? You mean to tell me that you ain't never heard of me? Where the hell have you been?"

"Excuse me," Lee Southgate started to say, "I'm sorry, but—"

"Where were you hiding when I took on Brakeman Shriver in Mobile? Didn't you even hear what I done to Burr Beaver in Houston, Texas? And you know damn well that Beaver, he went on to fight for the Championship of the World. You know they let that Burr Beaver have a shot at the Championship and I had already proved I was twice the man Beaver was."

So that's it! Just a punchy old prizefighter!

"That must have been quite a while ago, Mr. Thibault."

The old man giggled.

"Well, I guess so. I would say so. Likely you weren't even born yet, a young fellow like you."

"I guess that's why I never heard of you."

"That's no excuse. It isn't like I was just nobody. I was famous."

"Sure," Lee Southgate said, irritated. "You may be famous yet for all I know. I don't follow the fight game."

To Lee Southgate's surprise the old man winced away at that. He pressed his face flat against the glass of the rolled-up window.

"What's the use?"

It was a rhetorical question.

"Those were the days," the old man went on. "That was the time. It was the time of tall men. You won't believe it, but even me, a little old bird like me, I was a tall man in those days. It was good to be alive then. Nowadays there's nothing. This here is a bad time, a time of bitter children. There's not one good man among you anymore."

Then Lee Southgate was left with the heater to listen to and the road to watch and the sense that even though he had hurt the old man's feelings—and he was sensitive to other people's feelings and hated, usually, to hurt them—that he had accidentally saved himself from something bad, discomfort, trouble, some kind of real disaster. He could have been more polite with the old bum, feigned an interest anyway, but, obscurely threatened, he had told the truth. Lee Southgate was perplexed, baffled with himself. Why had he been compelled to offend the old man so?

It was early morning now. They had come out of the mountains of North Carolina and were in Tennessee, passing small farms and coming on toward Johnson City. Lee Southgate's appointment was in Chattanooga, but he felt so tired he decided after all that he would stop off in Johnson City at least long enough to get a barbershop shave.

"How far did you say you were going, old-timer?"

"I didn't say. But I'm trying to get as far as Chattanooga."

"I'm stopping off in Johnson City. I'll let you off anywhere you want."

"I want to go to Chattanooga."

Here we go, Lee Southgate thought. *Here we go again.*

"Oh, you'll get a ride easy from here on."

"I'm sick and tired of having to get in and out of cars and trucks and standing by the road and waiting for rides to come along. All I want to do is get where I'm going."

"You ought to take the bus or the train."

The old man certainly brought out the worst in him. Maybe

he was just tired out, worn beyond endurance, down to the bone marrow and the raw edges of his nerves. Truly he couldn't wait to get the old man out of the car and out of his sight.

As soon as they were in town, he pulled over and parked. People were already on the way to work, moving with purpose along the sidewalks to shops and offices. The mountains, the lonesome road, and the night seemed far behind. He felt much better.

"All right, Mr. Battling Bill Thibault, this is where you get off. End of the line."

Thibault, or whatever his name was, started to ease himself out of the car without a word.

"Why don't you take the bus from here on?"

No answer, but he stopped moving and waited.

"I'll tell you what," Lee Southgate said. "I'll give you enough money to have breakfast and buy yourself a bus ticket."

"What for? I ain't done nothing for you. What do I have to do for it?"

"Nothing."

"People don't give money for nothing."

Lee Southgate had an inspiration. Why not?

"Okay, I'll tell you what," he said. "I'll give you the money for your knife."

"What knife? I ain't got one. What do I need a knife for?"

"Show me what you're hiding in your right-hand pocket and I'll give you the money."

The old man's rat-face wrinkled with curiosity. Thibault had to think about it.

"You gonna give me some money just to look at my bad hand?"

Delicately he slipped his hand out of his pocket and showed it to the salesman. It was puffed and swollen out of all shape and proportion, red as a cooked lobster and the skin stretched taut, terribly infected. Southgate looked and saw that it seemed to throb with each pulse beat. The old man looked at it too for a moment, but impersonally, as if it were a separate thing, maybe a small sick animal, no part of him.

Lee Southgate, sickened and ashamed, fumbled for a wad of dollar bills without counting them. The old man snatched them and, without a word, stepped out of the car.

Southgate started the car and drove away in a hurry, not willing to glance back. And so he never saw, would never even imagine, the expression of simple childish pleasure and victory on the old man's face.

THE TEST

WE HAD WORKED on the helmet off and on all spring, and by June when school was about over it was finished. And we thought it was beautiful. It wasn't that much work really, but we made an occasion out of each afternoon that we spent together working on it. The three of us met in the secrecy of Bobby's garage, smoked until our heads were whirling, and talked about all the things we were going to do when we were finished. It had been just like that a few years before when the three of us tried to make a raft out of the pieces of a tumbled-down old boathouse. I wanted to float along the St. John's River all the way from Sanford to Jacksonville. Then the Mississippi. Then—who knows? —the Nile, the Ganges, the Amazon. When we finally got it put together and put it in the lake to see how it would float, it sank like a stone. Clearly, though, the helmet would be a useful device. My plan was to scour the lake bottoms for sunken rowboats. We'd raise them, patch, caulk, paint, and sell them. With all the money we got we'd buy a good-size yacht and cruise around the Gulf of Mexico searching for pirate treasure. Bobby was more practical from beginning to end. He was for taking it out to one of the popular swimming places—Rock Spring, Sanlando Springs, Palm Springs—and charging a quarter a head to use it for, say, fifteen minutes. By the end of summer we wouldn't be rich, not by a long shot, but still our pants pockets ought to be bulging heavy sacks of quarters. Chris, the Greek, had another idea completely. He said he just wanted to learn how to use it and to enjoy it. He would have liked, he had to admit, to go over to Tarpon Springs where most of the Greeks in the state live and become a sponge fisherman. But he had the grocery store waiting for him to finish high school, the bright rows of labeled cans, the stalls for fresh vegetables, the meat counter, the coat of sawdust on the floor, the flies and the hanging flypaper, the rich smells of the place all mingling together, and his father, a dark little man always smiling and rubbing his hands together and with one quick finger belling the music of his sales on the cash register.

All of us, then, were thinking of the diving helmet, not just as a means to something—money, adventure, pleasure—but as well as a means to escape from something. For instance, Bobby, the practical one, didn't need money at all. He came from the richest family in town, the banker's. After the disasters of the Depression my father thought it was the best joke in the world that his son should have the banker's son for his best friend. Whenever I'd ask permission to spend the night there or eat supper at Bobby's, he'd say, "Sure, by all means. Go on over there and really enjoy yourself. We might as well get something back from the bank."

"Hush up, Hugh," my mother would tell him. "Bobby is his friend. He doesn't have to worry about all that."

"I'm for friendship," my father would reply. "Let friendship thrive. But I reserve the right to take the ironic view of the situation. If you please." He never quite got over the hard times and the fact that he'd lost every cent of his savings, though he managed most of the time to maintain the "ironic view." He had been in the real estate business. Now he was a full-time inventor and spent most of his time in the study with a bottle. Bootleg whiskey then, but "the real stuff" off a boat that came by night to the coast and unloaded its cargo to dark waiting low-slung high-powered cars; these sped lightless over the rutted back country roads they knew by heart. Actual delivery was performed by a Negro washerwoman with a huge bundle of rags and bottles wrapped in a sheet and balanced on her head—which might have seemed mysterious and suspicious since nobody on our block could afford a washerwoman anymore and the wives could be seen any Monday morning hanging their own clothes out on the line, but the Chief of Police lived right down the street on the same block and got his liquor the same way. Anyway, there Father would sit with his bottle and his drawings and papers and plans and schemes. Some of them: an airplane, not a helicopter, that could fly backwards if you wanted it to, chewing gum that really cleaned your teeth so you didn't have to bother brushing them, a pill that turned fresh water into pure gasoline, a brand-new kind of coffee made out of acorns, a new kind of bulletproof glass. The funny thing is that a few years later when the War came along the latter made him a good deal of money. The Government used some part of his patented invention for the canopies and blisters of fighting airplanes. But meanwhile my mother taught school, my sister put off getting married (forever it turned out) to teach school too. And my brother dropped out of school and got a job with a shoe firm as a traveling salesman. No wonder then, when I recall it now, all my thoughts were of the Amazon River and searching for buried treasure.

With Chris, as I said, it was a different thing. His people were poor even before the Depression. His father had been an officer in the Greek Army; and when the Turks drove them out of Smyrna, he came to Florida and managed to open up a grocery store. He was a thin, dark little man with a clipped military mustache. Everyone said he had been a Greek aristocrat once. (Of course they say that about all the foreigners.) Now he and his wife and Chris, their only child, ran a grocery store. If it wasn't very prosperous, it was all his, and one day Chris would have it. Chris had to work only on Saturdays during the school year. But during vacations and the summer he had to work every day. Like lots of boys whose parents were foreigners, Chris was at once ashamed and protective of them, proud and embarrassed at the same time.

Bobby had furnished the basic item, a worn-out hot-water heater. It had a square piece of glass near the top where the pipe had fitted on, and that would do fine for the air line. He also furnished a jigsaw and metal files to smooth it down with. I furnished a garden hose. Chris had a bicycle pump and some rubber insulation that they use for the windows of automobiles. That was just what we needed for rough edges that would touch the body. Between smoking and talking about what we were going to do with it we did some work on it and finished up just the week that school ended. Chris was in a big hurry because he'd have to go to work right after the last day of school. We cut the heater in half and then cut out the sides of the top half so that it would fit easily over the shoulders and leave the arms free, like a sleeveless, sideless vest, with solid metal fore and aft. We filed and smoothed the jagged edges and fitted the strips of rubber insulation along the edges so it wouldn't cut. We rigged up a way to stuff one end of the garden hose into the hole on top and keep it there with a great blob of tightly wound friction tape on the inside. We stuffed the little hose of the bicycle pump inside the other end of the garden hose. I painted a skull and crossbones on the back of it. And there it was, a genuine diving helmet.

Now the question was, what were we really going to do with it? I was for starting immediately to explore the lake bottom for rowboats.

"It's full of sunk boats."

Bobby wanted to take it out and demonstrate it to the owners of one of the swimming places.

"If we make a deal right away, we'll have it made all summer."

Chris shook his head. "That's all right for you all," he said. "You can do what you want with it all summer long. But I want to have some fun with it first."

"What kind of fun?"

"What I had in mind," he said, "was doing something all three of us would always remember."

"Like what?" Bobby, the skeptic, said.

"Oh, I don't know," Chris said. "Something special, something a little bit risky maybe."

"Daring?" I perked up.

Bobby grinned in his superior knowing way and didn't say anything. He lit a cigarette like a gangster in the movies and blew a series of neat concentric smoke rings. After all, he'd been smoking a lot longer than we had. Anyway, they were his cigarettes.

"It's just this," Chris went on. "I know you guys have all kinds of plans for using the helmet. But I kind of thought that since we had talked about it so much and worked on it all together and all that, maybe we ought to do something special, just the three of us. We ought to make an occasion out of diving the first time, a kind of a ceremony."

"A ceremony?" Bobby scoffed.

I was Bobby's best friend, but I wasn't on his side now.

"We got to have a test anyway," I said. "We got to test the equipment and ourselves. They always do that."

"You can test it in a bathtub."

"Aw, Bobby," I said. "Let's do it right."

"Why is it so important to you, Chris?"

Chris shrugged his shoulders just like his father did. Chris talked with exactly the same accent we did and used the same words and might just as well have been born in Florida like the rest of us, except every once in a while he relaxed into some wholly alien gesture, something he did with his hands, a sudden facial expression, or that shrug.

"My people have always been great divers," he said.

That seemed to satisfy Bobby as a good enough reason.

"What did you have in mind?"

"Well, I was thinking maybe we might take a boat and the helmet out to Weikiwa. Maybe we could even get down inside that cave."

"Too dangerous."

Chris shrugged. I was delighted.

"I agree with Chris," I said. "Let's take it to Weikiwa."

"I'm against it," Bobby said, "but this is a democratic country."

We decided to go out there on Friday, the day of graduation. We weren't graduating, so we decided to skip that occasion—everybody dressed in white, long-winded speeches about the road of life, prayers made up on the spur of the moment that might last for half an hour, "Pomp and Circumstance" played badly by the Cherokee High School Band, and a whole lot of people (mostly girls) crying and carrying on. Bobby not only had a learner's license, he had his own car as well, a beat-up one, but it ran. We met at his house early that morning, shucked our white clothes in favor of something more practical, packed all the diving gear in the backseat and strapped Bobby's little rowboat to the top of the car. I brought a bottle of my father's scotch. (He'd never be able to remember whether he drank it or not.) Chris had some bread and mustard and cheese and baloney from the grocery store. It was turning out fine. We got in the car and drove ten miles out into the heart of the woods to Weikiwa Springs.

Weikiwa was once, years and years before, a fashionable swimming place. There is the ghost of a great bathhouse in the woods there, a haunted, crumbling place, a sagging pavilion, a summerhouse where the ladies could sit and watch the swimming. There's even a band shell where, I'm told, once on nice summer evenings music was played. The spring itself is a deep hole, a steep drop of ground going down to an almost perfect circle of water, an eye of clear sulfur water bubbling out of the mouth of an underwater cave. The spring is the source of a stream that winds away through a dense green jungle of palms and palmettos and water oaks and cypress, the trees covered with vines and the stream choked with green hyacinth plants. Farther along, up the stream a few miles, are some hunting camps, and if you go by boat to one of them, you'll see alligators and some of the biggest water moccasins you ever laid eyes on. Or imagined. You might as well be in Darkest Africa; it's easy to pretend you are. Weikiwa Springs is a lonesome, beautiful, abandoned place. I thought it was a stroke of genius for Chris to suggest testing the helmet there.

We got as near to the edge as we could with the car, and then we unlashed the boat and struggled with it down the steep overgrown slick bank to the fringe of sandy beach around the spring. We were sweating and panting by the time we got the diving gear down there too. I produced the bottle of scotch and opened it up.

"What'd you bring that for?" Bobby said.

"You have to break a bottle or something, don't you?"

"What does it taste like?" Chris said.

"It's not so bad," I said. "It's like cough medicine at first, but it feels warm once you get it down."

"We might need it," Chris said. "That water looks cold."

So we all took long brave swallows, made faces, grinned, and felt pretty good about the occasion. Chris made some sandwiches, and Bobby offered cigarettes. We sat on the sand and drank and smoked and ate. We started feeling good and laughing about the whole thing. Even Bobby.

"Just think," he said. "Here we are drinking whiskey, and all those kids in white suits are singing 'Onward, Christian Soldiers' or 'Jesus Loves Me.'"

"What's wrong with 'Jesus Loves Me'?" Chris said. He always wore a little gold cross around his neck.

"Nothing, I guess," Bobby said. "But this is a whole lot better."

We could all agree with that.

After a while Bobby put out his cigarette in the sand and stood up.

"Well, let's get going," he said.

But who was to go first? We drew straws for it. Bobby got first, I drew second, and Chris got the last turn. He looked sad, but when Bobby offered to trade with him, he said no.

"We got to do it the way the straws fell," he said.

We loaded the gear in the boat and put on our suits and paddled out to the middle of the spring. We looked down and you could see all the way to the bottom. The water sparkled with

June sunlight. We could see the sun shining into the mouth of the cave like a beam of light coming through the window of a church.

"Okay," Bobby said. "Here we go."

He slipped over the side and winced because the water was so cold. He looked very serious. He nodded his head that he was ready and held on to the boat with both hands while we slipped the diving helmet on him. Then he made a motion with his hand to start pumping and Chris grabbed the bicycle pump and began. Bobby waved a hand at us and slowly sank down into the lucent water. Chris kept pumping and I crouched over the side and watched him descending to the bottom. When he got there he walked along slowly, heavily, on his feet like a figure in a slow-motion movie. It was beautiful to see him way down there, walking along in pure brightness. But he didn't stay down long. He moved around awhile on the bottom, then he took off the helmet and swam to the surface. We hauled the helmet up by the hose while he hung on to the boat.

"You got to pump more air than that," was the first thing he said. "That bicycle pump doesn't do much good."

After we got the helmet in the boat he climbed in and sat there shivering, drying off in the sun.

"Another thing," he went on. "We did this whole thing without planning at all. We ought to have signals. And we ought to go up to the car and get the rope and use it for a lifeline."

We weren't about to go back to the car and get a rope before we had our turns. We did agree on some signals, though: one jerk on the hose meant to pay out more, two jerks to pump harder, three that you were ready to come up.

"How did it feel?" I said.

"Not so bad," he said. "You can't move around very much and the pressure hurts your ears."

"Do you think we can get in the cave?" Chris said.

"I doubt it. Not without some extra weight of some kind."

We weren't going to the car for a rope, but we didn't mind paddling back to the bank to scout around for some good-size rocks to weight us down.

Now it was my turn. I slipped into the water and had to holler it was so cold. My voice echoed in the still woods around us. They put the helmet over my head. It felt heavy and wet. The faceplate made all the world look watery and blurred. I took a big rock in each hand and started to sink down. I was a while getting my feet on the bottom. It was a long slow graceful fall like falling in a dream. I could hear the *squish, sqush, squish, sqush* of the bicycle pump, and the air filled up the helmet and bubbled out under my arms and shoulders. The white sand on the bottom was soft under my feet. I looked straight up and there the boat hovered above me on the surface like some kind of flying thing. The water was so clear it seemed of no more substance than the heat waves that dance on summer highways. I set down my rocks for a second and gave one jerk for them to pay out more hose, then I picked up the rocks again and started, like a creature made out of lead, toward the mouth of the cave.

The water boiled out of the cave and my ears were ringing from the pressure. I fought it and managed to slip inside a bit, enough so that the mouth of the cave was behind me. Inside the cave was dark and slippery, but a flow of sun streamed past me and lit up some places with a soft glow. I could see that the cave went back a ways, and then it was too dark to tell what happened. My head was full of rushing noises. I had to keep fighting all the time to keep from being pushed right back out of the cave. The air from the pump seemed very scarce and thin. I knew I couldn't get any farther, so I quit crawling and fighting and let the water wash me backwards out of the cave. When I was back on the bottom again and able to stand I signaled them to pump harder. I took a deep breath and shed the helmet and shot up to the surface. For a minute I just floated on my back and stared into the vague blue heart of the sky, dazzled by the hard light.

"How was it in there?" Chris yelled.

"Great," I said. "I got in the cave, but I didn't have enough weight to go anywhere. It was great."

"Come on," Bobby said to Chris. "Give me a hand with this helmet."

I swam to the boat and waited alongside while they hauled the helmet in.

Chris was smiling now. He had a plan. We paddled over near the entrance of the cave and threw in all the rocks we had collected. They splashed and seemed to float end over end to the bottom. He was going to have as much weight as he needed to keep him down.

"In a way I'm glad I got to be last," he said. "You guys tested it. Now I'm going to do something with it."

He dropped lightly over the side without splashing much or rocking the boat and held on. He had a big white smile and the gold cross around his neck glinted in the sun. For the first time I noticed how dark-skinned he was.

"I'm going straight in the cave."

"We should've brought a flashlight."

"Next time," he said. "Next time we'll bring one along."

"Be careful," Bobby said. "Don't get the hose fouled down there."

"Come on," Chris said. "Put the helmet on me."

We put it over his head, and I picked up the pump and started pumping. It was hard work and kind of tiresome. I pumped as fast as I could for him and Bobby kneeled and watched him go. He gave a jerk on the hose and Bobby paid it out.

"He's got a whole armload of rocks," Bobby said. "That's what we needed, more weight."

After that Bobby didn't say any more. There wasn't anything to see. Chris had crawled inside the cave. Every once in a while there would be a jerk and Bobby would throw in some more of the hose. Finally that's all there was to it.

"He'll have to come on back now," Bobby said.

I was sweating all over and my arms ached from pumping. I just nodded and kept on. Chris jerked on the hose again.

"We forgot to make two-way signals," Bobby said.

He peered over the side. The hose was taut. Then there were three jerks. He was coming up. We were relieved, but nothing happened. The hose slackened all right, but Chris didn't come up. Then there was a good deal of slack floating loose in the water. Bobby gave the hose a tug.

"You keep on pumping and I'll dive down and see if anything's wrong."

I was too tired even to nod by then, but I was worried about Chris and pumped as hard as I could. Bobby dived over the side, tilting and rocking the boat.

When Bobby came back up his face was white and drawn. He held up one end of the hose to show it to me. I felt like I was going to faint.

"Damn you!" he said. "Stop pumping. It isn't doing any good."

Chris was down there somewhere with no more air. We hoped he would come up, shooting up in a stream of bubbles from inside of the cave with a great big smile and a wonderful story about all the things he had seen. We didn't even think that it was sure to mean losing the helmet. After a minute or so (so quiet we could hear the squirrels scrabbling in an oak tree up near the ruined bathhouse) we knew we would have to go down and get him. We dived and dived, but even holding our breaths as long as we could stand it, we couldn't get far into the mouth of the cave. Spent, we clutched the boat and looked into each other's eyes.

"I'm going to get help," Bobby said. "Keep diving."

He swam to shore and I saw him grab up his pants and start scrambling up the bank. Just as I went down again I heard the car engine start. When I came up for air he was gone.

I kept on diving down until my lungs turned into something like tripe and my eyes felt like running sores. But I never could get inside the cave. When they came I was so weak they had to pull me out before they could get started trying to locate Chris. I remember when I got my feet on the ground I fought them to try and get back in the water again. They had to drag me to the ambulance and I was cursing them and yelling at them every step of the way.

The funeral was something else again. A terrible occasion when you didn't know whether to laugh or cry. It was at the Episcopal Church because there isn't any Greek Orthodox Church in our town. All of Chris's buddies were told to dress up in our Boy Scout uniforms and act as a kind of honor guard. We still wore the old-fashioned uniforms then, shorts and knee socks and the wide-brimmed, soft-crowned caps; and for high school boys it felt pretty silly. Chris never gave a damn about the Scouts anyway, but his parents did or at least they thought he did. They even buried Chris in a Scout uniform. At least he was First-Class. Bobby was an Eagle Scout, and I was the oldest Second-Class in the county, if not the country. We all had to file by the body in the undertaker's parlor and salute before they took it over to the church. There was old Chris with makeup on and, I swear, rice powder or something to make his dark face look lighter.

The church service wasn't so bad. At least it had enough ceremony to suit Chris, lots of flowers and music and prayer read out of a book instead of made up by some windbag. It was at the grave that everything bad happened. Chris's mother started carrying on in a foreign way, wailing a kind of tune, crying and wringing her hands. Chris's father had on his old Greek Army uniform with a lot of medals on it. It looked strange and didn't fit too well anymore. He put his arm around his wife, but he didn't seem to want her to stop wailing. Then when they lowered the coffin we all lined up and saluted and Lonnie Jones played taps on the bugle. Lonnie is the world's worst bugler (he used to drive Chris crazy at Scout camp), and I tell you I'd rather have heard anything, even a Bronx cheer, than Lonnie Jones playing taps over Chris's grave.

After the cemetery service was finally over we all filed by the grave and threw in dirt and started to leave. I was going to ride home with my family, but before I could get to them my father saw Bobby's father in the crowd. And that was a scene!

"You've got a nerve!" my father yelled at him. Daddy was drunk, I could tell. "You've got your nerve to show your face here. Diving helmets! It's your money that killed that poor boy and like to have killed mine. No, no, no, it wasn't your money, it was our money, *my* money, you crook!"

All the time my mother and my brother Joe, the traveling salesman, were trying to get my father back to the car. He didn't give them any trouble. He let himself be led along easily enough. But still he kept twisting around his red face to shout insults at Bobby's father. Bobby's father just stood there in the sun and looked at him proudly, as if he were beneath noticing. He looked at my father as if he didn't really see or hear any of it, as if he were lost in some graceful thought. He was a slim, distinguished man with white hair and one of the gentlest faces I've ever seen. He never raised his voice at anyone or got drunk in public or did anything that might possibly embarrass his family. Of course a few years later it turned out he was and had been a crook all along just like my father always said. And he shot himself. That's another story. I won't go into it except to say that even that gesture was frustrating to my father. He felt cheated, I guess.

"You see," he said when he heard the news that the banker had killed himself. "You see! People like that never get their just desserts. They have their cake and eat it too. Goddamn them all to hell!"

With all that going on at the cemetery I decided to walk home. Nobody was going to miss me in the excitement. And I cut across the graveyard, picking my way among the tombstones, old and new. I came over a little slope of ground and I found Bobby sitting under an oak tree smoking a cigarette. He gave me one too.

"Did you see all that?"

"Oh, I don't blame your daddy at all," he said. "I guess I'd be pretty mad myself if I was him."

"You don't feel like it was your fault, do you?"

He just shrugged. It was exactly like Chris's shrug. A real weary kind of a gesture, and for some reason it made the hair stand up on the back of my neck, and I felt a chill even though I was wringing wet with sweat in my Scout uniform.

"You don't feel responsible, do you?" I asked.

"Somebody's got to be responsible," he said.

"What do you mean by that? It was Chris's idea as much as it was ours. He wanted to go there and go down in the cave in the first place. It's a sad, terrible thing, but it isn't anybody's fault."

"That's the trouble with people like you, yes, like you and Chris both. And your daddy and my daddy too. You have all these crazy wonderful schemes and ideas. You don't care what the risk is. And that's all right for you. But somebody has got to watch after you all the time. And when you're all finished with whatever you're doing somebody else has got to come along and start to clean up the mess you leave behind. You people are babies in this world."

That was about the longest speech I ever heard Bobby make. He sat there puffing on his cigarette with all those Eagle Scout merit badges staring me in the face and grinning at me. There was some truth in it, but it made me mad.

"How does it make you feel to think like that?"

"It makes me feel old as hell," he said.

He stood up and brushed off the seat of his Scout pants and put out his cigarette. He tore it up and scattered the shreds of tobacco and wadded the paper up in a tight little ball and threw it away. (I was to learn what "field stripping" a cigarette was some years later.) He wasn't going to shame me that way. I deliberately threw mine still smoking into the grass to let it burn out of its own accord. Then, for some reason, he smiled at me and stuck out his hand to shake hands.

"Look," he said. "There's no use having an argument. Chris is dead and we can't change that. We can't ever change anything."

So I shook hands with him, and we put on our hats and started walking home.

THE VICTIM

AT FIRST there was an odor in the dry and dusty woods. Then it was in the leaves, a flicker of something unexpected like a sourceless shaft of light or the swift passage of a bird nearby, unseen. By the time they heard it unmistakably, the sparkling rush and white roar of water on rocks, they were already running. They blundered among the trees, tripped over roots and stones and fallen branches, thrashed like swimmers as they ran, and plunged headlong down a sudden steep slope, falling, rolling, bruised and bleeding from the rocks and the gnash of underbrush, but always rising and running on until they came to the edge of the mountain stream, fell on their bellies, pushed head and shoulders into its thrilling current, and gulped at it. The cold water was as cruel as fire to their parched tongues, cracked lips, their dusty throats.

They had been without water all day long.

Side by side they lay in the coarse sand and gravel, heads and shoulders thrust into the stream, the young man in khaki and the fat man, middle-aged, wearing the gray work uniform of the State Prison Farm. Almost at the same instant, like puppets, they raised their dripping heads and looked at each other and started to laugh. The cold water ran down them as, half-raised, they looked deeply into each other's eyes. The young man cupped a handful of water and splashed the other. The fat man, using his hands like little paddles, splashed back, and in a moment they were lost in a storm of splashing, wordless and wild.

They might have embraced then, they were so close, but the rifle lay between them like a sword.

Spent, they rolled over on their backs and looked into the bowl of the sky, blue as the heart of a flame with, here and there, the immaculate sculptured clouds of midsummer. A way off, behind them, back where they had come from, a buzzard circled in a slow lazy arc, then vanished behind the trees.

"I'm going to take off my shoes," the fat man said. "The hell with it. I'm going to pleasure myself."

He sat up, bending over the sag and bulk of his belly and, groaning a little, began to unlace his high-top work shoes. The young man grunted and looked at him, and it was then that the blued glint of the rifle barrel caught his eye. Very slowly, while the fat man struggled with the laces of his shoes, the young man's hand, poised high on its fingertips like a large, lazy spider, moved toward the rifle. When the fat man seized a shoe with both hands to tug it off, the young man snatched at the rifle, rolled away, cocked it in the moment that he was rolling, sat up, and snapped the safety off. The little click that the safety made might as well have been thunder. The fat man froze with one limp shoe dangling like a small dead animal in his hand, still not looking at the young man. His body seemed to turn to wax. Face and muscle began to melt, and he let the shoe slip from his fingers. Only his head turned, sad-eyed and hurt, the lips trembling like elastic stretched too taut, the rolls of fat below his face, where the tanned neck joined the fish-belly whiteness of his body in a ragged little horizon, shook. The young man saw sweat pop out all over his face at once and shine like a coat of grease.

The young man felt his own lips forming a slight smile.

"I'll take the knife too," he said.

"You got the gun," the fat man said. "I mean you got everything now. Why take the knife too? If you have the gun, what harm is there in a little jackknife?"

"Give it to me," the young man said. "And give it to me right. I want it."

The fat man mumbled to himself and dug in his pockets. His hand came up with the jackknife in it, and he edged his hand forward, palm up, fingers slack and useless, the knife resting lightly in his palm.

"Just drop it in the sand. That's right."

The knife fell and the fat man wiped his face with his sleeve. He rubbed his sleeve across his face, and gradually his face seemed to take a shape and color again. Even his eyes brightened.

"I should have known," he said. "I just got so thirsty I couldn't even think straight. I guess I got careless."

"Oh, you've been careless," the young man said. "Last night, the night before, you dozed off and I could've taken the gun then. I could have jumped you anytime in the woods."

"Don't forget I had the knife too. Don't forget that."

"You're a damn fool," he said. "I could've wrung your neck like an old stewing hen anytime I wanted to. And it wouldn't even be a crime. Just good riddance."

The fat man swallowed hard and quick lines of puzzlement troubled his forehead.

"If that's the truth, then why didn't you? If you could, why didn't you? That's what I'd like to know."

"I don't really know," the young man said. "I must have wanted to wait you out."

"Hah!"

"No, I'm serious. I knew if I waited long enough you'd forget yourself. You'd start to want something so bad you'd forget all about everything, what we were doing, where we were going, the whole works. People are like that. As soon as they start to want something bad enough they got one-track minds."

"You don't care much for other people. You got a fine contempt for them."

"Don't feel bad about it," the young man said. "I waited so long, I got so thirsty, I pretty near forgot myself. Now just don't you move."

He stood up and felt for the knife one-handed, the other hand holding the rifle, his index finger hooked over the trigger, the rifle hip-high, pointed straight at the body of the fat man, his eyes never leaving the other's. When his hand found the knife, he eased it into his pocket, then he moved back and away up the slope, crabwise, until he came to a tree he could lean against.

"That was all right," he said. "Now go ahead. Go ahead and soak your feet all you want to."

He leaned against the rough bark of the pine tree, wriggling his shoulders to scratch his itchy back, smelling the piney green sweetness, cradling the cool rifle in his arms; and the other turned his back to him and sat on a flat rock, dangling his bare feet in the water. The fat man wiggled his toes in the water like a child.

"You're a pleasure-loving old bastard," the young man said. "How did you ever stand it in jail?"

The fat man didn't answer. He turned his head and grinned briefly. He finished washing his feet and letting them dry in the sun and air. He put on his socks carefully, smoothing the wrinkles out, and he squatted on his bulging haunches and laced up his shoes, tied them in a neat firm knot. Then he stood up.

"All right," he said. "What now?"

"I dropped my pack up on the hill when we started running. I don't know just where, but it can't be far," the young man said. "Let's us stroll up there and pick up my pack and my canteen. Then we'll come back here and fix us something to eat. Unless maybe you aren't hungry?"

"I'm hungry all right."

"Lead off, fat man. I'm right behind you."

In a while they had a twig and brush fire going down by the stream. The fat man crouched beside it, stirring the twigs, blowing on the flames. The young man sat back against the tree and watched. They had two cans of beans, a little can of potted meat, some bacon, and a few pieces of bread. The fat man strung the bacon on a forked green stick and held it over the flame. Grease spat into the fire and the flame danced. There was a good crackling sound and the smell of bacon cooking.

"If you hadn't of been in such a big hurry," the young man said, "we'd be all right. We could've brought along my pup tent and the rest of my stuff."

"We never would've made it this far with all that," the fat man said. "We come a pretty good ways. I expect we're in Tennessee already."

"No we're not. We're still in North Carolina. Tennessee is a ways yet."

"I haven't heard the dogs all day. I haven't heard a single sound of dogs."

"I expect you will before long."

The fat man took the bacon off the forked stick and folded half the strips into a piece of bread. He came toward the young man, bent over, deferential, cautious, and handed him the sandwich. Then he backed down the slope again to the fire and fixed his own. He held it tight in his hands so that the grease could soak evenly into his piece of bread. Then he began to nibble at it in quick little bites like a squirrel with a nut.

"Stick the beans in the fire."

"How we going to get the cans open?"

"I'll let you use the knife."

"Both cans? Don't you think we better save one?"

"What for? Like you said, we're almost to Tennessee." The young man grinned and tossed the knife to him.

When the beans were warm, they ate them with their fingers, licking the sweet brown sauce so as not to lose a drop. They split the other piece of bread to wipe the cans clean. The can of potted meat remained unopened.

"Go ahead and have it," the young man said. "You're a big man. You need it worse than I do."

The fat man opened the can. Looking up, he saw the young man was busy mopping his can of beans with the piece of bread. He kept his eyes on the young man and very slowly slipped the knife back into his pocket. The young man made no movement.

"Look in my pack," he said. "There's a pack of cigarettes and some matches. Help yourself and throw it to me."

They sat where they were, facing each other, contented and refreshed, and they smoked.

A few days before, he had seen the fat man for the first time. The young man came down a road in the mountains with his pack and roll on his back and his rifle slung over his shoulder. It was toward evening and he came on a gang of prisoners working on the road. First he saw the guard with a shotgun, sitting on a canvas camp stool under a khaki umbrella, his pith helmet propped back on his head, his shirt open all the way down the front. Then he saw the prisoners nearby. In their gray uniforms, in the clouds of dust their picks and shovels stirred up, they themselves seemed to be composed of dust, walking and working piles of animated dust. He had the feeling then that if either he or the guard—who nodded with just a slight tip of his head to salute their mutual freedom—that if either one of them took a deep breath and blew, the whole gang of prisoners would disappear into nothing and nowhere like a dandelion or a thistle weed. The prisoners did not stop working as he passed between them—they were on both sides of the road—and no head raised, no eye, accusing or pitiful or serious, met his. He heard a kind of low moan or sigh which, as he listened, he took to be a song.

He had nearly passed by them when he encountered the fat man. The fat man came out of the bushes onto the road, bearing a wooden water bucket, and his uniform was astonishingly clean. He set the bucket down and unfolded a large colored handkerchief on the road in front of the young man, without a word offering him for sale some of the things which the prisoners had made—rings made out of toothbrush handles, bracelets made of bent spoons, and even a drawing or kind of painting on a piece of white cloth, made with ink and clay and some sort of coloring, maybe the juice of wild berries. It showed Calvary with Christ crucified between the two thieves, and, as the young man stooped to look at it more closely, he smiled to see that the artist had lavished most of his detail and color and attention on the thieves. They were naked and identical, crudely done, but clearly the same man, based on some real flesh and form. The

Christ was eyeless and vague as a store-window mannequin. The young man almost decided to buy it, but when he rose to ask how much it was worth, he saw that the man's eyes were looking past him, fixed with a kind of obsessive glint on the high-powered rifle. He dropped the cloth from his hands and stepped past the fat man, touching him flank to flank for one instant, feeling the heat of his body, smelling his short, sour breath.

That night he slept on a bedroll, alone in the deep woods. Near dawn he woke from a bad dream, a dream of running from something, a dream where gates and doors refused to open and all roads were a treadmill in reverse, to see the fat man standing over him holding the rifle. In the faint first light that came through the gloom of trees he could see the fat man smiling. He rose, still half asleep, and picked up his pack. The fat man motioned with the rifle, and he walked off into the woods with the fat man following close behind. Later in the gray deceptive light of dawn, a light like a splash of dirty water, they first heard the dogs.

Now the fat man was sitting by the ruins of the fire, the tin corpses of their meal. He was blowing smoke rings, large ones with little ones inside.

"I just thought of something," the young man said. "You could've killed me. You could've killed me right at first while I was still asleep."

"Sure I could," the fat man said. "But what good would it do me?"

"You could've sneaked away. I could have slept right on and just woke up without my rifle."

"Maybe so."

The young man put his cigarette into the sand, buried it neatly. He was, even now, dirty, unshaven, hatless, tired, surprisingly neat for a man out of doors.

"You were just scared," he said. "You were too scared to run away alone."

"Maybe," the fat man said, equally thoughtful. "Maybe that's the case."

"You would've killed me, but you were scared. You would've left me alone, but you were scared."

"Maybe that's right."

"You know one thing I can't stand about people—or maybe I ought to say one of the things I can't stand—it's fear. People who get scared make me sick."

"You don't scare? You weren't scared when you woke up and saw me there?"

"No, I wasn't scared."

"You would've been wise to be a little bit scared. Somebody else might have killed you."

The young man shrugged. "Well, here I am. I got the rifle, and I'm not any worse off for a walk through the woods. What about you? You ought to be scared now."

"I'm scared."

"If they take you back, they're going to take the bullhide to you. They're going to lock you in a sweat box for a while, and when you come out—if you come out—you'll never be a trusty again. They'll have you swinging a pick, full-time, in the hot sun."

"I can't help being fat."

"You make me sick to my stomach," the young man said. "Bury that stuff."

He pointed with the rifle barrel to the two cans, and the little can, so cleaned inside they shone, and to the ashes of the fire. The fat man kneeled and scooped a hole in the sand. He buried the cans and the ashes under a little mound.

"What did you ever do to end up in jail? What did you have guts enough to do?"

Still kneeling before him, the fat man laughed.

"I got involved in this rape case. I mean, it wasn't exactly rape when it happened, but it was her word against mine."

"I might have known it would be something like that. What were you doing before you got into trouble?"

"You might say I was a kind of a traveling preacher. I had the power of healing, too, for a while. But the Lord took it back from me."

"A kind of a hypocrite would be a better word for it. Preach one thing and practice another. And then get caught in a rape." The young man laughed.

"You don't allow much for other folk's weakness."

"Why should I?"

"Listen, the Good Book says we supposed to love each other. Now, if you love somebody, you surely going to have to tolerate a little weakness."

"I'll give it right back to you," the young man said. "The Bible says love thy neighbor as thyself, right?"

"That's right."

"Well, then, Mr. Convict Jailbird Fatman—"

"I got a name."

"Well, I don't want to hear it," the young man said. "Now, my point is this. If you don't love yourself, then what?"

"Oh, you bound to love yourself."

"Just suppose you don't. Just suppose for the sake of arguing that you hate yourself."

"I don't follow you," the fat man said.

"If you hate yourself, you got the right to hate everybody else in the world."

"I don't understand what you're talking about."

"The hell with it," the young man said. "Let it be."

Just then, far off, faint in the waning afternoon, they could hear the belling sounds of the dogs. The sounds were far behind them, but they could tell that the dogs were on the right trail. They stood up simultaneously and stared at each other, unsmiling.

"I guess you better get started," the young man said.

"You going to let me go? You going to let me be?"

"You better get going before I change my mind."

"Ain't you coming too?"

"For God's sake why?" the young man said. "I've gone along far enough with you."

The fat man stood, head down, shifting his weight from one

leg to the other like a small boy. When he looked up again there was a shy womanly softness in his face. He fumbled in a pocket and pulled out the cloth he had offered for sale.

"You can have it," he said. "I did it by myself, color and all."

He spread the cloth on the sand, smoothed it, then he turned and began to wade across the stream.

"You better go with the water a ways," the young man said. "So they'll lose the scent."

The fat man nodded without looking back. He went downstream awkwardly, wading in the knee-deep water, picking his way among the rocks. Once he stumbled on a wet stone and fell, but he struggled up to his feet and kept going.

"You hypocrite bastard!" the young man yelled after him. "You've still got the knife."

The fat man stopped. He still did not look back, but he nodded and reached in his pocket for the knife.

"You can have it back," he shouted back over the noise of the water. "I don't need it. I'll give it back."

"Keep it. Go on and keep it now!"

Then the fat man started to run in the water. The young man stood up. He dug the butt of the rifle into the hollow of his shoulder, sighted down the barrel, and fixed the gray diminishing back of the fat man in the tense slim V of the front sight. He took a deep breath, let out a little, and then held the rest. The barrel was steady. Gently he took up the slack in the trigger and began a smooth squeeze. He saw the fat man twitch and tumble with a great white splash, and then he heard the sharp report of the rifle thunder in the ravine and echo, dying away, in the woods. He heard the little *chink* of the ejected shell as it bounced off a rock by his feet. He stooped and policed it up, buried it under the sand. He picked up the picture and folded it and put it in his shirt pocket. Then he walked back to the pine tree and sat down and closed his eyes, listening to the dogs as they came, waiting.

GOOD-BYE, GOOD-BYE,
BE ALWAYS KIND AND TRUE

AT FIRST Peter Joshman hadn't known what to make of it all, how to take it. In the beginning came the scouts, surveyors, and engineers, crisp in khaki, their white pith helmets shining, driving state-owned trucks and jeeps, and supported by little galaxies of rodmen and assistants in T-shirts. They came to look at the lay of the land, studied it, measured it, marked it, and departed. Then (and it was not long afterwards) came the axes and chain saws, the bulldozers, and the dynamite. They shook the earth and rattled the windowpanes, jarred cups and glasses on the shelves, troubled old things from their accustomed places and left behind them a clay-colored raw swathe cut through the intense monotonous green of the pinewoods and across the field from west to east, like a new scar, so close he could have thrown a stone from his chair on the porch and landed it in the center with a little puff of dust. After that big machines, the rollers and levelers and graders, hurried through the early spring, smoothing the wound that had been made in his field of vision. There were men in khaki and explorers' helmets again, overseeing, writing and writing on their clipboards, and there were the young men, all lithe arrogance and bronzed bravado as, shirtless in the Florida sun, wheeling their huge machines, laughing brilliantly and shouting profanely at each other, they created a dusty chaos.

Inevitably convicts from the State Camp followed, sweating men, black and white, in gray prison uniforms with their shovels and rakes and pick mattocks, working slowly forward day by day along the smoothed earth, spreading gravel and finally the asphalt (that smelled at first good enough to eat), all under the scrutiny of the squat, relaxed, almost motionless guards who peered squint-eyed from beneath broad-brimmed hats into the glare of light studying the work, cradling their shotguns lightly in their arms like living things. One of the convicts, a trusty probably, had come to the house for a bucket of water and Peter Joshman jabbed with his cane in the direction of the pump.

"What's a man like you doing with a walking cane?" the convict asked him. "You ain't that old, is you?"

"I'm a wounded man."

"Somebody shot you?"

"Sure they did," Peter said. "In the War. I got a wooden leg, but you wouldn't know it."

"No, you wouldn't to look at you," the convict said. "Now you got it made, though, huh? Sit on your ass and draw a government pension."

"This here's my son-in-law's house," Peter said. "This here is his farm. I can't do no heavy work. I can't do much of nothing but sit in my rocker and watch things."

"Well, you going to have something to look at from now on with this new highway."

"I don't know as I can get used to what they done."

"Hell!" the convict said, moving now toward the pump. "After a while you can get used to most anything."

"You don't have to like it though," Peter Joshman said, laughing, surprised to hear himself laughing out loud like that. "No sir, you don't have to like it a damn sight."

They poured sweet thick asphalt and they rolled it and leveled it, and soon it was really a road. Pretty soon the tourists would be coming down it, making a shortcut to the East Coast with its splendid beaches, sun and waves, and the sand as white and fine as sugar there. Peter sat in his rocker, gripping his heavy cane with knuckles whitened from impotent anger, and saw them finish up the job. Some people seemed to like it fine. The children, his grandchildren, and all the devious wolf pack of them from the other farms around, ran when they could with shrill excitement—like a flock of little birds, they were so swift and aimless—around the fringes of all the action. They would be happy to see all the cars come by. And up at Evergreen, the nearest crossroads town, the gas-station owner, the storekeeper, and even the preacher took it for a good sign that now they were going to have a real paved highway passing through. His son-in-law, S. Jay, took it badly. They had gouged out a piece of his land, split one field in two, and though it meant some cash money for him, it meant fencing, too, and crossing the highway to do his work.

"What good does it do me, anyhow?" S. Jay grumbled. "I never go to the beach anyway, except on the Fourth of July."

"Get a new car, Daddy," the children hollered and pestered. "Get us a new car."

"Sure," he replied. "And while I'm at it I might just as well buy me a patch of ground on the moon."

"We could set up a stand by the road," his wife (old Peter's daughter) said. "We could make money selling garden vegetables and fresh eggs."

"This is nothing but a long lonely stretch of straight road," S. Jay answered. "Those folks won't even slow down. They got something else in mind. Fresh vegetables! Eggs!"

"Well, it's an idea."

"Won't anything come of it. Who's going to build you a shack to sell from?"

"And maybe the children could sell ice-cold lemonade."

"Lemonade!" S. Jay snorted. "Oh my God! You don't know nothing about this world, nothing at all."

Still, Peter thought that they ought to do something. It's hard, it's wrong even, he thought, to sit still and watch a great change, something new and something that will never, in one lifetime, be the same again, and not give at least a signal or a sign of approval or discontent. When the cars at last began to come, shiny new ones, and he could see the bright relaxed people in their bright unlikely clothes heading to and from the ocean, hear radios playing, hear the rhythms of their voices and occasionally a burst of their laughter, then he suddenly felt better about the whole thing. That was entirely different, a road with people on it. Suddenly everything was happening. He'd hear them coming, and they'd flash into his view, and tires humming or purring or swishing, and the sun exploding in little balls of brightness off the gloss and chrome of auto bodies, and, for a fabulous instant, he saw them in profile, lean as arrows in flight, going or coming, framed against the green pines, the rich green fields they crossed.

It came to him that he ought to participate, share in some way in the appreciation of that hurtling unbelievable moment of gleaming speed. He wanted to offer his benediction. So, he had the boys, his grandchildren, move the rocker out into the front yard, close to the road, under the shade of a mulberry tree where he could wave at them and they, seeing him, could wave back. They smiled and laughed, shouted or waved in solemn silence, and the children, the children always seemed to catch his signal and return it.

S. Jay was a little angry, even a little ashamed.

"It must be nice," he said, "it must be mighty nice to have nothing to do with yourself but sit by the side of the road and watch cars go by."

And Peter Joshman, in spite of himself, sensitive of his position as a paying guest in the house, lonely, too, fell upon self-pity grimly:

"Lose your leg sometime and see how much you like it."

"S. Jay don't mean any harm, Daddy," his daughter said. "You know how he is."

"Never mind about that leg," S. Jay said. "I don't grudge you a thing. But it seems like you could find something besides just sitting and waving at strangers. What do those folks mean to you anyhow?"

"They cease to be strangers when I see them pass by."

"Listen," S. Jay said. "Those folks are laughing at you. You're a joke."

"It don't do nobody no harm," Peter said. "It does me a whole world of good."

"It isn't even good for you, Daddy," his daughter said, siding at last with her husband. "You ought to sit in the shade of the porch, at least."

"They won't be able to see me from the road."

"Well, why don't you hang up a sign or something?" S. Jay said. "Run up a flag."

"Don't laugh at him, Jay," his daughter said. "It's wrong to make fun of an older man like that."

"He makes fun of hisself."

Still, it was S. Jay who put the notion in his mind. Why not sit comfortable in the shade of the porch and still have a way to communicate with them, the drivers and the riders? How to do this, with wit and wisdom, was his problem. Wisdom, yet; for what stranger, moving however swiftly over whatever strange or alien landscape, where he knows no one, owns nothing, between departure and arrival, is not touched, deeply, by a salute, a sign of some kind coming from a stranger by the road saying *I acknowledge you as flesh and blood, as a creature of dust and breath like myself.* Saying to himself like the children, his grandchildren, saying to himself, to be truthful, like the song they always sing at the end of Sunday school—"Good-bye, good-bye, be always kind and true." But to say this with wit because (and Peter Joshman knew this, though often irascible, embittered too, and, like everyone, self-pitying) he knew that any shared truth needs a disguise. Laughter will do. Otherwise, like Adam and Eve without the wit of fig leaves, the naked truth would shame to the quick.

The beginning was more or less accidental. An old dressmaker's dummy was in the barn from the days when first his wife and then his daughter, now another man's wife and the mother of her own children, sewed for a living. It was an easy thing to dress the dummy in his old-fashioned Army uniform, to place it on a stump at the edge of the road, to rig the right arm something like his own artificial leg so that, sitting on his rocker on the porch, he could at just the right time jerk a cord attached to the dummy's arm. And then up went that stiff right arm to wave in clumsy benediction, bringing in reply almost invariably laughter from the passers-by. Rain or shine, night and day, the wooden soldier sat on the stump and during most of the daylight hours Peter Joshman sat in his rocking chair, alert, attentive.

S. Jay, believe it or not, was tickled.

"What the hell!" he said. "The old man always was a little crazy. At least it keeps him out of trouble."

The children, never surfeited, wanted more of the same. And that was something to do with his evenings, to fashion a whole family to go with the wooden soldier, a plump wife and a child, a Negro servant in a white coat, to seat some, stand the others. What a spectacle when they all waved to you at once as you were passing by! By the end of a year since the road had been opened, this curious gallery was something to look forward to, a landmark almost, almost a work of art.

There were three of them, machines, motorcycles, three drivers, keen- and hard- and brown-faced as hawks, cut like figures from old coins, trim in tight Levi's and glossy leather jackets that caught like sails at the breeze of their speed, and behind them the three girls, each plump-thighed, straddling the lean, agile machines, each, hair blowing like the hair of mermaids in the waves, clinging to the wide-belted waists of the drivers. The road sang beneath them. The landscape fled, glazed, past the wind-whipped corners of their eyes. The sun dazzled off the asphalt in fragments like breaking glass. And the highway was theirs; they owned it, weaving among the placid and safe cars, slashing around and about them as, say, the trout, fine as a blade, moves among the drowned shadows of swans. The road sang for them, tormented, and the conventional landscape shivered and hurtled backwards, unnoticed.

Rounding a curve, the Leader came on a long straight piece of road. It stretched toward the horizon and vanished there, empty, glistening, a holy invitation and a challenge, and, hearing his companions coming behind him, he leaned forward, crouched, and opened up with a great soaring lunge of speed. He grinned, hearing his girl squeal, hearing his friends' and rivals' engines take on the same defiant tone, accepting his dare. Nothing on either side to contend with, only the green, shocked slash pines and ahead the regular pale fields of truck farms, a few shacks, and perhaps what was a few people bunched at one place like clod-footed dummies by the roadside. Give them something to remember, something to talk about, he was thinking, edging close to that side of the road so that he'd shower them with the noise and the dust of his passage. Let them have something to dream about. The Leader grinned to himself.

Peter Joshman was dozing. The road had been empty for quite a while. It was late in the day, not late enough for people to start returning from the beaches, but too late for ordinary tourists to be going there. Peter dozed and listened to the bees in the garden, heard a humming in his half-dream—louder and more profound now than the bees, and much nearer—blinked, looked slowly, and then saw the three machines in the very instant of their passing, almost too late to wave. And with a start he jerked his rigging of cords and all the wooden arms popped up at once waving wildly. Startled, the three seemed to explode, shot away from each other, skidded, reeled, whizzed, tilted on the edge of the drainage ditches on either side, amid the clear soprano of girls' screaming, somehow righted themselves unscathed, and resumed their proper course a half mile or so down the road, though he could see, laughing to himself, they were moving much slower now, abreast, in solemn formation going away.

When they reached the gas station at the crossroads called Evergreen, they stopped, pulled up under the shade of the roof, and dismounted. The three girls fled, rubber-jointed as drunks, to the door marked *Ladies*. The Leader leaned back, breathless, against a gas pump and spat into a rainbow smear of oil and grease by his feet.

"Jesus Christ! Did you see what I did?"

"A bunch of loonies!"

"What were they trying to do, kill us?"

"Christ!" the Leader again, recovered, composed. "I thought we was all gone. Liquidated, you know, dead."

They laughed together. Then they asked Smalley, who owned the station, what it was they had seen, and he told them about Peter Joshman and his wooden dummies.

"What is it with him?"

"What's he trying to prove?"

"I wouldn't know," Smalley said. "He sure gets a kick out of it."

"The son of a bitch liked to have killed all of us."

"This must be the first time you boys ever come down this road."

"Yeah, but we'll know all about it coming back."

There came at twilight a summer cloudburst. For more than an hour Peter Joshman had been watching the dark clouds massing, swelling. Just as the sun went down and the whole flat countryside seemed to glow with an inner light, the rain began to fall in rich thick drops, soon pelting the dusty yard, rattling on the roof, shining on the slick road. He watched half-sadly, his forlorn wooden figures, unable to come in out of the rain, standing, sitting, their weathered clothing steaming. Something would have to be done about them. Then he heard S. Jay come into the house by the back door, heavy-footed, stamping his feet, breathing hard from running across the field in the rain, and Peter stood up, stretched, and limped inside for his supper.

"Old-timer," S. Jay said, his wide young white-toothed mouth full of food, "how was your road today?"

"Is it Granddaddy's road?" one of the children asked.

"No, honey," his daughter answered for him. "The road belongs to the state."

"Be nice if it was your road," S. Jay said. "You could put up a tollgate out there. If you charged everybody who went by a dime, you'd be a rich man in no time. Then we could all sit on the front stoop and watch."

"Let's charge everybody ten cents, Granddaddy."

"You could at least charge them to look at your dummies," S. Jay said. "Maybe just ten cents a wave would be a good price."

"You-all hush picking on Daddy," his daughter said. "He loves those dummies."

"Well, that's something, anyway," S. Jay said. "It's nice to know he cares about something."

After the rain stopped it was cooler and Peter sat again on the porch, in the first dark, the first stars, watching the cars coming back. Sometimes if they happened to drive close to the shoulder of the road, their headlights suddenly picked up the group of wooden figures, bathed them in expensive light, and he in reply gave his cords a pull and blessed those night riders with a lacka-daisical wave.

The three, his enemies now, though he had no way to know it, were already on the road, returning. It hadn't been the day it might have been for them. Once they had arrived at the beach, they headed south, leaving the resort town with its motels and neon gardens, its drugstores and bars and camera shops behind them, the rows of cottages along the dunes, troubling the dust of a narrow road which ran along just behind the dunes, past even the forlorn and separate nigger beach and far on to a place where at last even the road ended, came to a circle centered on a huge clump of palmetto, the road ending abruptly at a clump of green growth, higher than any dune. Said to be an old Indian burial mound. They parked their motorcycles out of sight and climbed over the dunes to the beach.

"What did we come down here for?" one of the girls asked. Just like a girl.

"We're going swimming, ain't we?" the Leader said.

"I thought . . ." the girl answered. "But I didn't bring my bathing suit. I thought you said we could rent one."

"You know something," he said. "Neither did I."

The others laughed, but laughter did not work at all. With one of the girls reluctant, unpersuadable, the other two were forced by some immemorial tribal custom to side with her, to come to her defense, and in the end the three girls sat on the dunes and smoked and chatted with each other while the three young men frolicked, halfhearted, in lean tan naked exhibition amid the crisp surf. There was no hope for them and, after a while, the men, feeling foolish now, dressed and started back, grim, frustrated.

When they reached the resort town again, they met at a red light.

"That sonofabitch!" the Leader said.

"Who?"

"That bastard with the dummies by the road."

So with a mounting rage against the injustice of this afternoon, the three drivers, hating the hands now that clung to their belts, hating the rich, unseen knowledge of blown hair behind them, drove back the way they had come. It had been raining and the highway was slick and thrilling. They frightened their rivals in fat cars, forced them to clear the way.

Peter Joshman must have heard them coming. It was a solemn unison of buzzing sound that preceded the grim trinity of avengers as they came, slowing down as they passed through Evergreen, looking for their victims, three lights as bright and single as the Cyclops' furious eye, in formation as if passing in review. He must have heard them before he saw them and may have guessed then, for the first time, what was going to happen. Anyway, he didn't move. What could he do? From aimless, really impersonal malice like that of the trench mortar that shredded and took away his leg, there was no moving, only a waiting to suffer or, by sheer luck, to be saved. He may even have closed his eyes and not seen them when they stopped and fell on the foolish wooden figures in the dark. Shouting, cursing as they stripped off clothing, they broke the wooden bodies to pieces, stamped heads into the dust.

S. Jay heard them, though, and came out of his bedroom in his undershorts roaring, across the porch in one long-legged leap, his shotgun bursting forth, both barrels at once, an orange choleric mushroom against the astounded night sky, hitting nothing, or nothing important (one of the girls squealed like a frightened pig, but maybe it was nothing more than the noise and the shock of bird shot in the air). He ran toward them then, as they clambered on the motorcycles, stamped furiously on starters, cursing them as they fled down the road, knelt to reload, kneeling among the shattered corpses of the figures and the debris, the stuffing, glass eyes and torn clothing, but he was too late. Still in a rage, S. Jay fired again high and pointlessly into the trees, and the leaves sighed. He came back to the house slowly, dragging his gun butt in the dust.

"Sonofabitches!" he said. "Old-timer, they wrecked all your dummies."

"Maybe it's just as well."

"What do you mean, *just as well?*" S. Jay yelled at him. "It's my land, ain't it? I'll kill the son of a bitches if they ever come back."

"I say maybe it's just as well," Peter said. "It was a crazy idea in the first place. I let it get a hold to me and started to care too much. Nothing is worth caring that much about."

"I can't figure you out for the life of me," S. Jay said. "Ain't you going to try and fix them up again?"

"I don't know," Peter Joshman said. "I'll sleep on it."

Three

From
COLD GROUND WAS

MY BED LAST NIGHT

It is here, in this bad, that we reach
The last purity of the knowledge of good.
WALLACE STEVENS
—"No Possum, No Sop, No Taters"

THE OLD ARMY GAME

EVERYBODY HAS GOT A STORY about the Bad Sergeant in Basic Training. Sit down some evening with your buddies, and you'll find that's one subject everybody can deal out like a hand of cards. And that's not a bad image for it, because those stories, told or written or even finally mounted in memory, acquire a bright conventional two-dimensional character. All the people in them are face cards. Which seems to me as good a way as any to introduce Sergeant First Class Elwood Quince.

Lean and hard-faced, a face all angles like a one-eyed jack. Perfectly turned out, everything tailored skintight, glossy, spit-shined, and glowing. Field cap, almost white from washing and wear and care, two fingers over the nose. Casts a flat gray semi-circular shadow that way. Calls attention to the mouth. The thin tight lips. Open, you'd expect to see even rows of fine white teeth; instead you'd see them yellow and no good and all awry and gaping like a worn-out picket fence. And when he did smile, it was all phony, like a jackass chewing briars. Back to the field cap. Calls attention to the mouth and hides the eyes in shadow like a mask. The eyes—with the cap off and resting on a desk and his large restless hands patting his straw-blond hair, long and rich on top, but sidewalled so that with cap or helmet on he looks as shaved clean as a chicken ready for the oven, the eyes are peculiarly light and cloudy at the same time, like a clear spring that somebody has stirred up the mud in the bottom of with a stick. Can you see him yet? But he's standing still. Let's breathe upon him and let him walk because Quince's walk is important. He has two of them. The official walk when he's marching troops, in formation, etc. The former is conventional, ramrod, but natural. Well-trained soldier. The latter is really quite special. Light-footed, easy, insinuative, cat- and woman-like. Creepy. He seemed like a ghost to us. You always look over your shoulder before you speak because chances are he's right there behind you and everywhere at once.

Talk? Oh my, yes, he can talk. Arkansas mountain accent. Part Southern and part Western and a little bit nasal and whiny and hard on the *r*'s. Picturesque. Rural similes abound. Some extended to the epic proportion. For example, to Sachs, our fat boy from New York: "Sachs when I see you draggin' your lardass around the battery area, you put me in mind of a old woreout sow in a hogpen with a measley little scrawny litter of piglets sniffin' and chasin' around behind her and that old sow is just so tired and fat and godamn lazy she can't even roll over and let 'em suck." Also frequently scatological. Here is a dialogue. Sergeant Quince and Me. In open ranks. Inspection. He right in front of Me. I'm looking straight into the shadow his cap casts.

QUINCE: Do you know how low you are, boy?

ME   *(Learning to play by ear):* Pretty low, Sergeant.

QUINCE: Pretty low? No, I mean just how low?

ME: I don't know, Sergeant.

QUINCE: Well, then, since you're so ignorant, I'll tell you. You're lower than whale shit. And you know where that is, don't you?

ME: Yes, Sergeant.

QUINCE: On the bottom of the ocean.

(Quince passes on to the next victim.)

The tone of voice? Always soft. Never raises his voice except in giving commands. Otherwise speaks just above a whisper. You often have to strain to hear him.

When we arrived at Camp Chaffee, Arkansas (the Army's

mansion pitched in the seat of excrement now that Camp Polk, Louisiana, and Camp Blanding, Florida, are closed up tight as a drum, left to hobos, rats, bugs, weeds, etc.) we were assigned to take Basic Training in Sergeant Quince's outfit. I call it his outfit because the Battery Commander had some kind of a harelip and was as shy as a unicorn, stayed in his office all day. The First Sergeant had V-shaped wound stripes from the First World War, I swear, and didn't care about anything but getting a morning report without any erasures and also the little flower garden he had all around the Orderly Room shack that he tended and watered with a cute watering can just like Little Bo Peep's. Nevertheless Sergeant Cobb started out as at least a presence. Austere and lonely and unapproachable, but thought of and believed to be an ultimate tribunal where wrongs might be righted, a kind of tired old god we might turn to one day in despair of any justice or salvation from Quince, come to him as broken children, and he'd sigh and forgive us. Believed until there came a test one day. Sergeant Quince marched the whole battery, one hundred and sixty-odd men in four heavy-booted platoons, right across one side of Cobb's garden. By the time the First Platoon had passed by Cobb was out of the office, hatless, necktie askew and loose like a long tongue, eyes burning. (Ah ha! thought we of Sergeant Quince, the original "young man so spic and span," something unpleasant will sure hit the fan now.) But it didn't. Cobb stood there looking and then wilted. He watched his tended stalks and blossoms go down under the irresistible marching feet of Progress, Mutability, Change, and Decay. And he never said a word. He slumped and shook his fist, a helpless old man. Meanwhile Quince ignored him, counted a crisp cadence for the marching troops and grinned just like a jackass chewing briars. And our hearts sank like stones to see how the mighty had fallen.

So, though he was merely the Field First, it was Quince's outfit to make or break. His little brotherhood of lesser cadre revolved like eager breathless planets around him. From our first formation, we in rumpled new ill-fitting fatigues and rough new boots, he sartorial with, glinting in the sun, the polished brass of the whistle he loved so well.

"Gentlemen," he said. "You all are about to begin the life of a soldier. My name is Sergeant Quince. Your name is Shit."

War going on in Korea, etc. We would learn how to soldier and how not to get our private parts shot off by gooks whether we liked it or not. We would "rue the day" (his actual words) we ever saw his face or this godforsaken battery area. We would learn to hate him. We wouldn't have dreamed we were able to hate anybody as much as we were going to hate him. Etc., etc., etc.

"Let's be clear about one thing," he said, looking down from the barracks steps into our upraised, motley, melting-pot faces. "I hate niggers. They're black bastards to me, but I'll just call them niggers for short around here, during duty hours." (A Negro standing next to me winced as if he'd been kicked in the stomach.) "If anybody don't like it, let him go and see the I.G. I also hate Jews, wops, spics, micks, cotton pickers, Georgia crackers, Catholics, and Protestants. I hate all of you, damn your eyes."

I believe he meant it.

At this point, according to the conventions of the Tale of the Bad Sergeant, written or told, the story usually takes a turn, a *peripeteia* of a modest sort. You're supposed to be given a hint of his problems before moving on. So let's do it. I have no objection. But I reserve the right to call it giving the devil his due.

We were a crazy mixed-up bunch. Farm boys, black and white, from the Deep South. Street boys from the jungle of the big cities. College boys. Accidents: a thirty-five-year-old lawyer who got drafted by mistake, a cripple who was used for some weeks to fire up the boilers and keep the boiler room clean before his medical discharge finally came through. Two fat sullen American Indians . . . Mexican wetbacks . . . I remember one of these had a fine handlebar mustache. Quince walked up to him and plucked it. "Only two kinds of people can wear a mustache around here and get away with it," he said, "movie stars and cocksuckers. And I don't recall seeing your ugly face in any picture show. Shave it off, Pedro!"

So there we were. I'll give Quince this much credit. He wasn't the least bit interested in "molding us into a fighting team." His reach didn't exceed his grasp that much. He was merely involved in getting us through a cycle of Basic Training. We hated each other, fought each other singly and in groups in the barracks and in the privacy of the boiler rooms (with that poor cripple who was responsible for the care and maintenance thereof cowering in a corner behind the boiler, but armed with a poker lest he too became involved). We stole from each other, ratted on each other, goofed off on each other ("soldiering on the job" this is sometimes called in Real Life with good reason), and thus made every bit of work about twice as hard and twice as long as it had to be. And, if anything, this situation pleased Quince. He perched on his mobile Olympus and chewed briars while we played root-hog and grab-ass in the dust and mud below.

Strict? My Lord yes. I would say so. No passes at all during the whole cycle. GI Parties every night until our fatigues fell to shreds from splashed Clorox and the rough wood floors were as smooth and white as a stone by the shore. Polished the nailheads nightly too with matchsticks wrapped in cotton, dipped in Brasso. Long night hikes with full field pack. GI haircuts (marched to the so-called barber) once a week. Bald as convicts we were. Police Call was always an agony of duck waddling "assholes and elbows" on our hands and knees like penitents. How he loved Police Call! How he loved Mail Call! Gave out all the letters himself. That is, threw them into the packed hopeful faces and let us fight and scramble for them in the dark. Opened mail and packages when he pleased. Withheld mail for days at a time as a whim. Didn't make soldiers out of us, but tractable brutes. Brutalized, cowed, we marched to and fro like the zombies in mental hospitals that they haven't got time to bother with, so they pump them full of tranquilizers. And when we passed by, eyes front, in perfect step, he was complimented by any high-ranking officers that witnessed our coming and going.

Let me say this for Quince. I know another Sergeant who tried exactly the same thing and failed. He was of the same mold as Quince, but somehow subtly defective. In the end he had to fall his troops out of the barracks with a drawn .45. Not Quince. His lips touched to the brass whistle, even before he breathed into it, was quite enough to make us shiver.

A sadist too. Individually. Poor white, soft, round, hairy Sachs suffered indignities he couldn't have dreamed of in his worst nightmares. Once or twice was nearly drowned in a dirty toilet bowl. Sachs with the other fat and soft boys, "Quince's Fat Man's Squad," had regularly to participate in "weenie races." What's a weenie race? I think Quince invented it. The fat boys kneel down at the starting line, pants and drawers down. Quince produces a package of frankfurters, wrapped in cellophane. One each frankfurter is firmly inserted into each rectum. All in place? Everybody ready? Quince blows the whistle and away they crawl, sometimes a hundred yards going and coming. Last man back has to eat all the frankfurters on the spot. Tears and pleading move Quince not a whit. Nor puking nor anything else.

One time Quince lost his head about one barracks which had someway failed to live up to his expectations. He and his attendant cadre went raging through that barracks, tearing up beds, knocking over wall lockers, and destroying everything "personal" they could get their hands on: cameras, portable radios, fountain pens, books, letters, photographs, etc.

How did these various things happen? You're bound to ask. Didn't anybody go to the Inspector General, the Chaplain, write a Congressman or Mother? Not to my knowledge. Anyone could have, it's true, but all were very young and in mortal fear of the man. Who would be the first to go? No one went. And—*mirabilis*—nobody cracked up. If anything we got tougher and tougher every day. Gave our souls to God.

Or maybe—entirely justified in your contempt, "Don't give me no sad tales of woe"—you'll just say, "So what—what do you want me to do, punch your TS Card?" That would be to misunderstand. Agreed that in a century like ours these things are

small doings, negligible discomforts. It would be sheer senti-
mentality to claim otherwise. And I'm not cockeyed enough to
think that such events could arouse Pity and Terror. Nothing of
Great Men Falling from High Place in our time. A battle royal
in the anthill maybe. No, the simple facts, arranged and related,
my hand of cards, will never do that. But they are nevertheless
not insignificant. "Why?" you say. "Why bother?" Excuse me,
but Maxim Gorky said it once and better than I can, and so I
quote:

> Why do I relate these abominations? So that you may
> know, kind sirs, that all is not past and done with! You
> have a liking for grim fantasies; you are delighted by
> horrible stories well told; the grotesquely terrible ex-
> cites you pleasantly. But I know of genuine horrors,
> and I have the undeniable right to excite you unpleas-
> antly by telling you about them, in order that you may
> remember how we live, and under what circumstances.
> A low and unclean life it is, ours, and that is the truth.
>
> I am a lover of humanity and I have no desire to
> make any one miserable, but one must not be sentimen-
> tal, nor hide the grim truth with the motley words of
> beautiful lies. Let us face life as it is! All that is good
> and human in our hearts needs renewing.

Thus we survived, endured, lived through it, and finally the
cycle came to an end, a screeching halt. Last day on the Range
(rocket launchers) we fired $25,000 worth of ammunition into
the side of a hill as fast as we could, so that the Range Officer
could get back to camp early. If he didn't use the ammo all up,
he'd be issued proportionately less for the following day. We
were glad to assist him in his dilemma. We fired it away with joy
and abandon. What explosions! What flashes of flame and clouds
of smoke! It's a wonder we didn't kill each other.

That night we sat in the barracks packing our duffel bags. A
fine cold rain was falling outside. And we were quiet inside,
lonesome survivors, because somehow you never quite imagined
something like that coming to an end. It was a calm, respectable,

barracks-room scene. You could have photographed it and mailed the picture home to the family.

Up the steps, weary-footed, his cap soaking wet and his rain-coat beaded with raindrops and dripping, came the old First Sergeant—Cobb. He asked us to gather around, and he talked to us quietly. There had been a personal tragedy in the family of Sergeant Quince. *(That bastard had a family?)* His wife had been in a terrible automobile accident and was dying. *(A wife yet?)* He wanted to go home before she died. He had to arrange for some-body to look after the children. *(Children?)* The trouble was that this time of the month Sergeant Quince didn't have the money, even for train fare one way. He was broke.

"Why don't he go to the Red Cross?" somebody said.

Sergeant Cobb shrugged. "He ain't got time, I guess," he said. "I know he ain't a kindhearted man, boys. And you don't have to do this. It's strictly voluntary. But give a little something. He's human and he needs your help. Give from your heart."

He took a helmet liner off of the top of somebody's wall locker and held it in his hand like a collection plate in church. Some-body hawked and spat on the floor. I didn't think anybody would give anything. We just stood there and stared at Sergeant Cobb until Sachs pushed through to the front.

"Here's my contribution," he said. And he dropped a dime into the helmet liner.

Everybody started to laugh, and even the thick-headed ones caught on. Each of us put a dime in the pot. Ten cents for Sergeant Quince in his hour of need. Sergeant Cobb emptied the liner, put the dimes in his raincoat pocket, placed the liner back on top of the wall locker, and started to leave. At the front door he turned around, shook his head, and giggled.

"Don't that beat all?" he said. "They done exactly the same thing in the other barracks too."

Half an hour later we had the exquisite pleasure of looking out of the windows and seeing Sergeant Quince in his Class-A uniform with his double row of World War II ribbons stand in the rain in the middle of the battery area and get soaking wet. He cussed and cussed us and threw those dimes high, wide, and handsome and away. He wished us all damnation, death, and hell.

And this is where it ought to end. It would be a swell place to end, with the picture of Quince *furioso* throwing fountains of dimes in the air. Enraged and possessed and frustrated. Yes, Quince in insane rage, hurling our proffered dimes in the air, wild and black-faced with frustration and tribulation, would be a fine fade-out in the best modern manner. But not so. Not so soon did he fade out of my life. Nor, I guess, did I expect him to.

Sachs and I went on to Leadership School. What happened to the rest of them I wouldn't know and couldn't care less. But Sachs and myself took our duffel bags and waited in front of the Orderly Room. The harelipped Captain came out and painfully wished us well. We climbed over the tailgate of a deuce and a half and rode to the other side of camp where they try to make you into an NCO in three months flat or else turn you into jelly.

"Why are you going?" Sachs asked me. As if I understood at the outset why he was doing it. I had hardly even spoken to Sachs before that.

"Because that sonofabitch Quince is trash," I said. "I don't like to be pushed around by trash."

Sachs grinned. "You Southerners," he said. "You Southerners and all your pride and all your internal squabbles!"

I won't bore you with the sordid details of that next place except to say that they made us and we made it. It worked. Sachs shed thirty pounds, went at every bit of it with fury and determination and emerged as the top man in the class. Believe it or not. Many a husky specimen fell among the thorns and withered out of school, but Sachs thrived, grew, bloomed. I was in the top ten myself, and both of us made Sergeant out of it. We soldiered night and day like madmen. We learned all the tricks of the trade. When we were finished we were sharp. Bandbox soldiers. The metamorphosis was complete. Still, it's only fair to point out that we kept laughing about it. Sachs called it being in disguise and referred to his uniform as a costume. He called us both "the masqueraders." I called myself "the invisible white man."

One anecdote only of that time I'll insert. The Anecdote of the Word. It helps to explain the kind of game we were playing. One week early in the course I was doing badly and it looked like maybe I would wash out. I'd get good marks and only a few gigs one day, poor marks and many the next. The TAC/NCO wrote on my weekly report that he thought I was "a good man," but that I had been "vacillating." He was a college boy himself and used that word. Well, shortly thereafter the Company Commander called us both into his inner sanctum. We got shaped up in a big hurry and reported. His office was a room as bare as a monk's cell except for one huge sign on the wall that read "THIS TOO SHALL PASS." He, the Captain, was a huge hulk of a man, a former All-American tackle from some place or other, a bull neck, a bulging chest behind the desk, and all jaw, lantern and/or granite with the Mussolini thrust to it. He was dead serious. We were quivering arrows at attention in front of him.

"I have this here report before me," he said. "You say here that this soldier has been *vacillating*. What do you mean?"

The TAC gulped and patiently tried to explain what he had meant by means of the image of the pendulum of a grandfather's clock swinging back and forth. The Captain heard him out, nodded.

"Clerk!" he roared.

The Company Clerk came tearing into the room like somebody trying to steal second. Saluted. Quivered too!

"Get me a dictionary."

We waited in breathless anticipation. The clerk soon returned with the dictionary. Captain opened it to the *v*'s and followed his index finger, thick and blunt-ended as a chisel, down the line of words. Looked at the word a while and the definition. It was a pocket dictionary and defined as follows:

VAC-IL-LATE, *v.i.*, -LATED, -LATING. 1. Waver, stagger 2. fluctuate 3. be irresolute or hesitant.

"Nothing about pendulums," he noted. "Damn good word, though. Good word."

He wrote it down on a pad in capitals and underlined it several times. That was that. We were dismissed.

Now from within that Orderly Room issued forth each week reams of mimeographed material for the benefit of all students. Ever after that incident the Captain cautioned that those who wished to complete the course successfully *must not vacillate!* This got to be a standing joke in that mirthless place.

"If I catch any of you guys *vacillating* in the company area," the TAC used to tell us, "you've had it."

Sachs and I made it through, were transformed from anarchists to impeccable sergeanthood. We didn't end up going to Korea to be shot at either, but instead were sent to Europe to join a very sharp outfit where we would be able to maintain the high standards we had so recently acquired. Which we did for the rest of our service time. Sachs was so good he even made Sergeant First Class without time in grade.

More than a year later we were in Germany for maneuvers. It was the middle of summer and we were living in tents. In the evenings we used to go to a huge circus tent of a beer hall and get drunk. It was there on one hot night that we met Quince again. He was sitting all alone at a table with a big crowd of empty 3.2 beer cans around him. He was a Corporal now, two stripes down, and by the patch on his shoulder we knew he was in a mucked-up outfit, a whole division of stumblebums with a well-known cretin commanding. He looked it too. His uniform was dirty. His shirt was open all the way down the front, revealing a filthy, sweat-soaked T-shirt. Of course it's hard to look sharp if you're living in the field in the middle of the summer. But Sachs and I took pride in our ability to look as sharp in the field as in garrison. It took some doing, but we could do it.

"Let's buy the bastard a beer," Sachs said.

Quince seemed glad to see us as if we were dear, old, long-lost friends. Once we had introduced ourselves, that is. He didn't recognize us at first. He marveled at our transformation and good luck. We couldn't help marveling at his transformation too.

("This is the worst outfit I was ever with," he admitted. "The Battery Commander has got it in for me.") He bought us a round and we bought more.

Late, just before they shut the place down and threw everybody out, Quince went maudlin on us.

"I can't explain it, but it makes me feel bad to see you guys like this," he said. "I hated you guys, I'll admit that. Long before the dimes. But I didn't know you hated me so much."

"What do you mean by that?"

"To hunt me down after all this time and shame me. Soldiering is my life. It's just a couple of years for you guys. And here you are with all this rank looking like old soldiers. Sergeants! Goddamn, it isn't fair."

"Do you know what the Army is, Quince?"

"What? What's that?"

"I'll tell you what the Army is to me," Sachs said. "It's just a game, a stupid, brutal, pointless, simple-minded game. And you know what, Corporal Quince? I beat that game. I won. I'm a better soldier now than you ever were or ever will be and it doesn't mean a thing to me."

Quince turned his head away from us.

"You hadn't ought to have said that," he said. "You can't take everything away from a guy. You got to leave a guy something."

We left him to cry in his beer until they tossed him out, and walked back under the stars to our tents, singing the whole way. We sat in our sleeping bags and had a smoke before we flaked out.

"You were great," I told Sachs. "That was worth waiting for."

But Sachs was a moody kind of a guy. He didn't see it that way.

"You can't beat them down," he said. "No matter what you do. They always win out in the end. Sure I got in my licks. But he won anyway. *He made me do it.* So in the end he still beat me."

"You worry too much."

"That's just the way I am," he said bitterly.

"You don't feel *sorry* for him, do you?"

"Hell, no," he said. "You don't get it. The trouble is I still hate him. I hate him worse than ever."

And he stubbed out his cigarette and turned over and went to sleep without another word, leaving me to ponder on that for a while.

FARMER IN THE DELL

ELMER ADELOT is the Junior High School science teacher. He's skinny as a fence post, nearsighted, and wears glasses as thick as the bottom of a fruit jar, and he has not much more on top of his head than a patch of prematurely gray hair that looks like the head of an old worn-out wet mop left out to dry and bleach in the sun. Not that he's bad-looking after you get used to him. It's just that by no standard whatsoever could he be called a good-looking man.

Elmer is so shy, so modest, it hurts to tell about it. I remember years ago at Boy Scout Camp he used to wait around until everyone else was finished before he would go in the latrine or the shower. Lord knows how he ever got along in the Army.

Elmer is an only child and lived for years with his widowed mother, now gone to glory. She gave up on trying to interest him in marrying some nice girl. She gave up on the rest of us too. Sat up bolt upright on her deathbed and cursed everybody and everything. Called the Methodist preacher, who had come to pray over her, "a sugarmouth old hypocrite," swore she would lean down from the golden bar of heaven like Dante Gabriel Rossetti's blessed damozel and watch many a one of us, some of the least suspected, fry and stew in our own juice in hell. Old Lady Adelot weighed about two-fifty if she weighed an

ounce, and when they tried to bury her, the pallbearers slipped
in the mud and dropped her, coffin and all. The top flew wide
open and away she rolled to the edge of the grave in her white
evening dress, wearing her string of pearls, poised for one pre-
carious instant on that neat lip of earth, then rolled in, turning
over like somebody asleep, while we all stood there aghast, open-
mouthed, and the choir tried to keep on singing "In the Sweet
By and By."

"Ain't nobody going to push Old Lady Adelot into anything
unless she wants to go," somebody said.

"Amen!"

Is it any wonder Elmer has always been a little scared of
women, considering his natural shyness and the way his mama
was?

The kids at school will tell you about a different side of Elmer.
They don't think he's so comical. Once he gets in behind the
desk in the Science Room, he is a little tin god and everything
has got to be just so.

"You don't make mistakes in Science," he keeps on telling
them.

And if you don't print your name neatly in the upper left-
hand corner of your homework with the correct date on the line
underneath, he is just liable to tear up the paper right in front of
your face and give you a big fat zero for the day. He carries a
yardstick around the room with him to point with, and if you
don't stand up quick and speak up loud and clear when he calls
on you, he will bang you with that ruler across the knuckles or
your behind. If you happen to be a boy, that is. It's different if
you are a girl. All the girls' Science class say he is a perfect
angel.

Elmer's one great friend in the whole world is Johnny Sprat-
tling, called Jack Spratt since almost the day he was born.
Friendship is always a mysterious venture, but there couldn't be
two more different people than Jack Spratt and Elmer. Jack is a
big, husky, gregarious guy who looks something like Jack Carson, the movie star, and works as a traveling salesman for an
insurance company and couldn't be better made for the job. He

will stop you on the street corner any time of day and hold you up for half an hour while he tells you all the new jokes he heard on his latest trip. He was about the best fullback they ever had on the High School team and he might have been an All-American if he had gone on to college. The women are wild for him. He could, and probably did, have any of them he wanted to.

Which is what makes it hard to explain how he ever ended up marrying Mary West. Mary started out from the first being one of these dainty, prissy little girls. She grew up pretty enough and with a good figure, but still it looked like she was born to be an old maid. You would no more have thought of Mary West in a naughty way than you would write dirty words in a hymn book. She was one of the steady workers at the church. She taught Sunday school, sang in the choir, arranged altar flowers, and used to talk all the time about going to Africa and being a missionary. Still, she is the one he took for his wife. He courted and somehow convinced her. How I don't know.

One thing I do know. At the stag party we had for Jack just before he got married he got pretty drunk. "You probably think I am out of my head," he told us. "Well, I want something I can be sure is all mine. There's a lot of no-good guys just like me running around loose. And I want to be sure, you know. That's the important thing when you're a traveling man."

And that might be all there is to it. I don't know.

After the wedding and the honeymoon trip to Biloxi, Mississippi, Jack and Mary came back and set up in an apartment right near the Adelot house. Just across the street from it in a brand-new subdivision with apartments and little candy-box houses. Since they lived so near to each other and since Jack and Elmer had been good friends for so long, they used to ask Elmer over a lot for supper or a card game or to watch TV. The Spratts seemed to be happy enough. They didn't have any children, though, and they both wanted to have a family.

And everything goes along just fine until—

One hot Saturday evening Elmer calls Jack up on the telephone.

"Jack," he says, "they're working on the plumbing over here and the water is turned off. I'm just dying to take a cool shower. Could I come over and use yours?"

So Elmer gets his soap and a towel and even a bathrobe just in case he needs it and comes across the street. He finds Jack in the kitchen with his shirt off, all covered with grease, and he's got the washing machine disemboweled and parts of it spread all over the floor.

"I tell you," Jack says, "they just don't make things like they used to. Look at that mess!"

"Mass production," Elmer says. "That's the whole trouble in a nutshell—mass production."

"Mass production?" Jack guffaws. "I'm all for it. I believe in it. Why I guess I *mass produced* half the little ole gals in the county before I took on my ball and chain."

"I don't mean anything that way," Elmer says.

"You want a can of beer?"

"No, thank you," Elmer says. "I guess I'll just get in the shower."

He goes into the bathroom and shuts the door behind him. He is a little bit disturbed that the lock doesn't work, but anyway it is his best friend's house and Mary is uptown at the A & P. He hangs his clothes up neatly and climbs into the shower, making sure the curtain is pulled all the way across tight.

Meanwhile Jack is drinking a can of beer and looking sadly on the corpse and the scattered innards of the washer. It dawns on him that maybe he ought to run down to the appliance store before it closes up and ask Jack Smathers what to do next. He polishes off the can of beer in one gulp, grabs a shirt, and jumps in the car. Away he goes without a word of warning to Elmer Adelot.

Jack hasn't been gone a full minute when Mary arrives back in her car. (Jack is using the company car.) She picks up her packages in both arms and comes around the back way, staggering up the steps. One look at the washing machine and she plumps down the packages on the kitchen table and throws up her hands in dismay.

"Isn't that just like him?" she thinks out loud. "He tries to fix everything and he can't fix a thing. Well, maybe, this time I'll get a new machine out of him."

Since it is such a hot day and since she couldn't cook anyway even if she wanted to because of all the mess, she decides to prepare a cold supper. As she starts to set the dining-room table, she hears the shower running and, naturally, she thinks it is Jack, washing away the grease and the grime of his unfortunate mechanical adventure. On an impulse—a kind of bride's impulse still—she tiptoes to the bathroom, opens the door without making a sound, and steals toward the shower curtain. Without pause or warning she thrusts her arm past the edge of the curtain, feels for and finds the unsuspecting flesh.

"Ding dong bell! The farmer's in the dell!" she cries, emphasizing each word with the vigor of a drunken sexton. "Hurry up. Supper's ready and waiting."

Elmer Adelot freezes in a state of horror.

Smiling to herself, Mary goes back to the kitchen to get the cold cuts ready. And who should she meet, grinning, coming up the back steps to the kitchen with grease still on his face, but her husband.

There is a piercing shriek that can be heard for blocks around.

Shocked into action by the shriek—thoughtless instant action—Elmer Adelot bursts out of the bathroom forgetting everything, his clothes, his bathrobe, his soap and towel and the shower still running, just in time to plunge headlong past the astonished two of them. And outside he goes running for all he is worth down the sidewalk.

Mrs. Otis Bolgin, who just happens to be driving by at this time, looks twice at this dripping, naked apparition and blithely drives her car into a telephone pole.

Two small boys fall out of their perch in a tree house and almost break their necks for laughing so hard when Elmer runs by.

Elmer has run two or three blocks down the street when it begins to occur to him what he is doing. Now he is running back the way he came even faster than before, and this time all the way back he has acquired an audience. People have come running out on front porches or pressed their faces against front windows. Traffic has stopped cold. Children cry out for joy at the speed of the lean naked runner and a couple of small mongrel dogs are running too, snapping at the bare, elusive heels until he gets back to the apartment, slams the front door to behind him, and leaps past Jack and Mary.

After that he is in the bathroom, fully dressed, but he won't come out. He talks to them through the door while they beg, plead, and reassure him. He waits until after dark. They promise to turn their backs and close their eyes (since he still feels naked) and he sneaks out and across the street to his house.

He won't come out for a couple of weeks until some other incident has become the talk of the town. And that might be the end of it.

Except, of course, it isn't. Jack thought it was just about the funniest thing that ever happened since the world began. He told everybody about it endlessly, adding new imaginative details, sparing nothing. Now you might think that would be the end of the friendship between Jack and Elmer. Not so. After the initial shock was over, Elmer didn't seem to mind. Neither did Mary, which is more than I can understand. The Spratts (Sprattlings, that is) kept right on inviting Elmer over to their house for dinner or cards or to watch TV. And Elmer kept right on going to see them. He was even kind enough to take Mary to church or the movies once in a while when Jack had to be out of town.

Going through that experience seems to have changed Elmer slightly. It isn't anything definite, but there are some indefinable ways in which he seems to be a different person. More sure of himself, you might say.

Mary has changed too. She has taken to letting her hair grow long and full. She has changed her style of dress. The other day I ran into her at the drugstore. She was wearing maternity clothes.

"Mary," I said, "I didn't know you and Jack were expecting a baby. This is wonderful news."

"Yes, it's wonderful for us."

"What do you want—a boy or a girl?"

"I don't care, really."

"Well, what do you think it will be?"

"There's no way to tell for sure," she says, smiling nicely. "Science hasn't found the answer to that yet."

MY PICTURE
LEFT IN SCOTLAND

PROFESSOR DUDLEY STOOD UP and walked from his desk to the leaded window and looked out at the barbered green of the quadrangle, his fine profile outlined sharply against the glass. The student, sitting in front of the desk in a straight-backed chair, watched him out of the corner of his eye. The professor took a deep puff on his cigarette and blew a series of quick, admirable smoke rings. He was watching the brown squirrels on the lawn. Almost tame, they scurried about with plump devious energy and, somehow, reminded him of monks, the fat little ones carved in stone on the tower at Chartres. God, you almost had to be a mountain climber to see those monks.

"I suppose you want me to be completely honest with you."

The boy opened his mouth to speak, but his throat was so tight and dry that no words came. He ended by nodding.

"There are two ways a teacher can handle something like this," Professor Dudley said. "You can be tactfully honest. That is, more or less noncommittal. Search out whatever virtues there are and hold them up for inspection and praise. And try to ignore the naked, glaring faults. That's for the tender egos. On the other hand, if one mingles a little honey with the gall, one can say more or less exactly what one really thinks."

"Just tell me what you think, sir," the boy said. "I just want to know the truth."

"Good."

The professor grinned and sat down again behind his desk and picked up the manuscript. The title of this work was "The Signal Elm," which probably explained, he thought, why the student had sent it to him in the first place. He had received the manuscript, bulky and badly typed, in the campus mail a couple of weeks before, accompanied by a reticent, expectant note asking, if he had the time, would he mind reading it. The professor at once sent a note in reply saying that it would be a pleasure to read the novel and setting a date and an hour when they could meet in his office and discuss the manuscript. He added that it was always a pleasure to have the opportunity to look at the creative work of students.

"It's probably a confession of galloping senility, Mr. Grubb," the professor said, "but I don't recall ever seeing your name on any of my class lists."

"I never was able to take your course officially, sir," Grubb said. "I'm an engineer. But I come every year to audit your lectures on Matthew Arnold."

"Then you must have noticed," the professor said, smiling gently, "that from time to time I am guilty of repeating myself."

"The way I look at it," Grubb said, "is once you've really done the job on somebody like Arnold, you can't help repeating yourself."

"Well, that's one way of looking at it. Are you a senior, Mr. Grubb?"

"Yes, sir."

"Isn't it odd that we've never met before now?"

The boy smiled for the first time and shrugged.

Of all the sad and inarticulate gestures of mankind, the shrug was among the least appealing to the professor. Grubb could not have offended him more by picking his nose. The boy sat awkward and attentive in his chair, still bearing, after four years, the definable stamp of a metropolitan high school. There was something about all of them, the professor thought, something of the clumsy ponderous solemnity of the self-educated man. It must take some doing, a dark and vegetable tenacity like the potato's, to rise to the top in classes, each of thirty or forty, in public high schools of thousands, and at last to be accepted by good private colleges with the highest admission standards. In its own way it stirred one's admiration.

"It's a big school," Grubb was saying, apparently to break the silence.

"And getting bigger all the time, I'm afraid," the professor said. "Where did you prep?"

"I didn't exactly 'prep,' sir. I came here from high school."

"Did you? One of those that has a number for a name—PHS 53, like the one in your novel?"

"Yes, sir. More or less."

"Then it's an autobiographical novel?"

"No, sir, not really," Grubb said. "I mean it's somewhat autobiographical. But not completely."

"I suspected as much," the professor said. "Well, it's a wonderful thing."

"What's that, sir?"

"I say I think it's a wonderful thing for a second-generation boy, like the hero of your novel, the son of immigrant parents, to come up from the city streets like that. To fight and claw his way up from the anonymity of a big city high school and to end up in a place like this. It takes something. It takes persistence, patience, tenacity— Are you comfortable? Would you care for a cigarette? They're Italian—Nazionales."

"Thanks just the same," Grubb said. "I don't smoke."

"I have to admit something," the professor said, lighting his cigarette. "I have a confession to make before I can say anything at all about your manuscript. Years ago, already more years than I care to count, I aspired to be a novelist myself. After I graduated here and spent my tour at Oxford on a Rhodes, I chucked the whole thing and spent a year on the Left Bank just writing."

"Did you run into Fitzgerald? F. Scott Fitzgerald?"

"He died about the time I was in high school," the professor said glancing at his wristwatch.

"I'm sorry. I didn't mean—"

"Time," the professor said, "time like distance blurs things. A few years ago and I'd probably have been flattered to be thought to be a contemporary of the Lost Generation."

Mr. Grubb cleared his throat and looked down at the scuffed surface of his desert boots.

"Even after that," the professor continued, "when the cruel world had caught up with me at last and I was just another poor instructor on the treadmill, I kept at it for a while. *Mea culpa!* I have three unpublished novels in my desk at home."

"Gee, I never knew that," Grubb said. "That's really interesting."

"Not really 'interesting,' but the sad truth," the professor said. "Anyhow I've given you fair warning. Consider yourself well warned. Take any criticism I may offer with a large grain of salt."

"The way I look at it, sir," the boy said, "is if you've given it a good try yourself, you ought to be able to help me even more. I'll take my chances."

"Maybe so. *Unpublished* novels, though. Never forget that. Never forget I'm just a frustrated writer myself."

"Like I said, I'll take my chances."

Professor Dudley opened the manuscript and looked at it for a moment. He was an extraordinarily handsome man, tall, slender, immaculately casual. A crew cut shot with gray, fine features, clear blue eyes. As he studied the manuscript the cigarette between his fingers burned and the ash grew long. His fingers were stained from smoking. The boy looked away, staring at the bookshelves that ringed the room.

"All right," the professor said abruptly with his smile. "I'll tell you what. Since we've both come out in the open against sin and in favor of honesty, suppose I just read you the notes I made for myself when I finished reading the manuscript? I don't see how we can get a more direct, uncomplicated reaction than that, do you?"

"That suits me fine, sir."

"Now then," the professor said. " 'The Signal Elm,' a novel by David Grubb . . ."

Leafing through the pages, Professor Dudley had quickly grasped the outlines of the shopworn plot. It told the story of a young man's struggle to maturity and identity, starting from the confines of an immigrant Jewish family in Brooklyn. (Was Grubb Jewish? It seemed likely.) A family whose roots were in the Old World, baffled by the New. The story progressed until the young man was at last able to feel wholly a part of it, able to conquer it and, as well, to transcend the shadowing mediocrity of his background. At the climax the boy arose in a brand-new suit to deliver the Valedictorian Address at PHS 53 while his parents listened with gentle awe to his mastery of a language they had never really learned. The book ended in a subdued tone with the young man arriving at a green and only-dreamed-of campus, with possibilities for a bright new future ringing his head like a saint's halo of real gold. There were sections and occasional isolated scenes which were beautifully written. Sometimes the young stammer to the very edge of poetry almost in spite of themselves. Professor Dudley had not the slightest notion why this opus was called "The Signal Elm." Doubtless something had eluded him. He confined his brief critique to purely technical faults: stiff dialogue, overwritten description, crude symbolism, lack of clear-cut motivation for action, absence of well-defined development of what appeared to be the minor themes. On the whole the book itself and this present interview were precisely the material for the kind of anecdote Professor Dudley could tell so well, with mild self-deprecating irony, at a faculty party.

"I hope I haven't been too rough on you," he said, sneaking a quick look at his watch that he hoped did not go unnoticed. "I'm aware this effort means a good deal to you."

"Yes, sir. It means a lot."

"It should," the professor continued. "It's quite an accomplishment, particularly for a student who is not an English major. There are not many students around here who could write a better book than that."

"Thanks. I've been so close to it for so long—"

"Maybe that's the whole trouble. Maybe you're still too close to the material at this time. Why not let it sit a while? Why not try your hand at some other theme, some entirely different kind of story, something that will let you keep a little more aesthetic distance?"

"Don't you think I could revise? I mean, with your criticism as a guide—"

"No, Mr. Grubb, I don't. To tell you the truth, I don't think there's any hope at all for this one. You asked me for the truth. Remember, though, this is only my opinion. I feel that there is nothing you nor I nor anyone else could do to salvage this story. It would take a genius of another stamp—a modern Dickens, say."

"Yes, sir," the boy said.

"I can see you're disappointed. Don't be. You're young. Ever so much younger than you realize now. And you have written a novel. Even if it's not a good one, it's an achievement. Even if you never write another line as long as you live, you have done this much."

"I put everything I've got into this book," the boy said.

"Don't—I repeat—by all means don't take my criticism as gospel. Show it to somebody else on the faculty."

"I don't think that will be necessary. Everybody knows you're the best critic in school."

"The best critic in school? That isn't quite accurate," the professor said, handing him the manuscript and walking him toward the door. "But I suppose it is the little white lies, the happy little self-delusions that we all cling to and live by. I'm glad you sent the manuscript to me to read. Otherwise we might never had met. Perhaps we'll meet again. Do you play squash?"

"No, sir. I lift weights for exercise."

"Well, something will turn up," the professor said, offering his hand. "When you go out, please tell the young lady who's waiting in the hall to come right in. And, Grubb, don't give up. I'd like to think I'll see the day when I'll open a package in the mail and find an autographed copy of your first novel—perhaps even this one."

David Grubb looked at him, shrugged eloquently, and departed, closing the door softly behind him.

When the door closed, the professor walked over to his windows. He saw Grubb appear, ambling head-down along the crisscross walk and, particularly, he noticed an intriguing squirrel who paused in alarm by a tree near the walk, its paws poised together in an attitude of prayer, its great soft tail cocked in a question mark. He heard the door open and close behind him.

"Miss Palmer," he said, waving her to the chair, "I'm sorry I had to keep you waiting."

"You've always been so good about giving me time," she said. "I can't complain."

She sat easily in the chair, her fine tanned legs demurely crossed. She was blond and full-bodied as a ripe pear and her eyes were as clear and cool as rainwater. He gave her a cigarette and a light and moved behind his desk. He ruffled the papers in the top drawer and came up with a manuscript bearing the title "My Picture Left in Scotland: A Study of Ben Jonson," beneath which was typed "Submitted as Spring Term Junior Paper to the Department of English by Jenny Bell Palmer." He examined the wide-margined, beautifully typed pages, studiously frowning. He was aware that Jenny Bell Palmer had now shifted her position. She was sitting on the edge of her chair.

"With regard to your term paper," he said, "I think I'd better read my comments first."

He glanced at her. She wet her lips and nodded.

"This paper is a lucidly written close and comprehensive study of a single poem by Ben Jonson, and, within these self-imposed limitations, you have succeeded admirably. The reader is not entirely convinced that this eighteen-line lyric is deserving of such intense scrutiny or that the poem is as representative of Jonson's work as a whole as the writer seems to assume. This reader, not himself a specialist in the Renaissance period, would like to be led and encouraged by some cogent evidence to accept the validity of the implied assumption. On the whole, however, in spite of certain minor mechanical errors, this paper is an adequate realization of its intentions. A-minus."

"Thanks," Jenny Bell said. "Thanks a lot."

"Really, it wasn't so bad at all," he said. "You seem to be improving all the time."

"I liked doing this one," she said. "It's much easier to write about something you really care about."

"I am curious about one thing—why this particular poem happened to catch your fancy."

"I don't know," she said. "I guess because it's such a personal kind of a poem. I mean, you take something like 'Drink to Me Only With Thine Eyes.' That could have been written to almost anybody. In this one he seemed to have a particular person in mind. There was Ben Jonson in love with this young girl and he was worried because he was afraid *she* wouldn't love *him*. I thought maybe it would be more interesting if I wrote about it from the feminine angle."

"That's an interesting idea," the professor said. "I'm not sure it's clear in your paper, though."

"Oh the paper!" she said. "That's the whole trouble. As soon as I start writing a paper I—I don't know—I *freeze* up. An academic paper is such an *impersonal* thing!"

She had relaxed again, recrossing her marvelous young legs, and it occurred to him that at any moment all her youth and vitality might burst the shell of the skirt and cashmere sweater leaving her as nude and shining as an apple.

"Excuse me, did you say something?"

"Nothing, Miss Palmer, nothing at all. My imagination was simply wandering toward the riotous precincts of senility. Why don't we take a look at the poem together and see what you were really trying to do in the paper?"

He went to the bookcase, fumbled vague-handed for a moment, then returned with an anthology of Elizabethan and Jacobean verse. A quick flipping of pages and he found the poem. He presented the book to her and stood close behind her chair, close enough to detect the sweet fresh odor of soap. She must have showered just before coming to keep the appointment. Jenny Bell Palmer studied the poem silently.

"It's the last part especially," she said. "I mean, in the first part he just kind of states the facts of the situation. He says he is in love with her and she doesn't seem to love him."

"What about the last part?"

"Don't you see? I mean, it seems kind of self-evident to me."

"Suppose I read it aloud," he said.

He leaned over her shoulder, his hands gripping the chair, and in a soft voice, still haunted by the dim ghost of an acquired Oxford accent, he read:

> "Oh, but my conscious feares
>   That flie my thoughts betweene
> Tell me that she hath seene
> My hundreds of gray haires
> Told seven and fortie yeares.
> Read so much wast, as she cannot embrace,
> My mountaine belly, and my rockie face,
> And all these through her eyes, have stopt her eares."

"It sounds very nice when you read it like that."

"But what about the last part? It seems to me that the poet is only being realistic. After all, he is forty-seven years old, gray-haired, fat, and, as *Time* would say, craggy."

"That's exactly what I mean!" she exclaimed. "You notice he doesn't say word one about what the girl thinks. He's just being sorry for himself."

"Indeed he doesn't. How could he put her real thoughts in the poem? What man, since poor old Adam woke up and found Eve sleeping beside him, has ever known what the girl really thinks?"

"That's the trouble with men," Jenny Bell said. "Even the intelligent ones."

"I'm afraid the defect is irremediable."

"No, it isn't! Men just won't use common sense. Look how silly it is. There was Ben Jonson, *a very great poet*, all worried about what some silly girl was thinking about him."

"Otherwise no poem," Professor Dudley said. "It's just as well."

"I can't believe it."

"Let's face it," he said. "He does admit to a few physical characteristics that might be called impediments."

"When a girl falls in love with an older man, that part doesn't even enter into it."

"That's a very sweet thought."

Without moving an inch he could have bitten into Jenny Bell Palmer's pink, small, exposed ear. He turned away and lit a cigarette.

"It isn't just a 'sweet thought,'" she said. "Look, I have perfectly normal reactions to almost everything. Now my daddy, for example, he's ugly as sin, and I could easily fall in love with a man like him."

"And your point is that Ben Jonson was really a lovable old guy. Like Daddy."

"You make it all sound so silly when you put it that way."

"Ah!" he said, standing once again in strict profile by the windows. "What a good world it would be if all the illusions of the young and fair—"

"But it *is* a good world," she said. "Don't you think?"

Professor Dudley felt his lips relaxing into a slow smile. He returned to his desk, sprawled leisurely and unofficial on the edge of it, his long legs dangling, exposing below the creased line of his khaki trousers the neat loafers he wore, the subdued argyle socks, and the tan bulge of an athletic, tennis-playing calf. He looked a good deal younger than forty.

"I don't know why you do it," he said. "Every time we have an appointment you come in here, immaculate, bursting with youth and life. And you make me feel the weight of each and every one of my years, the burden of time I have to push around like the rock of Sisyphus. You ought to be ashamed of yourself."

"I never know how to take you," she said. "You're always teasing and kidding around."

"I'm not just kidding around."

"You don't look a day over thirty and you know it."

"And you—today you look as if you had just stepped out of a Renoir canvas."

"You ought to be ashamed."

"What on earth is the matter with Renoir?"

"I don't know," she said. "His women are all so—*sensuous.*"

"There you go again," he said. "Passing judgment on the basis of preconceived values. How am I ever going to make a critic out of you?"

"I don't know what you mean," she said, frowning.

"Take a word like that, like sensuous. The way you say it—*sensuous*—implies that it's some kind of a naughty word. Sensuous is a perfectly respectable neutral adjective and you know it."

"All right," she said. "But you know what I mean."

"Yes," he said. "I know what you mean."

He looked into her eyes. They were like water on a windless day, unclouded by complexity. If there was any emotion to be read in her eyes, it was only a mild, very mild anxiety. Perhaps it was only curiosity.

"Let's pursue the point," he said. "You find Renoir sensuous in some way that has connotations of naughtiness. Why?"

"Oh, I don't know," she said a little petulantly. "I just do, that's all."

"All right. Let me tell you how I feel about Renoir," he said, suddenly exuberant, theatrical. "I think Renoir is Paris in the spring, the sweetest, ripest, greenest city of April in the world. A long time ago I lived on the Left Bank, seeing everything for the first time with wide, intoxicated eyes. Drinking in every conceivable impression and experience like wine. Jotting down wild, irresponsible, inspired ideas for poems and stories and novels and plays. Somehow Renoir symbolizes all that to me, the lifeblood of youth, the time when every girl in Paris seemed to be a living still life made up of all the sweet fruits of the earth. And all of it lost, gone—"

"Oh *well*," she said. "You were being an artist. Artists are different."

"In what way? How are artists different?"

"You know what I mean," she said. "Like when I used to go to life class over at the Art Department. It was a mixed class, but once you got used to the idea of the nude model being up there, it was all right. Everybody just concentrated on their drawing. All except a couple of football players who signed up for the course and couldn't draw a straight line. They sat in the back and giggled."

"There are always football players who sit in the back and giggle. We have to try to ignore them."

"Oh, I ignored them all right. And, you know, one of them actually had the nerve to ask me for a date. Would you believe it?"

"Your point is well taken. I would believe it and artists are different."

But she had looked away from him, smoothed her skirt, and gathered up her books. And now she was standing. He thought he detected the faintest stain of a blush on her cheeks.

"I still don't like Renoir," she said. "I guess men do, though."

"I wish we had the time to discover why you really don't respond to Renoir," he said. "Perhaps another time. As it is the light is waning, it's already past five o'clock, and I must totter home."

"Christ!" she said. "I'm late for choir practice."

She started for the door in a rush.

"Hey, Jenny Bell," he called after her. "You forgot your paper."

Collecting herself, she returned and gracefully accepted the paper from him.

"I hope you will feel free to drop in anytime during the rest of the term to discuss your work."

"Don't you worry," she said. "I will."

She went out of the door, closing it gently behind her. He could hear her quick feet in the hall and, looking out of the window, he saw her racing across the quadrangle, scattering poor astounded squirrels every which way, her skirt blowing, her legs flashing. Diana, the huntress, without a thought in her head, and he was Actaeon, gnawed to pieces and devoured by his own hounds. He bit down on his lip until he could taste the light salt flavor of blood.

Professor Dudley walked home the back way, avoiding the main street of the town with all its little bustle of rush-hour traffic and late shopping. It was always better to be walking along the tree-lined, residential streets with their well-kept lawns and well-painted houses. It took a little longer, but it was only a few blocks either way. And he had come to think that walking easily in the green shade was a kind of ritual. He felt that coming home from the college he was like a deep-sea diver rising slowly from an arena of dark, dreaming beauty into the pitiless glare of sunlight and burning air.

When he opened the front door of the house, Ronnie stood formidably barring his way, arms akimbo.

"Susie broke my bicycle," he announced. "Mama is sick and we're hungry."

"Well, now," Professor Dudley said. "We'll have to see about these things, one at a time."

"I should hope so," Ronnie cried over his shoulder, fleeing.

The professor set down his briefcase and looked at himself in the hall mirror. Not *quite* like Dorian Gray. But somehow remarkably lucky, remarkably free from the lines of either his years or his sins. He adjusted his necktie and climbed the stairs to the bedroom. He knocked and entered, finding the blinds drawn and finding Vivian stretched out on the bed, her thin, pretty, troubled face buoyed up by pillows, etched with the pains of a headache.

"You know," she said, "it's not much help even if you know it's psychosomatic."

"No, I guess it hurts just as much."

"Regular soap-opera day here," she said. "First the goddamn dishwasher broke down right after breakfast and then I couldn't get the car started. I think it's the battery. I don't know what's the matter with it. Maybe it just won't work for me. One goddamn thing after another all day long. And then to top it all, Susie got the most awful gash in her head and had to have stitches. She was trying to ride Ronnie's bike down the steps at the park."

"I guess that's how she busted it."

"What?"

"The bicycle."

"Oh, I guess so."

He sat down on the edge of the bed and stroked her hand. Such pale slender hands with such exquisite, useless fingers. He used to call her his Rossetti girl, his pre-Raphaelite.

"How do you feel now?"

"Rotten," she said. "Just rotten. I can't budge. I feel like the top of my head is coming off any minute."

"Call the doctor?"

"What's the use? All he can do is tell me it's all in my mind."

He was possessed by an almost irresistible desire to shrug his shoulders. Exactly like Mr. Grubb.

"Why don't you go to sleep?"

"I am. I was just waiting for you to come in," she said. "How was your day?"

"Same old rot. Another day, another dollar."

"Pearls before swine?"

"You might put it that way," he said. "Have the kids had any supper yet?"

"Don't bother," she said. "Let them raid the icebox. They love it. Just like a picnic."

"I was being selfish as usual," he said. "I was thinking about me."

"There's a can of Spanish rice somewhere. You always like Spanish rice, don't you?"

"I'm a sucker for Spanish rice," he said.

The kitchen was, as he anticipated, a shambles. He put a bottle of scotch within arm's reach and got busy cleaning things up so that at least he could have the sink and the stove free. The main thing, he thought, the real distinguished advice I have for you this morning, students, is twofold. Point one: never, under no circumstances, no, never marry an intellectual woman. If you must marry at all, which, according to St. Paul, is debatable, then search far and wide for a plump, ripe, stupid, peasant woman. Keep her barefoot and pregnant and full of meat and potatoes. If, however, you are unable to locate such a delectable mountain, such a promised land for sowing and reaping and the raising of flocks, then let this be your guide: intellectual or not, never marry a woman who is more intelligent than you are. Now for point two. Let's see, what was point two? Ah yes, I have it right here and I shan't detain you one minute beyond the ringing of the bell. Mark this well. Keep your grubby, and I use the word advisedly, keep your grubby, cotton-picking, unwashed fingers out of the lively arts, lest, bitten by the bug or burned by a gemlike flame, as the metaphor may go, so to speak, lest you become infected with ambition and desire and then struggle yourself gray-headed and black in the face trying to be what you most patently are not. Most patently—

"All right, kids," he yelled. "Let's eat."

They ate canned Spanish rice with milk and bread and butter. He drank scotch. They seemed happy, Susie triumphantly bandaged and Ronnie eagerly pursuing the prospect of a new bicycle.

As a matter of fact, he thought, it might be something of an adventure to grow up in such a highly disorganized family.

"What are you going to do tonight?" he asked them.

"We're going to watch TV."

When they seemed to be sufficiently stuffed, he shooed them into the living room to watch TV and retired to his small study with the scotch. He poured himself a drink and listened awhile to the familiar sound of gunfire and battle cries coming from the living room. Then he picked up a copy of Arnold's poems from the desk and read through "Dover Beach" in a little under thirty seconds.

"You old fraud," he said, tossing the book aside. "You, Matthew Arnold, like all the rest of us. The truth is we all tried to volunteer for the ignorant armies, but they classified us 4-F. And now the only thing to do is to sit on the fence with the rest of the railbirds and jeer when they march by. You, too, T. S. Eliot. And you, too, Renoir, turning fat sweaty female flesh into

LOVE IS A COLD KINGDOM

As soon as i hang up the phone I get up and leave my desk. I tiptoe down the hallway, buoyant on the expensive carpet, hearing all around me, like the soft murmurs of confessionals, the monotonous rise and fall of human voices. Voices speaking to each other in hushed, confidential tones. Voices talking to machines, dictating. Voices talking on telephones. And, as always, the accompaniment, the faint, precise, impeccable rhythm of typewriters. Like the whispering together of a congregation of metallic insects. God knows they never stop. No doubt the last sound on Judgment Day will be a typewriter talking to itself. More likely the clicking of a word processor.

I enter the anteroom, still tiptoeing like somebody trying to sneak in late to a funeral, and come where I can stand behind Rena, our receptionist. She is a glossy thing, from the extravagance of her blond hair to the high shine on her high heels. Her hands, perfectly manicured, resting perfectly still on the desk beside a blank notepad. And she is staring straight ahead (behind her it can be imagined), her fine blank mask—the savage curve and pout of the lips, the eyebrows plucked and arched and sharply etched, eyelids blued with small dark wings, delicate wings, bruise-colored, the eyes wide and empty and deeply blue —a face that promises everything under the sun to you, you with your immortal manuscript in longhand, you with an undeniable talent for yodeling underwater or playing Chopin on the harmonica while standing on your head, you too, among all the thousands she greets with perhaps one great consuming idea in your brain like an inexhaustible pilot light; a face that promises everything you could possibly ask for, except, of course, self-respect.

I lean over close to whisper in her ear, troubled by the slight rising wave of her perfume. That ear is a perfect thing too. Like a glass flower. Or, better, like a seashell delicately whorled. You might think as you bent close to that little ear that instead of talking into it, you ought simply to kiss it. Out of pure joy that there could be such a thing in creation. Then you might think that maybe it ought to be listened to, just like a seashell. That would probably be the most honorable, the passive, appreciative thing to do—to listen. Maybe if you were very, very quiet and attentive, you could hear the long hush and sigh, the whole bone-scrawled history of the sea, songs of the drowned sailors, of the stars and the moon and the tides. In both cases you would be wrong, dead wrong. You might as well kiss the ear of a public statue. And if you kept very still and listened for a long time, as I did once, you would hear nothing. Nothing at all . . . .

"Don't move, doll," I say, jabbing my index finger between her shoulder blades, "I've got you covered."

Rena slowly raises her hands.

"What did I do to deserve this?"

"Nothing personal. Just a routine stickup."

"We don't have any petty cash."

"Who needs petty cash?" I say. "It's your approval I want."

Rena drops her arms and swivels around in the chair to face me with a swift, bright smile.

"You slay me," she says. "Always sneaking around the office and all."

"I got to sneak around, chickie babe. I'm allergic to lions."

(Inside joke: the boss's name is Leo.)

"That's no way to behave," she says. "If you don't want to get swallowed whole, you better break out the whip and the chair."

"I can't help the tiptoes. It's just the way I am."

"How are you?"

"Did I ever tell you I was a frustrated ballet dancer?"

"Ballet dancers!" she says. "Who needs them?"

"Them? What do you mean, them? Who's talking about them? This is supposed to be a personal conversation. I'm trying to find out who needs me."

"Well, lover, if you don't know . . ."

It can go on exactly like this. A form of communication, signals between isolate and separate souls in the manner of the medium. A conversation composed of snippets of bad dialogue from bad television plays. A couple of insects waving bristly antennae. It can go on like this in exactly this pace and tone until a man is ready to puke.

"Look," I say, "I just had a phone call and—"

"Congratulations! Bully for you! Who was it—Selznick? Susskind?"

Why fight the problem?

"Nobody. Just nobody. I mean capital N Nobody. Have you met anybody who's nobody lately?"

"Nobody is nobody," she says. "Everybody is somebody nowadays."

"That's where you're wrong, see? This guy that called me, he really *is* nobody. The last of the big nobodies. He's a national institution like the Vanishing Indian."

"So what am I supposed to do? Put up a tepee and get out the family wampum?"

"Look," I say. "He's a friend, that's all. Just a friend. We used to room together in college."

"I didn't know you were a college man."

"Where did you think I took my degree—the Garment District?"

"You could do worse," she says.

"Look, when he gets here—his name is McCree, Fergus Mc-Cree—when he comes in, don't buzz me or anything. Just send him straight back. I don't want to keep him waiting out here."

"What's so special about him? Why can't he go in quarantine like all the rest?"

"He's already had quarantine. They just let him out of the hospital—the booby hatch."

"So? So some of our best clients come here straight out of the booby hatch."

"You missed the point, the whole point. He's not a client, he's a friend."

(Exit line.)

"Wait," she says. "Just one thing before you go. Name me some place that doesn't have any phones."

"Why?"

"Because Mr. Barton said to tell anybody who calls that he's gone away to some place where they don't have phones."

"Okay. Tibet, Lapland, the North Pole—"

"I'm serious," she says. "How about the Virgin Islands? Do they have phones there?"

"Why don't we go there together and find out?"

I am saved because just then we both hear the buzzing sound of the elevator, and Rena spins around to greet the world with its briefcase and the holes in its shoes.

I tiptoe back to the cubicle from whence I came.

There are scripts and synopses piled high on my desk. In blue folders, in brown folders, in black folders, in notebooks, clipped and stapled and even dog-eared. All the raw wheat and the chaff, ready to be threshed, ground, milled, sifted, refined, and at last presented, all in a neat standard package like a loaf of bread (pre-sliced) to the great omnivorous Television Public. Think I don't like my work? Think I don't love my job?

I stand up again and walk over to the window. A superb view of nothing. A nice view of nothing special but the dull serpentine shine of one-way traffic. If there is anything in the world more depressing than the sight of a long line of one-way traffic coming from nowhere and going to nowhere, I'd like to know what it is. The sheep and the goats. The just and the unjust. The flowing stream. By I. P. Freely. *(Childhood joke: also the Spot on the Wall by Hu Flung Dung.)* All you have to do is fall in line and play along on your little instrument, whatever it is they gave you to start with, a banjo, a Jew's harp, a kazoo, or maybe a pocket comb with cellophane. Join right in the universal pointless hubbub and just keep tootling away until finally Gabriel raises his radiant trumpet and blows away the whole horrid mess with one fiery breath.

It must be McCree, old Fergus McCree who is responsible for this mood in me. The unspeakable sadness. The waste of it all. And, maybe, the shame. He, of course, would be the first one to laugh at my extravagant self-pity.

There is nothing, they say, like hard labor to ease the restive soul. So I sit down once again at my desk, a battered Ozymandias with a lone and hardly level waste of paper all around me. I go to work. I read:

> SIGNATURE: We see an audience, well-dressed, waiting in anticipation for a concert to begin. Men in tuxedos. Women in evening gowns and furs. The maestro approaches the podium. A scattering of well-bred applause.
> CLOSE-UP: The maestro raises his baton. As he brings it down instead of music we hear a shot. He topples crazily.
> CUT TO CLOSE-UP: A hand at the curtain, holding a smoking pistol.
> FADE OUT to First Commercial and Credits.

"A scattering of well-bred applause, my ass!"

And then I am thinking about Fergus McCree. A way, way back in the dim days beyond recall, a few short years ago, Fergus and I roomed together at Princeton. All four years. From the beginning to the end we shared a room in old Edwards Hall along Poverty Row. A strange combination it had been, a Jew who wanted to be a doctor and a Southerner with a crazy name. "You got any Scotch blood in your family?" I'd say. "Nothing but bourbon," he'd say, "but we have some Scotch cows—Black Angus." A Southerner with a taste for elegance and no money to support it, with the habit of arrogance and neither the physi-

cal equipment nor, really, the natural inclination to carry it off.
Just the habit. With the result that his eyes were always being
blacked and his nose was broken and his teeth were chipped.
Late at night he'd come rolling home from somewhere, singing,
drunk, and bloody, never self-pitying, in fact proud of his new
wounds. As for me, I'd still be up studying and studying subjects for which I had small aptitude and even less interest.

What joined us then was hate, I suppose. We were perfectly
agreed in our mutual hate of *them*, all the ones Fergus called "the
good guys." The clean-shaven, gray-flanneled, healthy-minded,
well-adjusted them. Sometimes we hated each other, too, but
never with the force of passion reserved for the rest of the
world. Somehow or other our friendship endured on that diet.
Looking back on it, though, I know it was a sour marrow bone
and we were a couple of snarling puppy dogs.

So much for all that. A few years have gone. No doctor I. I
work for my cousin Leo, who is in fact a graduate of the Garment District. He moved over to television when that was still
possible and often done, leapt for his life, then clung tenaciously
like an old barnacle in spite of (maybe because of) ignorance,
lack of taste, bad manners, aggressively conspicuous consump-
tion, and all the other well-known characteristics of the arche-
typal kike. He clung to his perch, lived in his niche, and he
learned. And the truth is that he is as good as anybody in the
industry now and could pass for a born Ivy Leaguer if asked to.
But he doesn't like to be asked. Which is why I, the sole Ivy
League blossom on our family tree, was hired in the first place—
"to give the joint a real Madison Avenue tone whenever we need
it."

I'm not complaining. I make a buck. And my little brother is
in medical school now.

Fergus, damn him. He was the boy with all the talent, my idea
of a real poet. Married and divorced. The Army. Sixty days bad
time in the stockade for going AWOL. Back to Real Life. Work
for a publisher. Fired. Work for a magazine. Fired. Teaching at a
boys' prep school. Nervous breakdown. Graduate school. Next a
sojourn in the state booby hatch. Poems? Zero, zip, none—

And now for some reason he is in the city and he has called me to say he is coming to see me.

"Is this what you really do for a living?" Fergus says, coming into my office. "Do you really have to *read* the things?"

"Sssh. The whole place is bugged. Lousy with hidden mikes. Just like working in the Kremlin."

He looks paler and thinner, if that is possible, and still bird- or squirrel-nervous, cocking his head this way and that as if he were listening to or for a sound you couldn't quite hear. He always used to claim he could hear those high dog whistles that you are not supposed to. He is smiling with his still-chipped teeth and he needs a haircut as badly as ever. His eyes, as always, are bright and clear and depthless.

"Sambo," he says, taking my hand, "I can see it agrees with you. You're putting on weight. You know what? You're going to wind up being one of the little round men. One of that whole swarming faceless multitude of wonderful little round New York Jews. I like that kind."

"You got me all wrong," I say. "I'm really one of the lean and pushy kind."

"Don't just stand there," he says. "Say something insulting."

"All right, Fergus, it's your turn. You look like the walking corpse of the Old South. You're hookwormed, pellagra-ridden, corncobbed, and segregated. Even if they did let you out, you look crazy as hell to me."

"Ain't that a shame? Don't that go to show you?" he says. "I thought I looked just like a Texas millionaire."

"Sure, and I'm a dead ringer for Bernard Baruch."

"Sam," he says, "I love you."

He moved to the window and stood there with his back to me, looking down at the traffic.

"Don't pay me no mind," he says. "You go right ahead and reject a script. Do something useful."

I glance at my watch. It is almost four o'clock. I start to tidy up my desk, making a leaning tower of Babel out of the unread scripts.

"Looks like it's going to snow," he says. "I love it when it

snows in this town. I forgot all about it. Isn't that a funny thing
—how you can just forget all about something, something you
really love? It's like the whole city and everybody in it was
falling asleep. The snow comes down all gray and soft like burnt
paper and then everything hushes—"

"Look," I say, "I've just about had it for today. What say we
go somewhere and lean over a drink?"

"You thought I was going to jump."

"What?"

"I said you were afraid I was getting ready to jump out the
window."

"Christ, go ahead and jump if you want to," I say. "Every
man to his own poison. A martini will do me just fine."

"The thing about you is, no matter what, you always say the
right thing."

The place where I take him (and I'll admit there may be a
little malice in this; we do know how to hate) is the current
favorite of the TV crowd. That is to say—if you haven't seen it
or one exactly like it—ostentatiously quiet, heavy with ersatz
elegance, some studio executive's idea of a gracious pub. Red-
jacketed waiters moving as deft and soft-footed as shadows. A
bar with all the very best liquor winking in appropriately subdued light. Two bartenders working behind the bar, one dark
and pretty, a dated Valentino, the other one, Hugo, with white
hair, thin lips, and the hard blank face of a croupier, currently
called "the best bartender in town," a very fast man with a
lemon peel. They were both so starched and white, so solemn
and floating, that they seemed a pair of high priests involved in
some obscure ritual or sacrifice. Soft, tinted, flattering mirrors
in which the fat boys swam like smallmouth bass and their
women, curvy at their tailored sides, as lean and predatory as
sharks or barracuda. All of it, everything, of course, in the fashionable worst of taste.

We sit down at the bar and order double martinis, watching
the white-haired maestro at work. He does have bravado with a
lemon peel. I'll say that for him.

"This way to the Egress," I say, toasting Fergus with the Barnum joke, how he got everybody out of his museum.

"No," Fergus says. "Let me make the toast for today. Okay? Here's the way it is with me and the world. I'm just like a groundhog, a cozy old groundhog safe in the ground. What I really want to do is to come on out. I want to poke up my head, out in the clean bright air, and say, 'Wake up all you stupid sleepyheads. It's spring! It's spring all over the place!' And you know what happens? Every time I stick my head up, all set to deliver my earth-shaking message, it's still the big middle of winter. Back to my hole in the ground."

"So, all right," I say. "Here's to Groundhog's Day."

"Amen. I'll drink to that."

"They ought to make more out of Groundhog's Day," I say. "In a commercial way."

"Like Mother's Day."

"We could be the ones to turn it into big business."

"Yeah, man," Fergus says. "We could sell cards and everything. Make it a kind of a universal symbol. The annual resurrection of Modern Man. I mean, pretty soon we'll all be living underground anyway. The groundhog is a great symbol for modern man, don't you think?"

"Fergus, did I ever tell you my plan to make a million dollars? The idea is to turn out a line of dolls, see? Like the old Shirley Temple dolls. Only these would be up-to-date celebrity dolls. Celebrity Dolls Incorporated. The kind you can stick pins in. Voodoo. A free pack of pins with every doll. There'd be Leonard Bernstein dolls and Johnny Carson dolls and David Susskind dolls—"

"What time do the celebrities start coming in here?"

"It's too early for celebrities," I say. "They only come out at night."

"Like witches and werewolves."

Soon we are talking about the old times, but they are far behind us. He gets to talking about all the crazy people he got to know, the attendants and doctors and patients, in the hospital, but his stories have too much edge. It's hard to be funny all the time about mental hospitals. And I try to tell him something about my job, about Leo the Roaring Lion, about Rena, about our writers, the rich ones and the poor ones, and, too, about my cousin David, who is worried that I lead a sheltered life and is always taking me down to the Garment District for a look at reality. Coffee and danish, quick sweaty deals, and the models you see who look like they stepped out of a Byzantine mosaic and talk like something chalked on a wall. Of course we laugh, we laugh and we drink, but there is a kind of hopeless humor about it all, a flourish and ruffles of weariness like the messages warships used to run up in signal flags to each other. HMS *Imponderable* to HMS *Repugnant:* "Matthew 8:29." *Repugnant* to *Imponderable:* "Jeremiah 13:23."

A couple come into the bar and sit down near us. The girl is dark-haired, thin, and pretty. The bullet-headed man wears glasses and a fixed expression of enormous boredom. The girl immediately turns to follow our conversation. The man sits clutching his drink and staring straight into the mirror.

"Are they celebrities?" Fergus says.

"I don't think so."

"They look like celebrities to me."

"That's the whole point," I say. "All the real celebrities are trying to look like people."

Fergus turns on his barstool to address them.

"Folks," he begins, "since fate has so kindly thrown us together and since none of us are celebrities, what we need is a good joke to begin with. The trouble is I don't know any jokes. I mean I used to know some, but then I forgot them all."

"I know a good joke," the girl says. "There was this old couple, real old, on their honeymoon, see?"

"Excuse me, ma'am," Fergus says. "Excuse me, but I have the floor and I haven't yielded it yet. Allow me to finish and we'll get back to your joke later on. As a matter of fact, mine isn't a joke at all. It happens to be a true story."

"I like true stories," she says, nodding. "Frankly, I prefer them."

"This happens to be the story of my life. You see, in the poor, benighted and unwashed area which I call home—"

"I bet you're from the South," she says.

"How did you guess?"

"Your accent, the funny way you talk."

"Funny?"

"You know what I mean," she says. "Well, go ahead."

"I can't. I'm afraid you have interrupted my train of thought with your acute observation of my provincial background. I've forgotten the story I was about to tell."

"That's rude," she says. "Here you had me all interested to listen to the story of your life."

Fergus smiles and shrugs.

"Excuse me," he says. "I beg your pardon. The truth is I suddenly realized it isn't an amusing story at all. I can assure you, you are not missing a thing."

He tips her a courtly bow and turns back to his drink. The girl grins and winks at me.

"What are your plans now, Fergus?"

"My what?"

"Have you got a job?" I say. "Do you need one?"

"What could I ever do?"

"You used to write poems in school, didn't you?"

"Is that a job nowadays?"

"I'm serious," I say. "You used to do some writing."

"Still do," he says. "Still do. Remind me to send you a bunch of my poems. At first, back in school, nobody but me could understand them. Now I can't either. Old buddy, I tell you I am about to arrive. One of these days I am going to be discovered. I won't forget you. When I'm a celebrity I won't forget my old friends."

"I've got this friend who runs an ad agency," I go on. "He owes me a couple of big favors."

"Do I look like I need a job?"

"I was just thinking—"

"What do I need a job for—money?"

"You could do worse," I say. "You can do various things with money."

"Indeed you can. Money begets money. Money begat money. In the beginning— Do you know what the forbidden fruit really was? You probably are a fundamentalist. You probably think it was an apple. An apple! Let me disabuse you. The real truth is it was nothing else but a little old stack of grubby green dollar bills. Or maybe not so little. A regular stinking compost heap of the stuff!"

"I'm trying to be serious for a minute."

"Don't," he says. "It doesn't become you."

"Look, Fergus, I know this guy will find a place for you. It would be easy for you, a snap. You'd get along fine as long as you didn't take it too seriously."

"I never take anything seriously," he says. "No, what I mean is, I take everything too seriously. Which, as anyone can see, adds up to exactly the same thing. Lack of discrimination. 'Lack of discrimination in love partners.' That's what one of the head-shrinkers said about me."

"What does that mean?" the girl down the bar asks.

Fergus turns again to include her in the discussion. Her boyfriend might as well have been carved in his place. He is still engrossed in the mirror.

"Since you have taken the trouble to ask me," Fergus says to her, "I'll tell you. Nothing. It doesn't mean a thing. It merely implies that in his opinion I have bad taste."

"Taste is always a matter of personal opinion," she says.

"Sam, do you know what my real trouble is?"

"No," I say. "What is your real trouble?"

"It's like this. I go around all the time with my lips puckered up waiting to greet the world. 'I greet thee, World!' That's all I want to say. The trouble is, when the time comes, I never know whether to spit or kiss."

"It isn't hard work," I start again, hopelessly. "I'm sure I can fix it up for you."

"Very good. Splendid."

"Why do you act like that?" I say. "You make people feel so bad. Why do you have to make everybody else feel helpless?"

"I said *splendid*, didn't I? A job is what I need. A job is what I am here for. I looked you up today expressly for the purpose of seeing if you could help me get a job. And if you do, I hereby promise to work hard and very conscientiously and save up a lot of money and go to Sweden."

"Sweden?"

"You've never been married, Sam, have you?"

"Not yet."

"Well, be that as it may, I have. Old buddy, I have been married."

"Marriage," the girl says. "What does that have to do with Sweden?"

"Nothing, ma'am," Fergus says. "It is entirely irrelevant, as anyone can plainly see. The point is that I'm going to Sweden. With all my ill-gotten gains. Quick as I get there, I'm going to buy me a great big high-powered speedboat and a great big high-powered set of binoculars. And then all I'm going to do is cruise up and down, back and forth and up and down, in front of the women's beaches and spend all my time looking at women."

"You don't have to go all the way to Sweden," she says. "You can go to Jones Beach. You can take a subway to Coney."

"You don't understand," he says. "I'm speaking of Swedish women."

"What's so special about Swedish women?"

"Ah!" he says. "You still don't understand, ma'am. I have heard the rumor that in far-off Sweden the ladies swim unadorned, in a state of nature, as God made them. That is to say, buck nekkid. Notice that I did not use the word *nude*. I didn't say naked either. I used the word *nekkid*. That is because I am a true-blue, barefoot, Southern boy. And that is why I'll never be able to pass for a Texas millionaire—too much blue blood. Anyway, as a part of my creed I believe, as is very meet and right so to do, in the ultimate, permanent segregation of saints and sinners on Judgment Day— Where was I?"

"In Sweden, baby, looking at the girls."

By this time the other conversations along the bar and in the room, the rise and fall and tremor of voices have ceased. Everybody seems to be watching us. Fergus is grinning and a light film of sweat shines all over his face.

"Thank you," he says. "And please don't misunderstand me. I hate to be misunderstood. You are probably under the impression that I've got a dirty mind. You are correct, I do have a dirty mind. But at present I am speaking metaphorically. Nekkid we come into this world and nekkid we go out of it. The way I look at it, metaphorically speaking, nekkid is all we are, what we really are. So what I am really trying to do is to be myself, the man I really am, a man without a fig leaf, so to speak. Are you with me?"

"Sure," she says. "As a matter of fact I like all-over sunbathing myself. It's supposed to be good for you."

"No offense."

"You left us in Sweden."

"Thank you, ma'am. Thank you for your close attention," he says. "After Sweden I'm heading straight for Finland. When I get there, what I'm going to do is take *saunas*. A *sauna*—that's a Finnish bath. You sit in a hot room and they whip you with birch switches. They are going to whip the devil out of me. Now, don't laugh, lady. It's supposed to be good for you. Just like your sunbathing. Let me explicate. The whole time I was languishing in the booby hatch—what you would probably prefer to call a mental hospital, like catatonic schizophrenia was the measles or something—The Funhouse of Mirrors is my real name for it. Because no matter where you look you see yourself reflected. Yourself fat, yourself thin; yourself masochistic, yourself sadistic; yourself manic, yourself catatonic; yourself screaming in a strait jacket or yourself senile and having to be fed and changed like a baby. As I was saying, the whole time I was in the Funhouse, I was looking for the cure. The real cure. I tried everything. Nothing seemed to work until I hit on the idea that the Devil is responsible. And he is— Where was I?"

"In Finland taking some kind of a crazy hot bath."

"Thank you again for your undivided attention," he says.

"Well, to make a long story short, as soon as I figured out it was the Devil's fault, the next thing I had to do was to figure out how to get rid of him. Our Lord, when He was around, once drove the Devil out of a madman into a herd of swine. Lacking Our Lord in person, so to speak, I was forced to try the more conventional scientific methods. Pills, electric shock, therapy, and all that jazz wouldn't even budge the Devil. So I sat back and imagined the only cure I could think of—all those pink and blond Nordic furies beating the Devil out of me with birch switches."

"Slavs," the girl says. "The Finns aren't Nordic, they're some kind of Slavs."

Fergus bangs his fist on the bar judicially to interrupt and say something. A few glasses hop, slop over, or overturn. Hugo, the white-haired one, appears instantly before us, deferential and soft-voiced.

"Is everything all right, gentlemen?"

"We're going to get something to eat, Hugo," I say. "We were just leaving."

"No, by God!" Fergus says to him. "Everything is not all right. Everything is all wrong."

Then he lowers his voice to a stage whisper again, ignoring a room full of raised eyebrows and the grinning pretty girl at the bar.

"Believe me," he says. "The world is going to the dogs. We're living in the last book of the Bible. It's the time of the hyena and the jackal. Wild pigs are going to pick our bones. They are killing each other and making each other suffer. The little children are suffering too, all over the world—"

"Take it easy, man," I say.

He looks at me briefly as if he is trying to recognize me, then smiles.

"It's all right, Sambo," he says. "I'm leaving. I'll admit the real reason I called you today was about a job. But I changed my mind. All I want to do now is ask you one question."

He pauses and waits for me.

"Okay, ask."

"Sam, my buddy, my old, old Jewbuddy, who is going to whip the Devil out of you?"

He gestures grandly and slips off the barstool, sits down hard on the floor, but bounces up again to his feet, straightens, hikes back his thin shoulders. He waves a benediction to all and starts for the door. After he gets his overcoat from the hatcheck girl, he returns.

"You people are probably under the impression that I am plastered," he says. "Let me assure you, even though I have been drinking martinis with this man, I am not drunk. My trouble is much simpler. My trouble is simply that I am crazy."

That produces quite a laugh, but when he turns to look at me there are tears in his eyes.

"Sambo," he says. "I love you like a brother. But it's snowing outside and I have to be alone."

"Give me a call, huh?"

"Sure, I'll do that."

"Who was that?" the girl asks me after he is gone for good.

"Nobody," I say. "Nobody you would know of."

"A writer?"

"In a way. Sort of."

"I knew it," she says. "I can spot one every time. They're all a bunch of creeps."

"John Irving was in here the other day," Hugo says confidentially.

"Is that so?" I say. "Which way to the Egress? I mean the phone booth?"

"In back."

Once inside the phone booth I start to have my troubles. Everything starts to go wrong. First I manage to drop a whole fistful of change on the floor. I know if I bend over to pick it up, I will never make it. I will just curl up on the floor and go to sleep. Finally I find a coin in my watch pocket, put it in the phone, and am able to dial the right number.

"Hello?" Rena says in my ear.

"Dollbabe, I want you to come live with me and be my love."

"Who is this?"

"Little Sir Tiptoe."

"Oh, it's you," she says. "You slay me."

"Come to me, doll. I need you."

"I'd just love to. But the thing is I already got a date."

"Break it."

"Don't be silly," she says. "Where are you?"

"In a phone booth."

"Where?"

"All right," I say. "So the phone booth happens to be located in a bar. So what?"

"Are you drunk?"

"Possible. Entirely possible. I mean a thing like that is a question of definition. Relative thing. Yes, as a matter of fact, I am a little bombed. I've been drinking with Nobody ever since I left the office."

"I like Nobody," she says. "He's kind of cute. Nervous, but cute."

"Never mind about Nobody. You're kind of cute too. I'd rather drink with you."

"Some other time, huh?" she says. "I'm right in the big middle of taking a bath."

"Take a bath with me."

"You're horrible."

"I promise it will be decent," I say. "I'll wear my fig leaf."

"That's fine for you," she says. "But what am I supposed to do?"

"You got a problem there. Tell you what. You can wear stars. Three gold stars. You come as the Gold Star Girl of the Year."

"What kind of girl do you think I am?"

"You really want to know?"

"I'm dying with curiosity."

"You're a goose girl, Rena," I say. "What I mean is in olden days you probably would have been a goose girl. Nowadays, in modern times, you are a glass girl. A glass goose girl and I would like to goose you—"

"You're a perfect riot," she says. "But I've got to hang up, I'm dripping all over the floor."

"Don't do that. You can't do that. This call is costing me good money. Give me a chance. Let me tell you all about money. Love is a cold kingdom and money is the key."

"That doesn't make sense. What is that bit from?"

"From nothing. It's a poem, a one-line poem. I just this minute made it up."

"Well, thanks a whole lot for calling, Longfellow—"

"Wait! Don't hang up on me! Just one question. Do you have time to answer one vital question?"

"That depends," she says.

"On what?"

"All right," she says. "Go ahead and ask your question."

"Tell the truth now. Be honest with me."

"Ask the question."

"Tell me the honest truth, Rena, has anybody ever tried to beat the Devil out of you?"

She hangs up on me. I look at all those coins on the floor and decide to leave them there. I am feeling a little sick, but I go back to the bar and have Hugo fix me another cup of cold poison.

"Something's the matter with your phone, Hugo. It doesn't work right."

"Yeah?"

"No matter what I say—and everybody knows I always say the right thing—I keep getting all the wrong answers. Hugo, do you know what the real trouble with the world is? People can't talk to people anymore. They don't know how. And they won't listen either. Not even on the phone. And you know what else? Here comes the best part. Listen, Hugo, the telephone was designed—by somebody like P. T. Barnum or Alexander Graham Bell—anyway *the telephone was designed for the sole purpose of talking and listening.*"

"Can you beat that?"

UNMAPPED COUNTRY

THE CAPTAIN PULLED his car off the road and got out and opened up a map. He spread it out on the hood, smoothing down the creases, and studied it. He was only a few hours away from a city and only a few minutes away from the highway, but the map showed nothing at all. The narrow dirt road he had been driving on dwindled away ahead. He had to make the choice of continuing to follow it or taking what was not much more than a rutted kind of trail that forked off to the left into the woods. He decided that he favored the dirt trail because it had to go somewhere. The road from here on looked like it might come to an end soon.

He folded the map and got back in the car, smiling. It was hard not to be smiling on a day like this, an April day in the Tennessee mountains. The air was fresh and sweet and warm, the sky was bright and clear. The leaves were newly green and he had seen dogwood blooming, wild puffs of white among the trees. With everything suddenly new, renewed, it was hard not to smile, not to feel good. It was hard to think of death. The Captain's impulse was to loosen his necktie and loll back his head and sing to the whole wide world. But he resisted that temptation. He drove along carefully, both hands gripping the wheel, silent and alone.

The Captain braked suddenly and the car skidded to a stop in the ruts. Deep mud ahead. And just beyond the patch of mud a choked mountain stream, water swirling in white mustaches around rocks. More mud on the other side. If he went ahead he would probably be up to the axle in the mud or else drowned out in the stream. He twisted around and backed up slowly until he found a piece of hard ground for the car. Then he got out, locking the car, and walked, glad that he was in uniform with his trousers bloused in his jump boots. Of course the high shine of the boots would get messed up with mud and dirt, but it was better than getting his whole uniform dirty. He skirted the edge of the mud the best he could and then crossed the stream, stepping from rock to rock, finding his way with care. The ruts began again beyond the fresh mud on the other side.

The path wandered close to the stream for a while in a dense cool shade. He could see in clumps, close to the earth, the leaves of wild strawberry plants, promising later on the small, pink fruit, the kind that set the teeth on edge just to taste them, they are so sweet. Then the path left the shade and went uphill, twisted away up a hill and dropped off again into a pie-shaped section of low ground. He was sweating by the time he reached the top and waited a minute to catch his breath. The ground ahead was cleared ground, stony, but cleared for farming. Across it in a shade of trees there was a ramshackle unpainted shack.

He was about halfway across the field, cutting diagonally toward the shack, when he saw the dogs coming at him. Two lean, mangy hounds, pale as twin gusts of smoke, coming swift and low to the ground and barking at him. He stopped still. A man, a tall man in overalls with an ax in his hands, came around from the back of the house and shouted. The dogs held up as if he had yanked them on a leash. He shouted at them again and they slunk back, obedient, to the edge of the porch, still snarling. Then behind the man with the ax the Captain could see children, two girls, barefoot and raggedy and shy, and a boy about twelve or fourteen, who was leaning his weight against a large stick. Looking closely, the Captain saw that the boy was

propped up on a homemade crutch. The three children continued to stare at him until a woman appeared and, seeming to
gather them into the folds of her full, long skirt, shooed them
back out of sight like a mother hen.

The tall man in overalls had not moved. He stood next to the
shack, holding the ax in huge, slack hands. The edge of the blade
caught the light and glinted.

"Hello," the Captain said.

There was no answer. The man might have nodded. There
was what might have been a briefest tip of his head.

"I'm looking for somebody. Wonder if you can help me."

Still no answer. The man seemed to tighten his grip on the ax
handle. He stared at the Captain, suspicious and hostile, but
with a kind of ease and pride too.

It must be his land, the Captain thought. *He must have cleared it
stump by stump, rock by rock with his owns hands—*

"I'm trying to locate a Mr. Cartwright that lives around here
somewhere. Edward T. Cartwright."

"Are you the law?"

"No, sir, I'm not a policeman."

"How come you're wearing that uniform?"

"I'm a soldier," the Captain said. "I'm in the Army."

"What army would that be?"

The Captain would have laughed out loud except for the expression on the tall man's face—still suspicious, still hostile, but
now also simply curious—that stopped even the beginnings of
laughter in the Captain's throat.

"The United States Army," the Captain said.

"Why didn't you say so?" the man said. "Come on over here
where I don't have to yell at you."

He mumbled something at the dogs and together they slid off
the porch like two streams of poured water and crawled under
it. He waited for the Captain to approach.

"I haven't done anything wrong," the man said. "Nothing
against the law as I know of. But a man can't be too careful—"

"No, sir. I understand how it is."

"I don't want anybody to have the idea, especially the government, they can come tramping across my land just any damn time they feel like it, without I give an invitation first."

The tall farmer was a powerfully built man. His wide heavy shoulders were stooped as if under the strain of a yoke of heavy weight and his hands were gnarled and misshapen. His hair was cut short and shot with streaks of gray. The Captain could not have guessed his age.

"I'm sorry to trouble you—" the Captain began.

"You say you're looking for Ed Cartwright?"

"That's right."

"Are you a friend of his?"

"No, I just want to see him about something."

"Do you know him? You know what he looks like?"

"If you can just tell me where I can find—"

"What do you want to see him about?"

The Captain started to speak and then checked himself. Never mind whose business it was. The farmer was making it his, and he might just as well play his part in the ritual interrogation or he would have to go all the way back to the place he had come from with nothing accomplished.

"It's about his son."

"Eddie? The boy's dead."

"I know," the Captain said. "That's what I came to see him about."

"Did you know Eddie in the Army?"

The Captain nodded.

"What was he to you?"

"I was his commanding officer."

"I'm Ed Cartwright," the tall man said. "Let's go around front and sit on the stoop. It ain't no use standing up to talk if you don't have to."

The farmer se. his ax against the wall and together they walked around to the front of the shack and sat down on the low first step. The Captain offered him a cigarette and he accepted it, pinching the end so he could grip it with his lips like a roll-your-own. He struck a kitchen match against the rough board and held a light for the Captain.

"He must not have been such a much of a soldier," Cartwright said, "to get hisself killed so quick."

"It was an accident," the Captain said. "It could have happened to anybody."

"Tell me about it."

"Don't you know? Didn't they give you the details?"

"Surely," Cartwright said. "They notified me and they give me the details. And then they even sent a sergeant with a box and a flag. I just want to hear you tell it, that's all."

A day on the Grenade Range. A cold raw grassless place under a low gray winter sky. The Captain stood on the range tower with the young Range Officer, stamping his feet against the cold. His lunch lay heavy in his stomach and the long afternoon was ahead of him. The Captain was a combat officer by experience and inclination, condemned for the time being to the boredom and frustration of training new recruits. You get them in their civilian clothes, wrinkled and dirty from a bus or train ride, shaggy-headed with their ducktails, sideburns, and pompadours, and so forth. You make them shave their faces and shine their boots. And you have a few weeks during which to try to turn them into something like a soldier. They come and go. You don't even have time to learn how most of the list of names you command corresponds with the faces in front of you before they are gone and you are starting all over again—

Below and at a little distance from the range tower six pits had been dug into the hard clay. Each with a sergeant instructor. Six at a time the men of the Captain's company come double-timing forward from a place to the rear and take places in the pits. The Range Officer calls off commands and instructions with his hoarse bullhorn. And left to right in steady sequence the recruits are to throw two live hand grenades over the top of the sandbagged pits and duck while a slight explosion rocks the startled earth. They are young and new to the hand grenade. Some of them are scared. Their palms sweat—

There is a sudden shout from one of the pits. The instructor is shouting something. The Captain looks and finds the Sergeant is locked in a furious embrace with a soldier, wrestling. The soldier has frozen from fear with the pin pulled and the grenade in his fist. Over the Captain's shoulder the Range Officer is yelling something into the bullhorn, something which is lost in a blur of static. Now the Captain is moving, swinging over the side of the tower and quickly down the ladder and so he does not see the grenade fall free, losing its handle, and roll into the pit. He does not see the recruit standing there still and stiff as a bronze statue or the Sergeant swooping, grabbing for the loose grenade. The Captain drops heavily to the ground and is already running forward hard toward the pits when the blast knocks him flat. Dazed, he staggers to his feet and runs on.

The accident has killed instantly a veteran sergeant and the recruit—Cartwright, Edward T., Jr., Private E-1.

The farmer listened to the story, quietly smoking. When the Captain had finished, he put out his cigarette.

"I told him. Don't anybody say I never told him. I said, son, you were born to be a dirt farmer. They won't be able to make you into no kind of a soldier. They can't make a soldier out of you. You're liable to get yourself killed or something. But that boy, he was nothing if he wasn't stubborn and willful—"

"He was only seventeen," the Captain said.

"Sixteen," Cartwright said. "He wasn't but sixteen. He was a big boy and he lied about his age."

The Captain looked at the man sitting next to him. He looked older than the Captain's father, a handsome, healthy, and successful lawyer who could still shoot the country-club golf course and break ninety. It startled the Captain to think that this man, worn by work and hard times, was probably nearer to his own age.

"Was he any good of a soldier?"

The Captain was tempted to lie. In his own defense as much as anything else. After all, the training cycle had hardly begun when the accident happened. He had known the name, one among many on a variety of lists that passed across his desk and on papers that had to have his signature. There had not been a photograph. He had looked at that name, even written it out carefully on paper, trying to rake his mind for any recollection of the face that went with it. He had looked at the faces of his whole company drawn up in formation trying to see if by *absence* he could recall the missing face. In combat men under his command had been killed, but he had known them. He felt an acute sense of failure. He should have known the boy. At the same time he could not repress a sense of outrage, anger that this guilt had been imposed on him by a stranger, a soldier he could not have known even by sight because of the hectic, inevitable confusion of the first weeks of training.

"It's hard to say in such a short time whether a man can make a good soldier or not," the Captain said. "He didn't get in any trouble while I had him. The men in his platoon liked him. He had some friends."

"He was a likable one all right. He always had friends. The only thing that surprises me is he stayed out of trouble. He was never what you would call a good boy. He had a kind of wild, restless streak in his nature. He never learned how to keep still."

"A lot of boys that age are restless."

"What? What's that?"

The farmer stared at him.

"What I mean is it's not such an unusual thing. Most boys that age are pretty much alike."

"I know what I'm talking about," the farmer said. "Don't you just sit here on my front steps and act like you knew more about him than I did. I'm his daddy!"

"I'm sorry. I didn't mean that. I was only—"

"A good boy! Would you call that 'a good boy' to go running off and join the Army and leave me here all alone with the wife and the girls and the other boy to look after? All of it falling on my shoulders. I need that boy bad this spring. I ain't hardly going to be able to raise a decent crop without him. What did he expect me to do?"

"You don't mean it that way."

It was a soft voice, the woman's voice. The Captain turned and saw her standing there on the porch behind him. He stood up.

"I do too!"

The farmer stood up, too, abruptly, and stamped away out into the bare, grassless yard, keeping his back turned to them.

"He was a damn fool to do like that," the farmer said. "To run off in the Army and get hisself killed."

"He don't mean a word of it," the woman said. "He is just hurting bad and he's got to try and hide it."

The farmer whirled and came back toward the porch, fury in his face.

"What I want to know is what's *he* doing here?" he said. "Can't they just leave us alone now? They done sent telegrams and letters and a sergeant with the box and the flag. Seems like it would all be over and done with. What's he trying to do, coming way out here all dressed up in his soldier suit?"

"He's doing the right thing, the Christian thing," the woman said. "It's what you would have to do if it was his boy that got killed."

"The whole thing is," the farmer said softly, "it was my boy that got killed."

Then he was gone. He passed by them and around the side of the shack and out of sight. In a moment they heard the ringing sound of the ax.

"Chopping wood," the woman said. "He'll chop awhile and work up a sweat and then be all right."

"I'm sorry to have upset you people," the Captain said.

"We haven't got any reason to be mad with anybody," she said. "Not even with the boy. He done what he thought was the right thing to do. I thank you for coming to see us."

She offered the Captain her hand.

"I wish we could ask you to stay for supper or something," she said. "Maybe some other time."

"Thanks just the same," the Captain said. "I have to try and get back to the post this evening."

"That's a pretty long trip."

"I've got my car down there on the other side of the stream," the Captain said.

"How about some coffee? I could heat up a pot of coffee."

"No thanks," he said. "I'll tell you what, though. I'd be grateful for some water."

"Help yourself," she said and pointed to the well.

She turned back into the shack. The Captain walked to the well and hauled up a bucket of water. He took a tin dipper off a nail and filled it. The water was sweet and cool and his mouth felt very dry. His tongue felt heavy. He stopped drinking. The sound of the ax ringing against wood had stopped. He looked up and saw the farmer coming toward him. He stiffened.

"She was right," the farmer said. "You done the right thing to come and see us. There's nothing to say, but you done right to come here and meet me face to face like a man."

The two men shook hands. When the Captain had finished drinking, the farmer took the dipper. He sloshed water around in it, splashed it on the ground, then dipped himself a drink. He sipped it and spoke to the Captain over the shiny edge of the dipper.

"That boy," he said. "I sure am going to miss him. He had a wild streak all right. No use pretending he didn't. But, you know, he had a light heart and a light heart is a rare thing in this world. He could make you laugh with his tricks and jokes and all. We used to go hunting sometimes. He used to be good with a gun. I don't see why he was afraid of a hand grenade. I don't see why—"

Quite suddenly the dipper slipped out of his fingers and fell with a splash. He seemed to sag on his feet. The Captain put his arm around his shoulders and held him while the farmer leaned against him and wept.

It was over in a moment. He blew his nose and drank some more water. He hung the dipper back in its place.

"I'm sorry to bust out like that," the farmer said. "It's a shame to have to watch a grown man crying."

"It's not the first time I've seen a man cry," the Captain said.

"Pray God you don't end up crying yourself."

The Captain walked back to his car. He went along slowly, taking his time. He loosened his necktie and opened his collar button. Near the stream he heard a rustling. It was the other

boy. He grinned at the Captain. He was a very thin boy with a
pale, pinched face, a face that was used to some dull steady pain.
But except for that sense of pain, like a shadow cast on the face,
and except for the game leg and the crutch, he was the image of
his father.

"What's that thing?" the boy said, pointing to the shiny little
parachute badge the Captain wore above his breast pocket.

"It's my jump badge," the Captain said. "It means I'm a paratrooper."

"So was my brother. He was a paratrooper in the Army."

"Is that right?"

"That's how come he joined up. So he could jump out of an
airplane. He told me so."

Jesus! the Captain thought. *If he froze with a live grenade in his
hand what the hell would have happened with him all hooked up and
standing at the door of a moving airplane?*

"A lot of them join up so they can be paratroopers," the Captain said.

"Did you know my brother?"

"A little."

"I wonder how come they didn't send his badge home along
with the rest of the stuff? I went through all the stuff they sent
us and there wasn't no badge like that."

"Maybe they made a mistake," the Captain lied. "Sometimes
they make a mistake like that."

"Maybe they lost it."

"Here, you take this one." The Captain unpinned the parachute badge and handed it to him.

"Can I keep it?"

"Sure," he said. "It's yours."

He stood there for a moment watching the boy hobble away
on the path, using his crutch well, moving along quick, holding
the small badge carefully in the cupped palm of his free hand,
looking at it. Then he turned back to the path.

For some reason he remembered something that had happened to him quite a while ago. He was a young recruit himself
then. The training company was about to move out on their first

twenty-mile hike with full field equipment. He remembered standing in ranks with the gray dawn just beginning to come over the camp, hearing a radio playing in the lighted mess hall, thinking about the sun that would be coming on soon. It was going to be a scorcher. The steel helmet felt heavy on his head and the pack was already cutting into his shoulders. His feet in his boots felt small and detached. Small-boned and separate from the rest of him. Then on the Orderly Room steps the First Sergeant was standing in front of them looking them over. Hard, tough, with the face of a clean-shaven prophet. An articulate man who pronounced the message the Captain now lived by.

"All right," the Sergeant said. "When I tell you to, you going to pick up your feet and move out smartly. I don't want to catch nobody worrying about when we going to get there. You ain't got nothing to worry about. All you got to do is keep picking 'em up and putting 'em down."

MORE GEESE THAN SWANS

THE FIRST PERSON to come and see us when we got back was Sam Browne. Good old Sam. It would be Sam, wouldn't it? Weeks later, after we were all unpacked with everything safely back on shelves, in closets and cupboards and drawers, the whole place looking as if we had never really been away at all, the others would begin to call and come over to welcome us back to the college. Not Sam. He arrived the very first night as soon as he saw the car in the driveway and the lights on in the house. Our trunks were still unpacked, trunks and suitcases with the usual labels of sabbatical travel in Europe were clogging the hall. White dust covers still shrouded most of the furniture. We were exhausted and the children, equally exhausted, were sound asleep upstairs in their room.

Sam would have waited until we got them safely to bed, partly out of his instinctive discretion, partly because he didn't like children, little ones, at all.

"Before it has reached a stage of decent articulation," he used to say, "the human animal is a bore."

He rang the chiming bell in front and stood there grinning, holding a bottle of good bourbon behind his back in the classic pose of the bashful lover with candy or a bouquet of violets.

"This house is not safe for habitation, not blessed," he said.

"You can't sleep here until there have been proper libations and rites. I have here the essence of the corn."

So we cleared away a few dustcovers in the living room, threw them in a corner like a pile of forlorn ghosts, and drank his bourbon out of our thermos cups and talked. Sam, ever tactful, asked us a few of the usual questions, then with his customary agility vaulted the hurdle of our complete ignorance and plunged into the subject of all we had missed at the college while we were away.

Sam can be a fine storyteller, given a certain kind of material. He can invest an anecdote, even a shabby one, with the magic cloak of myth or cosmic import. He can turn snatches of a brief conversation into a conspiracy. Seeing these things through his eyes can be a real pleasure. He's a kind of magician, able to turn the simple grays of reality into black and white or, at his best, into fabulous technicolor. He always reminds me of Dorothy in *The Wizard of Oz* (the movie with Judy Garland) when she has just been suddenly deposited by the tornado into a beautiful, improbable, exotic, colorful scene.

My wife doesn't like Sam much. Oh, she enjoys him and is often amused by him, but she just doesn't like him. Sam is a big man, ruddy from good food and drink and indestructible health, a very handsome man who has gone to seed and doesn't mind it much. He is a bachelor and always will be, I guess, one of that special breed of bachelors who seem to thrive in the taut, little, insular world of the Academy, free to drink with fraternity boys or the undergraduate poets or be a fourth for bridge or a last-minute escort for somebody who wants to go to the Spring Faculty Dance. He is a good teacher. But even though this is his environment, the one soil in our society where he can bloom and does, he manages to remain somehow a kind of spectator, a detached and mildly amused observer of the scene. It would be vulgar, the original sin in his vocabulary, to permit himself to become involved in anything that goes on. Maybe that is what my wife doesn't like about him, finally, his peculiar transcendence over us all.

He told us who had married and who had died. He described

in eloquent, mock-heroic terms the funeral of an old emeritus professor at which some very funny things involving two drunk gravediggers happened. He spoke of the birth of children, of failures and promotions, and of what happened when he had to introduce a well-known young poet who had come to give a reading of his poems.

"The thing is," Sam said, "the thing none of us knew is this— he stutters. He has a terrible stutter and he has to drink if he is going to talk at all. This particular evening he had indulged in a little too much fortification. When I introduced him, he rose, took one step, and fell flat on his face. All the students cheered and whistled—they loved it. When he began to read his poems the stutter was worse than ever. Then he fell down several times. What a catastrophe! Dean Marlowe nearly had an apoplectic stroke."

Sam chattered along aimlessly, and soon we were stifling yawns, not so much out of boredom as pure fatigue. Sam would notice something like that. A very well-controlled, well-squelched yawn would not escape him.

"You people, you weary world travelers, will have to trot off to bed," he said. "But I can't send you off to bed with my blessings on your very first night home without at least mentioning the Story of the Year. You'll be hearing about it again and again, to the point of tedium. But I do think you should have the Browne Version first.

"The truth is," he lowered his voice to a mock stage whisper, "we have had a scandal while you were away. A real scandal."

"Not a real scandal," Mary said. "Tell us about it."

"Here of all places! As a matter of fact it is the place that makes all the difference. Any other place, in any other *milieu*, it would have been just another little tale of woe and folly. Because it happened here, it is almost raised to the level of high comedy."

"Don't tease us," I said.

"Doubtless you will remember," he began, "that when you left there was some loose talk about founding a College Madrigal Group. Well, we did it. Hardeman got it going in September.

You can consider yourselves lucky you didn't have to hear us. Naturally I joined to play the recorder. I really couldn't miss out on a thing like that. Something amusing was bound to happen sooner or later. Well, the truth is, it was always amusing, rehearsing or performing. Something always went wonderfully wrong. There were fine, fierce clashes of temperament, sudden attacks of hoarseness, plenty of tears and feuds. I couldn't have asked for a better way to wile away a few evenings. It was every bit as good as I had hoped. I tootled away on my recorder, Jane Strong plucked on a lute, and everyone la-la-laed and hey-nony-nonnied. But, of course, I hadn't anticipated that anything real could happen in our little nest of songbirds.

"No doubt you still remember dear Susan Langdon?"

"Bunny?" my wife said.

"Alas, aptly named."

"*Bunny,* involved in a *scandal?*"

"Please, I'm getting there."

"Let Sam tell the story."

"Susan Langdon, called Bunny, model wife of the chairman of our History Department, Bunny of the long dark hair, the lovely cameo complexion, full-bosomed, voluptuous Bunny like a great, soft, spoiled cat."

Mary tossed her head with laughter.

"Who but Sam would ever describe Bunny that way?"

"We have to try to see things through her eyes, as she saw herself. You'll have to admit that she has always been amply proportioned and that she tended—I use the past tense advisedly —to favor exotic costumes, peasant blouses and full skirts, especially the Latin look."

"She dressed a little young," Mary said.

"She was young, young at heart anyway. We all saw her as you did, the faithful, respectable housewife, mother of three children, pourer of weak tea at the President's reception. Her only folly was the way she dressed, as if she were just about to sing *Carmen* or something. None of us could see that truth for a woman is exactly in her costume. Truth is not nudity, but its disguises. Truth for a woman is all in appearances.

"So the seven veils are the most important thing about Salome. So a woman is or becomes the perfume she selects to wear. Grant me that much as a working hypothesis anyway. I was as blindly naïve as anyone else. I saw Bunny in the conventional way. I never dreamed that any passion or discontent smoldered in that—I've already acknowledged it—significant bosom. Besides, she had such a sweet singing voice.

"It all began, as they say, when we decided to ask some townspeople to join us. They had displayed some interest and we were short of voices, recorders, and funds. Believe me, the latter was the deciding factor. For the high, stated purpose of improved town and gown relations, and with the idea of a new source of dues in mind, we asked some people from town if they would like to join us. The response was gratifying. Among these was Ernest Cooley, Cooley of all unromantic names, the lawyer."

"Cooley! But he's so young."

"Not so young, dear, but younger than Bunny."

"Come on, Sam, you can't mean it."

"Let him tell the story, Mary."

"Cooley, a short, thin, handsome man, nervous, one with great ambition and energy. Successful already, president of the Jaycees, director of the United Fund Drive, member of the Planning Board, active in the PTA. A veritable Roman candle out there in Real Life. He, too, married. In this case to a delicious little blonde with the improbable name of—I swear it's true—Queenie. A lovely unlikely triangle—Bunny, Queenie, Ernie—three babes in the woods.

"It did not begin as a triangle, and, simple, trusting soul that I am, I never dreamed it would be one. I introduced them the first time Ernie came to rehearse with us. He had been doing some legal work for me, some of the endless shoring up I have to do because of the ghastly state of Mother's will. Poor Mother! And it isn't as if there were any money involved. Over the years with all the lawyers and such I imagine I have lost money, but then, I've never been good at figures. I trust in the Lord and the lawyers. But I digress.

"I introduced Ernest Cooley to Bunny and I remember quite

distinctly that no signals flashed between them. I remember being amused. They looked so incongruous, she in her heels was much taller than Ernie, taller and rounder. I remember thinking as they smiled and shook hands and said the usual things I had never noticed how thin and wan Cooley was. Alongside that lovely ripe peach he looked like a lime twig.

"Nothing at all happened. He sang and she sang. I tootled. We all had a drink afterwards and drifted off our separate ways in the night. A few days later I happened to be in his office and he asked me casually about a few of the people, including Bunny. His tone was neutral, polite rather than interested. The name, Bunny, was just one of the others. Bunny did the same thing. I was having coffee with her in the Faculty Lounge while she was waiting for Everett to come along from a committee meeting. They were going to a cocktail party or something and I recall thinking how pretty she looked, all dressed up with everything just so. I don't think I had ever seen her look so pretty. She asked me all about the people from town. I was the link, you see, the liaison man. Ernie was mentioned, but not seriously.

"You can imagine how foolish I feel now. All that an aging bachelor has to call pride is his ability to make fine distinctions. I prided myself that I could tell the meaning behind the gesture. I was, of course, quite wrong. So let us say none of it was in vain. Like Job I have had the last stitch of my pride taken away, but I've learned that it isn't as bad as all that to know one's own inabilities. I was proud then and thought nothing of it.

"I was a long time learning. When the First Incident occurred I missed the point completely. We had been giving a little concert in the Parish House at St. Luke's. During the concert a few things, just the ordinary amateurish things, went wrong. They always did. After the concert Ernie Cooley was in a state, a rage. He was especially furious with Bunny, who, it seems had done something or other that made him feel foolish. He berated her unmercifully. Poor Bunny burst into tears. She couldn't understand what he was talking about at all. The curious thing, though, was the way that she stood there and let him carry on. He stormed out of the Parish House and I had to comfort her.

Later on he came back, apologized to everybody, and took Bunny and me out to a little bar in the country for a nightcap to patch everything.

"Bunny called me the next day, puzzled, and I explained to her that Ernie was a bundle of nerves and temperament and that she shouldn't take him seriously. She said she understood that, but that after all was said and done his bad manners were inexcusable.

"Things went merrily along. Ernie Cooley grew a little beard. I thought it was rather odd at the time, but probably some kind of defense mechanism against us. Ernie likes to be a chief in any group and it was a little awkward for the townies, mixing with the inbred academics. People started to tease him about his beard and how it was growing. He usually laughed and matched quips and insults with them. Bunny only teased him about his beard once. Quite by chance and in the spirit of things, she made some comment. To everybody's surprise it hurt his feelings. He turned on her.

" 'What's wrong with my beard? If there is anything wrong with it, if you don't like it, just say so. Don't needle me about it.'

"Bunny had no recourse but to turn away from him. I saw a little film of tears in her eyes and might have wondered about that, but I assumed it was merely her hurt feelings and the memory of the other time that bothered her. Over and done with as soon as it had begun. Afterwards everybody seemed very amiable and happy.

"Then came the picnic. Spring, time of the cuckoo and the turtledove. April, the cruelest month. The Madrigal Group had become very chummy by this time, *folksy* would be the word. We had even taken to wearing pseudo-Elizabethan costume for our concerts. (You can imagine how that was. I'm not at my best in Elizabethan costume.) We decided we had to have a picnic. Not the hard-boiled eggs and sandwiches kind of thing by any means. I held out and won my point for a really nineteenth-century kind of show, good food, good wine, under the trees, and not at an ordinary place. We finally picked Indian Springs. Maybe you know it? The forlorn ghost of a watering place about thirty miles from here. Very *Gothic*, a spring bubbling out of a rocky grotto, the ruins of an old hotel blending into the woods, shreds of an elegant bathhouse and pavilions. No doubt you people were basking in the sun at Positano or some such, but for us stay-at-homes Indian Springs seemed like a real adventure.

"I had to take Bunny because Everett couldn't or wouldn't go along. Everett isn't what you would call the picnic kind of man. He has always been possessed by the demon of irony. He has just enough of it to make him uneasy. So I had to take Bunny. Everybody had a fine raucous old time. Or so it seemed to me. We swam and cavorted like fillies, drank and ate well. We even ended up singing a little and came home weary and happy. At least the rest of them did. I had noticed something peculiar about Bunny when we first arrived. She wandered off in the woods to change into her bathing suit. When she came back to the Springs—really not to be believed in a dark, form-fitting, one-piece bathing suit, you would have believed in her as the voluptuous *femme fatale* then, Mary. I had never even imagined Bunny in a bathing suit before and I didn't know whether to be shocked or charmed out of my mind. A little of both would be a decent reaction. Anyway, when she came back, she looked flushed and upset, and a kind of pouty purse to her lips, eyes flashing anger, spots of color on her cheeks.

" 'What's wrong, darling?' " I said.

"She sighed, she started to say something, then put her hands firmly on her hips and looked out at the swimmers in the Spring.

" 'I am going to have a good time,' she said. 'I am not going to let anything spoil it.'

" 'What on earth could spoil it?' I asked.

"But already she had dived into the Springs, gracefully, with scarcely a ripple to prove where she had vanished. When she bobbed up again she was chilled and smiling. She laughed and seemed to be having a good time, and I thought nothing more of it.

"When we left it was much the same thing. She came back to the car as grim as Medusa. I tried to cheer her up with chatter and nonsense, but she was having none of that. Finally I even tried the radio, but she switched it off. I stopped by the side of the road.

"'What's wrong?'

"'Oh, just drive me home, Sam. Don't stop and interrogate me. Just take me home.'

"I was at once persistent and solicitous until she told me what had happened to her. This time she was completely dry-eyed. No tears, just cold anger.

"'That man,' she began. 'That horrible little man! When I went to change into my bathing suit, when we had just arrived, I was in the midst of undressing when I heard a little rustle in the bushes nearby. I looked up and there he was, peering out from among the leaves. With his beard and his thin face and his little, beady eyes he looked just like an animal, some kind of a rodent. The beard is what made me think of an animal, I suppose.'

"'Ernest? Ernie Cooley?'

"'I didn't know what to do,' she said. 'What do you do without making a scene? I decided that if I stared back at him, looked right into his eyes, he would be ashamed and go away. Well, he didn't. We stood there and stared at each other awhile. Then I ignored him and put on my suit. What else could I do?'

"'Nothing,' I said, 'under the circumstances.'

"'It was bad enough,' she said, 'but anyway I thought that would be the end of it. I imagined that he had "drunk his fill," so to speak.'

"'Imagine that!' I said. 'Ernie Cooley, a *voyeur*. A window-peeper!'

"'Don't make jokes about it,' she said. 'It isn't funny. To tell you the truth I was having such a good time at the picnic that I nearly forgot about it. Until just now, when we started home. I went back to where I had put my clothes, and do you know what he had done? He had tied everything in knots. Just like a nasty little boy. I was trying to undo the knots, so mad my fingers were trembling, when I heard that noise in the leaves again. And there he was in the same spot, beard and all, staring at me and *grinning* this time.'

" 'What did you do?'

" 'What could I do? I wasn't going to call for help or give him the pleasure of seeing me burst into tears again. I simply ignored him. And he simply stayed there. For all I know he may be there yet.'

" 'I doubt it,' I said.

" 'What should I do, Sam?'

" 'I don't know,' I said. 'I suppose you can tell Everett about it.'

" 'Oh, I *couldn't* do that. Everett would never understand.'

" 'No, I don't suppose he would,' I said.

"We drove on. I offered to speak to Ernie myself, to arrange some kind of an apology. Bunny wasn't interested. She had decided to let well enough alone, to forget the whole thing. Now that she had told me about it she felt better.

"I didn't know whether to laugh or cry. The whole thing was so absurd, hilarious, and sad. I didn't even know whether to believe her. It seemed entirely possible that she had made it all up. People do things like that, you know.

"Evidently she forgot about it. Relations were all very charming at the next rehearsal. I seemed to be the only one who remembered it, and, as the world knows, I have a dirty mind.

"Nothing new happened until the evening we were giving a little concert for the Ladies' Auxiliary of the Hospital, a charity affair, almost at the end of the term. We were all very grand in our costumes. We had just finished 'The Swan,' by Gibbon. That I must admit, is my great favorite. It has my favorite lines in English poetry.

'Leaning her breast against the reedy shore,
    Thus sung her first and last, and sung no more:
"Farewell, all joys; oh death, come close mine eyes.
    More geese than swans now live, more fools than wise." '

"Anyway we had just ended on that happy note when Ernie stood up and walked over and whispered something in Bunny's

ear. Heaven knows what he said. He took just about enough
time to say 'Let's go.' Then he stepped off the stage and walked
up the aisle and out of the room. She followed him. It was rather
unusual, but we went along anyway and managed to finish the
concert.

"It was the next morning before I found out what had really
happened. Very early—it was still pitch dark—the phone started
ringing and it was Bunny. She sounded calm and composed,
guarded even, as though maybe she had carefully rehearsed
what she was going to say. She asked me to please come at once
to the Timberline Motel. I asked her how soon she would like
me to be there and she said, still perfectly calm, that if I started
right now and hurried, that would be fine. I shaved and dressed
and had a cup of instant coffee—I detest instant coffee—and
drove out to the motel as fast as I could. I found them fully clad
and quite serious in Cabin Number Seven. Ernie made a wan
remark about lucky numbers, then lapsed into silence and let
Bunny do the talking. She explained that they had asked me to
come there because I, of all the people she knew, was Most
Likely to Understand. In a very matter-of-fact way, as if she
were summarizing the plot of a movie she had seen or a story
she had read, she told me that she and Ernie were very much in
love. She said that they were both unhappily married, that each
of them had given a great deal of thought to the matter and that,
weighing all, they had reached the conclusion that nothing was
more important than the chance for happiness they felt they had
together. They were planning to leave in a very few minutes to
have a kind of honeymoon together in a place Ernie knew of. Of
course, they planned to be married as soon as they were legally
divorced. I must not try to dissuade them or even discuss the
matter. It was settled.

"I ventured the impertinent question as to what, precisely,
they expected of me? Did they need my blessing or benediction
or what?

" 'No,' Bunny said with a sad, reproachful smile. 'Dear Sam,
we just want to ask you to do a favor.'

"She gave me two envelopes, one for Everett and one for

Queenie and asked me to deliver them. I protested that perhaps my position as a messenger might be misunderstood, that either Everett or Queenie or both might with all good reason be entitled to take a dim view of my part in the business, perhaps looking on me as the Pandarus of the little drama. Bunny assured me that all was thoroughly and tactfully explained in the letters. They had spent most of the night composing them. She said I had nothing to do except to deliver the letters. I thought it over a moment and agreed.

"They rose, put on their coats, and we all walked to the parking area.

" 'We have been thinking about this for months,' she said. 'Last night we both got the nerve to do it at exactly the same moment.'

"She seemed aware that I had noticed, with a curious glance anyway, that they had no luggage with them, just the clothes they had on and their costumes—which, by the way, they wanted me to return to the Madrigal Group. Bunny laughed.

" 'Not really planned, though,' she said. 'I don't even have a toothbrush with me.'

"I kissed her and waved good-bye as they drove away to live in sin. Then I went back to town and had a decent breakfast before I started the rounds with my epistles of doom.

"The funny thing was the way the two stay-at-homes took it. I was surprised; exactly the opposite of what I expected. Queenie, after serving me a cup of very good coffee while she read through the letter a couple of times, burst into gales of laughter.

" 'That nutty little bastard!' she said. 'Isn't that a damn fool thing to do? It takes the cake. Just like Ernie! Well,' still apparently highly amused, 'he is going to get the surprise of his life this time. When he comes back with big sad eyes, dragging his tail behind him, he is going to find the front door shut and locked.'

"Everett, on the other hand, fell apart like a card house. A professional ironist, an educated man, a wise man of the world in the best sense, he had always seemed to me perfectly rational, skeptical, fully aware that this is a world of fools and knaves.

Fully aware that this is a very bad old world and not likely to be a better one. Well, Everett read the letter and fell apart completely. Tears and a dreadful scene. Rage and self-pity, guilt and remorse, all in a wink like a chameleon moving swiftly from one color to another. He went into a state of shock. I called the college and arranged for someone to take over his classes and duties. I sat him down with a bottle of scotch while I bundled the astonished children off to school. By the time I got back he was thoroughly drunk and maudlin. He wanted to confess all, sadly, his inadequacies, their whole history of shabby troubles, his perfect contempt for her and his overwhelming need for her. And so on. It was obvious that the thing that bothered him the most was not her adultery, but the final and public way she had gone about committing it. It was a terrible blow to his pride for other people to know about it. He could never forgive her for the shame it was bound to cause him. He carried on in the high style like a cuckold in a Restoration play.

"It was all very sordid and depressing. I bled quarts of pure sympathy and finally he was drunk enough to be led up to bed. I left him snoring peacefully and went about my own affairs."

Sam paused to sip his drink.

"What happened?" I asked.

He shrugged.

"Not what you may imagine. Honestly, the rest is anticlimax. They came back inside of two weeks. Everything possible, it seems, went wrong. Ernie had taken her away to a rustic cabin by a lake in Canada. It should have been idyllic. But it rained the whole time and they were damp and cold and miserable. At night swarms of mosquitoes ate them alive. They both developed bad colds. Something happened to Ernie's car and they were at least ten miles from the nearest phone. In a very short time they were sad and homesick and quarreling bitterly.

"Ernie went straight home, bearded the lioness, and succeeded. She took him back. I saw them the other night at a little party and they seemed fine. It was all as if it had never happened, or, rather, as if something very amusing had happened to both of them. Happy as a couple of cherrystone clams.

"Of the others, I am sad to report no such news. When Bunny returned from her adventure, she stayed in a hotel a few days, wringing her hands and pacing her cage in the grand manner. I had to arrange a private meeting for them behind the Observatory. It was terribly theatrical, with the Observatory on one side of them and the old cemetery on the other and old Sam right in the middle of everything. They embraced and wept and thanked me profoundly. Everett led her off to the car and took her home.

"Now everything seems so different. Poor Bunny has aged about twenty years. Of course she dresses differently now, but she really seems to be an old woman all of a sudden, gray and sad. Everett is not much better. He is like a tired old man, palsied, one foot in the grave. They are in an absurdly perfect equilibrium, as if somehow age, decay, humiliation, and frustration were what they had to offer each other and what each one wanted most.

"It's really a little as if those breathless lovers who fled away from the cold castle in *The Eve of St. Agnes* had come dragging back later on, footsore and heartsore, disspirited and disillusioned, worn and weary. All the romance has gone out of the world. Even the Madrigal Group is *kaput*. There will be no hey-nonny-nonny next term."

"You bastard," Mary said. "What do you mean coming here to tell us that?"

Sam looked astonished, mumbled a few words, but Mary was already halfway out of the living room, headed for the stairs.

"On my first night home I am sick to death of it," she said. "Is that what you wanted?"

The question was rhetorical. She stamped up the stairs and slammed the door to our room. Sam looked at me, puzzled.

"I am sorry," I said. "She's tired. We've had a hard day and I guess she had a little too much to drink."

"No," Sam said. "I'm sorry. In a way it was very tactless of me. I had no idea Bunny and Mary were close friends."

"They're not. They hardly know each other," I said. "Forget it."

I poured Sam another drink and we toasted the year behind and the year ahead.

"That's a story you ought to write," I said.

Sam is our writer on campus; not really, but the nearest thing to a writer on the faculty. He has had a couple of stories published in places like *The Georgia Review* and he does a good deal of criticism and reviewing of current fiction. He has been working on a big novel for quite a while, and the people who have read parts of it say that it is very good, though not likely to sell many copies. One of these days he will finish it.

"No," he said. "Adultery is a fine subject for an anecdote, but not for art. It's too middle-class, the great sin and sport of the middle class. The middle class bores me, but, after all, what have we got around here?"

We talked awhile about the problems facing the English Department, who was in, who was out, the prospect of new faces. He was most affable and, at the door when he left, he told me to apologize to Mary for him.

"Not tonight, in the morning," he said. "Agree with her tonight."

When I came to our room Mary had turned out the lights and was pretending to be asleep. I knew that she wasn't, though. She is not very good at pretending and had forgotten to simulate the breathing of a sleeper. I switched on the light and she sighed and sat up in bed. I was taking off my shoes, my back to her.

"All right, say it," she said. "Tell me how silly I was. Say that my little outburst was uncalled for and that I deserve to be spanked."

"Don't make a big thing out of nothing. Of course I'm not going to be the outraged husband. I do wonder, though, what you have against Sam, why you don't like him."

"He's your friend, not mine."

"That's no kind of an answer."

"All right, I think he is a dirty old fag with a dirty old mind who revels in other people's misery and misfortune. I think he is destructive and malicious. I think Sam Browne is a vicious man."

"You don't mean that, Mary. You don't mean that at all."

"I know it," she said, and for some reason she began to sob. She cried, and I made an effort to comfort her.

"It's going to be so hard, so hard," she said. "I hate coming back to this place."

"There, there," I said. "Have a good sleep and you'll feel different in the morning. You'll get used to it again in no time."

TEXARKANA WAS
A CRAZY TOWN

WHEN I WENT BACK to the barracks for the last time to pick up my stuff, there was Mooney waiting on me.

"Well," he said. "You feel any better now?"

I didn't answer. I kept busy stuffing things in my duffel bag. I didn't want any trouble with Mooney. I knew how he felt, like I was running out on him.

"How does it feel to be a civilian?"

"How would I know?" I said. "I ain't even been off the post yet."

"You're making a mistake," he said. "You'll be sorry."

"Maybe."

"Maybe nothing!" Mooney said. "Listen here, boy. You've got it made here. You don't know it. You just don't know how it is. You don't know anything else but the Army. It's going to be tough out there for a guy like you, believe me."

"Listen, Mooney," I kidded him, "you came in the Army during the Depression. They had bread lines and all that then. People selling pencils on the street corners. Things are different now."

Mooney grinned. "I may look old," he said, "but I'm not that old."

"You look old to me."

"You don't know anything," he said. "What's the matter?"

"We've been all through this before."

"Never mind about before. I want to know."

"I just don't like being pushed around," I said. "And that's all there is to it."

"Who's been pushing you around? You tell me who's been giving you a hard time."

"Nobody," I said. "It's just the idea of the thing. I'm sick of it."

"Jesus Christ!" Mooney said. "That beats all."

Mooney was about the best friend I ever had. I knew him ever since I was seventeen and joined the Army. We had been in the same outfit all along. In the beginning Mooney was my Chief of Section on the howitzer. He made a soldier out of me. Now I was a Chief of Section and he was the Chief of Firing Battery. He could have been First Sergeant if he had wanted to. He turned it down because he wanted to be with the guns. Mooney was what you'd have to call a dedicated man with those guns. He really cared. That's why he just couldn't understand why I was leaving.

"What are you going to do?" he asked.

"I don't know."

"Maybe you can make use of your service experience and repair the old cannons in front of American Legion halls."

"Yeah, sure," I said. "And maybe they'll let me fire a salute on the Fourth of July."

"It's too bad you never learned how to play a bugle," Mooney said. "You could double up and play taps."

"I can always teach dismounted drill to the Boy Scouts. Or maybe I'll open a real high-class professional shoeshine parlor."

"You're crazy."

"I'd rather be crazy than chronic," I said. "You're chronic, Mooney. Nothing but an old chrome-plated chronic."

"Don't go," he said suddenly. "Change your mind."

I was all through packing and I was ready to leave. I didn't want to hang around talking to Mooney all day long. We had been through it all so many times before.

"It's too late," I said. "They already give me my mustering-out pay and my permanent grade of PFC—poor freaking civilian."

"What's everything coming to?" Mooney said. "What am I supposed to do for soldiers?"

"Hell, just grab ahold of a couple of those new kids and give them the sales talk. Maybe you'll convert some of them. If you signed up enough of them they might even make you Recruiting NCO and you could get yourself a bonus."

"You got ninety days," he said. "You got ninety days to change your mind. Just remember that."

"Okay," I said. "Just give me ninety days. So long, Mooney."

I stuck out my hand to shake hands with him.

"Don't give me that shit," he said. And he turned his back on me and walked away.

I didn't blame him. I guess I would have been mad, too, if I was Mooney. I knew how he felt, but that didn't help me a whole lot. He was my friend, a good one, and about the best soldier I ever saw. He was a great guy and you took him for himself. You just forgot all about Mooney being a nigger.

I didn't go home. What was the sense in that? I joined the Army in the first place to get away from that. They never would miss me. They've got a houseful anyway. Somebody told me jobs were easy to come by in Houston, Texas, so I went on down there and got a job driving a truck for an ice company. Now you might think in this modern day and age there wouldn't be a whole lot for an iceman to do. I mean with refrigerators and freezers and all. So did I. I was wrong. There was plenty for me to do all day, and there were plenty of people right there in a great big city who had an old-fashioned icebox.

That job lasted three days. The first day on the job the boss took me aside and told me what was what. There was one special case I had to worry about.

"There's a woman at this address, a real good-looking woman," he said, showing me the number on the delivery roster.

"Yeah?"

"Now, when you go in the house, this woman will be in the living room taking a sunbath under a sunlamp, buck naked with the door wide open to the kitchen."

"That's all right with me," I said. "I don't mind if she don't."

"Now you listen to me, sonny boy," he said. "You take the ice in and you put it in the top of the icebox. You don't look left and you don't look right. You don't stop and talk, even if she talks to you. All you do is put the ice in the icebox and get out. If you look, if you stop and talk, she's going to call up the company just as soon as you leave and I'll have to fire you."

"She must be a pretty good customer."

"Yeah," he said. "She's regular."

"Why don't she get herself a refrigerator?" I said. "That woman must be crazy."

"Don't talk like that," he said. "She's my wife."

I think that woman was crazy. She didn't need an icebox even if her husband did run an ice company. They had a nice house with air-conditioning and everything. The kitchen was full of all kinds of machines and appliances. And, to top it all, she had this great big funny old icebox. Well, I put up with it for two days, sneaking in and out of the kitchen like a dog. I couldn't see her, but I could hear the portable radio playing and see the glare of the heat lamp out of the corner of my eye and I could feel the heat of it. And I could tell she was just waiting to see what I was going to do.

The third day she tried to trip me up. I got inside and was just putting the ice in the icebox.

"Honey," she called out. "Would you kindly open a can of beer for me and put it by the sink so I can come get it when you leave?"

"Sure," I said.

It was a hot summer day in Houston, really hot and so humid the air seemed to stick to you. I was tired and I wouldn't have minded a beer myself.

"Don't you drink any of it."

"Don't you worry, lady," I said. "When I want to drink a beer, I'll buy it myself."

"You're kind of sassy," she said. "What's your name, honey?"

I came right up to the living-room door and leaned against the doorframe and just looked at her. She was laying on her stomach facing me, so she couldn't very well move to cover herself up. I'd say she was a pretty nice-looking woman, a little on the heavy side, but a nice, very nice ass.

"Pudding Tame, you bitch," I said. I figured I was as good as fired anyway.

"That's no way to talk to a lady," she said.

I lit myself a cigarette and looked around.

"I don't see no lady."

"You got a nerve," she said. "I'm going to phone my husband."

"You know what I'd do if I was your husband?"

"No," she said. "What would you do?"

"I'd whip your ass good and throw you out in the street where you belong."

I walked over and smacked her fanny so hard I left a print on it, all five fingers included, and then I walked right out of the house with her hollering rape and murder and everything else. I drove straight back to the company and gave the boss the keys to his truck.

"I'm sorry," he said. "But don't say I didn't give you fair warning."

"Mister, you can have this job."

"I'm sorry," he said. "I can't help it. It's just the way things are."

"The hell you can't!" I said. "You ought to knock some sense into that woman. And if she won't shape up, get rid of her."

"I can't help it," he said. "I'm sorry but that's just the way it is."

"Okay," I said. "Have it your own way."

At the end I almost felt sorry for him. He was just an old guy with a young wife. You know how it goes.

A few days later an oil exploration company hired me to drive a pickup truck for one of their crews. I was really hoping they would send me to South America or Arabia or some place, but they sent me up to Texarkana instead. Texarkana was a crazy town. I don't know how it is now and I couldn't care less, but it was a crazy place then. The state line between Arkansas and Texas ran right up the middle of the street and they said you could break the law on one side and then run across to the other and thumb your nose at the cops if you felt like it. One state, I forget which, was partially dry. You could buy only beer there. If you went across to the other side you could get beer and whiskey and pretty nearly anything else you wanted. Naturally it was heavenly country for bootleggers. On a still calm day you could see the smoke rising up from a half a dozen stills out in the pinewoods. The law wouldn't do anything about it or, anyway, I guess they couldn't.

About the same time I showed up there was another kind of crime that had everybody worried and worked up. Somebody took to killing off couples parked out in the woods. Whoever it was would sneak up on them in the dark, kill the man, rape the woman, and then kill her too. Then he would carve up the bodies with a butcher knife. All the newspapers were full of it. They called him the Phantom Killer and everybody in the area was supposed to be on the lookout to catch him. All this was in the middle of summer when everybody is edgy anyway. Life goes on the same everywhere, with or without no Phantom Killer, but I don't mind telling you it made the town a nervous, kind of suspicious place to be in.

All that part didn't bother me one way or the other at first, though. I was too busy on the job and getting used to the people I was working with to worry about what kind of a place I was living in. The whole crew lived together in a boardinghouse. We would be up long before daylight and out on the road, driving miles to wherever we had to work that day. I have to drive a pickup for Pete, the surveyor, and all his gear. We would drive way out in the woods or swamps somewhere and then run a survey for elevation and distance, setting up known locations, stations where the gravity-meter crew could come along later and take readings. The driving on those back roads was pretty bad, but I was used to rough driving. The only tough time I had was getting along with Pete. Right from the first day. Part of it was my own fault, I'll admit. He reminded me of my old man. Pete was a little scrawny guy like that and all puffed up with himself like a banty rooster. I guess he figured everybody was against him to start with, so he might as well give everybody else a bad time before they had a chance to do it to him. He went out of his way to let you know right away he thought you were dirt. The first time I ever drove for him he started in on me.

"What did you do before you came to work for us?" he asked me.

"I was in the Army."

"Yeah? I thought so."

I didn't say anything. Plenty of people have plenty of good reasons for not liking the Army. I even have a few good ones myself. When he saw I wasn't about to take his bait, he kept after me.

"Well," he said, "don't try any of your Army tricks around here or you won't last too long."

"Yeah?"

"I know how it is. I was in the Army. The idea is to get out of as much work as you can and let somebody else do it. That's right, isn't it?"

"I wouldn't know."

"Come on now," he said. "You know what I'm talking about."

"I hope you do," I said. "I don't."

"Just don't try any tricks on me."

Like I've said, one of my big troubles is I don't like to get pushed around by anybody. And another one is a quick temper sometimes. I pulled the truck off the road and stopped.

"What are you doing?"

"I'm playing my first trick on you," I said.

"I wasn't joking," he said.

"Now listen, you," I said. "I don't want any trouble with you. Let's get everything straight right now. You tell me what to do on this job and I'll do it. Just as good or better than the next guy. But let's just leave the bullshit out of it. They don't pay me to listen to you."

"You talk pretty big for a kid," he said.

"Try me," I said. "I'd just as soon whip your ass as anybody else's. Just try me and find out."

He shut up and we drove on. Later he asked me what rank I had in the Army and I told him sergeant. He said, "I might have known," or something like that. I let it pass. I let him get away with that. He was like my old man. He had to say the last word even if it killed him.

After that Pete didn't give me any trouble for a while. And I didn't bother him. Which is more than the rest of the guys on the crew. They didn't like him either and they always had some practical joke to pull on him. They made him pretty miserable I guess. The hell with it. I just worked with him and let him alone.

We always worked until pretty near dark and then we would drive hell for leather back to town. After we got back and cleaned up and had some supper, we would either go over to the cafe across the street and drink beer or else hang around the filling station.

The filling station was run by this one-arm guy that used to be in the Army away back. He had been a mule-pack soldier in the days when they still had mules and I liked to go over there and sit around and talk with him about how it had been in the old days. We could talk the same kind of language and I got to where I really liked to hang around there in the evening. Except for one thing. He had this nigger they called Peanuts working for him. Peanuts was tall and skinny and kind of funny-looking with great big loose hands and feet about half a block long. He wasn't very smart, but he was a good-natured simple guy and I got to where I couldn't stand the way they picked on him. Everybody played jokes on Peanuts. They would send him all over town on crazy errands like getting a bucket of polka-dot paint or taking the slack out of the state line. He never caught on. Once or twice somebody gave him a bottle of cheap whiskey and got him drunk. He would stagger all around the station singing and hollering and slobbering and carrying on until he just passed out cold. Whiskey put him out of his head. There would be a crowd of the guys to see this happen. They thought it was pretty funny, like seeing a pig drunk. In a way I guess it was funny too. Except a man is not a pig. So I made up my mind. I would rather sit in the cafe and drink beer by myself than to put up with a thing like that.

"What's the matter?" Pete asked me. "You don't hang around with the rest of the guys anymore."

"I'd rather drink beer."

"That Delma is a nice piece."

"Who?"

"Delma," he said, "the waitress."

"Which one is she?"

"Don't try and fool me," Pete said. "I know what you're up to."

"Well, you know a lot more than I do then."

To tell you the truth Pete put an idea in my head. I hadn't thought about it before, but there was this good-looking waitress working over at the cafe. And I was lonesome and horny as a jack rabbit and I figured that getting tied up with a woman wouldn't be such a bad thing. I never had a whole lot to do with women before I went in the Army. The only women I really knew anything about were gooks. I like them fine, especially the Japanese, but they sure are different from American women.

Delma was a pretty good-looking girl, short and stacked with dark hair and a good smile. Of course they all look good when you want one bad enough. It didn't take long for me to get to know her a little. When business was slack she would come over and sit in the booth with me. She talked a lot and joked. She was full of laughs about everything. She seemed all right.

One night, after I had been around Texarkana for a few weeks, she asked me if I wanted to go out with her.

"Sure," I said. "The only trouble is I don't have a car."

"We can use mine," she said. "I don't feel like working tonight. I feel like going out and having a good time."

She went back to the ladies' room and changed out of her white uniform and into a dress. She looked good in a dress. I never had seen her except in her uniform and so she looked like a different person. She had that clean, kind of shiny look American girls have when they're all dressed up to go somewhere. Like a picture out of a magazine. We got in her car and drove out in the country to some honky-tonk where they had a band.

"I don't dance much," I told her. "I never had much time to learn."

"That's all right," she said. "I'll show you how."

We tried dancing awhile, but it didn't work too well. So we sat down at a table and just drank and listened to the music. That Delma could really drink. I had a hard time keeping up with her.

"This is a pretty rough place," she told me. "A lot of really rough guys come here."

"Is that so?"

"You see that big man?" She pointed at a great big guy standing at the bar. "He is one of the toughest men in this whole part of the country. A big bootlegger."

"What did he do to get so tough?"

"They say he's killed two or three men."

I started to laugh. I don't know why. I just couldn't help it. I was drunk and it struck me funny to hear somebody talk like that, like he was some kind of a hero or something.

"What's so funny?"

"I don't know."

"Something must be funny."

"Is that what you have to do to get a name around here—kill somebody?"

"You better not let him catch you laughing at him."

For some reason that made me mad.

"I don't give a damn who catches me laughing," I said. "I'll laugh whenever I damnwell please and take my chances. Listen, I've seen bigger, tougher guys than him break down and pray to Jesus. I've seen plenty of great big tough guys that was as yellow and soft as a stick of butter. It don't take no guts to kill a man.

I've seen the yellowest chicken-hearted bastards in the world that would shoot prisoners. I've seen some terrible things. So don't come telling me about no big bad country bootlegger."

While I was sounding off like that she reached across the table and grabbed my hands and squeezed hard. She kept staring at me.

"Finish your drink," she said. "And let's go somewhere."

We went out in the parking lot and got in the car and necked awhile. She was all hot and bothered and breathing hard.

"Let's go somewhere," she said.

"Where do you want to go?" I said. "Out in the woods?"

"No," she said. "Not out there, I'm scared."

"What of?"

"I'm just nervous since all that Phantom Killer stuff has been in the papers."

"All right, you name it."

We drove even farther out the highway to a cheap motel. After I paid the man we went in the cabin and sat down on the bed.

"I've got to have a drink," she said. "Go ask the man for a pint of whiskey. He sells it and don't let him tell you he doesn't."

When I came back to the cabin with the whiskey all the lights were out.

"Hey," I said. "I can't see anything."

"Hurry up and get your clothes off," she said. "I'm so hot I can't stand it."

I climbed in the bed and we drank out of the bottle. You would never believe the first thing she said to me.

"Have you ever killed anybody?" she whispered. "Tell me about it."

I told her I didn't know. In the artillery you don't see what you are shooting at most of the time. They telephone or radio back when they have got a target for you to shoot at and then you just keep on shooting until they tell you to quit.

"I don't mean like that," she said. "I mean up close with a knife or something."

The only thing I could figure was she was drunk and had all

that Phantom Killer stuff on her mind. I could tell she wanted
me to say yes. I don't know why. I guess she wanted to feel bad,
dirty maybe. She wanted to pretend she was in bed with some
terrible man. Maybe she wanted to pretend that the Phantom
Killer was raping her or something. I was drunk enough myself
so I didn't care. So I told her yes I had killed a whole lot of gooks
with my knife. I made up a couple of long-winded phony stories
and that seemed to excite her. I'll say this for Delma, she was all
right in bed even if she did carry on, laughing and crying the
whole time until I was afraid the man would throw us out.

Later on, in the early hours of the morning, she got up real
quiet and started to get dressed. I sat up in bed.

"What are you doing?"

"Let's go," she said. "It's time to go home."

It was still dark. I snapped the lamp beside the bed and it
didn't go on. I tried the bulb and it was tight. I gave the cord a
pull and it was free. She must have yanked the plug out while I
was out buying the whiskey when we first came in.

"How come you unplugged the light?"

"What do you mean?"

"What's the matter with you?"

"I don't want you to see me," she said.

"I saw you when we came in," I said. "I know who you are."

"Not like this," she said. "You didn't see me like this."

Then she started crying. I thought the hell with it. Just the
hell with it all. And I got up and found my clothes and got
dressed in the dark. Before we went out the door she took hold
of me.

"Aren't you forgetting something?"

"What?"

"It's going to cost you twenty dollars."

"I'll be damn," I said. "I didn't know you were a whore."

"I'm not!" she said. "I'm not a whore. But I've got my kid to
think about."

"Your kid? I didn't even know you were married."

"Now you know," she said. "And it costs twenty bucks to
spend the night with me."

"That's a pretty high price."

Even if I felt bad about being fooled, I went ahead and gave her the money. What was the use of arguing? It was my own fault.

We drove back to town without saying a word. I turned on the radio and picked up some hillbilly music. We finally got to the boardinghouse and I pulled over to let her take the wheel. I got out and started to walk away. She called to me.

"Listen," she said, "you're not mad, are you?"

"Mad? Why should I be mad?"

"I just want to be sure," she said. "I don't want you to be mad at me."

"What difference does it make?"

"I just wanted to know," she said. "Will I see you again?"

"I don't know," I said. "How would I know?"

"Suit yourself," she said and she drove off.

I just about had time to put on my boots and work clothes before we left for work. I didn't even have time to shave. Pete was already waiting for me when I walked in the house.

"Where the hell have you been?"

"Go on out and wait in the truck," I told him. "I'll be ready in five minutes."

The others left without us. We drove out on the highway alone for an hour or so. Pete just curled up in a corner of the cab and went to sleep. I had a hard time staying awake myself, driving along the long straight road in the first light of the morning. The tires were humming. I nodded and rubbed my eyes and drove on. After a while I turned off onto a back road that led into swamp country where we had been working before. I drove as far as we had worked yesterday. Then I nudged Pete and woke him up.

"Where are the other guys?" I said.

"Where are we?"

He looked around a minute, blinking his eyes.

"Goddamn!" he said. "You went to the wrong place."

"I thought we were supposed to finish the line we were running."

"Yeah? You thought! Well, it's been changed."

"You could have told me."

"Drive on up the road and see if there's a place we can turn around. I think I remember a shack down the road a piece."

I started up the truck again and drove on.

"Well," Pete said, "while you were out catting around with Delma last night, you missed all the fun."

"What fun?"

"Peanuts," he said. "They beat the living hell out of him."

"Jesus Christ! What did they do that for?"

"They got him drunk last evening, see? Usually when he's drunk he's just funny. But this time he was kind of mean, mean drunk. Some of the boys egged him on and he was just drunk enough to swing at them. They gave that black sonofabitch a real going-over. Hell, they had to take him to the hospital when they got through."

"Jesus Christ!"

"You should've been there."

"I can't believe anybody would do anything like that."

I was thinking what a crazy terrible thing it was for some grown men to beat up a poor feeble-minded nigger like that. I was sleepy and hungry and hung over and it was all mixed up in my mind with all that had happened to me last night. Thinking about that married woman, Delma, and how she had to get herself all worked up by pretending she was in bed with some kind of a killer. She couldn't have believed it, but she needed to pretend that she did. Just like those men in town at the station had to pretend that Peanuts had done something to them and then beat him up to feel better. I felt so sick about everything in the whole world I wanted to die. I just wanted to fall over dead.

"Hey!" Pete yelled. "Turn in here."

There was a shack all right, just a patch of bare ground with the swamp all around it. It was all falling to pieces, but there were chickens running around the yard and a nigger without a shirt on was sitting on the front stoop picking at a guitar.

"The hell with it," Pete said. "He had it coming."

"Who?"

"Peanuts. They shouldn't let anybody that stupid run around loose."

"For what?" I said. "For what does anybody have things like that coming to him? Answer me that."

"I said the hell with it. Turn the truck around and let's go."

"I'm asking you."

"And I'm telling you to shut up and turn this truck around."

"All right," I said, turning off the engine and putting the keys in my pocket. "It was bound to come to this sooner or later."

"What are you going to do?"

"I'm fixing to beat the shit out of you."

I'll have to say he put up a pretty good fight for a little guy. He was tough. We fought all around the truck and all over the yard, rolling on the ground, kicking and punching each other. I was so tired and sleepy I felt like I was dreaming, but I kept after him and I finally got him down so he couldn't get up. He just lay there panting, all bloody on the ground, and I started kicking at him.

"You going to kill me?"

He looked bad lying there. He was too weak to move. In my blood and my muscles and my bones I never wanted to kill anybody so much. I wanted to tear him into pieces and stamp them in the dust. But I couldn't do it. When he asked me was I going to kill him, all of a sudden I knew what I was doing. I knew what had happened to me and I knew I wasn't a damn bit better than those guys that beat up Peanuts or Delma or Pete or anybody else. I was so sick of myself I felt like I was going to puke.

"I don't know," I told him. "I ought to."

I went up to where I saw a well and hauled a bucket of water and splashed it all over me. The nigger sat there and stared at me with the guitar hanging loose in his hands. I wonder what he thought was going on.

After that I splashed Pete with water, too, and I put the keys in the truck.

"Drive me back to town," he said.

"Drive yourself," I said. "I'm walking."

I was lucky to get back in my old outfit with my old job. I came into the Battery area on a Sunday afternoon. The barracks was empty except for a few guys on the first floor, broke maybe or without a pass, playing cards on one of the bunks. They were sitting around, smoking, concentrating on the game. When I walked in and went on through they just looked up and looked back down to the game. They were new since I left. They didn't know me and I didn't know them.

I climbed the stairs and went into Mooney's room. He wasn't there but the room had his touch on everything in it. It was bare and clean and neat. The clothes in his wall locker were hanging evenly. The boots under his bed, side by side, were shined up nice, not all spit-shined like some young soldier's, just a nice shine. I made up the empty bunk. I made it up real tight without a wrinkle, so tight you could bounce a quarter off of it if you wanted to. Then I threw all my stuff in the corner and just flopped down in the middle of my bunk. I felt like I was floating on top of water. I lit myself a cigarette and looked at the ceiling.

After a while I heard Mooney climbing up the stairs. He always came up real slow and careful like an old man. Once you heard him walking up stairs you would never mistake it for somebody else. He opened the door and came in.

"How many times do I have to tell you not to smoke in bed," he said. "It's against regulations."

"Don't tell me," I said. "I've heard it all before."

"You think you know it all," he said. "Let me tell you, you got a lot of things to learn."

"Oh yeah? I've been around. I've been outside. I've seen a few things since the last time I seen you."

"Did you learn anything?" he said. "That's what I want to know."

"Not much."

"Nothing?"

"There's one thing, just one thing I've got to find out from you."

He waited for me to ask it.

"Mooney," I said, "how come you're so black?"

Mooney looked at me hard for a minute. Then he leaned back, rocked on his heels. The whole room rattled with his laughter and it was good to hear.

"Sunburn," he said. "Son, I got the most awful, the most permanent case of sunburn you ever saw."

Four

From
A WREATH
FOR GARIBALDI

Is it any pleasure to the Almighty, that thou
art righteous? or is it gain to him
that thou makest thy ways perfect?

JOB 22:3

A WREATH FOR GARIBALDI
(A True Story)

THE BEGINNING WAS PERFECTLY CASUAL, offhand, pleasant. We were sitting on the terrazzo of a modern Roman apartment drinking coffee and thick, sweet, bile-colored Strega. It was an afternoon in late March, the air was fresh and cool, the spring sunlight rinsed and brilliant. The English lady, a poet and translator, was in the hammock and the rest of us sat around in wicker chairs—an artist, an Italian princess, another translator, an expatriate gentleman from Mobile, Alabama, who writes poems about monkeys. A usual crowd. . . .

The talk was about politics. A Pope had died, the new Pope had been elected amid rumors and fears—"*Un Straniero per Il Papa?*" all the headlines read for a while—and errors: white smoke pouring out of the chimney of the Sistine Chapel on the very first ballot because somebody had forgotten the straw to darken the smoke. The latest government had fallen. A coalition with more strength to the right (gossip had any number of known ex-Fascists among its members) had replaced it. The talk was of politics and, inevitably, the signs of the reawakening of Fascism. Mussolini was being treated with nostalgia and kid gloves in a major picture magazine. Another magazine had been publishing a series about the War, showing how they (the Italians) lost it by a series of "mistakes" and recounting moments of bravery and success wherever they could find them. There had been a television series on recent Italian history. Everybody had been waiting to see how they would manage to handle the whole big business of Fascism and the war. It was disappointing. They treated the subject like scholars from a distant land, or maybe outer space, with careful, neutral disinterest.

There had been other things too—the young Fascists making some headlines by dropping mice in tiny parachutes from the ceiling of a theater during an anti-Fascist comedy. There had been the "striptease incident" in a Trastevere trattoria when a Turkish girl took all her clothes off and did a belly dance. It was a very large private party, and most people missed that part of the show. More noticed the American movie star, one of the new sex symbols, who came with a buzz and hive of fairies (like Lady Brett?) and danced barefoot (like Ava Gardner?). In fact it never would have been an issue at all except that somebody took some photographs. The place was full of plainclothesmen who had come to protect the jewels, but they didn't go into action until the next morning when a tabloid appeared with the pictures of the belly dance. In no time the party was officially an orgy and there were lots of political implications and ramifications. It was the special kind of public prudery that interested the observer, though, the kind that had always been associated with the Fascist days. And there had been other signs and portents like the regular toppling over and defacing of the bust of Lauro di Bosis near the Villa Lante on the Gianicolo.

Something was happening all right, slowly it is true, but you could feel it. The Italians felt it. Little things. An Italian poet noticed the plainclothes policemen lounging around the area of Quirinale Palace, the first time since the war. At least they hadn't stepped up and asked to see his papers in the hated, flat, dialect mispronunciation of Mussolini's home district—*Documenti, per favore*. But—who knew?—that might be coming, too, one of these days. There were other Italians who still bore scars they had earned in police station basements, resisting. They laughed and, true to national form and manners, never talked too long or solemnly on any subject at all, but some of them worried briefly out loud about short memories and ghosts.

We saw Giuseppe Berto at a party once in a while, tall, lean, nervous, and handsome, and, in my opinion, the best novelist of them all except Pavese. And Pavese was dead. Berto's *The Sky Is Red* had been a small masterpiece and in its special way one of the best books to come out of the war. Now he was married to a young and beautiful girl, had a small son, and lived in an expensive apartment and worked for the movies. On his desk was a slowly accumulating treatment and script of *The Count of Monte Cristo*. On his bookshelves were some American novels, including Bellow's *Seize the Day*, which had been sent to him by American publishers. But he hadn't read them, and he wasn't especially interested in what the American writers were up to. He was very interested in Robert Musil's *The Man Without Qualities*. So were a lot of other people. He was interested in Italo Svevo. He was slowly thinking his way into a new novel, a big one, one that many people had been waiting for. It was going to be hard going all the way for him because he hadn't written seriously for a good while, except for a few stories, and he was tired of the old method of *realismo* he had so successfully used in *The Sky Is Red*. This one was going to be different. He had bought a little piece of property down along the coast of the hard country of Calabria that he knew so well. He was going to do one or two more films for quick cash and then chuck it all, leave Rome and its intellectual cliques and money-fed life, go back to Calabria.

Berto seemed worried, too. He knew all about it and had put it down in journal form in *War in a Black Shirt*. He knew all about the appeal of a black shirt and jackboots to a poor, southern, peasant boy. He knew all about the infection and the fever, and, too, the sudden moment of realization when he saw for himself, threw up his hands and quit, ending the war as a prisoner in Texas. Berto knew all about Fascism. So did his friend, the young novelist Rimanelli. Rimanelli is tough and square-built and adventurous, says what he thinks. He had put it down in a war novel, *The Day of the Lion*. These people were not talking much about it, but you, a foreigner, sensed their apprehension and disappointment.

So there we were talking around and about it. The English lady said she had to go to Vienna for a while. It was a pity because she had planned to lay a wreath at the foot of the Garibaldi statue, towering over Rome in spectacular benediction from the high point of the Gianicolo. Around that statue in the green park where children play and lovers walk in twos and there is a glowing view of the whole city, in that park are the rows of marble busts of Garibaldi's fallen men, the ones who one day rushed out of the Porta San Pancrazio and, under fire all the way, up the long, straight, narrow lane first to take, then later to lose, the high ground of the Villa Doria Pamphili. When they finally lost it, the French artillery moved in, and that was the end for Garibaldi, at least that time, on 30 April 1849. Once out of the gate they had charged straight up the narrow lane. We had walked it many times and shivered, figuring what a fish barrel it had been for the French. Now the park is filled with marble busts and all the streets in the immediate area have the full and proper names of the men who fell there.

We were at a party once and heard an idealistic young European call that charge glorious. Our companion was a huge, plain-spoken American sculptor who had been a sixteen-year-old rifleman all across France in 1944. He said it was stupid butchery to order men to make a charge like that, no matter who gave the order or what for.

"Oh, it would be butchery all right," the European said. "We would see it that way today. But it was glorious then. It was the last time in history anybody could do something gloriously like that."

I thought, *Who is older now? Old world or new world?*

The sculptor looked at him, bug-eyed and amazed. He had made an assault once with a hundred and eighty men. It was a picked assault company. They went up against an SS unit of comparable size, over a little rise of ground, across an open field. Object—a village crossroads. They made it and killed every last one of the Krauts, took the village on schedule. When it was

over, eight of his company were still alive and all eight were
wounded. The whole thing, from the moment when they
climbed heavily off the trucks, spread out, and moved into position just behind the cover of that slight rise of ground and then
jumped off, took maybe between twenty or thirty minutes. The
sculptor looked at him, let the color drain out of his face,
grinned, and looked down into his drink, a bad Martini made
with raw Italian gin.

"Bullshit," he said softly.

"Excuse me," the European said. "I am not familiar with the
expression."

The apartment where we were talking that afternoon in
March faced onto the street Garibaldi's men had charged up and
along. Across the way from the apartment building is a ruined
house, shot to hell that day in 1849, and left that way as a kind of
memorial. There is a bronze wreath on the wall. Like everything else in Rome, ruins and monuments alike, that house is
lived in. I have seen diapers strung across the ruined roof.

The English lady really wanted to put a wreath on the Garibaldi monument on the thirtieth of April. She had her reasons
for this. For one thing, there wasn't going to be any ceremony
this year. There were a few reasons for that too. Garibaldi had
been much taken up and exploited by the Communists nowadays. Therefore the government wanted no part of him. And
then there were ecclesiastical matters, the matter of Garibaldi's
anticlericalism. There was a new Pope and the Vatican was making itself heard and felt these days. As it happens the English
lady is a good Catholic herself, but of a more liberal political
persuasion. Nothing was going to be done this year to celebrate
Garibaldi's bold and unsuccessful defense of Rome. All that the
English lady wanted to do was to walk up to the monument and
lay a wreath at its base. This would show that somebody, even a
foreigner living in Rome, cared. And then there were other
things. Some of the marble busts in the park are of young Englishmen who fought and died for Garibaldi. She also mentioned leaving a little bunch of flowers at the bust of Lauro di
Bosis.

It is hard for me to know how I really feel about Lauro di Bosis. I suffer from mixed feelings. He was a well-to-do, handsome, and sensitive young poet. His bust shows an intense, mustached, fine-featured face. He flew over Rome one day during the early days of Mussolini and scattered leaflets across the city, denouncing the Fascists. He was never heard of again. He is thought either to have been killed by the Fascists as soon as he landed or to have killed himself by flying out to sea and crashing his plane. He was, thus, an early and spectacular victim. And there is something so wonderfully romantic about it all. He really didn't know how to fly. He had crashed on takeoff once before. Gossip had it (for gossip is the soul of Rome) that a celebrated American dancer of the time had paid for both the planes. It was absurd and dramatic. It is remembered and has been commemorated by a bust in a park and a square in the city which was renamed Piazzo Lauro di Bosis after the war. Most Romans, even some of the postmen, still know it by the old name.

Faced with a gesture like Di Bosis's, I find usually that my sentiments are closer to those of my sculptor friend. The things that happened in police station basements were dirty, grubby, and most often anonymous. No poetry, no airplanes, no famous dancers. That is how the real resistance goes on, and its strength is directly proportionate to the number of insignificant people who can let themselves be taken to pieces, piece by piece, without quitting too quickly. It is an ugly business and there are few, if any, wreaths for them. I keep thinking of a young woman I knew during the Occupation in Austria. She was from Prague. She had been picked up by the Russians, questioned in connection with some pamphlets, then sentenced to life imprisonment for espionage. She escaped, crawled through the usual mine fields, under the usual barbed wire, was shot at, swam a river, and we finally picked her up in Linz. She showed us what had happened to her. No airplanes, no Nathan Hale statements. Just no simple spot, not even a dime-size spot, on her whole body that wasn't bruised, bruise on top of bruise, from beatings. I understand very well about Lauro di Bosis and how his action is symbolic. The trouble is that, like many symbols, it doesn't seem to me a very realistic one.

The English lady wanted to pay tribute to Garibaldi and to Lauro di Bosis, but she wasn't going to be here to do it. Were any of us interested enough in the idea to do it for her, by proxy so to speak? There was a pretty thorough silence at that point. My spoon stirring coffee, banging against the side of the cup, sounded as loud as a bell. I thought, *What the hell? Why not?* And I said I would do it for her.

I had some reasons too. I admire the English lady. I hate embarrassing silences and have been known to make a fool out of myself just to prevent one. I also had and have feelings about Garibaldi. Like every Southerner I know of, I can't escape the romantic tradition of brave defeats, forlorn lost causes. Though Garibaldi's fight was mighty small shakes compared to Pickett's Charge—which, like all Southerners, I tend to view in Miltonic terms, fallen angels, etc.—I associated the two. And to top it all I am often sentimental on purpose, trying to prove to myself that I am not afraid of sentiment. So much for all that.

The English lady was pleased and enthusiastic. She gave me the names of some people who would surely help pay for the flowers and might even march up to the monument with me. The idea of the march pleased her. Maybe twenty, thirty, fifty . . . Maybe I could call Rimanelli at the magazine *Rottosei* where he worked. Then there would be pictures, it would be in the press. I stopped her there.

"I'll lay the wreath," I said. "But no Rimanelli, no press, no photographers. It isn't a stunt. As soon as you start mucking around with journalists, even good guys like Rimanelli, it all turns into a cheap stunt."

She was disappointed, but she could appreciate how I felt.

And that was that. The expatriate poet started telling a long, funny story about some German scholars—"really, I mean this *really* happened"—who went down to the coast of East Africa somewhere near Somalia to study the habits of a group of crab-eating monkeys, the only crab-eating monkeys left in the whole world. These monkeys swam in shallow water, caught crabs, and ate them. So down went the German scholars with a lot of gear to study them. They lived a very hard, incredibly uncomfortable life for a year or so and collected all the data they needed. Then they came back to civilization and published a monograph. The only trouble was that the ink was hardly dry on the monograph before the monkeys, perverse and inexplicable creatures, stopped swimming entirely, stopped eating crabs for good and all, and began digging for clams.

Everybody laughed and our host poured out some more Strega.

Then it was almost the end of April. The English lady was in Vienna. I had been working on a novel, one about politics in Florida of all things, one that nobody north of the Mason Dixon was to believe as probable (south of the line it was taken, erroneously too, as a *roman à clef*) and damn few people were going to buy. I hadn't seen anybody except my own family for a while. I couldn't get much interest or action out of the people who were supposed to help pay for the flowers. Some of them were getting kind of hard to get in touch with. I had a postcard from the English lady reminding me of it all and wishing she could be there to be with me. I thought a little more about Garibaldi, read about the battle in detail in the library of the American Academy. Remembered Professor Buzzer Hall at Princeton and his annual show, the passionate "Garibaldi Lecture," the same one every year, that drew enormous crowds, cheering students and half the Italians from Mercer County and Trenton. Hall could make you want to put on a red shirt and go out and die. I had some nostalgia about red shirts too. My grandfather had ridden with Wade Hampton's Redshirts in Reconstruction days in South Carolina.

I walked in the park of the Gianicolo many times. The American Academy, where I worked, was on Via Angelo Masina, and I had hunted for Masina, found his bust, and found it defaced. Somebody had painted out Angelo and painted in Giulietta.

I was going to do it all right.

Then somebody stopped in my studio for a drink. He said I ought to think about it, maybe it was against the law or something. But how would I find out whether I was breaking the law or not? By getting myself arrested? Then I remembered I had a friend down at the Embassy and I thought I'd ask him to find out for me, even at the risk that he would get very excited and patriotic. I called and we had a conversation that went about like this:

"Hello, John," I said. "Would you do me a favor?"

"What?"

"I'm going to put a wreath on the Garibaldi monument on the thirtieth of April. Would you find out if I'll be breaking any law?"

"All right," he said. "Don't call me, I'll call you."

Not even in his tone was there the suggestion of a raised eyebrow. Strictly routine. It would probably be the easiest thing in the world. Then he called back.

"Look," he said. "This may take a little time and doing. You sure you want to lay a wreath on the monument?"

"Well, I don't know . . ."

"Do you or don't you? I mean, if you do, we'll fix it up. It's a little bit complicated, but if you want to do it, we can fix it."

I shrugged to myself. "Okay, see if you can do it."

I wasn't going to be able to hide behind the long skirts of the U.S. Government. This wasn't the timorous State Department I was always hearing about. He now acted as liaison and as a buffer between me and the Italian Government. He, or his secretary, to be perfectly factual and to complicate things a little more, called me. There was a list of questions, some things they wanted to know before I got the permission. I would get the permission all right and it really didn't make much difference how I answered the questions, so long as I did not object to answering them in principle. She read the questions over the phone, completely matter-of-fact, and I dictated answers. There was quite a list, among them:

"Why are you laying a wreath on this monument?

"What special significance do you attribute to the thirtieth of April?

"Could there be any connection between the fact that the

wreath is to be put there on the thirtieth of April and that the next day is the first of May—May Day?

"How many people do you anticipate will participate in this ceremony?

"Will they march? Will there be banners, flags, music, etc.?"

And so on. The last question stopped me cold. I had also mentioned the bunch of flowers.

"Who is this Lauro di Bosis?"

I answered them all, each and every one. The secretary took down my answers, said she would relay them to Them and would call me back. A day or so went by before she called.

"It's all set," she said. "Go ahead and lay your wreath. They'll have police up there to protect you in case anything goes wrong. Just one thing, though, they're letting you do this with the full understanding that it doesn't mean anything."

"What?"

"They say it's all right because we all understand that it doesn't mean anything."

"Just a typical American stunt. No implications, some kind of a joke."

"That's the idea."

"Thanks a lot."

I was left with it in my lap then. If I put the wreath on the monument and flowers beneath the bust of Lauro di Bosis, it wouldn't mean a thing. If I did it, I was agreeing with that. They didn't care much about Di Bosis anyway. "Who was he?" they had asked. I thought they were just testing or being ironic in the heavy-handed way of governments. They were not, it appeared. I had replied simply with the information that there was a bust of the poet Di Bosis in the park. The secretary told me this was news to Them. Even if I did lay the wreath, it wasn't going to come close to fulfilling the intentions of the English lady. The hell with it. I would sleep on it and figure out what to do in the morning, which happened to be the thirtieth of April.

In the morning it was clear. The day was bright and warm and sunny. I walked over from my apartment to the Academy past the Villa Pamphili and along the route, in reverse, of Garibaldi's fallen soldiers. I passed by the English lady's apartment, the ruined house, the Porta San Pancrazio. Two horse policemen, mounted *carabinieri*, were in the shade of the great gate. A balloon man walked by, headed for the park in the Villa Sciara, which is popular with children and where there is a wall fountain celebrated in one of the most beautiful poems written in our time. Americans in the area simply refer to it as Richard Wilbur's fountain. I watched the balloon man go along the wall and out of sight, followed by his improbably bright bouquet of balloons. I had a coffee and cognac at the Bar Gianicolo and made up my mind not to do it. I felt greatly relieved. I thought she would understand under the circumstances.

But, even so, it was a long, long day. The afternoon was slow. I couldn't make my work go, spent the whole time fiddling with a sentence or two. I went for a walk in the park. Children were riding in high-wheeled donkey carts. A few tourists were along the balustrade looking at the vista of Rome. And there were indeed a few extra policemen in the area. I wondered what they thought they were looking for—some lone, crazy American burdened with a huge wreath—and what they would report when nothing happened, and who among Them would read such a report and how many, if any, desks it would pass over. I looked at Garibaldi. He wasn't troubled by anything. He was imperial and maybe a little too dignified to be wholly in character. He wasn't made for bronze. The traffic squalled around him and behind him the dome of St. Peter's hovered like a huge gas balloon, so light it seemed in the clear air, tugging on a string. If you went over to that side of the piazza you saw sheep grazing on a sloping hill beneath, with that dome dominating the whole sky. Once there had been a shepherd, too, with pipes, or, anyway, some kind of wind instrument.

I went on, took a look at Anita Garibaldi, another bronze equestrian, but this one all at a full gallop, wide open, a baby in the crook of one arm and a huge, long-barreled revolver in her other hand, which she was aiming behind her.

Diagonally across from Anita is the Villa Lante and the slender, lonely white bust of Lauro di Bosis. I went over and looked at him awhile. Pale, passionate, yes glorious, and altogether of another time, the buzz of his badly flown airplane like the hum of a mosquito and of not much more importance when you think of a whole wide sky filled with the roar of great engines, the enormous bombs they dropped, thinking of my sculptor friend losing all his friends (and in war that's all that there is) as they came up over the slight rise in the ground and rushed the village across an open field. . . . He said there was a tank destroyer captain with them. He had come along to see how it would go. He had been refused permission by Battalion to detach any of his idle tank destroyers to help the company out. He came just behind the assault, stepping over the bodies and weeping because just one tank destroyer could have taken the village and they never would have lost a man. Or thinking of all the brave anonymous men, bravery being a fancy term for doing what you have to and what has to be done, who fought back and died lonely, in police station basements and back rooms, not only in Rome but in most of the cities of the civilized world. It was a forlorn, foolish, adolescent gesture. But it was a kind of beginning. If Mussolini was really a sensitive man, and history seems to indicate that he must have been (perhaps to his own dismay), then he heard death, however faintly, the flat sound of it—like a fly trapped in a room. I looked at Lauro di Bosis for a moment with some of the feelings usually attributed to young girls standing at the grave of Keats.

And that was the end of it.

Except for one thing, a curious thing. That same night I had a dream, a very simple, nonsymbolic dream. In the dream I had a modest bouquet of flowers and I set out to try to find the bust of Lauro di Bosis and leave the flowers there. I couldn't find it. I had a sense of desperation, the cold-sweat urgency of a real nightmare. And then I knew where it was and why I hadn't noticed it. There it was, covered, bank on bank, with a heaped jungle of flowers. It was buried under a mountain of flowers. In my dream I wept for shame. But I woke then and I laughed out loud and slept soundly after that.

toward the depot and freight shed carrying all of her luggage at once—so much of it!—burdened comically beyond believing, and nearly beyond telling, like some kind of a circus clown. The train pulled away silently. Except for the two of them standing there in the sun with the suitcases, it was hard to believe that the train had stopped at all. After a while P. J. Florey, who sometimes doubles as a taxi driver, came over from his filling station to pick them up. There were wonderful complications in getting all that baggage into the trunk and the backseat. Then he whisked them away and out of sight.

Some kind of a clown, that's what Henry Monk was, always had been, and, everyone reasonably supposed, always would be. It was his vocation. He was like a grotesque dwarf, thick-torsoed, powerful-shouldered as big men twice his size with long loose arms dangling down and ending in huge, hopelessly awkward hands—they seemed to move, to live without coherence or even much relation to each other or the rest of him. Like wounded birds or a couple of fish on a string. He had a dented cannonball of a head with short curly hair clinging to it like some kind of fungus, squint eyes, red-rimmed and muddy, forever blinking, his lashes fluttering like the quick wings of insects. His lips were pouting, nearly colorless, and formed in bold exaggerated curves like those trick ones made out of wax that people put on for a joke. And his nose was peaked and warped and broken. Legs? They were incredibly short and thin and frail. Bowed, rickety, like bent pipes, they seemed incapable of sustaining the weight and bulk of the man above them.

When you looked at Henry Monk, you had to laugh. You were supposed to laugh. And all through the green years of growing up it seemed clear enough that Henry had not only borne this and fully played his given role—slapstick comic—in the strict unyielding pattern of the town, but he had seemed to relish it, to find some form of joy or at least security in being, like an ugly mongrel pup, the occasion of jokes, the source of crude comment and speculation, and, too, the somehow beholden receiver of the town's tousling, condescending, rough and curious affection. All that happened quite a while ago, way before the War.

When the War came along and Henry went to it, there was only general amusement that he thought he could be a soldier and some amazement that one way or another he passed the physical examination and was taken.

"Hell, all they want nowadays is bodies. They lay hands on you to see if you're still warm. If you are, they get a couple of doctors to look through you at both ends, both at the same time, and if they can't see enough to wink at each other, well, old buddy, you ain't nothing but a soldier boy."

"Maybe they're planning to use Henry for some kind of ex-per-i-ment."

So they laughed about it, and with bare country wit Henry was fixed in their chronicles; and then they forgot about him. Later, when they heard how he got a medal for some brave, unlikely thing done in a far-off, foreign land, they felt neither surprised nor cheated on their expectations of him.

"Henry, he's the kind that just don't know no better."

"What do he have to lose, anyway?"

"Most anything that happened to him would be in the nature of a im-prove-ment."

That he stayed in the Army afterwards to make a sort of a life out of soldiering caused at most a brisk shrug. He wouldn't be coming back. Well, what of it? There had been, and then only briefly, an empty place like a missing tooth. But, God knows, there were and always will be, world without end, amen, plenty of others to take his place—the strange, the weak, the drunk, the over- and undersexed, the feebleminded, the diseased, dwarfed, deformed, and dispossessed—to be offered up in propitiation, in true and perfect sacrifice, so that the safe, the sane, the whole might preserve at least some fragile notion of their self-esteem and human dignity.

Here then, after more than ten years, he was among them again, like the ghost of himself, and bringing with him a wife, a wife from Germany. Strangely, it was Ilse that the women hated. It was not just, not *only* that she was foreign. Even the perfect stranger has an allotted place here. It wasn't, either, because she was beautiful. There had always been young girls among them who bloomed, brief and mysterious, in roundness, softness, theatrical color, in rich hazy languorous desirability like peaches or, better, like some rare tropical plant or fruit, heard of from envied travelers, read about in a magazine or storybook once, seen in a picture show. There were always the older women of the tribe, those who themselves had possessed beauty once before the rigors of childbearing and raising, the long slow weathering of hard work, and, at last, the limp slack knowledge not of the years, but of the pure monotony at the secret heart of things, waved over them like a magic wand turning them wholly from splendid princesses to sharp-tongued stepsisters, from swans to ugly ducklings once again. These were the ones who knew too well how beauty fades and what a long time there is to live afterwards, gnawing the memory of its haunting visitation like a bitch with a sour bone. They could have tolerated even her pitiful vanities, her fancy clothes, her high head, gold hair shining, as she passed right by them without any sign of recognition. They knew already, with a brutal disinterest, discovering, like a sudden, deep-thrust wound, that she was old, old, old. In the beginning it was not these things that turned them against her. Or certainly not these things alone.

It was Henry. It was that she was Henry's wife. If Henry must marry at all, it was right, it was only natural, that he should choose one of his own kind, a girl clubfooted, crippled, cross-eyed, even crazy. Then together they could breed a whole family of genetic clowns. But this marriage asserted at least the possibility that he was in an obscure unguessed way a worthy man for any woman, even, maybe, for any one of them. Either it placed him on an equal status with their husbands, or, more urgent, more dreadful to contemplate, hauled down those husbands to his. Men, essentially brutes and beasts, of course, but good men and true still, could ogle her coming and going all they pleased, or, dozing after a big meal, drinking or dreaming, could summon up the swift incommunicable images of ecstasy, involving always and dependent on the myth of her imaginary naked perfection. Contemplating such a horn of plenty, they could whisper among themselves, joke, guffaw, or, for that matter, even speculate seriously, savoring it all they wanted to with vague lewd words on their tongues like raw oysters. That could be expected, countenanced, even encouraged; for that, after all, was to the eternal female consciousness at once a sly joke on the males and a bit in their teeth. But that they, husbands or lovers, should end up by having to envy Henry Monk. . . ! What became of your human dignity then? What happened if, instead of being a jest that some dark god spat into the dust and raised up to walk on two legs like a man, Henry became a creature secretly, mysteriously possessed of divinity, like one of God's chosen fools? Then the ugliness, deformity, bestiality—for beast he was—became things not for shame but for pride of any man, husband or lover, things they could strut for sharing. Then your human dignity, naked, dropped down on all fours and howled like a dog in heat.

And so it came to pass that when Ilse descended from the train and stood for one moment in the sun, wavering on those ridiculous heels, surveying the town with its clump of houses and small buildings like carelessly thrown-away cracker boxes, its dusty trees with leaves as limp as soiled money, its flags of washing on clotheslines signaling labor, monotony, and all the dreary sighs of lost and unfulfilled (not forgotten) desires, they (only faces then, pressed into gridded moons against the window screens) saw themselves for that instant wounded in her stranger's eyes, and since she was Henry's wife, they had to hate her from that time on.

"What on earth do you suppose she sees in him?"

"I wouldn't have the first idea. I'd hate to think about it."

"Of course, now, most of these foreign girls are just looking for a way to get to the U.S."

"There's plenty of soldiers to pick from. I mean it seems kind of crazy to single out somebody like Henry Monk."

"Oh, she's pretty, I'll say that for her. But if you get up close enough to her, you can see she wears a whole lot of makeup to hide the little lines around her eyes and on her neck."

"I never stood that close to her. I hardly ever see her, except once in a while at the store or in church."

"Who has, except by accident? I mean she's kind of distant, standoffish, don't you know?"

"I'll tell the world she don't look wore down and wore out, though. She looks as fresh as a young girl to me."

"It's the work, hard work and the cares of this world that wears you down, honey child. The lifting and bending and scrubbing and worrying, that's our cross to bear. She don't trouble much about that kind of thing. Did you know that Henry's the one that cleans house?"

"I wonder what she did before she met up with Henry?"

"What do you mean?"

"Well, I know he couldn't have very much, but she must have some money from some place to own all those nice clothes and things."

"I can just about imagine the kind of work she done before she got ahold of Henry. Some folks call it play, even if you do get paid for it."

The months of the first summer bled away, and the leaves paled and fell from the shedding trees like old wishes, were raked up into piles and transformed in gray shafts of smoke to dance briefly like genies released from magic lamps or bottles, or like some wild tongueless ghosts. And all that time, over fences, on back porches, over cool jelly glasses of buttermilk or lemonade or iced tea, in living rooms while sewing machines whirred like a field of locusts, while knitting needles clicked like cruel shears, gossip whirled around their unwitting heads like a cloud of insects around a light bulb. They couldn't have dreamed their names so much on everyone's tongue. The season changed under and around them, but they might as well have been on some remote seasonless island for all they knew of the climate, or the weather, or anyone else for that matter.

Henry worked at the garage and they lived in his family's (all dead now, gone to glory) little old house. The Army had someway taught him to calm his hands and use them well with tools.

Ilse stayed at home, wandered about vaguely in her wrapper all day long—for there were those who watched, keen-eyed, to see what she might or might not be doing, what she might or might not be wearing—playing the radio softly, watching the game shows on TV, drinking coffee and eating rich little cakes and cookies someone sent her regular as rain from Germany (who could picture her baking?) and shuffling the pages of the fashion magazines Henry brought home by the armload from the drugstore, shuffling the pages with a blurred speed like a deck of cards, then throwing them aside. Henry had little to say nowadays to the men who came to the garage or just loafed there. He did whatever work he had to do steadily, efficiently, and without complaining about anything, as if it didn't really matter what it was he was doing with himself and his time to make a living. Promptly when the five o'clock siren shrieked from the Volunteer Fire Station, he stopped whatever he was doing, packed his tools away, picked up his tin lunch pail, and started walking home like a shambling sleepwalker, passing known men, women, children without so much as a flicker of recognition on his face to prove he knew they were there. It wouldn't have been a surprise to anyone who saw him then, if he had simply walked through a house, a building, a tree, a parked car, any obstacle in his way that at least they believed in, just like you sometimes see in the movies. So, blindly he went home, stopping only occasionally at the drugstore to buy one copy of every picture magazine on the flowing rack, magnetized, hypnotized; and at his house he'd turn a sharp corner, a military corner, and without breaking the same restless pace move up the path splitting the now shaggy and weed-happy lawn ("Ain't it a crying shame the way he lets that old place just go to pieces?"), open the door, slam it, and lock it tight behind him. Then, seeming to happen all at the same time, in deft improbable furious simultaneity, all the yellow window shades came down and the radio was turned up full blast like the brass bands of doomsday over the aghast reverberating neighborhood houses.

"I expect you can about imagine what it's like for us, living right next door to them."

"Well, it's one thing to imagine something, and another to be right there with the radio booming and all."

"Thank the Lord for that radio! Think of the sounds it spares our ears."

"Have you heard them, really?"

"John has. You know how he is. Like a naughty little boy. Once in a while he tiptoes over there and puts his ear to the wall and listens."

"Men!"

"Oh well, that's just the way they are. There's no changing them."

"You can say that again."

"Do you know what John heard him call her one time when they were together like that? John says Henry called her 'my pretty birdie, pretty birdie in my cage.' "

"Would you believe it!"

Now this is a part of the strange truth about these two, these two lost ones, this beauty and this beast. Ilse has never been able to master more than a few words of English. It's no more translatable than birdsong to her. She has never learned to read much even in her own language. She has the mind of a young child. And who is Henry to teach her, anyway? All his life he's lived without knowing much of the brittle puzzling buzz and signal of words, inhabiting, instead, a dreamy place where images and feelings, even the vaguest of sensations, flicker with unheard-of swiftness like the first named birds of Paradise. And seldom these things coalesce, fall or fit into patterns like pictures or puzzles; and even when they do, they fly apart, fall to pieces because this world goes by so quick. He is one for whom reality is forever fluid, molten. And curiously, considering what the town thinks of him and what it has done to him, he's owned still by a kind of eyeless innocence that could convert even a sponge of vinegar into something sweet and inexpressible as the juice of a plum on the tongue. Besides, when he speaks, his tongue trips over words like a pratfalling clown. So he keeps quiet. Ilse, for all her sculptured conventional beauty and all her pretty clothes, is, or was anyway, as inwardly deformed as he is outwardly. She was stupid and bitter, brimming with hate. He sensed this right away, the first man to know it, when he stumbled upstairs with her to her room in Munich, when she was still a whore and any man, even one like Henry, could dare, could try and find out who she really was for a price. This knowledge of the truth of her lay between them like a shining blade for a long time, but now Henry has converted her and when they are together the flesh speaks for both of them and the grappling of love is joy. Why then have they come here? It's Ilse's idea to return to the place of his first wounds and try to heal them. And Henry's vision of this world is too complex to allow for something so dangerously simple as a rational malice or perverse jealousy. It would never occur to him that anyone would envy him, just as he'd never imagine that his wife's shy stupidity, bafflement, her wounds and weakness, so lightly disguised in wiles of languor and vanity, are not at once apparent to any observant beholder.

The winter settled in. The sky was a splash of dirty water. The days were shorter and needled by chilling rains. The trees shivered, some of them as nude as picked bones. Dogs huddled by fireplaces, slept close to the ashes and fading embers and dreamed, gold-eyed, while late, late, the passing freight trains cried out into the frosty night the names of places, towns and landscapes and climates, no one here except perhaps a few hopeful children ever dreamed of seeing or would see. Grumbling, uttering, sometimes calling out, husbands and wives in chilly sheets, cold flank to flank, slept the troubled sleep of the dead.

Toward the end of the gray season the words of the women had a cutting edge.

"Why did Henry Monk ever have to come back here?"

"He used to be such a nice boy, funny-like. He could make you laugh."

"He ain't funny anymore."

"Maybe he just came back here to show off his fancy wife."

"If that's so, why does he keep her shut up so tight in the house."

"Thank the Lord the last of his kin have gone to glory!"

"Pity his poor old mama if she'd had to live to see what become of her boy."

"It's the wife that changed him. You can bet on that."

"I wonder what their children will look like—him or her?"

"Who said anything about children?"

"She's not the type. Having kids is hard on the figure."

Spring came like a fierce beast, clawed at the frozen earth and turned up a nest of buried treasures and desires. Everywhere wildflowers spread like a rash, a plague. The trees were on fire with new leaves and blossoming, and bird songs rang in the air like dropped coins. Wind came from the south, through the dense, pine-dazed woods, over the river where the fish sometimes flashed and glittered like surgical blades in the fresh sun. Those winds were like new wines. Even the sky tugged at its breezy moorings like a gas balloon. Transformed, blood and sap, in bush and flesh, rose and burned together. Flesh rode hard on spirit like a cruel horseman. March was a tidal wave. By the middle of April the town was wholly submerged. And now they stumbled like divers in vague green precincts of the deep sea. And they drowned. . . .

Every year at just about this time there was a picnic. All the little town, everyone who was able, left in a procession to go over the roads and through the pinewoods to a quiet cleared place by the river. That was a day for you! All day the men played games and fished and, furtively, drank, and the women cooked and prepared huge tables of food. Before that evening meal was served it was the custom for the women to leave together to bathe in the river. Then, after the numbing satiety of the meal, late at night just this once a year, there was dancing—lovemaking and fighting in the shadows—and there were fireworks, the wild antic arcs of skyrockets bursting overhead in incandescent perfect stars as if all the least and lost wishes of the

heart were new and known again for once and all, and to be had
for the asking. Now even a preacher would turn up a bottle and
dance like the devil was pinching his joints and bones. There
was always time enough for regret later.

"Do you think they'll come too?"

"Who?"

"Henry and the German woman."

"Not liable to."

"Maybe we ought to call on her and invite her."

"When Henry was a boy he made a lot of fun at those pic-
nics."

"He's changed now."

"Maybe so."

"We'll see."

So the women called on Ilse Monk while Henry was at work,
talked to her through the screen door at least, and painted such a
picture of the pleasures of that day that she couldn't imagine
refusing to come.

The procession of cars, wagons, trucks, bikes, even the school
bus, went off the highway and through the woods to the place
where pine trees, sweet gum, and scrub oaks had been cleared
away down to the riverbank. The clearing was hedged with the
bright green of the woods, and all around wild dogwood burst
like puff-ball smoke explosions. The men set up trestles for the
long tables and built cooking fires. Then through the afternoon
the women worked while the men were fishing, playing softball,
pitching horseshoes, and firing their rifles and pistols at floating
things in the river. Ilse was left alone to wander like an ineffectual ghost among the busy women. Dressed in the white she had
worn when they had first seen her, she walked about smiling,
watching what they were doing without understanding any of
it.

Late in the afternoon, with the meal prepared, the women
went off by themselves to bathe in the river. They went in single file along a snaky path that struggled through the deep

woods for maybe a quarter of a mile before it climbed a steep rise. At the top of this, overlooking the river, there were the ruins of what had been a church once. From that spot the path ran down swiftly and steeply through an old, forgotten nigger graveyard, the forlorn tombstones leaning and tilting at wry angles. There was a narrow sandy beach at the edge of the river, a kind of cover, a fine hidden and sheltered place, and there the women, young girls, wives, old women stripped off their clothes and waded out into the slow river, still thrilling with some of winter. Soon they were splashing and shouting in shrill voices, drunk with the pleasure of it, almost dancing. The men did not trouble their privacy, and only some of the young boys, peering from the trees and shrubs with amazed eyes, saw all of what happened.

Ilse had not seen them go. Not needed, she had wandered off in the woods, and she came on that path by accident. She followed it, unknowing, to the place, and she stood at the top of the little hill seeing them, all shapes and all sizes, shed of their clothing like winter skin, in the clay-colored water. When she came suddenly upon this scene, she laughed.

Perhaps it was the sound of her laughter, perhaps only the sight of her, elaborately dressed, tall on the hilltop, perhaps, at just that moment, only a desire to transform her from the stranger and spectator (like some visiting goddess) into a sharer, but whatever the first cause, they soon let their long-stored feelings possess them. Her laughter became to them a kind of profanation. Some of them stumbled dripping all the way to the top of the hill and, taking hold of her, urged her toward the bank. At first she laughed more loudly and resisted. Then more of them came running. They swarmed over her, ripped her clothes until she was as bare as they. For a moment, panting, aware of what they had done, they drew back in a circle and looked at her. She stood still as if carved there in stone on that spot, but then she threw back her head with a flash of gold hair and shrieked like a wild animal. All at once they were bearing her overhead, high in their hands, into the water. They baptized her amid a tangle of swarming bodies, of squirming legs like a nest of snakes, a thrashing fury.

As soon as the men heard that terrible shriek, they came running through the woods. Henry ran with them on his frail legs. Coming to the place, he tripped over a grassy tombstone, fell and rolled end over end down the hill, rose and fought through the storm of bodies and lifted her up in his arms. Nearly drowned, she huddled against him like a child.

Just then it went silent. The men fell back along the path to make a way for him, the women crouched down in the water or covered themselves with hands and arms, touched with shame. But, following the powerful torso, Henry's dwarfed, absurd legs emerged from the water, bowed and shaking with the strain of the burden, and then someone began to laugh. Then another. Then everyone was laughing at once, men and women, shameless, delirious, wildly relieved. They were rolling with it, falling on their knees and backs with it, dancing with it, some nearly drowning with laughter.

Henry ran up the steep path and turned away, blundering among the trees, pursued by the sound of laughter like hounds, unaware, unable to grasp the simple truth that now he had paid them a debt, that now, purged, they could freely offer him, if not love, then at least his rightful place again in the only world they knew about or cared to believe in.

BREAD FROM STONES

I DO NOT KNOW much about rich people. I have been among them sometimes and was always more or less accepted because I am Southern and it is all right to be Southern and poor if your ancestors were Southern and rich. Still, I find them very strange.

I can give examples. Once I was invited to luncheon at the country house of some rich New York people, and it happened that I sat between a successful Dutch businessman and his wife. The only memory I keep of him is of a round bright blond head bent busily close to a plate of food. I remember his wife more clearly. She was an astonishingly beautiful woman, delicate, fragile, and pale-faced with wide amazed eyes like an expensive china doll. She told me that she was deeply involved with Eastern philosophies, that she had been for years, and that she was continuing her studies at an American university while her husband was here. I was really interested in what she had to say because I don't know anything about Eastern philosophies. She talked to me in a kind of whispered breathless urgency like a child sharing a very solemn secret. I tried vainly to follow the words and all of the veiled nuances her voice implied. But I couldn't. Chiefly because the whole time she was talking to me her little sharp-nailed hand was as busy as a spider, exploring my thigh and groin under the table. Of course, after we rose from the table and went our separate ways I never saw or heard of her again.

Or take the time I took a girl to call on her uncle who was a rich Texan. He lived on a yacht, an enormous one as white and pretty as a birthday cake. He was anchored not far from New York and we drove up the Hudson to call on him. As soon as we came on board he invited us to join him in a drink.

"This is a nice yacht you have," I said.

"You think so, huh?"

"Yes, sir, that's what I think." I didn't know what else to say.

"Well," he said, "the yacht's all right. If you've got to live somewhere a yacht is as good a place as any I guess. Personally I can't stand living in a house."

"Did you ever try a trailer?"

"Boy," he said gruffly, "you don't understand much. Don't ever trust your snap judgments about people and things. You probably are under the impression that I am a happy man. Look at me."

He was a big, handsome, red-faced man lolling comfortably in a deck chair. The first thing he reminded me of was a great big teddy bear. Which, offhand, is about the happiest thing I can think of.

"You look happy to me."

"Well, you're wrong."

"Okay."

"Dead wrong!" he went on. "My personal tragedy is as follows. All my life all that I have wanted to be is a cattle rancher. To make a long story short, every time I would buy a cattle ranch, the damn fools came along and drilled and struck oil. Whamo! There went the cattle ranch."

"Are you still trying?"

"Hell, no," he said. "I quit trying years ago. What's the use?"

I have no idea where this general discussion would have led and maybe ended, because just then the girl interrupted us.

"Uncle Ed," she said, "do you remember when I was a little

girl and I used to come and visit you and one time you said you would give me a quarter if I learned 'Break, Break, Break'?"

"Sure do," he said. "She did it too. She memorized that poem and earned the quarter."

"I've never forgotten it."

"Think you can still say it?"

"Oh yes."

And without hesitation she began to recite. I was watching her, a picture of intense concentration as she summoned up the melancholy of the poem. Then I heard him gasp for breath. He sat there for a minute or so quietly after she had finished, and then, apparently the victim of a sudden impulse, he jumped to his feet, trotted down the deck, and disappeared into a stateroom. He came back after a while, all smiles, waving a check so the ink would dry.

"Here," he said to her. "Take this. It's the least I can do."

It was a check for more money than I can make in a month or two.

Afterwards, when we were driving back to the city, she seemed pensive and a little sad.

"What's the matter with you?" I said.

"It's all so pathetic," she said, "so tragic."

"What is?"

"Being rich," she said. "It must be tragic to be very rich."

"Yes," I said. "I reckon it must be."

I couldn't see any point in arguing with her. That wasn't what I had in mind at all. She got most of her ideas on the subject from a passing familiarity with the works of F. Scott Fitzgerald. Anyway, I couldn't care less about it one way or the other. I have never had to be around rich people that much.

My cousin Raymond was always trying to be around rich people. He had even been slightly rich once or twice himself. Raymond was one of the black sheep of our family. Almost any old Southern family has its quota of black sheep, and I could tell you something about that general subject too. But it is beside the point. Take my word for it. Raymond ran away on his way to

Yale and spent the money for his tuition in New York. Then he
became a professional ballroom dancer. Raymond was a wonderful dancer, I'll say that for him. He was tall and broad-shouldered and slender and darkly handsome. And he looked just fine
in a white tie and tails. The family didn't object to his dancing
even though they wished he had gone to Yale. Or at least managed to get as far north as New Haven. They did object, however, to the fact that he changed his last name to a Spanish one.
He maintained that his new name was much more exotic than
Raymond Singletree, and nobody could disagree with him on
that. The crux of the matter was: did Raymond need an exotic
name to be a dancer? He seemed to think so. The other members
of the family did not. The other thing they disapproved of was
his dancing partner, Vivian. She was a glazed, beautiful blonde,
absolutely perfectly equipped for a nightclub dance team, but all
the hierarchy of aunts insisted that she was fundamentally
"common." Raymond said they were married, but nobody took
that assertion at face value. Oh, he had a grand old time before
the War, dancing in nightclubs all over the world, his pockets
jingling and bulging with easy money. Then the War came and
when he returned home from three years in the infantry, ETO,
he was ravaged, his face gray and deeply lined and most of his
hair gone from wearing a steel pot on his head so much of the
time. Meanwhile Vivian had left him for a 4-F saxophone
player. And the last of the money was gone.

One week with Christmas coming soon, I ran into him on the
street. He was skulking along the sidewalk. He had on an ill-
fitting, cheap trench coat with the collar turned up and he wore
a snap-brim hat pulled down over his eyes. He looked for all the
world like a gangster in an old-fashioned grade-B movie.

"Raymond!" I said. "Where are you going—to a masquerade
party?"

"I beg your pardon," he said. "I'm afraid I don't know you
from Adam's house cat."

"Don't kid me," I said. "You're Raymond Singletree and you
know it."

He stood there glaring at me fiercely under the brim of his hat while the quick crowds flowed all around us.

"All right," he said at last. "So what if I am?"

"I'm glad to see you, that's all. Where have you been and what are you up to?"

"I've been down and out," he said. "Down and out. At the moment I'm on my way over to stick up Macy's."

I started to laugh.

"Don't laugh," he said. "It isn't a laughing matter. I've got it all figured out and I think I can get away with it."

"All right," I said. "But before you go and rob Macy's how about having a drink with me, just for old time's sake?"

He glanced furtively at his wristwatch.

"Why not?"

Once I got him into a booth in a bar and he had a drink in his hands, it was clear that he was dead serious about trying to stick up Macy's single-handed. He explained that he was flat broke and that it was especially awkward for him to be so broke at this time because he had a marvelous opportunity to get his hands on a couple of million dollars. All he needed was to get his good clothes out of hock and a little extra pocket money.

"This couple of million," I said, "is it a sure thing?"

"It's a woman," he announced simply.

Raymond had always been a lover and I had to admire his beautiful, resigned honesty about it. He went on to tell me that this particular woman was the daughter of a famous financier. She was divorced and she loved to go out drinking and dancing with him. He added sententiously that it was a crime for a man in his position to let such an opportunity go begging.

"You were really serious about robbing Macy's, then?"

"Sure," he said. "It's the only way."

And with that grim remark he fished out a huge Army .45 pistol and plunked it down in the middle of the table.

"Get it out of sight," I said. "Don't you know it's against the law to carry around a gun like that?"

"Oh," he said. "Sorry."

And he put the pistol back in his trench-coat pocket.

"Are you crazy, Raymond? Don't you have any idea what you're doing?"

"Sure I know what I'm doing," he said. "I'm taking a chance to get some money. I'm sick of being poor."

"You make me tired," I said. "You don't have to be poor. You could make a living doing a lot of different things. You could always teach dancing. Arthur Murray's would probably be glad to hire you."

"Arthur Murray's!" he said. "Oh my God!"

"All right, forget about Murray. You could do any number of things."

"I don't want to make a living. I want to be rich."

"Listen," I said, "nobody in our family, nobody, has been rich since the War Between the States."

"That's it!" he said. "That's it exactly. All my life I've had to hear all about the wonderful old times they had down on the old plantation. *Etc., etc!* Well, I had to grow up in a crummy furnished apartment eating off of fine leftover old china with fine leftover old silver. My old man divided his time between dodging bill collectors and telling me what a privilege it was to be a Singletree. The chosen people. The hell with it!"

"That's the spirit," I said. "The hell with it."

"No," he said. "Not right. Not correct. On the contrary, I am going to show them."

Here it was with Christmas coming on, and I hadn't even seen Raymond for years. It should have been a wonderful reunion. It should have been like the old times when both of us were new in New York and we would meet once in a while in some bar. And over a drink or two we'd hatch fantastic conspiracies, the conspiracies of two lonely Southern boys a long way from home. I had always admired Raymond. I admired him for his looks, his attitude, his talent. And when I went to work for the bank, how I used to envy him his nimble feet and the bright, bitter world of the nightclubs I couldn't afford to go to, and the shining, kiln-baked finish of his dancing partner. Once in a while in those days I would get a postcard from some far-off place—from Paris, Mexico City, Montevideo. I still keep one he sent me from Rio.

It is an aerial view of the harbor in brilliant color. I remember sitting in my room and just staring at it for a long time while the rain fell heavy on the gray city outside. All that it said was "This is the life. You ought to try it sometime. As ever, Raymond."

"Raymond," I said. "I'll tell you what. I'll buy that pistol from you."

"Why?"

"I want it."

"It's worth a lot of money," he said.

"How much?"

"I could make do with a couple hundred dollars."

"I guess it's worth that much to me," I said.

I gave him all the cash I had with me and wrote out a check for the balance. He seemed to be very grateful and promised he would get in touch with me soon. After he left I went into the men's room and put the pistol in the wastebasket, hidden underneath a pile of used paper towels. I often wonder what the janitor, or whoever it was, thought when he found it there. The damn thing was loaded and everything.

A few months later I heard from Raymond again. It was in early April, I think, because I remember walking from the bus stop and noticing how beautiful the first frail green leaves were in the park. Raymond was waiting for me in front of the apartment building. He was parked right in front in a sleek, shining, low-slung sports car. He looked quite different now. He was wearing an expensive sports jacket and an ascot. He had some kind of a wig on that looked perfectly natural. He appeared to be about ten years younger, and he was all smiles.

"Hey you!" he said. "You're coming with me."

"Okay."

I didn't have anything else to do with myself, so I just got in the car. We eased out into the traffic and tore away with a spectacular growl of pure horsepower.

"Like it?"

"Sure," I said. "Whose is it?"

"Mine," he said cheerfully. "It's all mine."

"Where are we going?"

"To meet Sonya."

"Who?"

"Don't you even remember?" he said. "She's the one I was telling you about at Christmastime."

"You're not married, are you?"

"Not yet," he said. "Not just yet."

We drove on downtown and left the car in a parking lot.

"Listen," he told me as we walked along, "there's one little thing I ought to tell you. She's Jewish."

"So what?"

"I knew you wouldn't disapprove," he said. "Some of the family wouldn't understand, but I knew you would. Anyway, she is descended from Spanish Jews, and that makes it all right."

We went into a cocktail lounge and climbed a set of wide, carpeted stairs. She was sitting at a table waiting for us. She was a tall, handsome woman, a little gray, a little fat, but elegantly dressed. And you could tell she had been beautiful as a girl.

"Hello, honey," she said. "Raymond told me all about you. You work in a bank."

"Yes," I said. "That's about the size of it."

"You're kind of cute," she said. "Raymond said you were terribly serious, but I think you're kind of cute."

Evidently she had been drinking steadily while waiting for us, but she ordered another to celebrate our arrival and to be sociable.

"You know what?" she said to me. "Raymond dances divinely. He dances like an angel. He can dance even better than Rumpelstiltskin."

"Who the hell is he?" Raymond said. "I never heard of him. What kind of a name is that, anyway?"

"He's in a fairy tale," I said. "But I think—I hope—Sonya has got him mixed up with somebody else."

"Sure," she said. "I always mix them up. Like the names of popular songs. He was the first one I could think of. What I mean, I guess, is it's all kind of like a fairy tale."

"I don't get it," Raymond said.

"But you do," she said to me. "You get it, don't you?"

"Sure," I said. "It's something like Cinderella."

"Right," she said. "That's exactly right. More or less . . ."

Everything was very pleasant until we started to leave. When we got up I noticed that she was wobbly on her high heels, but Raymond didn't seem concerned about her, so I didn't worry about it. At the top of the stairs she tripped and then over and over she went, rolling slowly down the stairs in a great soft blur of shiny clothes and pale flesh. When she hit bottom, she just curled up like a big comfortable cat going to sleep.

The manager came tearing over waving his arms and shouting. He was terribly excited. He thought she might be dead or something.

"Get up, baby," Raymond said. "You're drawing a crowd."

"Don't want to," she said. "Wanna go sleepy-bye."

"Go get a cab," Raymond told me. "It will be a lot easier to get her home in a cab."

I walked up the street until I found a cruising taxi. When we pulled up in front of the place, Raymond and a couple of waiters heaved her into the backseat like a sack of meal. Everyone seemed calm and collected by that time. Strictly routine.

"Listen," Raymond said, "thanks a million."

"Anytime."

And I stood for a moment and watched the taxi drive away.

It was the middle of summer before Raymond got in touch with me again. I was sitting in my apartment one Saturday afternoon considering what in the world to do with myself. In the morning I had walked in the park and watched the children playing and the old men on the benches sleeping or just staring. There wasn't even the least ghost of a breeze to stir the listless leaves. I was thinking maybe I would take in a movie, any air-conditioned movie, when the phone rang and it was Raymond.

"Hey, old-timer," he said. "How's it going?"

"All right, I guess."

"Well, cheer up. We're going for a weekend in the country."

"When?"

"I'll be right there," he said. "Grab your toothbrush and let's go."

We drove out to Long Island in the sports car. It was fine with the warm air blowing over us and the trim feel of light-headed speed. Almost like sailing. Raymond looked good, suntanned, fit, and healthy. He had dispensed with the wig.

"No hair again," I said.

"Why should I try and fool myself? I'm not a kid anymore. I might as well look my age.

"By the way," he added. "Don't get the wrong idea about Sonya from last time."

"I didn't get any idea," I said. "She was drunk."

"That's what I mean," he said. "See what I mean? She drinks, sure, but getting drunk like that is a rare occasion. A very rare occasion."

"Okay, if you say so."

"Believe me, it's the truth. Sonya is all right. She's had her share of troubles, though."

"I expect so."

The estate we went to, carefully secluded by a few acres of piny woods, was fantastic. It was one of those turn-of-the-century châteaus. It had been added to since then and, in deference to the times, a couple of TV aerials perched like metallic scarecrows on the roof. The wide slope of the lawn had been gouged for a swimming pool. Sonya came running down a pine-needly path to greet us, bright in slacks and an Italian T-shirt and closely followed by two poodles. They gamboled awkwardly around her like a pair of spectacular wind-up toys. As she ran toward us through the light and shadow that flickered through the leaves, she seemed like a modern burlesque of Diana, the huntress. It wouldn't have surprised me a bit at that moment if she had been carrying a bow and arrow. She seemed glad to see us there and she was quite sober. She led us inside into rooms that had an oaken heaviness and the gloom and clutter of too much furniture and too many things. It was almost as if somebody had won a whole lot of prizes at a carnival. Except, of course, that everything was very expensive.

"This is a crazy, kooky place," Sonya said. "But I love it. My mother was an Italian opera singer. My old man had some taste, I think, but he humored her. As a matter of fact, I don't think he gave a damn about anything as long as she was happy. She was like a big overgrown child, a baby. Spoiled but beautiful, very beautiful."

"Wait until you see the plumbing," Raymond said. "It's better than a high-class whorehouse."

He was right. My bathroom was an extraordinary place. The walls and even the ceiling had colored mirrors so that the whole room rippled with a broken sourceless light. It was like being underwater. The toilet and the basin and the bidet and the enormous sunken tub were made of black marble, and all of the pipes were some kind of gold plate. The bedroom was a dream of the Orient filtered through the consciousness of the end of nineteenth-century America. I listened for the sound of a gong or the tinkle of little bells and sniffed for the only thing lacking, the odor of incense. On the walls there were a few small portraits of desperately ethereal pre-Raphaelite young ladies. And directly above the wide bed there was a painting of a boyish, almost sexless Pandora covering her slim nubility in shy, decorous astonishment as a swarm of evils ascended, batlike, from the open box.

We settled on the lawn in deck chairs and enjoyed tall cool summer drinks. After a while a governess brought Sonya's little girl to meet us. They were dressed to swim, the governess chaste and dumpy in a single-piece bathing suit, the pale child like a butterfly in her frilly swimsuit and water wings. She looked at us with sad questioning eyes as if she didn't know whether she was going to be patted or spanked.

"Say hello to the nice people, honey," Sonya said. "Can't you say hello? You can say hello to your Uncle Raymond. She's shy. She usually speaks right up and says hello. I don't know why, but she's a little shy today. All right, honey, you run along and have a nice swim before your supper."

The little girl scampered away, immensely relieved, and we

could hear her shrill voice as she shouted to her governess above the noise of splashing.

"I invited some people for tonight," Sonya said.

"I thought you said this was going to be a quiet weekend," Raymond said.

"I thought it might be more fun for your cousin if we had some kind of a little party."

"Don't worry about me," I said. "Anything is fine with me."

"These people," she said to me, "are a little bit *kikey*, but you may find them amusing. I gather from Raymond that you've had a kind of sheltered life."

"Sheltered?"

"You know what I mean," she said, smiling. "Going to a nice respectable college and then working in a nice respectable bank. I mean, it might be fun for you to see the other half. These people have lots of money, though. Oh yes, lots and lots of money . . ."

I do not remember whether we had any supper or not. I think not. We just kept on drinking and before long things stopped being sequential and chronological and took on a montage aspect. I remember that when people finally began to arrive they were all dressed as hillbillies and cowboys. It turned out Sonya had invited them for a square dance. With a sudden reckless fury we cleared a large room—the music room, I guess, because there were two grand pianos—stacking everything on top of everything else in one corner in a heap as if for a huge bonfire. Somebody put on some square-dance records and Raymond began to call the dance. The room whirled and turned around us as we stomped and sweated. Everybody seemed to be as happy as can be. Then I remember crawling up under one of the pianos to get a little rest. I curled up there on a folded rug and watched the dizzy cycle of feet and legs, like a tribal dance, all around me.

I must have dozed off because quite abruptly the room was empty and silent. I came out from under the piano to find the floor littered with shoes and odds and ends of clothing. A brassiere was festooned on the ornate chandelier and a record was spinning aimlessly on the turntable. I tried to switch off the hi-fi, but only succeeded in starting it again. Square-dance music roared in the room. I went outside for a little fresh air. Then I heard laughter and voices from the swimming pool. I walked down to have a look and stood teetering and unsteady at the edge staring into the darkness of the pool. There could only have been a few people swimming, but the pool seemed to be packed and swarming with bodies. It reminded me of a huge tank of fish.

"There he is!" somebody said. "I knew he was still alive."

"Push him in."

"Push the sonofabitch in the pool!"

I remember that it seemed desperately important not to be pushed into the pool. I fought off clutching hands and sprinted across the lawn to the house. Somehow I found my room. Leaning against the closed door in the dark, panting, I heard soft voices in my bathroom and the sound of splashing in the black marble tub with the gold-plated pipes. I flopped on my bed and, as the room began to spin around me, I fell asleep.

Sunday was depressing. The guests had all gone home, and we three had hangovers and were a little on edge. There was a rather solemn luncheon outside on a terrace at which the governess and the little daughter joined us and we all strove to be pleasant to one another. Late in the afternoon Raymond drove me back to town. It was a long wearisome ride in the weaving, stalling lines of Sunday traffic.

"Boy, you sure tied one on," he said. "How do you like it? Some place!"

"I think you can do better than that, Raymond."

"What do you mean? Didn't you have fun? Didn't you have a good time?"

"Sure," I said. "It's not that. I just wondered if you really want to live that way."

"What way? We spent a weekend in the country, that's all."

"You know what I mean."

"The trouble with you is you've got no imagination. You're so damn middle-class. You get all upset by anything out of the ordinary. If anything is fun, it's got to be bad. You end up by moralizing everything."

"Maybe you're right."

After that weekend I didn't see or hear of Raymond for quite a while. I heard from her, though. She called me up late one night. She was drunk, but nevertheless she made good sense.

"Why do you have to spoil everything?"

"Who is this?" I said.

"Sonya," she said. "You come along and ruin a perfectly good thing. Perfectly good."

"I don't know what you are talking about."

"Yes you do," she said. "You damnwell do know. You know what Raymond wanted you to do? He wanted you to approve. That's all he wanted out of you and you wouldn't."

"What is all this?"

"I said he wanted you to approve. The idiot! He wants some little sign of approval from that crummy *Tobacco Road* family of his.

"Talk about life on the old plantation!" she went on. "You make me sick! Don't you want anybody else to have a good time ever? For Christ's sake, you would think it was royal blood or something. Who the hell does he think he is—the Duke of Windsor?"

"No," I said. "I don't believe he thinks that."

And on that happy note she hung up on me.

I sometimes wonder about myself. I have no idea why, without even trying to, I manage to get involved in things. The truth is I really didn't care what Raymond did with himself. But when I think about it, it seems worse somehow than caring strongly one way or the other. Just being neutral, disinterested, indifferent, just watching the things that happen to other people, you can acquire your share of guilt. That happens to be ironic, when you think about it, because that is the one thing—guilt, responsibility, call it what you want to—I was most anxiously trying to avoid by means of my neutral strategy. I guess the truth is that nobody but a saintly hermit can be really immune. And even that vocation is a career of danger and daring. Take St. Anthony, for example.

When the summer was over I bought myself a dog, a little beagle pup. It was a selfish thing to do. A beagle is so full of natural energy and has such a fine sense of smell that it's a shame to keep one cooped up in a city. But I wanted one, and in a way he reminded me of my childhood when there were always plenty of dogs around the place. I tried to give him enough exercise in the park. I used to take long walks there early in the morning and in the evenings when I got home from work. Early in October I was walking the dog in the park. It was foggy with chill in the air and all the paths in the park were strewn with the rich debris of autumn, the damp blown leaves, the broken twigs and branches. Into autumn's melancholy and desolation came Raymond, stepping suddenly in front of me from behind a tree. He held up his hand to stop me, like a traffic cop. Or the Ancient Mariner . . .

"I've been hanging around here all week long trying to get up the nerve to speak to you," he said. "I've been following you every morning."

"That's the silliest thing I ever heard," I said. "Why didn't you just come up to the apartment?"

"I wasn't sure you would understand."

We began to walk along the path together.

"That's a nice pup," he said. "A real nice puppy dog."

"Yes," I said. "He's a good one."

"Listen," Raymond said. "That gun. You remember that pistol I sold you last spring?"

"Yes."

"I have to have it back."

"Why in the world . . . ?"

"I have to go out West."

"You won't need a gun, Raymond," I said. "The Indians are all on reservations and all the cowboys are on television."

"Very funny!"

"If you need money," I said, "why don't you sell the car? You just can't decide to go out and rob some place every time you're a little short of cash."

"Oh I couldn't sell the car. I just couldn't do that. Go out to California without the car! Sonya gave me that car. It's all I've got left."

"Whatever happened to Sonya?"

"We broke up," he said. "The last I heard she was running around with some musician. Probably a goddamn saxophone player. It seems like all my women end up with saxophone players."

"How much do you need?"

"A couple of hundred, that's all. But the thing is, I couldn't just take it from you. I've got a little pride left."

"Okay, suppose we make it a straight loan?"

"No, I'd feel like you were just giving it to me."

"We could write it all down and make it official."

"In that case," he said, "maybe it would be all right."

"Come on up to the apartment and let's have a cup of coffee."

We drank some coffee and I typed up an extremely official-looking statement to the effect that Raymond Singletree owed me two hundred dollars. Then I wrote him a check for it.

"Well," I said, "California ought to be great."

"It is great," he said. "I always had a fine time there."

"I'd like to go there someday myself," I said. "What do you expect to find out there?"

"Find?"

"Do?"

"Oh, I haven't got the slightest idea," he said cheerfully. "Something will turn up. It always does."

I had no more news of him until the springtime when I received a scrawly letter from Los Angeles. "Things are going pretty good out here," he wrote. "I am running around with this photographer's model. She is really gorgeous. You ought to see her. She is a little mixed up, but who the hell isn't? What would I ever do with myself if women weren't so crazy about dancing? She makes a good living and we are planning to pool our resources and open up a fancy camera shop here. It ought to go over big and we will make a killing. We might even get married. I will send you a picture of her in my next letter. Take care of yourself, old time.

"By the way," he added in a P.S., "I have not forgotten about the money I owe you. I will enclose a check for the full amount in my next letter."

Naturally I haven't heard a word from him since then, but I'm sure he will turn up again one of these days, broke, down on his luck, and still believing that his luck will change and something, some miraculous and shattering revelation, will occur to atone for all the sad waste of the past. And I imagine I will help him out again. Not that I believe the same myth that he does. Not that I think we could change things much one way or the other or would even if we could. I have been living alone and working in a bank too long to believe anything like that. Still, it makes me feel better that somebody I know believes it.

WOUNDED SOLDIER
(Cartoon Strip)

WHEN THE TIME CAME at last and they removed the wealth of
bandages from his head and face, all with the greatest of care as
if they were unwinding a precious mummy, the Doctor—he of
the waxed, theatrical, upswept mustache and the wet sad eyes of
a beagle hound—turned away. Orderlies and aides coughed,
looked at floor and ceiling, busied themselves with other tasks.
Only the Head Nurse, a fury stiff with starch and smelling of
strong soap, looked, pink-cheeked and pale white as fresh flour,
over the Veteran's shoulders. She stared back at him, unflinching and expressionless, from the swimming light of the mirror.

No question. It was a terrible wound.

—I am so sorry, the Doctor said. —It's the best we can do for
you.

But the Veteran barely heard his words. The Veteran looked
deeply into the mirror and stared at the stranger who was now
to be himself with an inward wincing that was nearer to the
sudden gnawing of love at first sight than of self-pity. It was like
being born again. He had, after all, not seen himself since the
blinding, burning instant when he was wounded. Ever since
then he had been a mystery to himself. How many times he had
stared into the mirror through the neat little slits left for his
eyes and seen only a snowy skull of gauze and bandages! He

imagined himself as a statue waiting to be unveiled. And now he regretted that there was no real audience for the occasion except for the Doctor, who would not look, and the Head Nurse—she for whom no truth could be veiled anyway and hence for whom there could never be any system or subtle aesthetic of exposure or disclosure by any clever series of gradual deceptions. She carried the heavy burden of one who was familiar with every imaginable kind of wound and deformity.

—You're lucky to be alive, she said. —Really lucky.

—I don't know what you will want to do with yourself, the Doctor said. —Of course, you understand that you are welcome to remain here.

—That might be the best thing for any number of good reasons, the Head Nurse said. Then to the Doctor: —Ordinarily cases like this one elect to remain in the hospital.

—Are there others? the Veteran asked.

—Well . . . the Head Nurse admitted, there are none quite like you.

—I should hope not, the Veteran said, suddenly laughing at himself in the mirror. —Under the circumstances it's only fair that I should be able to feel unique.

—I am so sorry, the Doctor said.

Over the Veteran's shoulder in the mirror the Head Nurse smiled back at him.

That same afternoon a High-ranking Officer came to call on him. The Officer kept his eyes fixed on the glossy shine of his boots. After mumbled amenities he explained to the Veteran that while the law certainly allowed him to be a free man, free to come and go as he might choose, he ought to give consideration to the idea that his patriotic duty had not ended with the misfortune of his being stricken in combat. There were, the Officer explained, certain abstract obligations which clearly transcended those written down as statute law and explicitly demanded by the State.

—There are duties, he continued, waxing briefly poetic, which like certain of the cardinal virtues, are deeply disguised. Some of these are truly sublime. Some are rare and splendid like the aroma of a dying arrangement of flowers or the persistent haunting of half-remembered melodies.

The Veteran, who knew something about the music of groans and howls, and something about odors, including, quite recently, the stink of festering and healing, was not to be deceived by this sleight of hand.

—Get to the point, he said.

The High-ranking Officer was flustered, for he was not often addressed by anyone in this fashion. He stammered, spluttered as he offered the Veteran a bonus to his regular pension, a large sum of money, should he freely choose to remain here in the hospital. After all, his care and maintenance would be excellent and he would be free of many commonplace anxieties. Moreover, he need never feel that his situation was anything like being a prisoner. The basic truth about any prisoner is—is it not?—that he is to be deliberately deprived, insofar as possible, of all the usual objects of desire. The large bonus would enable the Veteran to live well, even lavishly in the hospital if he wanted to.

—Why?

Patiently the Officer pointed out that his appearance in public, in the city or the country, would probably serve to arouse the anguish of the civilian population. So many among the military personnel had been killed or wounded in this most recent war. Wasn't it better for everyone concerned, especially the dependents, the friends and relatives of these unfortunate men, that they be permitted to keep their innocent delusions of swirling battle flags and dimly echoing bugle calls, rather than being forced to confront in fact and flesh the elemental brute ugliness of modern warfare? As an old soldier, or as one old soldier to another, surely the Veteran must and would acknowledge the validity of this argument.

The Veteran nodded and replied that he guessed the Officer also hadn't overlooked the effect his appearance might have on the young men of the nation. Most likely a considerable cooling of patriotic ardor. Probably a noticeable, indeed a measurable, decline in the number of enlistments.

—Just imagine for a moment, the Veteran said, what it would be like if I went out there and stood right next to the recruiting poster at the Post Office. Sort of like a "before and after" advertisement.

At this point the Officer stiffened, scolded, and threatened. He ended by reminding the Veteran that no man, save the One, had ever been perfect and blameless. He suggested to him that, under the strictest scrutiny, his service record would no doubt reveal some error or other, perhaps some offense committed while he was a soldier on active duty which would still render him liable to a court-martial prosecution.

Safe for the time being with his terrible wound, the Veteran laughed out loud and told the Officer that nothing they could do or think of doing to him could ever equal this. That he might as well waste his time trying to frighten a dead man or violate a corpse.

Then the Officer pleaded with the Veteran. He explained that his professional career as a leader of men might be ruined if he failed in the fairly simple assignment of convincing one ordinary common soldier to do as he was told to.

The Veteran, pitying this display of naked weakness, said that he would think about it very seriously. With that much accomplished, the Officer brightened and recovered his official demeanor.

—I imagine it would have been so much more convenient for everyone if I had simply been killed, wouldn't it? the Veteran asked as the Officer was leaving.

Still bowed, still unable to look at him directly, the Officer shrugged his epauleted shoulders and closed the door very quietly behind him.

Nevertheless the Veteran had made up his mind to leave the sanctuary of the hospital. Despite his wound and appearance he was in excellent health, young still and full of energy. And the tiptoeing routine of this place was ineffably depressing. Yet even though he had decided to leave, even though he was certain he was going soon, he lingered, he delayed, he hesitated. Days went

by quietly and calmly, and in the evening when she was off
duty, the Head Nurse often came to his room to talk to him
about things. Often they played cards. A curious and easy intimacy developed. It seemed almost as if they were husband and
wife. On one occasion he spoke to her candidly about this.

—You better be careful, he said. —I'm not sexless.

—No, I guess not, she said. —But I am.

She told him that she thought his plan of going out into the
world again was dangerous and foolish.

—Go ahead. Try it and you'll be back here in no time at all,
beating on the door with bloody knuckles and begging us to be
readmitted, to get back in. You are too young and inexperienced
to understand anything about people. Human beings are the
foulest things in all creation. They will smell your blood and go
mad like sharks. They will kill you if they can. They can't allow
you to be out there among them. They will tear you limb from
limb. They will strip the meat off your bones and trample your
bones to dust. They will turn you into dust and a fine powder
and scatter you to the four winds!

—I can see you have been deeply wounded, too, the Veteran
said.

At that the Head Nurse laughed out loud. Her whole white
mountainous body shook with laughter.

When the Veteran left the hospital he wore a mask. He
wanted to find a job and wearing the mask seemed to him to be
an act of discretion which would be appreciated. But this, as he
soon discovered, was not the case at all. A mask is somehow
intolerable. A mask becomes an unbearable challenge. When he
became aware of this, when he had considered it, only the greatest exercise of self-discipline checked within him the impulse to
gratify their curiosity. It would have been so easy. He could so
easily have peeled off his protective mask and thereby given to
the ignorant and innocent a new creature for their bad dreams.

One day he came upon a small traveling circus and applied for
a job with them.

—What can you do? the Manager asked.

This Manager was a man so bowed down by the weight of weariness and boredom that he seemed at first glance to be a hunchback. He had lived so long and so closely with the oddly gifted and with natural freaks that his lips were pursed as if to spit in contempt at everything under the sun.

—I can be a clown, the Veteran said.

—I have enough clowns, the Manager said. Frankly, I am sick to death of clowns.

—I'll be different from any other clown you have ever seen, the Veteran said.

And then and there he took off his mask.

—Well, this is highly original, the Manager said, studying the crude configuration of the wound with a careful, pitiless interest. This has some definite possibilities.

—I suppose the real question is, will the people laugh?

—Without a doubt. Believe me. Remember this—a man is just as apt to giggle when he is introduced to his executioner as he is to melt into a mess of piss and fear. The real and true talent, the exquisite thing, is of course to be able to raise tears to the throat and to the rims of the eyes, and then suddenly to convert those tears into laughter.

—I could play "The Wounded Soldier."

—Well, we'll try it, the Manager said. I think it's worth a try.

And so that same night he first appeared in his new role. He entered with all the other clowns. The other clowns were conventional. They wore masks and elaborate makeup, sported baggy trousers and long, upturned shoes. They smoked exploding cigars. They flashed red electric noses on and off. They gamboled like a blithe flock of stray lambs, unshepherded. The Veteran, however, merely entered with them and then walked slowly around the ring. He wore a battered tin helmet and a uniform a generation out of date with its old-fashioned, badly wrapped puttees and a high, choker collar. He carried a broken stub of a rifle, hanging in two pieces like an open shotgun. A touch of genius, the Manager had attached a large clump of barbed wire to the seat of his pants.

The Veteran was seriously worried that people would not

laugh at him and that he wouldn't be able to keep his job. Slowly, apprehensively he strolled around the enormous circle and turned his wound toward them. He could see nothing at all outside of the zone of light surrounding him. But it was not long before he heard a great gasp from the outer darkness, a shocked intaking of breath so palpable that it was like a sudden breeze. And then he heard the single, high-pitched, hysterical giggle of a woman. And next came all that indrawn air returning, rich and warm. The whole crowd laughed at once. The crowd laughed loudly and the tent seemed to swell like a full sail from their laughter. He could see the circus bandsmen puffing like bullfrogs as they played their instruments and could see the sweat-stained leader waving his baton in a quick, strict, martial time. But he could not hear the least sound of their music. It was engulfed, drowned out, swallowed up by the raging storm of laughter.

Soon afterwards the Veteran signed a contract with the circus. His name was placed prominently on all the advertising posters and materials together with such luminaries as the Highwire Walker, the Trapeze Artists, the Lion Tamer, and the Bareback Riders. He worked only at night. For he soon discovered that by daylight he could see his audience, and they knew that and either refused to laugh or were unable to do so under the circumstances. He concluded that only when they were in the relative safety of the dark would they give themselves over to the impulse of laughter.

His fellow clowns, far from being envious of him, treated him with the greatest respect and admiration. And before much time had passed, he had received the highest compliment from a colleague in that vocation. A clown in a rival circus attempted an imitation of his art. But this clown was not well received. In fact, he was pelted with peanuts and hotdogs, with vegetables and fruit and rotten eggs and bottles. He was jeered at and catcalled out of the ring. Because no amount of clever makeup could rival or compete with the Veteran's unfortunate appearance.

Once a beautiful young woman came to the trailer where he

lived and prepared for his performance. She told him that she loved him.

—I have seen every single performance since the first night, she said. I want to be with you always.

The Veteran was not unmoved by her beauty and her naïveté. Besides, he had been alone for quite a long time.

—I'm afraid you don't realize what you are saying, he told her.

—If you won't let me be your mistress, I am going to kill myself, she said.

—That would be a pity.

She told him that more than anything else she wanted to have a child by him.

—If we have a child, then I'll have to marry you.

—Do you think, she asked, that our child would look like you?

—I don't believe that is scientifically possible, he said.

Later when she bore his child, it was a fine healthy baby, handsome and glowing. And then, as inexplicably as she had first come to him, the young woman left him.

After a few successful seasons, the Veteran began to lose some of his ability to arouse laughter from the public. By that time almost all of them had seen him at least once already, and the shock had numbed their responses. Perhaps some of them had begun to pity him.

The Manager was concerned about his future.

—Maybe you should take a rest, go into a temporary retirement, he said. People forget everything very quickly nowadays. You could come back to clowning in no time.

—But what would I ever do with myself?

The Manager shrugged.

—You could live comfortably on your savings and your pension, he said. Don't you have any hobbies or outside interests?

—But I really like it here, the Veteran said. Couldn't I wear a disguise and be one of the regular clowns?

—It would take much too long to learn the tricks of the trade, the Manager said. Besides which your real clowns are truly in hiding. Their whole skill lies in the concealment of anguish. And your talent is all a matter of revelation.

It was not long after this conversation that the Veteran received a letter from the Doctor.

—Your case has haunted me and troubled me, night and day, the Doctor wrote. I have been studying the problem incessantly. And now I think I may be able to do something for you. I make no promises, but I think I can help you. Could you return to the hospital for a thorough examination?

While he waited for the results of all the tests, the Veteran lived in his old room. It was clean and bright and quiet as before. Daily the Head Nurse put a bouquet of fresh flowers in a vase by his bed.

—You may be making a big mistake, she told him. You have lived too long with your wound. Even if the Doctor is successful —and he may be, for he is extremely skillful—you'll never be happy with yourself again.

—Do you know? he began. I was very happy being a clown. For the first and only time in my life all that I had to do was to be myself. But, of course, like everything else, it couldn't last for long.

—You can always come back here. You can stay just as you are now.

—Would you be happy, he asked her, if I came back to the hospital for good just as I am now?

—Oh yes, she said. I believe I would be very happy.

Nevertheless the Veteran submitted to the Doctor's treatment. Once again he became a creature to be wheeled into the glaring of harsh lights, to be surrounded and hovered over by intense masked figures. Once again he was swathed in white bandages and had to suffer through a long time of healing, waiting for the day when he would see himself again. Once again the momentous day arrived, and he stood staring into a mirror as they unwound his bandages.

This time, when the ceremony was completed, he looked into the eyes of a handsome stranger.

—You cannot possibly imagine, the Doctor said, what this moment means to me.

The Head Nurse turned away and could not speak to him.

When he was finally ready to leave the hospital, the Veteran found the High-ranking Officer waiting for him. A gleaming staff car was parked at the curb, and the Veteran noticed by his insignia that the Officer had been promoted.

—We all hope, the Officer said, that you will seriously consider returning to active duty. We need experienced men more than ever now.

—That's a very kind offer, the Veteran said. And I'll certainly consider it in all seriousness.

flip, heads or tails, just for the fun of it. As I say, Harry and I were about the same age and size, but he had dark hair and I was redheaded; and in temperament and interests we were from the beginning just the opposite. So I used to think (if you can call the flow, the torment and joy, the visionary dance of a child's mind thinking) that we were really somehow the same person somehow and that when I looked at him I was really looking at myself, changed and different, strange and wonderful, the way your own face and body comes back to you as a stranger from one of the crazy mirrors in the Funhouse at the Fair.

It was just a child's notion, and by the summer that Harry came to be with us I wasn't a child anymore and not a man either. If I remembered that idea at all it was something to laugh at. Still, like all the other cockeyed, cross-eyed visions from the knee-high world of children, it had some truth in its distortion.

Not a child anymore and not yet a man. In the fall I would be sent back, according to the family custom still followed by those who could afford it, to military school. In that curious cold greenhouse the flowering from boy to man was supposed to be accomplished. I wasn't happy about it. I had been there. Suffered and survived. Conformed and thus gained some freedom. At least that was one lesson from the world of men, though you either learned it by accident, tripped over the truth as you might bump into and fall over a piece of furniture in the dark, but known room. Or else you were hurt and broken. What happened was that you stifled your impulse to rebel and followed an urge to conform. Very slowly it dawned on you that you were now anonymous. Nobody knew who you really were. You were just another pale-faced, gray-uniformed body passing up and down the cold stone halls of the barracks named for an Episcopal bishop, standing in ranks, marching on the parade ground, or sitting in a classroom with your compass and sharp pencil trying to prove that Euclid was right. Meanwhile you, the real you, were far away and somewhere else. You pushed the flesh and bones that bore your name through a thousand motions and activities every day. In a while these became routine and habit, and you could prod yourself along, all the separate and integral parts, careless and thoughtless as a shepherd with a flock of calm sheep grazing. You were free as a bird or a beast. The rebels charged windmills, battered at closed doors and high walls with their bare heads and were always bloodied and always finally bowed. You never had to bow. Of course your body did obeisance to custom and ceremony. But while your flesh knelt before some honored institution your spirit was dancing jigs and hornpipes and thumbing its nose at everything under the sun.

There was another lesson to be learned, not yet but soon after, as inevitable and abstract as those theorems and corollaries of Euclid: that all the other survivors were doing exactly the same thing. That would be a chilly realization when you knew that all the others, like yourself, were ghosts in the flesh, countries, counties and continents populated by gray ghosts while, invisible, the world of spirits was a tumultuous chaos. Then you'd have to learn to live with that too.

But none of these things was much on my mind when Harry came to stay with us. I just thought that it would be good to have him around and show him things. I envied and admired him by that time. He had grown tall and slender and handsome. Everyone said he looked Spanish (the last of the Spanish blood in our family) and all agreed he was the best-looking one in the whole family. He had his own car he had put together out of old parts from a junkyard, and he drove it down. (I still had a bike.) He brought guns and all kinds of fishing tackle with him. Up in his part of the state there was still lots of wild, wide open country, and he had spent most of his spare time in the woods. When he arrived, I helped him unload the car and carry all the stuff in the house and up to his room on the second floor. My father greeted him on the front porch and saw the rifles and the shotgun, and he didn't say anything but welcome.

When we got everything up to his room, Harry piled it all in a corner and flopped down on the big double bed and smoked. (I wasn't allowed to smoke yet.)

"Daddy must like you a lot," I said.

"How come?"

"He doesn't allow any guns in the house. But he didn't say a word when he saw yours."

Harry laughed. "He doesn't care. He just feels superior and doesn't care."

"Oh, I don't think that's it."

"Or," Harry went on, ignoring my idea, "maybe he just feels sorry for me. It's exactly the same thing as feeling superior."

"I just think he wants you to feel at home."

"Well, it's a good thing," Harry said. "If he said anything about my guns I would've turned right around and hopped in the car and left."

"Where would you go to?"

Everything I said seemed to tickle Harry.

"Somewhere. Oh, I'd go somewhere," he said. He bounced up and down on the bed and then turned over on his stomach. "You know? I think I'm going to like it here. This has got my room at home beat a mile."

We were off for a summer of it, it seemed. Harry had lots of tales and plots and plans and ideas. Harry was bored and restless, fidgety and as calm as a stone in the sun at the same time. Harry had caught tarpon all by himself off the East Coast, and he had killed more than one buck in the woods. He was a strange and wonderful kind of blood kin to have. He could make you want to show him everything you cared about, and as you were showing it to him you knew all the time he'd be scornful and either by laughter or silence make you ashamed of it and yourself. Beautiful things could turn shoddy from one of his skeptical glances. He could laugh about anything. He even got the giggles when we went to St. Luke's Cathedral for Holy Communion. He held it all back while we were still kneeling at the altar, but when we went out the side door to go back to our pew, he ducked in the dark little room where they keep vestments for the acolytes and started to laugh.

"What's the matter?"

"I can't help it," he said. "I got to thinking that's probably the only way I'll get a drink the whole time I'm here."

"That's sacrilegious."

"So what?"

Harry was brave, there was no doubt about that. He would take any kind of a dare my friends and I could come up with. He dived off the top of a high light-pole at Rock Springs and somehow he didn't break his neck. He drove his car wide open up and down the main drag through all the red lights and the cops couldn't catch him. (Not then, anyway. They knew whose car it was all right.) He did whatever he felt like whenever he felt like it.

He used to talk a lot about wanting to be in the Army. The real Army. He scorned military school.

"I'll be glad when I can get in," he said. "I know everything there is about guns and I can really shoot a rifle."

The proof of that was that whenever he felt cranky and like being alone, he'd go down to the lake at the end of the street and shoot snapping turtles. When they poked their little black heads above the surface he'd fire a shot and hit one most every time.

I thought it was fun to have him around.

That same summer Joe Childs came back from reform school. He was a lot older than we were, but he had been in the same grade with me all through the public schools until I went away to military school and he got sent off to the reform school at Raiford for trying to set fire to somebody's house. He was one of the barefooted, shambling, overage, shaggy-haired, snaggle-toothed, dull-eyed cracker boys who always came to school in overalls and never took a bath. They brought their lunch in paper bags and ate outside under the trees by themselves instead of in the lunchroom where everybody else ate. Cornbread usually. They bullied everybody else, carried knives, were cruel to Negroes, cripples, stray dogs, and old maids. They smoked in the latrines. When they got caught at it the Principal beat them on the bare skin with a piece of rubber hose. But they were famous for never hollering or breaking into tears.

"Him? I don't pay him no nevermind. My old man draws blood when he swings a strap."

Joe Childs was big and ugly and slow-witted. He had a lazy yellow smile all the time, but he could be cruel. When we were still in grammar school and his age and size made a lot more difference, he used to make some of us bring him a meat sandwich every day. If we didn't, he beat us up. I used to beg my mother and Edna, the cook, for a meat sandwich. If they wouldn't make one for me I'd either have to play hookey that day or take a beating. I'd go dragging to school with my heart in my throat like a wad of sour grease and my feet like two heavy lead weights. It was hard to go ahead and go when you knew you were bound to take a beating.

Finally, after a long time of it, I broke down and told them why I had to have a meat sandwich every day.

My mother was really angry and all for telling the Principal, but the funny thing was that my father didn't get mad at all.

"That poor boy hasn't got anybody looking after him," he said. "Tell Edna to fix an extra meat sandwich every morning."

I'll never know, I guess, whether that was the right thing or not, or whether that was just feeling superior and sorry at the same time the way Harry said. At the time, anyway, it was a great relief. My father carefully explained to me that Joe Childs's father was a veteran of the First World War. He had been gassed and he couldn't do much work anymore. His wife had run away and disappeared when Joe was still a baby. He drank a lot.

When Joe Childs got back from reform school, or anyway the first we knew about, it was on a day when some of us were out at the Old Fairgrounds playing ball. (Harry didn't come with us. He couldn't see any point in games.) Joe Childs came running up out of a pit they had dug there years before, before the Depression, to put in a big municipal swimming pool. All they did was dig a hole in the ground. There were two other guys running along with Joe Childs. There were five of us, and I was standing with my back to the bushes around the pit knocking flies out to the others. I heard somebody or something thrashing in the bushes behind me and I twisted around to see what it was. And there stood Joe Childs, smiling that lazy yellow smile, and there were the two others, strangers to the town as far as I knew, on either side of him.

"Chunk me the ball." That was the first thing he said.

I threw it to him and he bounced it in his palm a few times and then put it in his pocket.

"All right," he said. "I'll take the bat too."

I wasn't going to give him the bat even if it meant a fight. He was big, but we had them five to three, and the other guys had run in from the field and gathered around me.

"Don't you hear me, boy?"

I put the bat in my hands like a club.

"You'll have to take it if you want it."

All three of them reached in their pockets at one time and came up with big, long-bladed jackknives. I had had knives pulled on me before, and I was scared as soon as the sunlight hit the open blades and glanced off them. All of them grinned at our surprise.

"Go on and give him the bat."

I handed it to him and he pushed me down.

"We don't want no kids from town coming out here and playing ball," he said. "You come out here again and we'll cut you wide open. Get!"

We turned around and started to walk across the field to where our bikes were parked, downcast and mad.

"Run, goddamn you! Run!"

And we ran all the way to our bikes, hopped on, and pedaled away for all we were worth until we were out of sight.

I told Harry all about it that evening.

"You just let them walk over you like that?"

"What else could we do?"

"I'll tell you what you can do," he said. "You get another bat and a ball from somewhere and go back out there tomorrow afternoon."

"We couldn't do that."

"Don't worry," Harry said, laughing. "I'll come along too. Let's see if they'll try and pull a knife on me."

The next afternoon we all piled into Harry's car and drove out to the lonely Old Fairgrounds. We started to play ball in the same spot. We played a little while, so tense and waiting for

what we knew was going to happen that we could hardly catch
or hit the ball. Pretty soon, sure enough, the three of them came
running out of the pit, blundering through the bushes like runaway animals. This time they had their knives out already.

"I thought I done told you all," Joe Childs said. He was red in
the face he was so mad.

Harry came walking straight toward the three of them.

"What's the matter with you, waterhead?"

That made Joe Childs even madder. He did have a big head.
He started for Harry, but before he could even move a couple of
steps Harry calmly reached in his pocket and took out a little
pistol. I didn't even know he had it with him. No wonder he
was so sure of himself. He didn't wait or just wave it around
either. When he pulled it out he shot—WHAM! (Every one of
us jumped!)—about an inch or so in front of Joe Childs's bare
foot. The three of them stopped like somebody had jerked them
backwards on a leash. Joe Childs turned as pale as the belly of a
catfish. One of his buddies broke out in a sweat all over and the
other one wet his pants.

"Throw down them knives."

They dropped them in the grass.

"Okay," Harry said. "Let's all go down in the pit."

We picked up the knives and followed behind him. He
marched them down in the pit and made them line up in a row
with their hands up in the air. Just like the movies. We saw that
they had built themselves a lean-to shack down there, and there
were cans and bottles all around. They must have been living
there.

"You know what you are?" Harry said.

They didn't say anything. The one who had wet his pants
shook his head, but none of them said a thing.

"You're trash, white trash," he said. "I'd just as soon shoot you
as not. Understand that?"

They all nodded.

"Now," he said. "All together—*We're trash! We're trash! We're
trash!*"

They stood in front of him with their hands in the air and

shouted over and over again that they were trash until Harry got tired of laughing and listening to them. He grabbed hold of my arm and pushed me right in front of Joe Childs.

"All right," he said. "Hit him."

I had been raised never to hit anyone first and especially somebody who couldn't hit you back. I couldn't do it. But Harry kept yelling in my ear until I finally hit him in the face.

"Hit him! I didn't say *tap* him. Hit him!"

I hit him a little harder. Joe Childs shook his head and had to spit blood on the ground. Harry kept on nagging me until I hit the other two. The last I really teed off on and he sat down. One by one we had to hit them, and after the first go-around we began to get in the mood for it. Then we were possessed by it. Round and around we went, hitting them until their faces were all cut and bruised and bloody, and they were begging for us to quit. When they wouldn't get up off the ground to be hit again we kicked them until they would. We hit them until our hands hurt. When their faces got too bad we started to hit them in the stomach and the ribs. They got sick all over the ground and cried like babies.

In the end, once we had really got going, Harry had a hard time stopping us. They just lay on the ground and moaned. The strange thing was that all of us, who hadn't even dreamed of doing anything like that before, felt wild and exhilarated and good about it.

Harry kicked the lean-to over and we jumped up and down on it and smashed it to pieces. Then we piled everything they had on top of it and stuffed magazines and paper in wads underneath.

"You," Harry said to Joe Childs, prodding him with the point of his shoe. "Get up."

He struggled to his feet and moaned. He staggered and looked like a dog trying to walk on its hind legs and we laughed at him.

"You're the one that plays with fire, ain't you?"

He kept both hands over his face and mumbled something.

Harry gave him a pack of matches and told him to start a fire. He knelt with trembling fingers and touched a match to the wadded paper. It caught and the dry wood caught, too, and then there was a good crackling fire. After everything was burning good he made them empty their pockets and throw everything on the fire. Then we took them out of the pit and made them run, across the Fairgrounds and away from town. They were weak, running and falling down. We yelled and hooted after them, and Harry shot at them a couple of times, just over their heads. They picked up a great burst of speed when he did that, and we got to laughing so hard we fell on the ground and rolled over and over.

Then we climbed in Harry's car and drove it as fast as it would go, wildly, out in the country and all over the county. We laughed and sang and joked. It was like being drunk.

It was only late that night when I was alone in my room trying to get to sleep that I started to feel bad. I got up and went down the hall to Harry's room and woke him up to talk about it. He sat right up when I touched him, switched on the bedside light and smoked and listened to me. He laughed at my doubts and shame.

"They asked for it, didn't they, pulling knives on you like that?"

"Sure," I said. "It isn't that simple, though. It isn't that I feel sorry for them or anything. They probably would do the same to us if they could. It's just I didn't know I had it in me to do like that."

The answer he gave me has stuck, because, in a curious way, in the next years the whole wide world seemed to be asking itself the same question and getting the same answer. And once tasted, that doubt and shame is with you, on your tongue always. Harry puffed his cigarette and looked at me. For once he wasn't smiling.

"Well, now you know," he said.

That ought to be the end of it, but it isn't. I don't know how I would have ended up feeling about Harry and myself if he had stayed on for the rest of the summer. A few days later he got a telegram that his father was in a bad way, and he had to go to Baltimore. My father bought him a ticket on the plane and he left. And I didn't see him again. His father lived on through the summer and didn't die until I was already back at military school and couldn't come back for the funeral. I wrote him that I was sorry to hear about that, but I didn't get any answer.

Of course I thought about him and that terrible thing we had done a lot. Since he wasn't there anymore except as I chose to remember him, I usually made him the villain of the story, the one who had put us up to it, rather than the one who had made me see the potential of evil and violence in myself. For which, I guess, I should even have been grateful.

Then along toward Christmas, not too long before vacation, I got a letter from home which said that Harry had accidentally killed himself on a hunting trip. That seemed strange because he knew so much about guns and how to take care of himself. And I knew that the truth must be that he had killed himself, though I couldn't have said why. Except that maybe he knew too much about himself and other people too early.

But the strangest thing of all was how I felt when I surmised this. At first I was just plain numb, the way you always are about confronting a brute and sudden fact. But then one night after taps and after the midnight bed check when the beam of a flashlight crisscrossed our tranquil sleeping faces, I sat up in the cold dark and cried silently. It was a great deep loss to me all of a sudden. As much as I hated the memory of what had happened in the summer and still burned with shame at the injustice of his scorn and laughter, I felt that something had been taken away, stolen from me, that in some wordless way he had cheated me. I wept like a woman deceived and forsaken by a lover.

Five

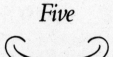

NEW
AND UNCOLLECTED

Nobody gets to choose what yoke to wear.
DAVID SLAVITT
—"The Calf and the Ox"

SONG OF
A DROWNING SAILOR:
A FABLIAU

GHOSTS?

Sure we have our share of ghosts in old Paradise Springs.
Name me any place that is not haunted by all that has happened
there. A place like Paradise Springs, a small town dying slowly
in bits and pieces, in spite of many schemes and plans, occasional transfusions of new blood and new money, has lost or
forgotten the reason it came to be there in the first place. Still, it
has been there for quite a long time, and if now it is drying and
shrinking slowly like a beached and stagnant pool left behind by
the withdrawing tide, there are always shards and signs (a piece
of conch shell, a broken sand dollar, a stiff dead starfish and
maybe even the squiggle of minnows and other small fry) to
prove that the sea was once at home there.

The modest truth is that we have our share of ghosts from all
the ages of the land. Nobody knows them all, but it is not beyond the limits of even a lazy imagination to picture them. In
the pinewoods and hammocks of the county, driven back by
new and old roads, by farms and ranches, shrinking always before the music, the gleaming gigantic eye of the saw blade,
tamed by paper mills and turpentine camps; taken also by the
old Army camp, not used now but not utterly abandoned either,
kept intact for some future and perhaps inevitable time of war;

among those trees, moving in lean Byzantine dimensions across the mosaic of light and shade, surely there are the last baffled, outraged ghosts of the Redmen. And no doubt as well there are the fleeting, smoke-colored, holy spirits of the beasts they hunted. Also, some would claim, there must be the clanking armored ghosts of the bearded, bright-eyed Spaniards (each now as rusty as the Tin Woodsman in *The Wizard of Oz*) who came and lived and died and left so little behind them.

In the town itself there are all the other dead, the troubled and the carefree alike. For instance, you will find some who believe in the ghost of a Union soldier, probably a far-straggling deserter from Sherman's Army up in ravaged Georgia, poor boy who, drunk and all by himself, captured the almost manless village one night by the light of a full moon; who rode up and down the dusty street firing his pistol in the air, singing his head off, alive and kicking until an old lady shot him out of his saddle, off his horse, and into glory, with a single shot of an antique squirrel rifle. They say that her shoulder was black and blue from the bruise of the shot for the rest of her life.

And you would not want to forget the top-hatted, tail-coated ghost of the high-living banker who hanged himself back in the bad days of 1929.

Oh, there's many of them, the ghosts of our place, and most of them have at least some patch of earth to call their own, marked by a headstone of one kind or another.

With the exception, of course, of Adam Peterkin. Adam, the handsome blue-eyed sailor boy, drowned in the far-off Indian Ocean. And perhaps of all our ghosts, all those among the dead who will not or cannot rest easy until Judgment Day, those wanderers, hunters and hunted, Adam paid the strangest visit to our town.

Katie Freeman, bless her mountainous, quivering, uncorseted, seismic, untroubled flesh and bones, she is the one person alive who knows them best. Born with a sixth sense (they say), she easily learned the skills of tea leaves, of palms, the riddles and mysteries of a deck of cards. If anybody in Paradise Springs really knows what the dead are up to, what they are seeking, what they have lost, what their worries and concerns are, it is Katie Freeman. The funny thing is that none of it, none of this knowledge, troubles her. She is as calm and careless as a saint, kindhearted and easygoing. She loves living, is fond of beer and bourbon whiskey and deep-fried foods. True, she has been called a witch, even in this advanced day and age, but then only from a certain stern pulpit and only on certain Sunday mornings. And we all know that that same hellfire and brimstone preacher himself has visited Katie Freeman from time to time to gain some news of his first wife, the one who fell from the top of a tall mulberry tree at a Sunday school picnic so many long years ago. Even that is not what we would be inclined to call a clear-cut case of hypocrisy. Nobody in his right mind would begrudge the Preacher the right to his official position and his official words delivered from the pulpit on a Sunday morning. Who knows? Katie may be a witch, but she chooses to deny it. And that's good enough for me.

"All I am is a kind of a messenger," she explains. "You might say I'm a kind of a long-distance operator, hooking up the circuits between this world and the other one."

"Don't it ever give you bad dreams, Katie?"

"Lord, child, I sleep sound and sweet, just like a baby."

"But don't you ever get weary, just plain tired of it, passing messages back and forth between the quick and the dead? Doesn't the burden of all that trouble weigh you down?"

"I reckon I can stand it if they can."

"What do dead people talk about mostly, Katie? What's on their minds?"

"Oh, well, a whole lot of different things, you know. Nothing out of the ordinary. Mostly it all boils down to the same old things that living people would have to say for themselves if the chance came along. *We have suffered and made other people suffer*, they say. *We are sorry.*"

"That doesn't make a lot of sense to me."

"Maybe it does and maybe it doesn't. Anyhow, child, that's the long and the short of it."

And now, concerning the late Adam Peterkin. . . .

Poor Adam, he was certainly the best-looking young man in town. He was so nearly *beautiful* (the women say) you wouldn't believe your eyes if you didn't know him and saw him pass by. Many a girl and grown woman would have given not much less than her soul to the Devil himself in return for the right to possess such a fine, unblemished complexion, such blue-bright eyes, such rich hair, blond and shiny as corn silk, and such a pair of improbably long eyelashes to flutter. And the pity was that Adam Peterkin squandered the time of his youth and good looks in the fruitless, elusive courting of the one woman in the whole county he could never have—Lucy Birdsong. Lucy was a nice-enough-looking girl, attractive, well-shaped, well-groomed, and well-dressed. But she was born with the soul and vocation of a nun, and she kept it that way. In a strictly Protestant town like Paradise Springs, not a Catholic church in the county and only one small Episcopal chapel to represent the middle way, this meant Lucy Birdsong was born to be an old maid.

Lucy was a vague and dreamy kind of a girl and was happy just as she was, happy being herself, and she never even got close to seriously considering the possibility of getting married. So Adam courted her in vain until he learned, in some kind of slow-dawning revelation, that nothing he could ever do or leave undone would win her to be his wife. And he left town, for good and without good-byes, to be a sailor. And he never came back, though every once in a while somebody or other received a colorful postcard from some exotic place, usually asking about the health and welfare of Miss Lucy Birdsong.

Then along came the news that Adam's ship had gone down in the Indian Ocean. And later on another sailor from the ship came to Paradise Springs to try to find Adam's family and tell them about it. Adam Peterkin was the last of his family, and so he told the story to us who had known him. It seems that if only Adam had known how to swim he would have been all right. Everyone else was saved. That's a strange thing, isn't it? To have been a sailor on the high seas all that time without even know-

ing how to swim. It gave people something to talk about for a
time, until something else interesting came along and it would
be forgotten; no, not so much forgotten as filed away in the
dusty archives of the memory, the little footnotes of our history.

One summer night, one of those breathless midsummer evenings when even the leaves on the trees are as limp as old soiled
dollar bills and the wings of night-flying moths and insects beat
stiff and dry, like tinfoil, in the tepid air, Lucy Birdsong suddenly appeared at Katie Freeman's house. Now, the truth is *that*
was a real surprise to Katie, and she isn't easily surprised. Because of all the living people she knew of, Lucy Birdsong was
the last she ever expected to have need of her services. She
knocked on the door and Katie was so surprised she couldn't say
anything—for once. She just gulped and stepped aside, holding
the door, so Lucy could walk in.

First, though, you better get a rough picture of the place, the
house, or, let's be honest, the shack where Katie lived, out beyond the edge of town. Outside it's all sagging and propped up
here and there with cinder blocks and old two-by-fours. It's unpainted and weather-worn. It could just as well be a nigger
shack over in Black Bottom. And inside it's a complete mess, but
not exactly what you'd expect from the outside. It is a fantastic
clutter of rich, strange, extravagant, and even foolish things.
The first thing you would probably notice is the vast bed, long
and wide with tall brass bedsteads, and all covered with a spread
of what looks to be dark crimson velvet. There's that bed and
then a large dark oak table, round, with tall straight chairs
around it. There's a high dresser with a tall mirror and the top
of the dresser seems to be all glittering and pulsing with little
lights like an open jewel box. Step closer and you can see it is
cluttered and covered, deep with odds and ends. Oh, there are
iron curlers, hairpins, hatpins, perfume bottles, cosmetics, sea-
shells and shotgun shells and bullets of all sizes and calibers;
there are stamps, photographs, picture postcards, ball-point
pens, combs and brushes, eyeglasses, magnifying glasses, filled
ashtrays, movie magazines and paperback books, keys and coins,

paper clips and staples, old letters, silver spoons, medicine bottles, demitasse cups, matchboxes, cigarette lighters, and also a Colt .45 automatic pistol, loaded and shiny. Why you could lose a rattlesnake on top of that dresser and never find him again until he bit you. There is a great big black electric fan always turning and blowing up a storm, and there's a long tall rattan rocker that Katie likes to sit in when she feels like sitting and rocking awhile. There are lots of stray cats, but they come and go. Her only real, full-time company is the parrot, Lancelot, in his ornate gold-gilt cage hanging from the ceiling.

And Katie herself. Knock on the door sometime and you'll nine times out of ten find her wearing a fancy silk Chinese dressing gown and a pair of laceless sneakers for slippers. And nine times out of ten she'll have a can of beer in one hand and a paper fan from Fishback's Funeral Home in the other. And if you happen to be somebody she knows, she'll most likely be right in the middle of a one-sided conversation with Lancelot. One-sided because that parrot won't talk back.

—Kitchie, kitchie-coo, Lancelot, you no-account lazy sonofabitch. Why can't you learn to say something? How come you just sit there and look and listen all the time? You know what I think? I think you are just waiting, biding your own sweet time until you get a real good chance, a perfect chance to embarrass old Katie. Then you're going to rear back and cut loose and shame us all. What I need around here is a real talking parrot, dammit. Maybe I'll get me another one that talks. I got about half a mind to have you stuffed. It wouldn't make no difference at all and it would cut the cost of feeding you. You know something, Lancelot? I had me a crow one time, a ordinary plain old black crow, and he could talk. He could as good or better than most people. Most people around this godforsaken town, anyway. I even taught that crow to recite "The Gettysburg Address" and we were planning to go into show business when he up and died on me. . . .

Well, then, into this setting came Miss Lucy Birdsong, a real surprise.

"Take a seat, Miss Lucy. Care for a can of beer?"

"No, thank you, ma'am, I never touch alcohol."

"Oh it isn't the alcohol," Katie said. "I take it now and then because it's carbonated. Helps the gas on my stomach."

"I make it a rule not to indulge in any alcoholic beverages."

"Well, you never know about a thing like that," Katie said. "Some people do and some people don't. I can't keep up with all their habits. . . . Hot one, isn't it, Miss Lucy?"

"My daddy said the thermometer got up past a hundred to-day."

"I used to think I was going to get me an air conditioner. But I think I will get a thermometer one of these days. It might be a comfort to know just exactly how hot it really is. You know, I had one once. I used to keep it on the back porch. . . ."

Katie noticed that Lucy Birdsong wasn't listening too well, and Lucy looked worried. Her hair was a little bit frizzy and disheveled. There was a spot of dirt on her cheeks. Katie felt a little sorry for her in spite of herself.

"Is something troubling you, Miss Lucy?"

"Miss Katie," Lucy said, frowning. "Do you know if there are any strange ghosts in town?"

"No new ones that I know of. Unless you want to count Old Man Bill Robinson that died of liver trouble or that little nigger boy who drowned in the Springs last Thursday."

"I'm not referring to people like that," Lucy said. "I mean strangers. Are there any strange ghosts around?"

"Not that I know of."

"Are you sure? Is there any way to be sure?"

"Is it real important to know?"

"Yes, ma'am."

"All right, then, Miss Lucy. I can see by your look that you're sincere. I'll tell you what I'll do. I will ask around among my friends in the spirit world and see what I can find out."

"Oh, thank you, Miss Katie!"

"I can't promise anything, now, honey. I don't promise you a thing, but I'll damn sure give it a try. That's the best I can do for you."

"I really can't thank you enough," Lucy said, rising, hurrying out into the dark.

"Think nothing of it, honey," Katie called after her.

A week or so went by, and of course Katie didn't do anything about it because, practically speaking, it was impossible. As all the world knows, it is one thing to establish communications and carry on a conversation with a known and familiar ghost. But it's something else again, altogether different, to seek and search the invisible air for the traces of a spiritual stranger. However, Lucy Birdsong came back, and when she did she was looking worse than she ever had before. She was pale and drawn, and she, who had always been so proper and careful about her appearance, looked now like a worn-out country wife, a slattern. Her pretty blue eyes were red-rimmed, swollen, and bloodshot. Her fingernails were bitten and her hands seemed to want to tremble.

"Have you found out yet, Miss Katie?"

"I think you must have been imagining things."

"I couldn't be imagining it!" Lucy cried. "It's got to be the truth."

Katie Freeman sighed, long and deep, and resigned herself to a mess of somebody else's troubles.

"All right, now, Miss Lucy. You are going to have to be straight with me. You are going to have to tell me the whole truth—or a pretty fair share of it anyway—if I'm going to be any use to you."

"Oh, I couldn't do that!"

"I reckon you're going to have to."

"I can't!"

"Why not?"

"Because it's all so—embarrassing. . . ."

Katie Freeman snorted through her nose and couldn't help chuckling. Lucy Birdsong then commenced to snuffle and cry. Kate shrugged, went and found some kind of a handkerchief, and then put her arm around Lucy and tried to comfort her.

"Now, don't you be embarrassed with me, honey child," Katie said. "No need to feel that way. Why, you'd be surprised, shocked probably, at the kind of things I usually have to listen to. Just as a matter of course. And I'm talking about listening to the living and the dead. . . ."

"It's just too awful, Miss Katie."

"Well!" said Katie sternly. "If it's too awful to talk about, even in front of me, and I've heard pretty near everything that can be said about everything that can happen, why then it's for damn sure too awful for me to do anything about."

And at that Lucy began to cry and carry on in a much more dramatic manner. But nevertheless, somehow, Katie managed to get a story out of her. It seemed that someone—and it had to be, could only be a ghost—was sharing her bed nightly with her. Touching her, holding her close and tight in a way that she had strictly intended never to happen for as long as she lived and breathed. At first she had thought that she must be dreaming it all: the cold hands, cold kisses, the cold invisible body next to hers. Maybe the heat of midsummer had gone to her head. Maybe she had a touch of fever or the vapors. To stop her dreams, or whatever it was, she prayed, she went on a meatless diet, she wore a rough and scratchy woolen nightgown, even at this time of year. But it did not stop. And gradually she realized it was a ghost, a ghost who would not be discouraged, no matter what. Night after night—and now she would lay awake all night to be sure she wasn't dreaming—a ghostly lover came to her bed, and there wasn't a thing she could do about it. I mean, where can you run and hide from a ghost? If she called for help, who would believe her? Who would ever understand?

"Have you been to see that nice little Dr. Ehrenpreis, the psychiatrist?" Katie asked. "He's Jewish, of course, but he seems kind of sweet-natured."

"I don't want to end up at the Funny Farm in Chattahoochie. Not *that!*" Lucy bawled.

"Can't say as I blame you," Katie answered. "You know, when I first began to make contact with the spirit world and all, I thought maybe I was losing my mind. And I hadn't had a real vacation or a change of scene in a long time. So I got some people to commit me and went up there to lay around and take a load off my feet. Only they just don't leave you alone to pull yourself together and work things out. Those people have gone modern, and they fill you full of shots and pills. They shock you with electricity and they make you take all kinds of silly tests, like you was back in kindergarten, and they keep you busy weaving baskets and finger painting and all that. Worst goddamn vacation I ever had, I'm here to tell you! I had this roommate and she was a sweet thing, but she had gotten the idea somewhere that she was a poached egg and if she didn't find a piece of toast to sit on she was liable to break and run all over. . . ."

"Miss Katie, I am not joking," Lucy said primly.

"Well, I'm not joshing either," Katie said. "But you've got to admit, honey, you're in a mighty unusual situation."

Lucy Birdsong shook her head and wept some more.

"Who do you think it could be?" Katie asked finally.

"How should I know?"

"Don't you even have the slightest idea?"

"No, ma'am."

"Come on now, girl," Katie said. "If anybody wants to get in the bed with you that much, dead or alive, you damnwell know who it is. And don't you try and pretend otherwise."

Lucy blew her nose and hung her head. Katie lifted her chin and looked her in the eyes.

"All right, Miss Kate. You win. I am almost positive that it is the ghost of Adam Peterkin."

"My goodness, he's come a long way if it is Adam."

"He is the only one who would do a thing like that."

Kate opened herself a fresh can of beer and took a few swallows, thinking about it. She took off her sneakers and propped her bare feet on the table in the path of the fan, and she wiggled her toes so she could think better.

"What do you want me to do?" she said at last.

"You tell Adam Peterkin that if he loves me, if he ever did love me, then please, please quit what he's doing before I lose my mind."

"This sure is an interesting case," Katie said cheerfully. "I'll see what I can do for you."

Adam Peterkin was quite a good while answering Katie's most effective, most urgent summons. But, at last, everything worked and he appeared before her in a filmy vision, sullen and angry, yet withal still as handsome as ever in his dripping-wet sailor suit. He was, of course, thoroughly drowned.

"Don't you look nice all dressed up like a sailor!" Katie exclaimed. "It sure does become you."

"I am sick and tired of it," Adam said. "These pants don't even have pockets. I wish I had died wearing something else."

"No pockets?" Katie clucked. "That's a shame. How come they don't have no pockets?"

"Miss Katie, what do you want me for? You've been calling and calling. . . ."

"It's a good thing you reported in of your own free will," Katie said. "I was just about ready to call on some of my old-time spirit friends to persuade you."

"It's not that I don't want to talk to you, Miss Katie," Adam said, more politely. "You are the first living soul I've had a chance to talk to since I got drownded. I mean, somebody to really talk to. A Chinese medium in Shanghai summoned me up one time, but it must have been some kind of a mistake or an accident. Anyway, we couldn't understand each other for beans."

"Shanghai, China!" Katie said. "My, but you must have been some interesting places."

"Well, when I was living, I got around to practically everywhere you can think of. Except the Caspian Sea. I never made it there."

"Do tell."

"Miss Katie, you get to see all them places, and it's all right. It's an experience and I'm not complaining. But after a while it gets just like everything else. You feel like if you've seen one, you've seen them all."

"That's not how I feel about it."

"Miss Katie, I never should have left Paradise Springs in the first place. It's just as easy to die here."

"I've never been anywhere much besides this little old town," Katie said. "I guess the only real traveling I've ever done is in my rocking chair. I'll bet you I've rocked my way thousands of miles in that old chair."

"If it suits you, don't complain."

"I'm not bitching, boy," Miss Katie said. "When you get to know me better, you'll find out that complaining isn't a big part of my disposition."

"I didn't mean . . ."

"It's just that I'm interested," Katie continued. "Curious, don't you know? I'll bet you that the least little old thing you could remember about some strange place like Shanghai, China, would give me more than enough to think about and ponder on for a week."

"That's not exactly why you summoned me up tonight, though, is it?"

"Not exactly."

"What is it all about?"

"I've got something to tell you."

"Oh, yeah?"

"What became of your manners? Did you lose them in the Indian Ocean?"

"Excuse me, Miss Katie. I beg your pardon. What do you want to tell me?"

"I think you've already got an idea or you wouldn't have been so rude."

"I said I was sorry."

"Never mind about that," Katie said. "What I want to know is aren't you ashamed of yourself for what you're doing?"

"No, ma'am, I'm not," he said. "I'm not a bit ashamed of myself now. What I'm ashamed of, what embarrasses me to even think about, is how I was before. Carrying on like a lovesick puppy. Moaning and groaning and gnashing my teeth over one silly girl. And then running away and getting myself drowned in the ocean. If I had've done what I'm doing in the first place, none of this would ever have happened."

"Oh, that's an old, old story," Katie said. "That's what they all say."

"I ain't studying about the rest of them. I'm speaking for my ownself—me, myself, and I. I was nothing but a fool the whole time I was alive."

"You're acting like a fool now too."

"How do you mean?"

"It's one thing to carry on a little communication with the living, messages and warnings and blessings and the like. But I can't see any excuse for what you're up to. What do you want from the poor girl?"

"Nothing," he said. "I don't want a thing she's got to offer."

"What will it take to get you to leave her alone?"

"Don't you worry about that, Miss Katie. I'm done with her. I'll never bother her again."

"Lord, Lord, Lord . . ."

Katie sighed her sigh and shook her jowly, full-moon face right at him.

"What's wrong with that?"

"Sonny boy, you don't know the first thing about women."

"I know all I want to about her, if that's what you mean."

"I am speaking to you of the character and the ways of woman in general. Which naturally even has to include Lucy Birdsong. You don't know nothing about women and you never did."

"I'm always willing to listen and learn," Adam said.

"Just about the worst possible, the meanest thing you could do right now is to leave her without even any explanation."

"What do I care?"

"It would drive her out of her wits for pure shame."

"She drove me out of mine."

"She'll get even with you some way, in this world or the next. Any woman would and you better believe it."

"Miss Katie, I just don't care about her anymore."

"Adam, you are good and dead. Lucy's got long years of living ahead of her. The worst that can happen to you has already happened. Show her a little charity at least."

"All right, Miss Katie. You've gone and persuaded me," he said. "What must I do now?"

And so it was agreed that Katie would deliver the message. Katie would tell her that what Adam Peterkin was really after, all he really wanted, was a grave of his very own in Paradise Springs, along with a proper headstone and somebody to kind of look after it and maybe put some flowers on it now and again. Which, as you can guess, was a solution which saved Lucy's natural modesty and preserved her natural feminine vanity at one and the same time. Lucy was very pleased. She bought a nice shady plot for him in the cemetery. She ordered a fine marble headstone, specially made, with an appropriate quotation from the poetry of Robert Louis Stevenson carved on it. And ever afterwards she put fresh flowers on the grave at regular intervals.

And that, anyway, is Katie Freeman's version, her explanation of the undeniable fact that Lucy Birdsong did get to looking pretty puny and distracted during that long summer and that she did, indeed, buy a grave and a headstone for the late Adam Peterkin, and that shortly thereafter she regained her old composure, her straitlaced serenity, her old self.

You can take it for what it's worth and what you may want to, considering the source.

—What about Adam Peterkin? somebody is sure to ask. What became of him?

Go ahead and ask. Katie Freeman won't say where he may be now or what he's up to, waiting, biding his time until that final shiny trumpet call summons us all. She says that is privileged information and nobody else's business. So she will merely smile and shrug her shoulders if you ask her.

Some of the gossip, people who will speculate and gossip about anything under the sun, and take a dim view of it and put the bad mouth on it, some of these have some pretty outlandish theories on the subject.

But even in the face of that, you have to admit that Katie Freeman has the last word.

"Let them think and say what they please," she says. "There's not a whole lot of good in any of them."

SWEETER THAN THE FLESH OF BIRDS

"AFTER ALL," Jane said, "it is my own money. It isn't as if I were taking anything away from you or the children."

Her husband sighed and shrugged, wounded by misapprehension and misunderstanding. They were having breakfast in the kitchen, a white, bright, tidy, pleasant place in the morning sunlight. She was sitting at the table, still wearing her wrapper, but her hair was neatly brushed in place and her face was made up for the day. She was a woman who found neatness and control easy. She would not lose her outward composure, her quiet and tested certitude, if at that precise moment a loud bugle at the end of the block had proclaimed it was the Judgment Day.

Howard stood next to the stove, sipping coffee that was too hot to drink in a hurry. But, of course, he was in a hurry, and it showed all over him from the little stains of dried mud (from yesterday's rainstorm) on the tips of his shoes to the tiny fleck of shaving soap just below his left ear. She could see it all at a glance and she knew that he could feel, as always, her calm, objective scrutiny of him. Naked or clothed, drunk or sober, he wasn't likely to cause her to raise her eyebrows. Not that she was judging him. She made no evaluation. She simply looked and saw him exactly as he was this morning and would be on so many others yet to come.

Around them swirled the relentless noisy action of the two children getting ready for school, bolting breakfast, looking for their books and mittens. But this was habitual as well. The truth is that Jane and Howard might just as well have been on a desert island a little larger than the stove, alone with a single stylized palm tree and their thoughts.

They always moved into this kind of intense and bitter vacuum when they had to deal with the problem of John.

"It's your money all right," Howard said. "And you're free as a bird to spend it any way you want to. That's not the point."

"If it isn't the money, what is the point?"

"I don't really care about the money," he said. "I wouldn't care even if it had to come out of our own savings or household money or what-have-you. It's the idea of the thing that worries me."

At this she smiled. It was a pleasant, knowing smile that wouldn't be named a sign of sarcasm by a stranger.

"I suppose," she said, "you see it as a matter of principle."

He had finished his coffee now and had his back to her as he bent over the sink to rinse out the cup.

"No, I don't quite mean that. What kind of an argument could I come up with against charity in principle?"

"It isn't charity. It isn't as if John were a beggar with his palm stuck out."

"I think beggar would be a charitable word for it. Maybe you'd prefer *parasite* or *confidence man?* Personally, I'm inclined to favor *bum.*"

Howard always looked more attractive to her, at once more manly and forceful, when he had been needled into fighting back on her own terms. Another time except breakfast and they might have gone on, beginning to quarrel mildly enough as now, but moving on through a kind of intricate, emotional disrobing into an open rage that might end anywhere, as likely as not in some act or office of love. But it was the morning. The children had to get off to school and he had to go to work.

"That's the trouble with you," she said. "You just don't understand how it is with a close family."

"Oh, I had a perfectly normal family," he said. "It was a mere and fortunate geographical accident that it didn't turn out to be a *Southern* family."

"More's the pity."

Then they both laughed because this little turn in the argument, though as real and thorny a boundary between them as a strand of barbwire, signified, by the accumulated rules and precedents of the game, that the discussion was over.

So they laughed at each other, reserving judgment for another time, and then in a breathless moment they were all going. Howard kissed her and ran out of the back door toward the garage, hat on the back of his head, buttoning his overcoat as he went. The children clattered once more around the kitchen in a jerky dance and galloped off like a pair of heavy ponies, slamming the front door with window-shaking finality behind them. She was left alone with a second cup of coffee and time to think ahead with pleasure and some amusement about what her brother John would be needing the money for this time, and how he would go about wheedling it out of her.

John was ten years older. If he had bumbled through three marriages in less time than it had taken most men to discover the woe of one, if he had already failed in more schemes, projects, businesses, and ordinary jobs than were worth counting, it had not always been so. Far from it. In the beginning he had seemed blessed with the pure shine of luck, bound for success. Her most vivid memory of him this morning was almost chivalric in its persistent and abstract beauty. She was only a girl then and John was away at the State University. They had all driven over to see him play in the homecoming game. She drank coffee in a paper cup that morning, her first coffee, because there was nothing else, and then with the strange warm feeling inside her and the sweet taste on her tongue, she sat in the stadium and saw him make three spectacular touchdowns against Georgia Tech, a lean, small, whirling dervish in the gaudy orange and blue uniform of the University, dainty-footed, agile, dancing across the clipped green field with its freshly chalked yard lines, a field so green and flat it might have held the armored knights of Sir Walter Scott. Later, in college herself, she would read *The Faerie Queene* and incongruously picture all those allegorical adventures taking place on just such a field.

She had been an awkward, plain, growing girl then, and he had been the laughing, dauntless, magical, imperious emblem of all possible fulfillment, all pride and honor.

They waited in the long shadows by the field house after the game. When he came out he was in the midst of a laughing, back-slapping broil of the other players and the heavy, jowly alumni with their hats and cigars. But he broke free of them, too, and sprinted over, took her up in his hands, and tossed her high and light as a doll for one dizzying instant in the air, caught her and set her down as lightly as a leaf falling.

"How's my baby girl? How did you like that, Janey girl?"

For that moment and some others like it she would never cease to be grateful. Nor would she ever quite be able to forgive him now. She would not let anything change it for her, though, not even when he was expelled from the University only a few months later for cheating—*that* caused some gnashing of teeth at home—not even when, over the years, he seemed determined to follow his newfound vocation as a swaggering, arrogant, foolish, and weak buffoon. Not even now, when she was a grown woman with children of her own. It gave a kind of bitter sweetness to all her old memories now that the world was so new and changed.

She finished her coffee and looked at the kitchen clock. She would have to get busy. Even though the house was always shipshape, there were many little things to be done. She wanted the whole place as neat and dustless as a good museum when John arrived.

Even though he said on the phone that he would be by "sometime in the middle of the morning," he came at noon to be in time for lunch. She counted on that and had a good lunch ready for him.

John seemed a little shabbier, softer, fleshier, balder, and grayer than the last time, but he still had an easy smile, that winning smile. Often, after he was gone, that would be the only memory he left behind, like the vanishing Cheshire cat. They had moved since he had come last. Howard moved up, and they moved farther out into the suburbs. So she showed him all around the house and he ably and tactfully noticed the nice things she had done with the place. She offered him a drink before lunch and was somehow pleased when he declined, even though his color, the little veins around his nose and a slight tremor of the fingers showed he was begging for one. She was amused, but deeply pleased, too, because his abstinence seemed to prove the ritual importance of the occasion to him. Of course, before he went back to the city, beginning at some bar near the station and continuing on the Club Car, he would more than make up for it. But, for the time being at least, he was willing to deny himself and pretend to her.

During lunch he managed to approach the subject openly.

"I'd say it looks like the best chance I've had in a coon's age," he was saying. "Silberman says it's almost a sure thing."

"Silberman?"

"My partner."

"And what does this Mr. Silberman have to offer you besides sage advice and counsel?"

"It isn't the way you think, Jane. Silberman is giving me a great opportunity. He could give it to anybody else, but he likes me. He wants to help me. We get along and he's doing me a favor."

"No doubt," she said. "No doubt this Silberman has an inbred and deeply charitable disposition."

"Let's leave him out of it, then."

"Why? Why leave him out? It's his idea, isn't it?"

"You're a wonder," John said, laughing.

"*Well, isn't it?*"

"You don't even know what the plan is. You don't even know anything about Silberman except his name. And already you're competent to pass judgment on the whole thing."

"You'll have to admit, John, that I have had a certain amount of vicarious experience with these 'things' in the past."

"This is different," he said. "Just let me tell you about it."

"I really don't want to know," she told him. "Spare me the sordid details of the Great Silberman-Singletree Treasure Hunt. Just let me go to my desk and write out a check for what you need—if I have enough in the bank."

She rose from the dining-room table and went to her writing desk in the living room. She opened her checkbook and sat waiting with her pen poised. He followed and stood behind her, looking over her shoulder.

"How much do you think you need?"

"You really would give me a check right now, without even knowing what for, wouldn't you?"

"Haven't I always? Have I ever let you down?"

"Not exactly," he said.

"How do you mean that—*not exactly?*" She twisted around to look at him.

"Look," he said. "You offered me a drink before lunch. Could I have one now?"

"Just tell me how much money you want."

He sighed and turned away, looked out of a window at the yard.

"What would you say," he said softly, "if I told you I didn't come here just for money?"

"I'd probably say you were lying."

"Suppose what I really wanted was your blessing and not a dime?"

"There's an old proverb," she said. "It goes 'Beware of lying, for it is sweeter than the flesh of birds.' "

Inexplicably, John laughed. His laughter was sudden, loud, and crude in the dustless, well-kept room.

"God Almighty, Jane! Where did you get that one?"

She shut her checkbook, put the top back on her pen, closed the desk, and stood up. She was stiff with stifled anger.

"I will be happy to give you what I can," she said. "I am happy to do what I can if you will only tell me how much."

"I'm sure you are," he said. "Now that we're talking about the truth, I'm sure you are happy to give me the money."

"What is that supposed to mean?"

"I guess it means I don't want it this time. I guess it means I'd rather go back empty-handed and face Silberman and get the immemorial horselaugh than to take another check from you."

"You're getting mighty proud in your middle age."

"Proud?" he said. "Pride, that is it, isn't it? You'll let a man have anything, anything under the sun except his pride. Lord, I'm just the ne'er-do-well brother. What kind of a life does poor Howard have around here?"

"That's quite enough," she said, feeling her hands tremble a little and hating herself for it.

"I'm sorry," he said in a moment. "You know I didn't really mean that." Then: "Maybe I will have that drink now, if you don't mind."

"Help yourself."

He poured himself a drink and then they sat down and chatted easily about the family. He had been out of touch with everybody and she told him all the news. Soon it was nearly time for his train and she called a taxi for him. They did not mention the check or the reason he had come to see her. But when the taxi tooted its horn and he was at the door saying good-bye, she gave him a ten-dollar bill. She stuffed it into his coat pocket and saw his eyes film with quick tears before he turned from her and ran, still light-footed, after all, still graceful, down the walk to the cab.

She shut the door and leaned back against it, breathing deeply. John would be back. He would come back again all right. Or maybe he would not come; he would write and then she could send a check in the mail.

Now she was alone again. In an hour or so the children would be home from school. She had an hour to read or sew or write letters or phone somebody. But she felt tired, beyond doing anything.

She climbed the stairs and went into their bedroom, rummaged in her bureau drawers until she found what she was looking for—a yellowing snapshot of herself at the age of ten, a plain girl with pigtails, short skirt, skinny legs (one with a bandage), and bony knees, a sad little girl with an apprehensive, frightened look. She looked at herself in the picture and wept for herself and all the tricks and ravages of time, silently and hopelessly.

But when she raised her head and saw herself in the mirror, already red-eyed and puffy from weeping, she put the picture back where she had found it. She went into the bathroom to wash her face and be ready for the children when they came home. Maybe she could take them somewhere. Perhaps they could read a story or play games. She really ought to think of something nice for them to do this afternoon.

THE INSECTS ARE WINNING
(Two Versions of the Same Tale)

I.
THE MOTH

Now THE MOMENT OF TRUTH is near. The young matador, theatrical in his suit of lights, has dedicated the killing and he is working the bull close with the muleta. He stands poised like a dancer and the dark bull moves to the inaudible tune of his least gesture. There is a long gasp from the crowd at the dangerous beauty of each pass, followed by the exaltation of their roared *olés*, one roar overlapping the other like the sound of stormy surf. Then the moment itself arrives, the bull fixed, his great head lowered, and the young man rising on the balls of both feet, sighting along the delicate deadly blade in lean profile. He goes forward, graceful between brutal horns, sword easing home, seeking and finding death; and, triumphantly, he spins around grinning with sweat gleaming on his face as the bull's legs bow and cave behind him. The uproar of the crowd crackles with portent like the sound of distant summer thunder.

"Okay, honey," Grace says. "This is where we came in."

The truth is that a full five minutes have passed by since the exact place in the picture when they first entered the close darkness, stumbled into their seats, and looked up together into a flat, rectangular, transfigured world of improbable joys and abstract, riskless dangers. During those last, precious five minutes, ever since the scene he remembered flashed into view again,

Harry has been sweating with a vague anxiety that Grace, wholly involved, may discover herself and wake to what is happening before he has had a chance for the second time to see the climactic moment of the killing. For those five minutes he has been completely aware of her, aware of her intense, palpable concentration at his elbow, aware of the solidity of her flesh, of the breath of life in her. Still, wishing and hoping against the inexorable flow of time and the gradual gray dawning of her self-consciousness has not spoiled it for him. Now that he has succeeded after all, if anything the possible danger of being detected and deprived of pleasure has added a furtive zest to it.

"Sure," he says. "Let's go on home."

He stands up and moves along the row just ahead of her, mumbling *excuse-me-please's* as he wriggles through a squirming nest of legs around his ankles, and he waits at the end of the row while his wife, struggling with her coat, hat, gloves, and pocketbook, runs the same gauntlet to join him. They walk up the slanting aisle under the long beam of light, still fountaining its bright configuration of images, through the lobby where a pimply young usher, apparently surprised by them, cups a cigarette in his palm and looks away. Outside they stand under the glittering sign, dazed by the sudden winter air and all the sad burden of reality.

"It wasn't such a bad picture," Grace says. "I don't like to even think about them killing animals. But the rest of it was fine."

Harry grunts something, not a word, in reply, lights a cigarette, and they start to walk past mounds of frozen slush, the remains of last night's snowfall, which seemed bound to annihilate everything, all known shapes and forms and images, under the white, unspeakable weight of its silent purity, to the bus stop. Harry's car is in the garage again. Trouble with the transmission. That thought and the loneliness of the late street have released in him the sullen demon of self-pity.

Not for him the joys of the bullring. Not for him the brilliant band music reproduced with stereophonic clarity, nor a life that can sparkle to unmistakable identity in the magic light of a thousand urgently attentive eyes. Not for him the dark lady of the oh-so-perfect skin and bones who bestowed luminous glances on the matador while he risked hide and hair for her. Not for him the never-to-be-forgotten moment when the two embraced in a spontaneous excess of passion and the camera showed a close-up of her sharp enameled nails digging into his bare back, and then the whole scene blurred and faded out to the music of many violins. By God, there are not any merciful fade-outs and transitions in his life. Neither violins nor brass bands will ever play a musical accompaniment to any action he performs.

"I wonder why they do a thing like that?" Grace says.

"Who?"

"Those bullfighters. Why do they do it?"

"For money," Harry says, chuckling. "It's a way to make a buck. What else?"

"Oh, I don't think so," she says, seriously. "You wouldn't catch me doing it for all the money in the world."

"It's a gimmick. You gotta have a knack for it. It's a talent like anything else."

"I don't care about talent," she says. "I wouldn't go in there and take a chance on getting stuck by those horns for anything."

"Don't you worry about it," he says. "You won't ever have to."

"I know that. I was just wondering."

"Well, don't worry about it. It was only a movie."

Hell, Harry thinks, if Grace ever got in there they'd put horns on her and let her be the bull. They could starve her and steam her out and massage her for a month and they would still never cram her into one of those little skintight suits.

"What's so funny?" she asks.

"I was just thinking how you'd look as a bullfighter."

"Huh!" she says. "I guess you think you'd look like some kind of a movie star yourself."

The picture of himself in the same role is equally absurd, and not so funny. Harry does not need to be reminded that by any standard he is an undistinguished man, a soft-bodied, tired little man with lines around his eyes and a double chin and thinning hair and an apprehensive, earnest, hardly memorable countenance. It is hard enough for him to love himself without the added discomfort of knowing that he is unlovely to others. Of course, he thinks, neither of them is exactly what you would call a handsome specimen. Neither of them has ever had a chance to win a beauty prize.

Grace has always been fat. But when he married her, her very fatness seemed to be a ripe and buxom promise of mystery. And she had a beautiful, creamy complexion in those days and the peculiar, healthy odor, a sweetness like fresh bread, of a fat woman. When he married her he was possessed by the erotic fiction that somehow he was going to wake from all that sleeping flesh an undreamt-of energy and enthusiasm precisely proportionate to its mass. He went to the nuptial bed like a rodeo rider. Whatever the magic was, though, it had eluded him. She was discovered to be (and so she remains) a big lazy woman of easy bovine pleasure in no way similar to the wild white mare of his adolescent hopes and fears. She is, as she has put it to him so often, only human. At least she has the comfort of that certitude. Harry is divided, split in carnival images of himself, on the one hand as the favored child of shining gods and on the other as a naked, squalid thing of aging flesh and blood, a little lower than the beasts and lacking their elemental dignity and simplicity.

"So if you're so hot for a movie star, why didn't you marry one?"

"I didn't say I like movie stars," she says. "Anyway, I never met one."

The bus hisses to a stop for them, and while Harry is fumbling for the right change, she finds two seats for them toward the back. Harry can be so rude sometimes. He is so moody. And the really disgusting thing is how easy it is to hurt his feelings. It is an anguish to her, to be asked endlessly to offer sympathy and pity and praise. Jesus, what happened to all the real men in the world?

What once in girlhood was a dreamy world of burnished armor and naked swords has dwindled to become a world of fists. The tightly clenched, grubby, sticky hands of little boys who are wearing the bodies of grown men like Halloween costumes. In those gone days there was so much of the sweet contentment and mystery of the world contained and always to be found in a piece of cake. Grace did not love herself then, but she still loved what she might become. When she became a woman, though, the few men who were drawn to her, the only ones she met, were all like Harry. Fidgety little sparrows who hopped all around her solidity and good health, pecking. Mosquito men! How she longed for a creature with an arrogant body like a statue made of bronze or stone to bruise herself against! She dreamed a tall lover with a whip in his hands who would come and beat down and subdue her unruly white flesh while, free at last, her spirit awoke and flourished like a rose.

Harry came along at last and was a diplomatic compromise with reality. For some reason he obviously wanted her, and thus she managed to exact the tribute of marriage from him. Maybe then, she thinks now, it was partly her own fault that from the beginning he treated her like a kind of shrine, a sanctuary. At first he approached her on tiptoes and then misbehaved with mild blasphemy like a naughty boy in Sunday school. By this time it is only a weary ritual.

"I don't know why every time I get on a bus I never have the right change," Harry says. "All day long my pockets are like a big sack full of quarters and nickels and dimes. Then whenever I really need some change, like getting on a bus, all I can find is folding money."

"Why didn't you ask me?" Grace says. "I've got lots of change."

"Isn't that just like a woman?" Harry says, and for some reason he smiles.

Harry is not an expert on the subject. There have not been many women in Harry's life. In the heyday of adolescence, the flush of puberty, he suffered a long, groaning, and secret desire for the girls' gym teacher at high school, Miss Janet Ellsworth. She was trim and vigorous, a flashing montage of well-muscled legs and hard, high buttocks as she taught the girls to play basketball and volleyball in the gym. Aloof, shining, and magnificent. Completely unlike his plain older sister who always seemed to be cringing, who was always on the verge of crying about something. And completely unlike the gray thin shape of his mother, a woman who seemed so universally weary with living that she was always about to fall asleep on her feet. Miss Ellsworth, dear Janet Ellsworth, was bright and blond. She was real life. Huntress, sorcerer, witch, and fairy princess, she appeared in a thousand filmy disguises and shared countless adventures with him in dreams and daydreams.

The pity was that Miss Ellsworth never knew of his passion for her. Once and once only he steeled himself and determined to confront her with simple truth. Miss Ellsworth, I love you. I worship you. If it will make you happy, cut off my silly head and use it for a basketball. . . . He waited around the gym until the last period was over and the last students drifted away to the lockers and the shower room. He waited behind the empty bleachers, tense and vague and bodiless, feeling as if he had a high fever. Then he walked swiftly and opened a door with her name on it. For one instant a shining vision in fact of Janet Ellsworth, surprised in all her blond and austere purity. Angry, but unhurried, clouded but casual, she covered herself with a towel.

"You might at least knock, boy."

"I . . . I'm sorry . . ."

"Looking for something?"

He shook his head and backed out of the room and ran all the way home and shut himself in his room, tears of shame and rage brimming in his eyes, warm on his cheeks. But once alone there with the door shut he felt the shame vanish to be replaced by a yawning languor and a sly smile. *Looking for something? You might at least knock. Something? Somebody? Knock, boy! Knock, knock, knock . . .*

There have always been other Janet Ellsworths, all of them infinitely desirable, all emphatically unobtainable, hovering in his consciousness like a gauzy harem. Janet Ellsworth in innumerable transformations has stalked, light-footed, the fleeing days of his manhood. Take, for example, the most recent manifestation, the new receptionist down at the office, a divine, supple creature with a full-lipped, pouting indifference to the desires of men and the envy of women. Only the other day she looked up and caught him staring, transfixed, while she smoothed and adjusted her stocking on a marble thigh.

"Enjoy yourself, pop," she said, laughing out loud. "You can look but you can't touch."

And Harry could have swooned on the spot out of the huge force of his love and hate for her.

Reality has been somewhat different for him. The first time had been with a new girl in the neighborhood, dirty and, as he now knows, feebleminded. Four boys took her into the excavation for a new building. In the breathless dark she started to laugh hysterically and spoiled everything for him. As a grown man he has known whores and still from time to time takes that solace, but by now the only real pleasure left in it, the little shudder and wince of guilt, is growing tedious also.

"Money!" Grace is saying to him. "You talk about your pockets full of money. What I'd like to know is where does it all go to?"

"You tell me," he says. "Prices are so high these days."

"Think you'll get a good raise this year?"

"Maybe," he says. "You never know. It depends."

"That's what you always say about everything—*it depends.*"

"Well, it does."

"On what? What does it depend on?"

"You wouldn't understand," he says, looking away from what he takes to be her accusation. "It just depends. On a lot of different things."

"Mother was right."

Grace's mother was exactly right. "This Harry may make you happy," she told Grace. "You never know about a thing like that. He may even make you a decent husband. But one thing for sure—he won't make you rich."

"He may not get rich," Grace said, "but he's got a good steady job and an excellent opportunity for advancement."

"Sure, baby, he's got plenty of chances. We all do. Everybody does. But he won't get too far, if you know what I mean. Money is just like sex in a man. You get where you can almost smell a winner. Harry smells like a loser to me."

"Oh, Mama!"

Still, her mother had always been tolerant of Harry. More than that. Just the last time she came for a visit they decided to splurge and Harry took them out to dinner at this very expensive restaurant. Everything went along fine until the check came. When the waiter presented the check, Harry had to go and put on his reading glasses and take out his ballpoint pen and double-check every item on the bill. Right in front of the waiter! With the waiter just standing there! The waiter was a young man, darkly handsome and cool in his crisp, starched jacket. He stood aside, supercilious and amused, supremely contemptuous.

"They know how to add," Grace said.

"Let him be, baby," her mother snapped. "Money don't grow on trees."

"But, Mama," Grace whispered. "It's so embarrassing. They don't try and cheat you in a place like this."

"Sometimes they make a mistake," Harry said without even looking up.

"I'd rather pay the bill and save the embarrassment."

"So who do you think you are?" her mother said. "Doris Duke? The Duchess of Windsor?"

"Jackie Onassis," Harry added, chuckling.

"Let me tell you something, baby," her mother told her later. "I'm just an old woman now—no, don't interrupt me, it's the truth—but I think you got yourself a pretty good man, after all. You ought to appreciate him more. You could have done worse, a whole lot worse. When you get my age you'll find out that's the best you can ever say about anything. *That you could have done worse.*"

"What do you hear from Flora these days?" Harry is asking her on the bus.

"What in the world made you think of Flora?"

"I don't know," Harry says. "She just popped into my head."

"It's funny you would think of her right now."

"Why? I can't explain it. It's just the way my mind works."

"Just like that?" Grace says, snapping her fingers. "Up pops Flora?"

"Listen, what are you supposed to be—a psychiatrist or something?"

"I just don't see how you can be riding along on this bus and all of a sudden you're thinking about Flora."

"Forget it. I just wondered, that's all."

"I haven't heard a word from her," Grace says. "Not since last Christmas. She's probably in Mexico or Bermuda or some place interesting. The Christmas card came from Key West."

Flora used to be Grace's best friend. They worked together at the Luxuria Beauty Salon before Grace married Harry. She had been Grace's friend since childhood. It is hard for Harry to picture Flora as a child. Flora must have sprung into this world full-blown and thirty. It is hard for him to imagine her old either. She will always be the same—tough, cynical, good-looking, rootless, and ageless. When they were first married they saw a lot of Flora. The Luxuria wasn't far from where they first lived and when Flora got off work she would come over to see Grace. Harry would get home later and find her there. She often stayed for supper and after. The two women had so many private jokes, signs and signals, swift allusions to the past, that it made Harry feel uneasy, like a stranger in his own house.

"Why doesn't she just get married and settle down?" Harry says abruptly.

"Who? Flora married?"

"What's so funny about that?"

"You never did understand Flora, did you?" Grace says. "She's not the domestic type."

That's the truth, Harry thinks. That is the plain damn honest truth.

Flora was always taking wonderful trips on her vacation even in those days. She had been to Mexico and Cuba and Nassau. She favored the sunny, southern climates.

"Harry, you ought to take Grace South sometime for a vacation," she used to say. "You can't even imagine how great it is."

"I can imagine all right," Harry would answer. "What I can't imagine is where the money for a jaunt like that is going to come from."

"Go now and pay later."

"That's easy for you to say."

"You depress me," Flora said. "Talking so poor all the time. You're making good money."

"That's easy to say, for a person without any responsibilities."

"What kind of responsibilities have you got? I ask you!"

"You don't know the half of it," Harry said. "Grace hasn't been too well and we've got all these doctor bills and expenses."

"A trip would do her a world of good."

"Well," Harry said, "maybe if I save up a little this year. . . ."

"If you wait to do the things you want, it's always too late."

"We just can't afford it now."

"You ought to be more adventurous."

"Sure, sure," Harry said. "I ought to be more adventurous."

"I mean it," Flora said. "One thing that makes me sick is to see a perfectly normal healthy man wasting his life away in some office. Getting all pale and gray in the face like a prisoner or something. Losing his muscle tone. Getting a big soft rear end like a woman's and a potbelly, just from sitting behind a desk all day long."

"Muscles! What am I supposed to do? Buy me a shovel and go out and dig ditches?"

"Man," Flora would then usually say with a solemn dignity, "was made to be a hunter and a fisher and a lover. A builder of cities and a warrior."

"And I'm supposed to do all this hunting and fishing and loving on my present salary."

Looking for something? Somebody? You might at least knock, boy. Knock, boy, knock, knock . . .

"I never could figure out what you saw in her," Harry tells Grace.

"Who, Flora? Are you still thinking about her?"

"She leaves me cold."

"That's funny," Grace says. "Most men think she's very attractive. She has a real way with men, even at her age."

"If she's so attractive, why can't she find herself a new husband? Answer me that one."

"You always bring that up. Flora isn't looking for a new husband."

"Okay then," Harry says. "You tell me. What is she looking for?"

"Oh, I don't know," Grace says. "She just wants to have a good time out of life, I guess. To enjoy life, that's all."

"Personally I think she is a bad influence. She always was a bad influence."

"That's the silliest thing I ever heard," Grace says. "Flora is the best friend I ever had."

Harry is painfully remembering one brief moment with Flora. They were alone in the apartment. Grace had gone to the store to get something for supper. Harry was trying to read the paper.

"It's a shame about you two," Flora said. "A crying shame."

"How's that?"

"I mean it's just a shame that you two can't have any children."

Harry folded the paper. When he tried to shrug, the weight of the world descended on his shoulders.

"Well, you know," he said, "I guess you can't have everything."

"Here we are!" Grace says. "This is our stop."

They get off the bus, breathing ghosts in cold air. They climb the stairway to their apartment. Harry fumbles a minute with the reluctant lock, masters it, and they go inside. The air of the apartment is close and warm. Harry yawns. The odor of dinner haunts them like a forlorn family ghost.

"See? See what I mean?" he says, sniffing. "It stinks in here. That's why I always like to leave the kitchen cleaned up."

"Never mind," she says cheerfully. "I'll go take care of it right now."

While she cleans up the kitchen, whistling, nibbling at leftovers more out of habit than hunger, Harry settles down in a chair to read the paper.

Here is what will happen next. She will clean up the kitchen and then it will be time to go to bed. Grace will undress in the bathroom as she has always done. She will put on a long, shapeless, warm winter nightgown. She will rub cleansing cream on her face and fix her hair. Then she will wait quietly for him in bed, staring at the cracked plaster of the ceiling with its map of well-known imaginary continents and countries. She may turn on the radio and listen to late music. That will be a bad time for him when he stares at his familiar enemy in the mirror, looking over the top of a glass of water on the shelf, a glass in which Grace deposits her dental bridge to soak overnight. The bridge, a rude, simple twist of metal, rests at the bottom of the glass like some submarine creature in an aquarium, somnolent and vaguely dangerous. Looking at it nightly in the same astonished and vexing instant that he greets himself in the mirror, Harry dons a crown of thorns.

Thinking about these things, Harry folds up the newspaper, laying column of disaster upon disaster, wars upon rumors of wars, and goes into the bedroom. He is going to listen to the weather report. He sits down on the edge of the bed and snaps on the radio. There is a flash and all the lights go out. He swears, feeling his way out of the dark room.

"What happened?" Grace calls.

"Must have blown the fuses or something. Maybe the power is off."

"Wait a minute," she says. "I'll light some candles."

A moment later she appears, smiling in the soft glow of two tall candles in candlesticks.

"I think candles will be fun," Grace says. "We hardly ever use them."

She puts the candles on the table beside the bed. The little flames flicker and dance like the quick, forked tongues of a pair of snakes. They cast huge shadows in the room.

"It's kind of romantic, don't you think?"

"Yeah," Harry says. "Like a tomb."

Grace carries one candle with her into the bathroom. Harry takes off his shoes and rubs his feet. While he is undressing, he can hear Grace humming a tune above the sound of water running in the basin. He throws his clothes over a chair and puts on his pajamas. Then he lies back on the bed smoking a cigarette, trying to blow smoke rings inside one another. Wheels within wheels.

She emerges, her round, smiling face gleaming with cleansing cream, her hair pinned in place. Harry rises and goes into the bathroom. He looks at himself in the mirror. Looks at the dental bridge in the glass of water. And then begins to brush his teeth.

"Harry! Harry, come quick!"

He spits, rinses his mouth, and opens the door to the bedroom.

"What's the matter?"

"Look!"

"It's only a moth."

"I can't stand them."

"They don't hurt anything," Harry says. "The light attracts them."

"Please, Harry, I can't stand it. Kill it for me please!"

A single moth has come from somewhere and now circles the candle flame, fluttering toward it and away. Grace huddles in the bed clutching the sheets. Harry picks up the newspaper, rolls it into a tight cylinder, and comes toward the candle. He tiptoes close, stalking his prey. He swings, misses, and the moth darts aside, filling the room suddenly with the shadow of huge wings. Cunning now, Harry stops moving, freezes until the moth returns, lured by the flame. Even with his back to her he knows that Grace is watching him. Now the moth is moving close to the flame again, graceful and erratic, as Harry slowly, very slowly, raises his weapon and cocks his arm to strike. He studies his enemy in a bright clean fury of concentration. Then swings fiercely, catches it in flight and smashes it to the floor. It flutters and then is small and brown and still.

"Thank you. Oh, thank you, thank you . . . !"

"What's the matter, honey? Is something wrong?"

"Thank you, thank you, thank you . . . !"

"Can't you tell me what's the matter?"

Grace shakes her head. "Nothing is the matter, please."

She feels the tears rolling down her cheeks, rich and warm and strange, and she feels the whole weight of her body shaking with sobs. She doesn't know why she is crying. She doesn't feel like crying at all. She feels light-headed, empty of any emotion at all, except, perhaps, a slight and altogether unfamiliar sense of joy.

II.
AT LEAST THEY'LL
HAVE CANDLELIGHT

LUCILLE IS RESTLESS. During the day, especially in the morning, she hardly knows what to do with herself anymore. After Sam leaves for work she eyes the small disorder of breakfast dishes, a tan film of coffee in the cup's bottom, fragments of fried egg hardening on the plate, the crumpled, stained paper napkin, the crushed cigarette, and she feels almost physically sick. She feels dizzy and heavy, the way they say pregnant women are supposed to feel in the morning, but she isn't pregnant. Fat chance of that after five years! She's thinking about doing the dishes now and getting them over with; she's thinking about washing the curtains in the kitchen (they're as gray as a ghost); she's thinking about calling the plumber to fix the leaky faucet in the bathroom. But even as she's thinking of these things, she knows she's not going to. In just a minute she's going to leave everything just the way it is and go back to bed for a while. She won't go to sleep. She'll just lie there studying the map made by cracks in the plaster on the ceiling and wondering for the thousandth time what continent it reminds her of, studying the ceiling with a blank indifferent mind, hugging her pillow like a child and hearing the sounds of the waking world around her.

After a while the radio clicks on in the apartment next door. (They got walls so thin in this building you can hear everything,

I mean everything.) They always play it too loud, as if they weren't really listening at all, as if they just wanted plenty of sound to reassure them. At first it used to annoy her to hear the radio next door blaring like that. Suppose she wanted to sleep or something? But now it is a ritual part of her morning. If the Seegars happen to be away, she misses it, and the harsh hacking cough of Mr. Seegar too.

Now she's thinking about men. She hears Mr. Seegar's cough and she can picture him, bulked and pendulous as an old woman in his soiled, sleeveless undershirt, reaching for the morning paper and the milk bottles. He's retired or something. Mr. Seegar. Doesn't work, anyway. She thinks of Sam. She can see his rumpled silk pajamas on the floor like a corpse. A real extravagance those pajamas. Ridiculous too. He's heavy, not like Mr. Seegar, but soft and heavy. In silk pajamas, his uniform of love, he looks like some kind of a clown.

"It's the line of work I'm in," Sam has said to her jokingly. "Now, if you want me to look like Charles Atlas or Jack La Lanne, why I'll give up my desk at the office and start digging ditches. I'll get all kinds of muscles and you can take in washing to make ends meet."

"I didn't mean it that way," she has replied. "I made a general remark to the effect that a man's body ought to be a beautiful thing. I just said that when a man does the things his body was meant for, it's beautiful."

"You'd have a lot of time to think about beauty if I spent my days digging and lifting. You'd have a lot of time to hang around the beauty parlor," he has said.

"Why do you have to take offense at a general remark? Why do you have to apply everything to yourself?"

"Skip it."

Sam's good to her, it's true. He works hard and long and is very conscientious. They appreciate it, too, at the office. He's making some progress, advancing, but it takes too much out of him. He's tired, tired, tired in the evenings. He comes home slumped, weary. He'll sit in the kitchen and drink a bottle of beer while she fixes the supper. Afterwards they'll sit around and watch TV or maybe they'll go down the street to the early show, and once a week he'll go out and play cards with some of the guys from the office. Lucille thinks about Sam and his life and she feels a little sad and guilty, as if maybe she's to blame for it all. There are always two sides, like they say, and she's to blame for a lot of things, she guesses. When a marriage breaks up they always blame the woman anyway, so what's the difference? But so is he. So is he to blame. He doesn't have to be so miserable. He could put his foot down. He could really tell her a thing or two. He could tell her, "I don't go to work eighteen hours a day just to come home to a sloppy house. You better get in gear and clean this place up!" Or something like that. He could say, "So, you been to the beauty parlor today? Well, I'm sick to death of coming home to a cold supper just because you like to go out in the afternoon and get your hair done." Will he ever say anything like this? No, indeed. He'll come home and say not a word about the mess the apartment is in, no matter if she even calls it to his attention, saying something like, "Honey, I'm sorry everything is in such a stew."

"Oh, it's all right."

Later on he'll ask where something is, and when she can't find it, he'll just stand there looking hurt, and never a word. And when he sits down to cold cuts and a can of something, she'll apologize, saying she spent all afternoon at the movies or the hairdresser's. You'd think he'd take his belt to her.

"I like you to have a good time," he'll say. "I like you to look nice."

He'll eat salami and cheese sandwiches and drink a glass of beer and never complain. Later on in the evening, though, he'll go in the kitchen and scramble himself some eggs.

Sometimes, in a pure exasperation, Lucille will be direct with him.

"Sam, you ought to be more aggressive."

"So, what am I supposed to be—Clint Eastwood or somebody? I'm supposed to slap you around and holler or something?"

"Don't be silly. I mean you ought to stand up for your rights more."

"I'm happy."

Lucille wants to say, "Well, I'm not," but she never does.

Sam is a good man. Almost everybody likes him. He always has a smile and a good word. He never has arguments. Mr. Seegar, now, he has some pretty radical political opinions, so much so that hardly anybody can listen to him for more than a few minutes. Not Sam. He'll stand there and listen and nod from time to time, saying, "Maybe you got a point there," or "You could be right, I guess." Sometimes Lucille wishes more than anything that Sam had some enemies or even some crackpot ideas like Mr. Seegar. To be so mild-mannered, to be so kindly, seems to her to show a lack of discrimination.

But this morning Lucille sighs and feels guilty. Why should she always be trying to change and improve him? She remembers what her mother said:

"You better be happy with what you got, baby. Ignorance is bliss."

Lucille starts thinking about her mother. Maybe she will get a letter from her today. And this is her excuse for thinking about the postman. Isn't that funny? She knew when she climbed back in bed and clutched the pillow to herself that she was going to end up thinking about the postman. But she had come to it gradually and naturally. Now, he's a type that disturbs her.

The postman, whatever his name is, and she isn't going to ask, is broad-shouldered and narrow-hipped. He has a mass of unkempt red hair and a quick bright smile that worries her. It's malicious, knowing, and a little contemptuous, she thinks. He arrives daily this summer with a sweat-wrinkled shirt open at the collar showing a tuft of fine red hair on his chest, his cap cocked a way back on his head, and a swagger, not a little boy's swagger, not the swaggers she has seen on men who are just overgrown little boys, their silly strut that says *Look at me, everybody, look at me!* No, his is the natural rhythm of a young man secure in his manhood. Sometimes she imagines what it would be like to be his wife, to hear the clickety click of his tapped heels as he turns in from the sidewalk to where he lives. To be suddenly aware of his presence in the house, the odor of a pipe, the sound of him moving indifferently among the objects and furniture in the living room. She has an idea that for some reason she should furnish the house they lived in with a lot of delicate little feminine things. So he would prowl around uneasy there, necessarily break and bruise things. Isn't that a crazy idea? Lucille has a vague sense of hopeless desire, unrealized, impossible, when she thinks of the postman. It is very close to love. It makes her a little ashamed.

But Lucille has still more to be ashamed of. Why is it that she always happens to be taking a bath or something when he arrives and rings the doorbell? And she must get up and wrap a towel around herself and pad barefooted and dripping to peer around the door and take the mail. (He's supposed to leave it in the mailbox, but ever since the first time, when it was a Special Delivery or something, maybe postage due, he's brought the mail directly to her door.)

"Why," he said that first time, handing the envelope around the door to her, brushing her hand with his, as quick and light on her flesh as the shadow of a wing, "why I've interrupted your bath. And you're as pretty as a peach."

She slammed the door and leaned against it, listening to him laugh as he went out. Fresh thing! Nevertheless, the same scene has been repeated and never without some remark—"Ah, the Goddess of Cleanliness," or "So, once again we have Miss Bubble Bath"—inane, but italicized by his quick, arrogant smile. There is nothing more to it than that, and never will be (she hopes), but it makes her ashamed of herself to have this odd little compulsive feeling, ashamed, too, for Sam.

This morning she's determined that at least that won't happen again. Suddenly she flings off the covers and starts to get dressed. There's plenty to do. There's, Lord knows, enough housework to discipline herself. She makes the bed hurriedly, picks up Sam's socks and underwear, his shirt, and puts them in the bulging laundry hamper. For nearly a half hour she dusts and straightens until—what is it?—she suddenly feels very tired, trapped in the apartment. Is it the sound of someone whistling outside? She wants to get all dressed up, hat, gloves, and heels, and just go somewhere.

Naturally, just when she's in the middle of dressing again, the doorbell rings and it's—who else?—the postman again. She throws on her robe and goes to the door, opens it, and peers around. He's standing in the hall on the other side, leaning against the wall, smiling.

"Hello there," he says. "Sorry, no mail today."

"Well," she says, "what did you ring for then?"

He laughs. She sees that he has a large gold filling in one tooth.

"Just wanted to say hello."

"Hello, then," she says and she slams the door in his face.

The nerve! The nerve of some people! She walks back to the bedroom and, catching sight of herself in the mirror over her dresser, she sees that she is smiling for the first time this morning.

When she finishes dressing, she sits in front of that mirror to put on her makeup. The telephone rings. It's Sally Rose, her friend from the beauty parlor. Sally is one of those ageless blondes that men seem to like so much. She must be thirty-five if she's a day, but she looks younger unless you look at her very closely. She's a friend Lucille has never told Sam about—he wouldn't approve at all. Sally's divorced and she's a little wild. Of course most of the time she's just like anybody else. She sticks to her job as a manicurist, faithfully, day by day. Oh, she has a date once in a while and she likes to take a drink now and then, but as far as anybody is concerned she's perfectly respectable. She has a kind of cool, composed manner most of the time, and the women who go to the beauty parlor like her well enough to tolerate her good looks, though they wouldn't trust her, probably. Sally has a little boy going to Junior High School. Lucille's relationship with Sally is simple—Sally talks and she listens. Sally often tells Lucille about things which might not be so apparent.

"You're so sweet and pretty and innocent," Sally has said. "I feel like I could tell you anything about myself. A person's got to have someone to talk to once in a while, if you know what I mean."

Lucille is the only one who knows all about Sally's vacation last year. Sally took her vacation in the middle of the winter and she came back deeply suntanned.

"Well," a lot of the women said, "I think I'll get a job in the beauty parlor. Vacations in Florida yet!"

Sally just smiled nicely. "A person ought to have some fun once in a while."

How could anybody disagree with that?

But Sally told Lucille how she really spent her vacation.

"You know Mr. Rogers?"

Mr. Rogers is an elderly businessman—he must be sixty-five at least—who comes into the adjoining barber shop a couple of times a week and is one of Sally's steady customers for manicuring. He's in real estate or something like that. He's always very well-dressed and dignified-looking, and he jokes around a lot with Sally. It seems that Mr. Rogers took Sally to Bermuda with him on a business trip. That was how she spent her vacation.

"Wasn't it awful?" Lucille asked, wide-eyed.

"What do you mean?" Sally said. "Bermuda?"

"No," Lucille said, "not exactly."

"Oh, oh," Sally laughed. "You mean that part. Don't be silly. Jack is just a dear sweet old man. Why, he's just like a little boy."

"I wish Sam would take me on a trip like that."

"Why not, honey? You only live once. Tell him you want to go."

"Oh, he wouldn't. In the first place there's the budget and everything. And even if he did, it wouldn't be any fun. He'd mope around about how much everything was costing."

"Husbands," Sally said. "They're hell."

"Don't you ever want to get married again?"

"Not this kid," Sally said. "I've had all that before."

Today Sally says she's bored stiff. It's her day off and she wants to do something.

"Why don't you come on over?" Sally asks.

"I've got so much I ought to do."

"Nuts," Sally says, "you're just too lazy to budge. I'll tell you what, let's go swimming."

"Oh, I couldn't."

"Well, come on over anyway. I want you to see my new bathing suit. It's a howl. Just grab a cab and come on over."

"Okay," Lucille says.

Sally's apartment is small, neat and trim as a ship. She keeps it that way all the time.

"I envy you," Lucille says. "If I could just get my place picked up once, I'd keep it that way."

"Lord, it's hot," Sally says. "Sit down and take a load off."

Sally goes in the kitchen and comes back with a couple of glasses.

"Not so early in the day," Lucille protests.

"It's nothing but a little gin and quinine water, honey. It'll help you to cool off."

They sit and sip their drinks for a moment, then Sally gets up and switches on the record player.

"Thank God for that machine," she says. "I'd go out of my mind on my day off if I couldn't have a little music."

"I'm going to get Sam to buy me one," Lucille says. "One of these days."

"How is Sam?"

"Oh, he's all right. Same as ever."

"Let me show you the bathing suit Mr. Rogers got me. He saw it advertised in some man's magazine and he ordered it for me. It's a riot."

Sally goes into the bedroom.

"Just be patient," she calls.

In a minute she comes out wearing a little-bitty red bikini bathing suit. She takes a turn around the room swinging her hips like a chorus girl.

"How do you like it?"

"It sure shows off your figure."

Sally laughs. "The old goat," she says. "He's getting senile."

"You wouldn't wear it, would you?"

"Why not?" Sally says. "Oh, not around here, I guess. But in Bermuda I would, sure."

"You going to Bermuda again next winter?"

"I may be going lots of places."

"What do you mean?"

Lucille has known all along that Sally wants to tell her something important. That's why she called up in the first place. Like everything else in life, you have to kind of sneak up on it.

"The old guy wants to marry me."

"Sally!"

"No kidding."

"Are you going to?"

"I don't know," Sally says. "He's got piles of money."

"But what about your boy?"

"They'd get along somehow," Sally says. "Anyway, the old man can't live forever."

Sally sips her drink and her mouth draws tight. She looks harder and older.

"The hell with it," she says. "When you get my age you'll understand. I get so tired, tired, tired, putting on a clean white starched uniform every day and going down there and working on people's dirty fingernails. You don't know how ugly hands can be. Sometimes I think there's nothing in the world but dirty hands. I'm fed up. I want to live a little."

"Well," Lucille says, "I think it's wonderful."

"No you don't," Sally says. "You do not. I know what you're thinking. But you're still young and you don't understand."

"Yes I do," Lucille says. "I think I understand how you feel."

Strangely, Lucille's disgust is mixed with envy. For one thing she'd suddenly like to have the freedom to choose to do even something like that. And she wishes Sam was making more money so they could go places and see things. Even if they could afford it, Sam would have to change. She winces inwardly picturing him in the setting of some tropical hotel, the rustling of rich palm trees, the candlelight, an orchestra playing, beautiful suntanned people sitting under the stars, herself in an expensive off-the-shoulder white evening dress, and Sam, Sam awkward and self-conscious in dinner clothes, not knowing exactly what to say to the imperious headwaiter, carefully adding up the check at the end of the evening. It makes her feel ashamed of him. Her mother would feel differently about it. Once Sam took them out to an expensive place for dinner when her mother was visiting. When they had finished, Sam examined the check in great detail. He even put his glasses on to read it.

"Oh, Sam," Lucille said, "they know how to add."

"Sometimes they make mistakes," he said.

"What's the difference?" Lucille said. "It's so embarrassing."

"What's the *difference?*" her mother said. "You'll learn what's the difference one of these days. One of these days you'll be glad Sam's got common sense."

Sam smiled. "You got to understand," he said. "It's good sound business to know what you're paying for."

"You'll see how it is when you get my age," Sally is saying bitterly.

"You always talk as if you are so ancient," Lucille says. "You make me tired."

Sally laughs.

"There's life in the old girl yet," she says, and she struts around the living room once more before she goes to change out of her bikini.

They end up having lunch and then spending the afternoon talking about whether or not Sally is going to marry Mr. Rogers. One minute she's praising him to the heavens. The next, she's calling him the old goat. Then she's on the defensive, saying she has a perfect right to do what she wants to do and why shouldn't she live a little. Then she's vulgar, telling Lucille all the jokes she knows about young women married to old men.

"I think you ought to go ahead and do whatever you want to," Lucille says finally.

"Well, maybe so," Sally says. "I just don't know. Right now I'm playing it coy."

Suddenly it is four o'clock. Lucille must hurry home if she's going to get some dinner for Sam. She sits in the back of an extravagant taxi, feeling depressed, upset. Poor Sam! Here she's dawdled away the whole afternoon talking with that woman while there are a thousand things to do at home. She'll make it up to him some way. She's been all wrong about Sam. She's lucky to have such a good sweet man like that. She gets out at the grocery store to shop for dinner. She buys a couple of steaks and some ice cream. She hurries home.

Once inside the apartment she's suddenly let down again. It's so hot and stuffy. The windows have been shut ever since she left. She throws open all the windows and changes into more comfortable clothes. She goes into the kitchen and washes the breakfast dishes and begins to fix dinner.

It's nearly six by the time Sam gets home. She hears him coming. When he gets to the door, he knocks. He always knocks. Why does he always have to knock at his own door, I ask you?

"Sam?" Who else?

"Yeah," he says, walking in. "What a scorcher today," he says. He looks wilted, worn out and sweated through.

"Rough day?"

"Those people are crazy," he says. "They blow their tops about everything. Every little thing has got to be a crisis."

"Want a beer?"

"I'd love a beer," he says.

She gives him a bottle from the icebox. He likes to drink it from the bottle when he first comes home. He takes the beer with him while he goes back to change out of his office clothes. She hears water running in the bathroom, and then, at last, she hears him whistling.

"Lucille," he calls, "did you call the plumber?"

"Tomorrow," she says. "I'll take care of it tomorrow."

"Okay."

Why doesn't he come charging into the kitchen and give her hell? She's furious about that leaky faucet. He comes into the living room. She can hear him padding around in his bedroom slippers. He turns on the TV to watch the news. She smells the cigarette he has just lit. Lucille is nervous now. This is the part of the long day that's the worst. She wants to, she has to do something a little different; so she puts four tall dinner candles on the table. At least they'll have candlelight!

"What's the big occasion?" he says, bringing the empty beer bottle back to the kitchen.

"I just thought it would be nice," she says, "to have candles for a change."

She looks at Sam. He's wearing a short-sleeve sport shirt now.

"Well," he says, conscious of her gaze, "I guess I'll have to put on a coat and a tie for this meal."

"You don't have to put on anything," she says, hearing her voice rise. "Come any way you want to."

"Wouldn't think of it." Sam pads back to the bedroom.

The windows are all open but there's not a breath of breeze and the candle flames are tall, orange, and untroubled. They sit down and she looks at Sam in the candlelight and she feels exhausted. She'd like to go to sleep forever.

A moth has come from somewhere and flutters in sharp darts around the candle flames. Its wings beat a quick staccato as it veers near the flame and then suddenly away.

"Sam!" she cries. "Get it out of here. I can't stand them."

"It's just a little moth. It can't hurt you."

"Please!" she says. "I can't stand it flying around."

They are both standing up now looking at each other.

"Oh all right," he says.

He goes into the living room and comes back with a newspaper. Lucille stands watching him. He moves on tiptoes toward the moth, swings the paper swiftly, misses. The moth flutters away.

"Kill it, Sam! Kill it!"

Sam comes around the table, swings and misses again. The moth flies away. The flame is troubled, trembles like a dancer.

"Please, Sam, kill it."

"Take it easy," he says. "Wait."

She can see that he's panting a little now as he moves around the table after the moth. She sees his eyes are bright with intense concentration, his hand is poised. Expertly he swings and catches the moth in flight, dashes it to the floor.

Lucille doesn't know why but she begins to cry.

"What's the matter?" Sam asks.

"Oh, thank you," she says. "Thank you, thank you, thank you!"

And then there is only the sound of her own stifled choking as she sobs, crying not so much out of pure weariness as for a sense of joy which she cannot understand.

LAST OF
THE OLD BUFFALO HUNTERS

I HAVE NEVER BEEN a close friend of Professor Harvey Peters. Nor can I be numbered among his enemies. There are plenty of both. There are those who find him endlessly amusing, his eccentricities charming, his modest successes laudable, and his petty failures lovable.

"He could have been a good scholar," one of his friends will tell you, "if he hadn't been scared to death to take a chance on anything."

"He's just lazy as hell," his enemies say.

As it is, his academic reputation rests squarely on half a dozen anthologies, compiled with the judicious use of scissors and paste, all with sound introductions and adequate notes, published over a span of twenty years. The last of them was mildly "popular" in purpose and made a serious bid for a wider audience. And it was safely remaindered a few months after publication.

His admirers marvel over his inconsistencies as one does over the ambiguous activities of a ne'er-do-well uncle. For instance, Harvey is passionately devoted to social causes. He will sign petitions, organize committees, write letters to editors, senators, and congressmen, send checks to funds for this and that, and read *Time* regularly just to work up the necessary rage to stir him to forceful action. In a moment, like a magician, he can summon up the whole specter of the Depression, from bread lines to Bonus March. Lest we forget! He has battled indefatigably for social justice since the days of Sacco and Vanzetti.

Don't misunderstand me. I don't find anything unusual or amusing in all this. The irony begins with the simple fact that Harvey Peters is a real old-fashioned snob, an elegant man, a stylish man, even a moderately wealthy man, a gourmet (he founded the College Escoffier Society), a sheltered man, one to whom the least hint of hoarse and sweaty vulgarity would be about as welcome as a fist in the face.

Picture this paradox. Harvey is outspoken, vehement, and articulate in his criticism of the South and its curse of invincible ignorance. Yet he remains an awe-struck, sentimental admirer of the Old South and likes nothing better, as the years roll around, than to be invited to spend his spring vacation in the company of well-to-do Southerners in the spacious arena of some well-preserved antebellum house in Virginia or the South Carolina Low Country, there to sit on the classic rocking chair on the classic verandah, to sip a classic julep, and to stare with satisfaction across a wide, barbered lawn (where classic barefooted darkies move to and fro) at the flagrant white excess of the early dogwood.

An anecdote will serve to illustrate his stance. A few years ago we were fighting (as we are still) a losing battle with our railroad passenger service. The trains, then, as now, were too few, too late, and wildly overcrowded. In the heat, the thunder and lightning of a protest meeting, Professor Harvey Peters arose to give us his point of view.

"Last Friday, coming back from the city," he began in his rich, Roman senator's voice, "it was with the greatest of difficulty that I succeeded in getting a seat in the parlor car. God knows what it was like for those poor people down in the coaches!"

Enemies? He has plenty. They will tell you flatly and unequivocally that Harvey Peters is "a brag and a drone and a tank of air." They insist his reputation is a mansion with a false front built upon the shifting sands of pure lethargy and improbability. They see both his democratic vistas and his aristocratic affections as simple sham. They go on to say that he has the backbone of a jellyfish and the soul of a rag doll. His inefficiency is criminal and his service to any good cause is The Kiss of Death.

And I . . . until recently I pooh-poohed both his friends and enemies. I maintained that they were all making much ado about a plump, pink-cheeked, tweedy, moderately intelligent and modestly successful Walter Pater Professor of Belles Lettres at our college.

That was before the book came along, the novel. And now you can't be neutral. You have to have a feeling one way or the other about it.

One of his students returned from a stint in the Peace Corps with the manuscript of a novel in his duffel bag. A reputable publisher promptly accepted it. Harvey was charmed and delighted and could talk of nothing else over coffee or the lunch table. For young Roy Kelly was the first of a whole long procession of bright and literary young men, protégés guided and guarded and shepherded and advised by Harvey, to have anything accepted by a publisher. There had been twenty years of them, one or two young men from each class, carefully selected, entertained, their talents cultivated and nurtured. The others had written their books, which had been duly rejected by all the publishers; and then, usually following a short and happy siege in the Village, they had one by one capitulated. They had surrendered unconditionally and gone into the ranks of Business or Advertising or, perhaps haunted by some gray vestige of interest and dedication, they drifted into publishing, where they soon had the pleasure of rejecting other people's manuscripts.

So goes the world.

But now at last Roy Kelly—lean, handsome, well-bred, well-dressed, intelligent, and sensitive—had returned from Africa and somehow had turned the magic trick. Harvey Peters was justified. Though he had not yet actually seen the manuscript, he was confident that it was a very superior first novel. He allowed as how he and Roy had often discussed the subject—the problem of how a young man, lean, handsome, well-bred, well-dressed, and well-to-do, growing up in a thoroughly corrupt and decadent society (ours) eventually, and chiefly by means of a long night spent in a second-rate motel with a married woman and an automobile accident in which his best friend is killed, finds himself. Harvey couldn't wait to receive his inscribed advance copy.

About a month before the publication date Harvey suddenly dropped the subject. He was very busy teaching a number of courses and with committee work. (One of these was his own creation—the Lightening Committee, a group of earnest professors making a close study of how much time was being lost by their colleagues through committee work. A perfect Peters paradox.) He did not mention Roy Kelly's novel, nor did anyone venture to remind him of its imminent appearance.

When the book finally did come out we all knew why.

A Field of Fists is a pretty bad book any way you want to look at it, though I don't imagine Harvey Peters was very much concerned about its literary value. I doubt that he got far enough into the book to make a critical judgment. He must have quit reading right after the third chapter, which was exclusively devoted to the merciless, heavy-handed satire of a Professor of Belles Lettres in a small college. The name of the professor in the book was Hervey Pierce. He was depicted as an officious ass, a phony, a loudmouth, stentorian, naïve, foolish, and vaguely vicious man. His house, his things, his tastes were exposed to cruel ridicule. Even his wife was not spared. It was, in short, a personal disaster for old Harvey.

It might have been worse if Harvey had read on past the third chapter, because then he would have found, unkindest cut of all, that he was never mentioned again in any role or capacity whatsoever.

You can imagine how it was.

"Serves the old fraud right," the enemies said. "Of course, it is a little crude, but you'll have to admit young Kelly nailed his ass to the cross."

"Someone should give young Kelly a public thrashing," the friends said. "He broke Harvey's heart."

Me? I read the book and its locally famous third chapter and I remembered the one time that I had met Roy Kelly. It was at a cocktail party at Harvey's house. I was more or less offended to start with. I don't like getting drunk in the company of students and the only reason I would ever go to a party at Harvey's is to get bombed on his good liquor. I had reached the age of thinning hair and a thickening waistline, a time when it is not at all unusual to despise the young and the fair. Kelly's lean, tanned good health (he looked as if he ought to be wearing a blazer and carrying a couple of squash rackets under his arm), his pleasant self-confidence, and his glib literary talk bored and annoyed me.

But when we all left at the same time he offered to drive me back to the campus in his new sports car. I was torn between the wild horses of my pride (I didn't own a car at the time) and my curiosity. I accepted and we drove back to school together swiftly along the country road with the fine air of a spring twilight flowing over us. He was a little tight and excited about everything. It was his last semester. He began to talk about Harvey Peters.

"You'll never believe this," he said, "but I really love that old bastard. He's been good to me and you can't help but love him. But it *is* all kind of pathetic."

"Pathetic? How's that?"

"Oh, you know what I mean," Roy Kelly said. "He's so out of place. I mean out of time. He's like an old whale stranded on the beach."

"Sort of a poor man's Moby Dick."

"I'm serious," he said. "That was a bad analogy right off the top of my head, but I'm serious. The thing is, he just doesn't belong in a time like ours. In this day and age he's so helpless and hopeless and ineffectual, the only way you can see him is as a comic character."

"Like the stranded whale?"

"No, that was a bad one, I already admitted that. Say he's like the last of the old buffalo hunters. A kind of an academic Gabby

Hayes with a scrubby beard and a broad-brimmed hat and no teeth and a powerful, lever-action rifle, riding round and round in some fenced-in park looking for the old, lost, wild game. Only the thing is there isn't any wilderness anymore. Just public parks and cultivated pasture with a few Black Angus cattle moping around for decoration."

That is all I remember of Mr. Roy Kelly's conversation. Like a lot of people, he talked a little bit better than he wrote. Or maybe he should have written his book drunk.

One day later on I was having coffee in the Faculty Club and I just happened to have a copy of the novel with me. (I was returning it to the library. I wasn't about to *buy* the damn book, even for a few laughs.) I saw Harvey Peters come in and head for my table. I managed to get the book hidden under Douglas Bush's *English Literature in the Earlier Seventeenth Century*. Apparently it wasn't noticed because Harvey sat down and drank his coffee and talked amiably about trying to raise some money to come to the aid of a convicted ax murderer. I even promised to give him a check for five dollars for the cause. Just as he rose to leave, however, he reached across and tapped the back of *A Field of Fists* with his finger.

"Never let them write a book about you," he said. "Don't live that long if you can help it."

I looked at him, thinking that he had come to terms with his disappointment and now found refuge in the tragic pose. I was wrong. His expression was sad enough for tragedy, but it was mild too.

"You know," he said, "so many, many things have never worked out right for me. I was born to be a buffoon, a kind of amusing fool. There's a very precise word for it in Yiddish, but I forget what it is. It's a stock character in Yiddish literature. The book didn't really hurt me much. It all started, all that, so long ago. . . .

"When I went to college—it was a small, poor college upstate —we didn't have all the amusements they have now. I guess we had more of mischief than anything else. When winter came around, every freshman had to prove himself a man by riding a sled down a really fierce, icy slope. There was one very bad turn and there was one tree that you had to miss. The infirmary was full up and half the class was wandering around on crutches. I was scared to death of the whole idea; but it had to be done. I kept putting it off and putting it off until there were only a couple of us left who hadn't done it. Finally I steeled myself against the inevitable, and I did it with half of the student body looking on. I hated doing it, but I did it anyway and I did pretty well too. A nice smooth run. No bumps, no bruises, no scratches.

"The trouble was that after it was all over I felt that I had earned the right to a little shred of pride. But they never even gave me that much. When they saw my pale face and my knees trembling, more from pure relief and joy than anything else, they laughed. Oh, it was hilarious! By doing the thing I had earned myself even more of a reputation as a coward and a buffoon than if I had refused to do it at all."

He looked at me with the same mild, sad, serious expression, as if he wanted me to say something or, perhaps, to ask a question or change the subject.

"What do you think of that?" he said finally. "Do you know I have never told a soul that story, not even my wife?"

I smiled and shrugged. At that moment I could have bitten my tongue in two because I was neither a friend nor an enemy and there was nothing right for me to say or do.

WHAT'S THE MATTER
WITH MARY JANE?

MILDRED GLANCED across the room. She looked past tense, close-packed heads, all bobbing like floating apples and most of them gashed, bitten it seemed, here a mouth open, there the flash of good teeth. Here a smear of red lips, and everywhere tongues. Tongues fluttering, lolling and loose, all talking, talking, talking to each other at the same time. Didn't anyone bother to listen anymore? Did anyone ever stop talking and for one bright moment become nothing more than a pair of eyes, a pair of attentive ears, five alert senses devoted wholly to concentration on something or somebody else? Or did they clothe themselves, disguise themselves in words? Was there anything worth saying? She felt empty. "Empty as a broken bowl of everything save light and air," she recalled a line from one of her husband's poems.

Looking across all that, feeling now as bodiless as a ghost or a shadow, she watched her husband and the actress. They were talking, too, both at the same time it seemed. They had found themselves a quiet corner, a corner anyway, for no zone in that small, walk-up apartment could be called quiet. The actress was sitting, regal, in a comfortable armchair. Mildred's husband, Bill, sat on the arm, his legs dangling, his body half-twisted toward the actress, so that Mildred saw him in profile.

She watched her husband's jaw moving. He wouldn't just be chewing gum, would he? The actress stopped talking for a moment, and even appeared to be listening to him. She was a tall, big-boned, handsome woman who seemed not only able to listen, but to react as well. Good training. The best-trained ones always react well. Now the actress was saying something to him, intently, slowly, as if weighing her words with care. Bill's jaw stopped moving as he gave her all his attention.

Who would have imagined she could listen to anything but the fluent music of her own rich voice?

The two of them over there seemed out of place. There they were with the whole room whirling and dancing around them, with cigarette smoke swirling at the level of the ceiling like a convention of genies just freed from the prisons of their bottles. There they sat while faces and bodies were joined together and swept this way and that by a fickle wind. Only they seemed anchored, at ease and safe. It made Mildred furious.

Then looking more closely at her husband with a critical eye —what he called her "First Sergeant's look"—she noticed even at this distance the gaping hole in the side of his wool sock. She had knitted them for him. Why would he wear them if there was a hole in them? She should have darned them, would have if she had only known. Why didn't he tell her? Maybe it was deliberate, an intent to shame her. Then it occurred to her that perhaps they were the only clean pair of socks he had. She was not, she was the first to admit, a good housekeeper. They didn't teach you the joys and sorrows of that. You didn't major in sock-darning at Smith.

Sometimes when she thought about the way she treated him, she felt so sad she wanted to cry. He didn't have to put up with it, though, did he? Why didn't he stand up for his rights?

"You about ready for another, doll?"

Smiling, she turned her attention to the young actor. His face —pale, intense, angular, Jewish, bright-eyed—blurred and swam near her. Like a face on the television screen going in and out of focus. The head of the actor, as if ghostly, disembodied, came close and then receded, as if he were on a swing. Up close he looked vaguely double, superimposed upon himself.

"You look like a Picasso!" she cried, laughing.

His fine brows wiggled. "Is that—good?" He had taken her empty glass away from her.

"I shouldn't," she said, eying the glass. "I've had enough already. But we come to town so seldom these days. . . ."

"Don't make excuses," he said. "Just stand there and look pretty. I'll be right back."

Swift, dimensionless, suave as a shadow, he was already gone toward the kitchen, edging easily through the crowd. A lean, hungry barracuda knifing through a school of fat, contented . . . what? Well, fish anyway. Just fish. She couldn't remember the names of anything right now. Especially the names of fish. The stereo was blaring a popular tune from one of the new musicals. She knew it by heart, but she could not recall the title. And what was his name? Gold? Silver? It had something or other to do with precious metals or perhaps a stone. Stone would be better. Diamond, how would that be? He was all angles and subtle, sharp creases, etched lines. His face was pale as milk, but his dark eyes brimmed with an inner source of light, the overflow and excess of whatever hidden fires consumed him. A cruel glow, she concluded, compounded of pure and ruthless ambition and appetite, of boundless ego and an insatiable self-esteem.

Well, what did she expect an actor to be made of? Bells and cockleshells? Snails and tails?

Entirely without his knowledge or consent, the poor boy had been involved in their lives, the center of a shabby domestic crisis less than a week before. He had appeared in a minor role on a TV series. He had impressed her then, playing the long-suffering and inarticulate younger brother of the leading man. He seemed so fragile and vital. His inability to articulate the profound feelings, which so obviously swept through and racked his being like gusts of fire, seemed to her fine and clean in spite of Bill's sotto voce comments, his dry ironic vivisection of the play, the plot, the characters. Billy was seldom at a loss for words. He wavered between a kind of acquired irony and a painfully natural talent for announcing the obvious in a periodic, sententious style.

She had watched the young actor's high-boned, exotic face, framed in the glowing TV screen, and she glimpsed a whole magic world of fire and ice. She was offended by her husband's good health, his rational composure, his words, words, words. Impulsively she jumped up and cut off the television. His reaction was merely sympathetic curiosity.

"Why do you always have to spoil everything?" she said.

"What seems to be the matter, Mildred?" he said, unruffled and solicitous.

"What's the matter with Mary Jane? She hasn't an ache and she hasn't a pain!" she shouted at him.

She left him, ran up the stairs, and fell on their bed. She buried her face in the pillow and enjoyed the luxury of tears. She heard him turn on the TV again. After a while she fell asleep where she was. When he came to bed later, he gently undressed her and tucked her in. He was businesslike, efficient, and quick with buttons and snaps and zippers. She was aware of all this, and when she lay between the cool, clean sheets, still with her eyes closed, she waited for his first hesitant amorous touch. She lay very still for a long time and listened as he settled into a deep sleep and began to snore.

Now she was here and talking to the same actor. So many were here in the room. Nobody really famous, of course, but many recognizable faces and names. And he, Bernie—that was his name after all—was articulate enough in person, and he was tough, aggressive, the proud possessor of the armored sensibility worthy of, say, an old snapping turtle.

It was silly, she supposed as they chattered along inanely, silly to be here at all, mingling among people their own age who were really doing something. Their host, who was a classmate of Bill's, was currently directing an Off-Broadway production. In this room there were actors, writers, other young directors, chic exciting women, and once earlier in the evening a well-known producer had passed in and out of the room, smiling tolerantly on one and all, benignly receiving the homage that was due him.

Bill was an Assistant Professor of English at a small New England college. Thus she, Mildred, became a Faculty Wife, turned out to perfection in her modest, decently expensive dress, her sensible shoes (for walking in New York), her hair cut short and designed mainly to demand a minimum of attention. More than two hours away on the unpredictable railroad (Bill didn't trust their old car to make it all the way there and back), they did not often come to town anymore. With his eight o'clock classes, spent urging sleepy freshmen not to split infinitives and not to dangle poor helpless participles, it was very difficult to come in for an evening. It seemed to require so much planning, so many arrangements.

It had not always been that way. When they were first married and Bill was a graduate student at Princeton, they were only an easy hour away from the City. They lived in the Project then, the University housing development of drab, converted, one-story barracks, and they were poor and happy.

He wrote poems in sullen rebellion against his assigned task of tracking the Bestial Footnote to its ultimate lair, against the horror and the day when he might produce a Footnote himself. Mildred acted with the Theater Intime and even allowed herself to think of a career in the theater. They had friends in New York, at Columbia, and in the Village, and there were long wonderful nights, parties where the talk was deathless and vibrant with significance . . . surely they had at least talked well in those days.

Now, a few years later, Bill had two scholarly articles to show for all his dreams and pains, one in *PMLA* and another in *The Journal of English and Germanic Philology*, both sound and solid examples of scholarship. He had invested in a depressing stack of separately bound offprints which he kept to send around to colleagues and rivals in his field—the Seventeenth Century.

Now she winced at that inevitable, and perfectly neutral, academic question: "And what century are you in?"

The infuriating, wholly inexplicable part of it was that Bill seemed perfectly satisfied now. He talked fondly of his students, gossiped amiably about his colleagues, wished and worked for eventual promotion and tenure, and looked forward nervously and eagerly to the regular dinner parties they gave with that aim in mind. That slothful beast, Security, was in view.

"You ought to come down more often," the actor was telling her. "Play hookey for a weekend sometime. I'd love to show you around. I can get seats for a play and I know a great little restaurant . . ."

That, of course, was one alternative. Other faculty wives availed themselves of it. They called it coping. Mildred tried to picture it as she listened to him. She saw them smoking joints in the lobby of a theater between the acts. How he would listen to her! He would smile and nod and his eyes would be bright. She saw, vaguely, the denouement, a little scene played out in his apartment, whiskey, and the tape deck softly playing the appropriate music, a roommate conveniently absent. Even the perfect little shudder of illicit pleasure it gave her now seemed hardly worth the trouble. Suddenly she felt very tired.

"It would be very nice," she told him, "but I probably won't be back for quite a while."

"Why?"

"I'm pregnant," she said.

His eyebrows twitched almost imperceptibly, reflexively, but his smile never wavered. She could tell him very simply the truth, that she had lost two babies in miscarriages and that in a few months the doctor would not let her travel at all. But he was very young and he was very arrogant.

"I'll be wearing maternity clothes in no time," she added. "Would you like me to come for a weekend in maternity clothes?"

"Sure," he said. "Why not?"

But already he seemed more preoccupied with his drink than before. She smiled and looked away, back toward Bill and the actress. They were still talking. There was a crash in the kitchen as something or someone fell heavily, a sound of shattering glass, then loud laughter. Neither Bill nor the actress reacted.

Nor paid heed to the pounding noise of the music. Nor the heat and smoke of the room. Nor the gray winter wind prowling like a hungry wolf just beyond the windows.

It was easy to understand Bill's fascination. The actress was glittery, deeply involved in Real Life. Tall, in fact too tall for Bill in her heels, she was conventionally pretty and adequately voluptuous. Bill was probably haunted by the dim adolescent vision of An Affair. Poor old Bill! If Mildred's intuition was sound, the actress was quite sexless. No doubt she was inordinately fond of little stuffed animals.

What on earth did she see in Bill? Probably, Mildred thought with a certain pleasurable malice, he represented what she would call "class." That would be very amusing. It was Mildred who had been a debutante, and it was because of Mildred's family that they happened to be listed in *The Social Register*. A curious triumph for Bill, since he had never even heard of it before they were married. Now it was Bill who refused to let their annual subscription go by. He said that on an Assistant Professor's salary it was his last shred of dignity, like Englishmen on remote tropic isles dressing for dinner. Bill was pure, solid, yeoman middle class from the wilds of the Middle West. Like many others before him and since, he had come East from a small Middle Western college, lost in the vast inane distances of that Somewhere. He came to graduate school in Princeton, and there he acquired, almost to the exaggerated point of parody, all the local tribal habits of dress, of speech and conversation, even of thought.

It was doubly amusing, for Mildred had married him out of rebellion against her own family, precisely because he was what he originally was. Now, as though to compound the ironies, he had let himself become a kind of a caricature of the young ambitious academic, the kind of young man that nostalgic, aging Full Professors smile on. Maybe the actress thought that Bill might one day write a play for her. More likely, though, he was just a good listener. That particular sort of blind, bland worship, the horse who gratefully accepts the sugar lump, the wide-eyed, wet-eyed cow who licks the salt from your palm, was what the actress thrived on. As an orchid feeds richly on thin air. . . .

On the subject of thin air. When Mildred turned back the young actor was gone. Vanished into it. A dance of filmy smoke filled the space where he had been. Maybe all his pale fires had suddenly consumed him and all that was left of all his energy and hungers was a little smoke.

The room was whirling a little now. Bits and pieces of shredded conversation fell on her ears like senseless, intimate, lewd whispers. She started for the bathroom. . . .

Later she found herself in the bedroom lying in and among a shaggy flock of overcoats. After a long, dizzy time she was awakened by a gentle shaking. She opened her eyes, sat up stretching, and smiled at Bill.

"Poor girl."

"Don't poor girl me," she said. "I've been having a lovely time. I just happened to get plastered and I passed out."

She moved to a mirror and put on lipstick and ran a comb through her hair.

"Almost as good as new," she said, winking at herself.

"I'm sorry," he said, helping her into her coat. "I should have been looking out for you."

"Don't go around being sorry all the time. Don't . . . !" She stopped. Her voice was loud. Her tongue felt thick and heavy trying to shape words.

He buttoned his overcoat and walked behind her. The host had disappeared, and the last of the beached and stranded survivors of the party ignored them. Bill shut the front door quietly behind them, the best thank you and farewell he could muster under the circumstances. They went slowly down several flights of stairs. He held the door for her and she stepped out into the cold air. There were fine snowflakes falling, beautiful in the light.

"We can stay over at a hotel," he said. "Or the Princeton Club."

"Why?"

"I'm afraid we're going to miss the last train."

"Who'll take your classes?"

"They can get along for once without me."

They walked along the quiet street. Bill was watching for a taxi, but there was none in sight.

"Tell me all about the great lady of the theater," she said. "You two seemed to be having a very intense little tête-à-tête."

"She's having a hard time finding any work this season."

"Maybe if she took up another line of work . . ."

"What's the matter with you? I only talked to the girl."

"She didn't talk to me."

"Please," he said. "You're shouting."

"Very well," she said in a stage whisper. "How's this?"

Then they stood silently at a corner waiting for a traffic light to change. When the light changed Mildred bolted across the street, laughing, and he followed running behind her. The wind cut into their faces and carried her laughter away. Once they were in the partial shelter of the buildings in the next block, they slowed down to walk again.

"She's good-looking," Mildred said, "if you like that type."

"I didn't say I . . ."

"She'd have to wear flat heels with you. I don't think she'd like that."

"Why do you have to make such an issue out of everything?" he said. "Didn't you have a good time?"

"I had a marvelous time," she said. "That nice boy asked me to come down some weekend and shack up with him."

"What did you say?"

"I told him I'd love to, but I'm pregnant."

Bill put his arm around her, hugged her tightly, and laughed.

They decided to walk awhile before going uptown. Now the cold air felt good and clear. They went down a few blocks of bars, nightclubs, coffee houses, and little theaters, moving leisurely through the press of people and the sudden island of carnival atmosphere, staring in windows and blowing little foggy ghosts of breath.

"I bet everyone at school is sound asleep now," she said. "They're all dreaming about tenure."

"Want to stop somewhere and have a drink or some coffee?"
She shook her head. "Let's just walk."

At a corner they stopped to look at the tinted posters flanking the entrance of a little strip joint.

"It's so cold," Mildred said. "They should at least let them have goose pimples on."

The doorman, a shabby field marshal, cupped his gloved hands and called to them to come on in, the last show was going on. They passed by and crossed the street. From the other side they could see just a glimpse of the inside. They saw the sparse crowd and the little tables. Then the lights blinked and dimmed and a spotlight fell brightly on what must be a small stage or platform. A girl appeared in the light. She began to sway and dance to the sound of music which was completely stifled by the heavy glass door.

"Let's stop and look," Mildred said. "I've never even seen one."

The doorman across the way eyed them a moment, then stamped his feet and clapped his hands together, looking away.

They stood watching as the girl, cool, moving as if to an elegant, subtle melody, danced and peeled off her elaborate costume. Finally she bowed to what must be applause. Then she smiled widely and began to dance to a different tune, a different, more frantic rhythm. There was a kind of blurred flashing white frenzy they saw.

"There she is practically naked," Mildred said. "And here we are all wrapped up in our overcoats and freezing. And there's only a little glass between us."

"Like the snow and the roses."

"What?"

"In that poem by Louis MacNeice."

The girl finished, bowing again to unheard applause.

"Is that all?" Mildred asked.

"I guess so," Bill said.

They were walking along again, talking into the wind. Far off a ship hooted in the harbor and the snow was beginning to fall more heavily now, damp flakes swarming around the street-lamps like soft, huge moths.

"Wasn't that strange," she said, "watching someone dance to music that you can't hear?"

"If you can't hear it, then it isn't music."

"Don't be philosophical."

"I wonder what they were playing?" he said without much enthusiasm.

After that he was silent and so was she. She was beginning to feel sorry for herself, for all the mess and clutter she created out of things, for her cluttered, untidy life. Then she was saved by a happy, silly thought.

"That's me, Bill! I'm exactly like that girl."

He looked at her, but said nothing.

"I dance and dance," she said. "And nobody else can hear the music. Nobody knows the name of the tune."

"That's a pretty fancy reaction to a striptease," he said.

"You wanted to be a poet," she said. "You used to write poems. Whatever happened to you?"

He stopped walking, grinned, and started to say something—"We can't always do . . ." He closed his mouth and the wan grin vanished and all of a sudden there were real tears in his eyes. She could not remember ever seeing him cry.

"I'm a bitch," she said. "I don't know why I said that."

"It's a legitimate question."

"Poor Bill," she said. "I love you, but I did a terrible thing. I sent you off to a party with a big hole in your socks."

He took her in his arms and kissed her. Their lips were cold. Then he put his arm around her and they walked away leaning their heads together. He was lost in a dream, a deep-sea diver in a perilous sea, searching amid wrecks and bones for some lost, glittering treasure. She in her separate dream, with only a few bright sequins for costume, dancing and dancing before a mirror as wide as the sky.

A RECORD
AS LONG AS YOUR ARM

RAY, OLD BUDDY, one of the things I'll never be able to forget is the look on your face when you strolled into your bedroom and discovered me there with your wife.

You were supposed to be away for the whole weekend with the Debate Team. Only they called it off, and so you got back home a little after midnight Friday. Walked into the house happily, already slipping out of your clothes, with a whole unexpected, unplanned weekend ahead of you. You were tiptoeing (you thought maybe she would be asleep). Otherwise we would have heard you, I think. Maybe. Actually we were each and both reaching that state of being where the explosion of a bomb in the driveway or the front yard wouldn't have distracted us. If we'd heard at all. You tippy-toed into your own bedroom, switched on the light, and got about halfway into some familiar, cheery greeting when you saw that smile and cheer were being wasted on the large, inadvertent, pale and glowing moon of a bare ass. Mine. . . .

After that things began happening kind of quickly. But I can, by some oversimplifying, impose an order and sequence on events. Geraldine is free of me as if repelled by an electric shock. She has got the sheet all around her—thus even more fully exposing me to chilly light and chill air—and she is trying to curl up under the pillow. You, still without a full word, have turned toward the bureau and snatched open the top drawer. I have not yet moved. Not purely out of shock and fright, mind you, but also because I can vividly imagine a large, blue-black, shiny, well-oiled, well-kept revolver, probably a .38 Police Special, resting in the bureau drawer just beyond your fingertips. And naturally I am amazed that you would have a gun in there. You know how strongly I feel about the necessity for gun control. My position on the possession of handguns has always been quite clear. Politics and ideology aside, however, I am thinking that I am sure enough about to be shot at, but with luck I may yet come out of this alive. I am betting it all on the fact that you are (1) completely surprised, (2) naturally a little nervous, (3) basically nonviolent, (4) hopelessly inept with mechanical things, (5) and probably a lousy shot. My first thought is that I must begin by offering you a target, something to shoot at, but which, if hit, will likely do the least permanent damage. Hoping that luck, thick muscle, and adequate fat will save my vital organs, banking on the expectation that one good clean messy hit will bring you to your senses, I therefore exaggerate the somewhat awkward position which Geraldine has left me in, trying with the facility of a contortionist to curl up completely behind that largest of muscles. Hoping that the bland bare sight of it will so enrage you as to cause you to miss me altogether.

Instead of a shot, however, in this timeless instant, I listen to your deep breathing and some considerable rummaging in the bureau drawer. Things start landing on the floor. I decide I'd better sneak a peek, even though it may be my last one. Therefore I shift my strategy and my stance slightly, rising up higher. To view you more or less as, say, the center sees the punter on fourth down.

At which point, precisely, you turn back toward the bed, twist, rather; twist your head to look at the bed. Our glances meet. Upside down, of course. And I am happy to see that you are empty-handed.

What else can I do, then, prior to resuming my original position, what can I possibly do but wink?

"Geraldine!" you shout.

Muffled noise from beneath the pillow.

"Where the hell is my fucking gun? I left it in the top drawer."

Ah, a familiar domestic situation. In a trice and a twinkling Geraldine is back in charge.

"Well," she says clearly and distinctly, "I haven't touched it. Try the bottom drawer."

Clutching her sheet—in fact all of the sheets pulled out from under me in one smooth deft yank—she is now rising with every intention, it seems, of helping you search for the gun.

Wrapped in her cloud of sheets, she is suddenly between us.

And I? Off of that bed in a roll. Scooping up my undershorts like a third baseman handling a hot grounder. Out the window without wondering if it's open or not.

Discovering, a good hundred meters away from the house, that indeed it had been open and all I have wrapped around me is the screen and its frame. A picture entitled "The Wages of Sin" is moving twinkle-toed, screen and all, through a series of almost identical backyards in the Whispering Pines Subdivision. Tangling blindly with rows of hedges while trying to take them like low hurdles. In one case having a memorable encounter with a portable outdoor grill on wheels. Which sails me along merrily as far as a blue plastic swimming pool, through which I thrash and splash, half-drowning, while packs of dogs begin to bark and various lights come on.

I shall pause in my headlong flight through the awakening neighborhood, suspenseful and pathetic as it may be, to say, "Meanwhile, back at your house . . ."

Now, Ray I have to confess that this next part is not purely imagination. I got it from Geraldine the next time we met. I do not give my unqualified credulity to her version, of course. Geraldine, bless her heart, has a tendency to lie grandly when she can or has to. And when she cannot, she will certainly do a little needlepoint upon the plain pattern of truth. So I do not believe that part of her story—how later she managed to con you so that, when the time for apology could no longer be deferred, it was you who apologized. And then were deeply grateful for her forgiveness.

It's possible, I'll grant you. Perhaps also true, but I prefer not to accept it. Nor, for that matter to think about it very much. However, I am willing to accept other elements as basic facts.

The two of you together searched through the bureau for your pistol. No pistol. In your perfectly understandable anger and dismay, you turned on Geraldine and accused her of having hidden the damn thing, just in case this ever happened.

Very dumb move, Ray.

She denies it. Did not touch, has not ever touched that damn dumb fuckingpistol of yours. Would not either. Being as how she, for one, knows how to respect another person's goddamn privacy. Then she reminds you how you were down in the basement, cleaning the pistol, a couple of days ago.

Maybe, you allow. But you wouldn't have just left it down there.

Yes, you did. You did! Because you got a phone call from the Dean. You had forgotten all about that—the meeting of the Committee on Educational Policy. You had to haul ass over there, fast as you could.

Now you remember it all—the call, a wild, fast drive over to school in the Triumph, tearing up four flights to the Dean's Office, two clumsy steps at a time, bursting into the room a half hour late and suddenly all those astonished, hostile faces looking at the doorway and you standing there in work clothes, panting, both hands all grubby with oil and grease.

Down you go to the basement, Ray, to look and see for yourself. And I go with you, even now. Feeling it all. Stiffness and the slight vague pain in your bad leg. Stooping at your height, under the low ceiling, moving toward the worktable. Where, sure enough and just as you left it, there's the pistol amid rags, an oil can, toothbrush, patches, and a stiff wire brush for the bore. You stand there a moment, testing the cool, pure, clean weight of it. Then a brief flash of inspiration, a flicker of a smile. Yes, she has got you cold, dead to rights and right back in your place. But you smile to yourself, poor deluded Ray. You climb back up the basement stairs. Slow, regular, noisy. Conveying decision and direction. Clump, clump, clump, the ever-so-slight drag of the gimpy leg, through the kitchen, diagonally across a piece of darkened living room, and back into the bedroom.

To find her changed into her best nightie, sitting at her dressing table, back to you, but able to see you enter in her mirror. What happens next I can't claim to know; but either, without missing a stroke with her hairbrush as you approach, she informs you that you'd be a whole lot more scary if that gun were loaded; or equally likely, she reacts with operatic fright, so convincing that you immediately reassure her by showing her the gun is not loaded, whereupon you find yourself having to apologize for frightening her half out of her wits.

In any event, apologize you will, must, and do. And now you are ready to talk about it, to discuss the whole thing.

She is not ready, but a light is in her eyes. She's got an idea. John Towne is lucky to be alive. He needs to be taught a serious lesson. You can agree on that much, if she keeps talking and you don't stop to think about it. If you had shot me when you first came in, you'd have been within your rights; if you proceed to shoot me now, however, even assuming you do find the shells for the pistol, it will technically be first-degree murder. Geraldine says she hates the thought of you in jail. She needs you. She needs you near and available. Maybe you could get off on grounds of temporary insanity, but . . .

You are practically hypnotized by then, Ray. What's more, she has an even better idea. The two of you should get in the car and drive over to my place. I should be there by now. You will wake us up and scare the wee-wee out of me with the big gun and making a horrible face like you did when you came sneaking back in the bedroom trying to be funny. You can take the clothes and shoes I left behind, and hurl them on my living-room floor, enjoy fully the look on Annie's vapid, pretty face as she discovers, at long last, the truth about the two-faced, two-timing, sonofabitching sex fiend and monster she is married to. Then turn with pride and dignity and leave them to each other. She has all the money, such as it is, you know. A taste of poverty will serve

Jack right. At that point, Ray, you accept her logic. Partly because it is better than doing nothing, and no question, you do love that Geraldine. And who wouldn't? She may be a little tacky, but she is a truly first-rate piece of ass.

So you gather up my clothes and get in the station wagon. Solemnly, with even a certain stiff ceremony to the occasion. I bet you even held the door open for Geraldine when she climbed in.

It is, or will be, important you are not driving the Triumph. You are behind the wheel of a John Wesley College wagon, the one you checked out earlier to drive the Debate team.

I'll bet—I can actually see it happening—you haven't driven two blocks before Geraldine, her spirits and confidence now fully restored, has punched on the radio and is humming along with the music of an all-night record show.

Meanwhile, Ray, I had made it safely home. Out of Whispering Pines, through the fringes and edges of town across town, skirting the campus but using the park and the cemetery to good advantage, part way along the railroad tracks, and finally home, over the plowed field behind our (Annie's) literally Colonial house. The real thing, only all furnished in blond Swedish and Danish and probably Finnish modern, with rugless, highly polished, wide-board floors, damn few *objets*, barish light-colored walls. Only a very few choice pictures and prints hanging, and those changed regularly. Fresh cut flowers, artfully arranged. Some old musical instruments that nobody plays, mostly stringed things all out of tune. Pots and ceramics made by Annie herself, together with a few elegant examples of her stitchery. And not to forget the brick and board bookcases; the big stereo setup that can rattle every windowpane in the house. The nursery for Allison, not out of *Winnie the Pooh* at all, but instead as sparse as everything else, with strictly functional toys. One bare cold bathroom upstairs with a high, claw-footed, stained, wheezing turn-of-the-century tub. A toilet with an honest-to-God chain pull. And ancient, scratchy towels (oh long before Margaret Drabble tried to make them popular!). Hardly a mirror in the whole house except for the one in the bathroom—small, old, distorted, badly lit, silvered—over the medicine cabinet. Where, if you peeked, you find it as neat and bare as a GI's footlocker. Only the most basic toilet gear, a bottle of Listerine, and a bottle of aspirin so old that the tablets were crumbled to powder.

Did I mention the bedroom? Most of it occupied by our big, low bed. Which was really only a mattress and an inner spring set up on wood blocks.

Maybe that's what first attracted me to Geraldine. Such a good old simple broad, you know? Everything phony and wonderfully cluttered. Fancy bathroom with all the latest equipment and the soft, colored toilet paper, the covered seat for the john, the cute and vulgar stack of reading material. I think you even had a bidet. I may be wrong. But when I try to picture your bathroom, I always see a bidet gleaming there. And who could forget the full rich medicine cabinet of Geraldine Wadley? I picture everything I can imagine and then I multiply by two. Then add a little forest of pill bottles, every kind of prescription from a couple of dozen different doctors. All about half full. And Geraldine had big soft, expensive, wraparound towels just like in the movies.

Ray, I have to admit I really liked your bathroom.

So, anyway, winded, battered, and bruised, toes stubbed and feet full of splinters, eyes teary from twigs, I find myself home at last, sneaking in. Why do I sneak? She's wide awake, reading a book in the living room. Oriental kimono, smoking a Schimmelpenick cigar, reading a book and listening to Segovia.

When I come in, Annie looks over the top of her book and reacts. Very cool, as ever and always.

"Hi, Jack, is anything wrong?"

"I'm afraid I may be in a little trouble."

"Oh . . . what kind of trouble?"

So I explain how I was in the Library working late as usual. And how I got a phone call from Geraldine Wadley. All frantic about how some kind of an animal is loose in the house. Big bat or a flying squirrel or something like that. Ray is away on the

Debate trip and she is scared out of her mind. Would I, as a very big favor, please, please come out there and get rid of it?

I was, naturally, playing on every decent chord I could reach. Annie loves animals. All kinds of animals indiscriminately. Supreme contempt for any woman who is frightened of any animal. Besides which Annie has always had a dim view of Geraldine. Convinced Geraldine is a slut and a hussy and a Jezebel. Cheap and tawdry temptress. Two-dollar whore, etc., etc., etc.

Of course, Annie liked you a lot, Ray, and thought you were patient and long-suffering.

I continue to create my simple fiction. I get out there (never mind how, Annie doesn't ask) to your house and discover a flying squirrel is indeed in the basement. In passing I mention the fact that Geraldine greets me at the door wearing only her panties and bra. Insisting that she was so upset and panic-stricken that she probably forgot all about her personal appearance.

Knowing better, Annie smiles and permits me to continue my tale.

Well, Geraldine has this big pistol and she wants me to shoot the flying squirrel. I will have none of that. Truth is, I couldn't bring myself to kill a flying squirrel. But I explain it to her in more practical terms. I am liable to shoot up her lovely home. A .38 slug could easily carry over to a neighbor's house. Anyway the explosions will wake up the whole subdivision. What I will do, I say, is catch the beast and release him outside.

"Catch a flying squirrel? You?" Annie laughs at that.

"Scoff as you may and must," I answer her. That's exactly what happened. In the limited space of the basement I was able to run the bugger down and trap him in an old badminton net. But not before I ripped my trousers on a nail, dirtied my shirt, and soaked my shoes in water leaking from the ancient hot-water heater.

After I set the squirrel free in the yard and returned, Geraldine seemed very grateful. She insisted that the least she could do was to sew up the rip in my trousers and run the shirt and socks through her washer and dryer. (Annie is sternly against dependence on appliances.)

I remind Geraldine that it is getting pretty late and that the Library is already closed. I better go on home as is. Nonsense, Geraldine insists, wouldn't dream of sending you home like that. What would Annie think? I am urged to go into the bedroom, hand my stuff through the door, stretch out, relax, watch TV or something. And she'll be through in a jiffy. Should I call Annie? No use worrying Annie about it. She's probably asleep by now anyway.

In trusting innocence I did as she suggested. I did, however, notice that while I had been crawling around down in the basement she had modified her outfit. Changing into a black, powdery, filmy sort of a peignoir. And once I was inside the bedroom I noticed (one each) panties and bra draped across a chair. But I honestly never stopped to think . . .

"You're too naïve," Annie concludes.

"Maybe so," I am willing to concede.

I stretched out on their bed. Since I share my dear and loving wife's supreme contempt for TV and since there are no books in the bedroom, merely some old copies of *Cosmo* and *Mademoiselle* . . .

"She has always dressed too young."

. . . I dozed off briefly. Eyes tired from my long hours of study. An intimate touch, the odor of an unfamiliar perfume waked me. There she was, on the bed beside me, as bare-assed as Eve in Eden, an amorous glint in her eye if I ever saw one . . .

"That bitch!"

But wait. Nothing really happens. Then suddenly everything happens. Who drives up, lights flashing across the bedroom walls, but my good friend Ray? What will I do? If I try and explain everything, will he believe me?

I never had a chance to decide what was the right thing to do. For just as Ray came whistling and limping into the house, Geraldine made a unilateral decision. She hollered rape at the top of her voice. Ray came into the bedroom just in time to see me bail out of the window.

God knows what will happen next. They might even call the police.

Now, Ray, here is where Annie really surprised me.

"What happens next, sport, is that you get some clothes on, and we will drive over there and straighten the whole thing out."

"Don't you think it might be better to wait until morning? Let things cool off a little?"

"No."

"I'll see Ray at school tomorrow anyway and tell him the complete story. No use your getting involved too."

"Don't be such a coward," Annie says. "Whenever something serious happens in our lives, you always try to avoid it. Usually by comedy. You will go right to the center of a scene and then cop out with a gag line."

"Show me a gag line and I'll go after it like a dog chasing a stick," I say.

But there is no getting out of it. I get dressed to go. I am thinking, what the hell, Ray will never shoot me down in front of Annie. And she will attribute your fantastic story to your sense of misguided nobility—the desire to protect Geraldine's (ho-ho-ho) reputation.

I give it one last try, though.

"We shouldn't go off and leave the children all alone."

"Nonsense," Annie says. "I woke up Andrew. He is perfectly capable."

And away we go. Laughing and scratching.

Here comes the next problem of that evening. Happens that our car is in the garage. Guy was supposed to have it ready, but he didn't. We have a loaner. Good enough. Not long at all, a few blocks maybe, as we drive toward Whispering Pines, our heap drives right past a John Wesley station wagon. But we think nothing of it. We are looking for a sporty red Triumph. You are on the lookout for a new Pinto not an old Plymouth.

Ships that pass in the night . . .

We get to your place, hang around awhile. Then decide maybe you went to our house. We go back, passing without noticing, almost certainly, a John Wesley station wagon. You arrive home and find Annie's crisp, curt, cool, condescending, and correct note. We get home to find Andrew highly amused by something.

"Mr. and Mrs. Wadley were just here. Mr. Wadley had a gun with him. He said Daddy is a very bad man and he's going to shoot Daddy."

I get myself a big drink. Annie lights up a cigar and considers the situation. Since they haven't called, it behooves us to go back and try again. As we drive away, I hear, faintly, our phone begin to ring. Annie doesn't hear that well, especially when she is thinking. Andrew won't answer it, you can count on that. He hates the phone.

I think I could save us all a lot of trouble if I drove into a telephone pole or something. Except the local cops know me too well already. They will nail me for drunk and reckless driving. Engine trouble? Annie knows more about cars than I do. The whole thing is, Annie likes Ray and Ray likes Annie. And I . . . ? Well, I like Geraldine all right. As a friend, I mean. And I am willing to forgive and forget the way she treated me. What the hell? Annie will work it out. Then we'll all get drunk together and watch the sun come up. Fix breakfast . . .

Well, Ray, we missed you twice again, going and coming. Then everybody quit trying. I know from Geraldine (believing about half of it, of course) what happened with you all. Thoroughly beaten down, frustrated, you were ripe for a long serious talk. Tears and a plea for forgiveness from her. An appeal to your emotional maturity and natural generosity. Promises for the future.

About that unfortunate incident in the office. Knowing you had an eight o'clock class, I came early. Not to ambush you, as it may have seemed. Nor to go through your desk. I figured that, since we share the same office, I'd better get there first, take what I needed, and cut out. I won't brazenly sit there, I told myself, with my very presence an insult to Ray, until we have straightened it all out. I'll just get what I need from the office, enough for a couple of days. By the Wednesday Department Luncheon everything will be okay, I'm sure.

It was my thought that prior to the Luncheon I would give you the benefit of a wide berth. At the Luncheon I would be as friendly as can be and you would have to respond in kind. Because our Chairman likes that. A friendly Department is a good, productive Department, he says. I intended to make sure he was standing right there when I greeted you effusively and then asked you how the Debate trip went. Not out of irony or a vulgar desire to rub it in. Shock, yes. To shock you into wakeful attention and the possibility of a meaningful dialogue. You would understand my effort to communicate. Being a genuinely sensitive and intelligent guy, you would be amused too. What dramatic irony! You have to stand there and kill me with comradely kindness. One pout, one snarl or sneer, one snotty remark, and you would be on the Chairman's shitlist. Unfriendly guys have no future at John Wesley. And least in the English Department. And you were still trying to hustle yourself a promotion.

Lest I sound cynical and cruel, let me remind you of the truth that if you play a role well enough, becomingly, as it were, it becomes you.

Trouble was, I overslept. And then I forgot that my watch was running slow. Even so, I probably would have had plenty of time to collect my things and get out before you got there. You never in your life arrived one second early for your eight o'clock class. Except on that particular morning . . .

I got to the office, quickly packed my briefcase, and was ready to leave. Felt suddenly a little sad, like I sensed an unhappy ending. Reached for a cigarette. Had forgotten. Remembered you kept a pack somewhere in your desk. Went and sat in your chair to rummage and find . . . one cigarette, that's all. Among some papers a glossy shine, the edges of some photographs caught my eye. Took a look. Some pleasant Polaroid shots of Geraldine. Flipped through the pictures. Whoa there. Flash of flesh! Geraldine in buff, inimitable birthday suit, taking various and sundry poses. Pretty good horn shots. A natural model. Couldn't help looking, Ray. Once I found them, I mean. Admittedly, it was wrong to poke around in your desk drawers like that. But I found them only by accident.

I thought maybe I would take one, just for a souvenir, so to speak. Which one? Preoccupied, I spread the pictures across top of desk to pick and choose. Put one in my pocket. Figured the next time I was with Geraldine I'd show it to her. Tell her you sold it to me for two dollars. Geraldine sometimes a very gullible person. I was sitting there laughing out loud imagining the possibilities of that scene when you walked in on me.

I was not laughing at you or Geraldine.

Intended to put pictures back where I found them and leave.

Unfortunately, with pictures in hand like a hand of cards, I never had a chance. You came in and made your own erroneous inferences.

You threw your attaché case at me.

Started around desk after me. I went under the desk, diving and crawling, and made it to the hall. Hall full of students going to class. Bells ringing to add to confusion. I staggered into wall across the way, caught myself, and turned around. You gave me mouthful of knuckles and my head banged hard against wall. Saw pinwheels and stars of light. Trying to duck and to keep from falling. Second blow grazing my ear and side of head.

Bent over, I started to come up with a punch. Then realized I was still holding onto the photographs. Checked my swing. From my position—please try and see it from my point of view —I was helpless. Head ringing, mouth and lips bleeding. All I could see was your two legs firmly planted, solid and set to hit me again. What could I do?

I swear to God, Ray, I never meant to kick you in your bad leg. Second, and by the same highest authority, with my head and eyes down I never even saw that the students had grabbed you and were holding you. Not until you yelled from the pain and fell to the floor. By then it was too late for anything.

I hurled the pictures away and ran off to the parking lot.

Ray, I doubt that you ever fully understood about your unpleasant interview with President Butterman. Objectively speaking, I don't look too good on that one. And I'll be the first one to admit it.

The thing is, the mitigating circumstance, I was desperate. I checked with old Butterman's secretary, Grace. Remember Grace? Not bad; not good-looking; high-spirited and eager to compensate for her lack of beauty by energy, activity, and a sense of adventure. She always responded with enthusiasm and took my intentions for exactly what they were—polite and strictly political. Within those rational limits we got to be good friends.

Grace told me that I didn't have a prayer. She said Butterball was planning to drop me anyway because I still didn't have my Ph.D. She also told me that Butterass hadn't decided what he was going to do about you. You had about an even chance to be allowed to stay on. There were some advantages for him if he did that. For one thing, he would have you permanently over a barrel if not in it. He would have another grateful slave on the faculty.

I want you to know that it was more to wipe that possum grin off his ugly face than to hurt you personally that I did what I did.

Grace told me that your appointment was set for Friday afternoon. That gave me time. I typed the letter over at her place, and then she drove me down to the P.O. so I could mail it off Special Delivery. I have found that many people are inclined to attach an undue importance, certainly a significance which is not intrinsic, to the fact that a letter arrives by Special Delivery.

I'd rather not quote it or fake it, if you don't mind. A confession doesn't have to be completely embarrassing to be efficacious does it? Indirect discourse will have to suffice.

I said to Butterworth that much as an apology seemed to be called for in view of my unseemly behavior, much as good manners and, yea, even honest self-interest demanded of me at least a measure of regret, a show of repentance and contrition, yet I had no intention of so honoring him. As far as I was concerned he could stick it up his ass now and forever after. That the only time I ever wanted to see his name again was when I would read

his obituary. Which, statistically speaking and barring unfore-
seen accidents and the whims of Fortune, I would almost certainly live to read and enjoy. However, I continued, I would like
to do him one last favor before I faded from the scene at John
Wesley. I would like for him to know something he really ought
to know, lest he should mistakenly misinterpret the Geraldine
Wadley Caper and surmise that it must be a one-shot misfired
adultery, chiefly distinguished by its comic elements, and very
unlikely to recur. Lest he, like stupid, well-meaning Raymond
Wadley himself, might reach the conclusion that a single and
wholly exceptional infidelity, nipped in the bud, so to speak,
might, in the manner of some broken bones, not only heal, but
also weld the original union more firmly than before. Geraldine,
I hastened to assure him, was no character out of conventional
women's magazine slick fiction. More likely out of Olympia
Press.

I then made a list of fourteen members of the faculty who I
knew for a certainty had, at one time or another during the
current academic year, had one or more rolls in the hay with the
aforesaid lovely Geraldine, adding that the list was woefully
incomplete, since I did not choose to include members of the
Athletic Department, the coaching staff; nor did I wish even to
venture even a guess as to whether the entire football team or
only the starting lineup had so indulged. Furthermore, I added,
in the case of undergraduates, it was practically a professional
venture on Geraldine's part. I wished only to call attention to
the amateur amatory activities of this charming faculty wife.
However, should he wish to check through his sources and
spies, his undergraduate stoolies, he might well inquire whether
or not a number of compromising photos, not at all unlike the
enclosed, of the aforesaid Geraldine Wadley were not at this
very moment in well-thumbed circulation in dormitories and
frat houses.

I added that I was doing him a hell of a big favor because with
a piece of nymphomaniacal dynamite like that in his already
partially corrupted University community, a scandal of really
major proportions was, by all odds, likely. And the only reason I

was doing this was that when it did hit the fan and nothing at John Wesley was left spic and span, he would have no bitch or whine or hand-wringing coming, and I should be entitled to laugh my ass off at his acute discomfort. . . .

By Friday when you appeared, innocent enough, in your best dark suit, with all the dignity an aggrieved cuckold can muster, you had already had the ax, just like me, only you didn't know it. Not knowing any of these things, you must have wondered at the ease and audacity with which he simply fired you. You had probably prepared yourself against the eventuality of being told that you would not be promoted or, even, if worse came to worst, being told that at the conclusion of the current academic year your services would no longer be needed. But—virtually unheard of!—to be fired on the spot. And not gently, but curtly and gruffly. And for what? For "moral turpitude." That old bugaboo, define it as you will, like "incompetence." Defined in this case, neatly and irrevocably as attacking with fisticuffs a fellow member of the faculty—*in the presence of students!* Never mind why. There is no sufficient cause of justification. For, even should violence have been a legitimate response to whatever wrong Mr. Towne may have done you, it should never, ever have taken place on University property and in the presence of students. Therefore he had no alternative, as chief administrator of this institution, save that of asking you to leave quietly and without untoward theatrics or rancor; for surely you must acknowledge the justice of his decision? Adding that it might well serve your self-interest to accept this verdict gracefully in view of the fact that every time you applied for a job in the academic world in the future, or for that matter in any other field of endeavor, the matter would sooner or later come up and he, Butterman, would be asked confidentially for an explanation of the details and for an evaluation of the man, you, Raymond Wadley. He, Butterman, would then be personally grateful if, upon leaving this office and this campus, you, Wadley, would demonstrate those qualities of patience and fortitude he knew you to possess at your best moments. Your resigned acceptance and self-control would be matched, he promised you, by a willingness on his part to forgive, forget, and to do everything in his not altogether inconsiderable power to assure you a decent second chance in the academic world. In fact, as a token of his faith in your ability to rise above this one surprising lapse, he was willing even now to get on the phone to a friend of his, the Chancellor of a small but honorable agricultural and mechanical institution in South Dakota, and arrange for a job for you there, perhaps at a slight, temporary reduction of salary, but money isn't everything and we all have to tighten our belts and put our shoulders to the wheel from time to time, nobody being perfect. . . .

According to Grace you shook hands with him, gratefully, Ray, tears in your eyes. And he walked you out of the office, the reception room, and the building, briskly to be sure, but with his arm around your shoulder like a real pal.

By Friday night, thanks to her many friends and my many enemies (plus, I guess, my own track record, which helped to impose a certain pattern on the circumstantial evidence), Annie had pretty well figured out everything that happened. At least she knew all she wanted to know.

"You are no damn good, rotten to the core," she told me. "It is bad enough, by all known standards, to fuck your friends' wives. But you don't stop even there. You have to find a way to fuck your friends too."

I had time to get in only one good solid slap across her face when the phone started ringing. She ran to answer it. I lit a cigarette and stood there trying to think of the proper rare quixotic gesture which would work as an effective apology when Annie came back, rubbing the side of her face and looking furious.

"That was Geraldine."

"Geraldine who?"

"Women can be a problem," she said. "They tend to get involved in spite of themselves."

"Oh goddamn . . . !"

"Are you going to beat her up too?"

Bad scene, Ray. Boring and bad. Best I could hope for from then on was a reconciliation. Fall-back position was "a few days for both of us to think it over and sort things out." Which I got. We agreed to separate for a while, beginning the next morning. I could take the car and go somewhere. She was quite comfortable at home, thank you.

Saturday morning I drove out to the Finlandia Sauna. Ready to sweat until I became a pure spirit and could vanish or fly away. There was one of the college wagons parked out there, but it meant nothing to me. I figured a couple of coaches had come to bake out the Friday-night booze. I undressed, noticing some clothes on a hanger but not paying any attention to them either. Grabbed a towel from the stack and slipped into that dry, hot, wonderful, wood-smelling, low-ceilinged little room. Parked my butt gingerly on a hot bench, sweating already, before I looked up and saw you. I must have jumped and started to get out of the room by instant reflex.

"Aw, sit down, Jack," you said. "Can you think of anything sillier than a couple of old crocks like us fighting it out, bare-ass, in a sauna bath?"

"It's my nerves, Ray," I told you. "I guess I just can't take it like I used to. It's been a rough week. Let's see . . . I lost my job and my best friend and I'm about to lose my wife and kids. Old age, Ray. A few years ago I could have taken it with a shrug. Now it kind of smarts."

Well, it was, for an hour or so, like old times. We sweated a lot. We had a few inconsequential laughs. We even stopped at a place down the road on the way back to town and drank a couple of beers together. Nothing like a freezing cold can of beer after you've had a sauna bath.

It was then, with the two of us sitting in the Wesley wagon, drinking beer, that you told me how you and Geraldine had agreed it was better to break up for keeps. You were very calm and sensible about it. She would go off and visit her Aunt Clara this weekend, leaving you time to pack up your things and anything else you felt you wanted. All she wanted was the little red

Triumph. Which is why, of course, you were driving the Wesley wagon.

We finished our beers. Shook hands and said good-bye. You drove off to pack up. And I drove to Boston to be Geraldine's Aunt Clara for the rest of the weekend.

We had a wild weekend. Never left the hotel room. Couldn't break it off until Tuesday. (Or maybe, I think now, she may have planned it that way, to give you a whole extra day in the empty, lonely house in case you changed your mind.) We got back to your house after dark. She went in first to look around. Came to the doorway and motioned me to come on inside.

"He left everything!" she said. "All he took with him was his own clothes."

"Oh yeah?"

"I was afraid he would take the TV or the stereo or something, just for spite. But he didn't. It proves I'm right."

"About what?"

"About people," she said. "Trust them and give them freedom and responsibility and they do the right thing almost every time."

"It just proves Ray is a good guy."

"He's a sweetie pie," she said. "Just a sweetie pie."

I grabbed her up in my arms and carried her, laughing and kicking, into the bedroom. Dropped her on top of the bed. Started pulling and peeling her clothes off.

"As I was saying here the last time when we were rudely interrupted . . ."

That seemed to amuse her. Still, Geraldine made me turn the photograph of you, which was on the bureau, to face the wall. That girl was not without a certain sensitivity.

Since folly is, in fact, the subject of this little true confession, I would be lying, Ray, if I didn't say to you that you were a damn fool to do what you did. That fact in no way mitigates my own folly or lessens my need for confession. But goddamn it, Ray, I have been terribly hurt by what you chose to do. Ever since. Did you stop to consider the probable effect on Geraldine and me? Or on other people? If you didn't, you damn well should have.

And if you did, then anything you may have hoped to achieve has been deeply undermined by the punitive and vindictive nature of your action.

I refuse to let guilt cripple me. Sure I have gone right ahead making a wake of mischief behind me, getting into trouble and out of it, goofing off and fouling up. Just like I did before then. And like I guess I am bound to keep on doing for as long as I live. For better or worse. I am the same person. But nothing has ever been quite the same since then.

It must have been around two in the morning when I woke up and wanted a smoke. Out of matches. Geraldine got up, slipped on a robe, and went into the kitchen to fix us something to drink. We looked everywhere for matches. No luck.

"Try the basement," she said. "We used to keep some down there in case that damned old hot-water heater conked out."

I tried the light, but the bulb was out. Stumbled down dark stairs and felt my way toward the hot-water heater. Stubbed my toes on something hard. Felt it in the dark. Felt and hefted it. And then the other one right beside it. Both of them heavy.

"Geraldine," I called. "He left his suitcases in the basement."

I groped in the dark, trying to find the heater and the matches.

"Jack?"

I looked back and saw her framed in the doorway, backlit by light from the hallway.

"Did you say he left his suitcases down there?"

"I believe so. Wait till I light a match."

"I wonder why he did a thing like that?"

"Wait until I can see something . . ."

Ray, I already knew as clearly as if I had seen it in noon sunlight. But I was praying my mind's eye had deceived me this time. I found the matches. They were damp. The first couple wouldn't strike.

"I'll go find a flashlight," she said.

"Just a minute."

The third match caught and flared. I held it up. There were the two suitcases all right. And there, too, over in the corner just before the match went out, there you were. Sprawled and lying in the corner like a broken doll.

"Is he still alive?"

"I don't think so," I said. "Go get that light and I'll take a good look."

While she hunted for the flashlight I came back up and swallowed the drink she had fixed. She gave the light to me and I was sent down again. Ray, you and I both have seen our share of blood and gore in the wars. So I wasn't worried about having to look at a stiff. After a time you learn that the only blood and gore you are entitled to feel anything about is your own. I put the light right on you, Ray.

"He's been dead quite a while," I said.

You had done a job of it, taking half of your face and head. You had, evidently, sat down in a little deck chair, which lay nearby, taken that pistol of yours, and put it in your mouth. And then at some point, early or late, you pulled the trigger. Very brave, in a way. Because there is always the chance that you'll live. I couldn't do it that way, myself, Ray, not with a pistol. For fear I might flinch or twitch and botch it. I stood there looking at you, admiring your courage. On the floor, bloodstained (oh there was plenty of that), there was a framed portrait photograph of her. You must have been holding it in your free hand when you pulled the trigger.

"Is there a note? Do you see a note anywhere?"

Geraldine was right beside me, her face pale and drawn in hard, tight lines of shock. She looked old, Ray, hard and old. I could see what she was going to look like in twenty years. Or less.

"I don't see anything. Maybe he left one some place else in the house."

"Maybe . . ." Then she said, "I wonder if his life insurance has a suicide clause."

She turned back to the stairs and started up slowly.

"That was the only good . . . the only really good picture I ever had taken in my whole life," she said. "And he ruined it."

"I doubt if he wanted to."

"Want! Want!" She shouted at me. "He never knew what he wanted!"

By then she was sobbing and I was sick. Vomiting all over the basement. Puking my guts out. I couldn't cry. But my stomach, the seat of truth, reacted for me. Not out of squeamishness and not even from shame. Not then, not yet. But from sorrow. And not just sorrow for you, but for the three of us. For all of us. For Annie and the children. For all the children you would never have. For scratchy towels and big soft fluffy ones. For television and stitchery . . .

I kept on vomiting until I had the dry heaves. Until there was nothing left to come up. Then I was over it. I went and sat in the kitchen and discussed calling the police. She wanted me to leave first, but I explained that within five minutes they would know I had been there anyway and then there would be some bad trouble.

"He's been dead since sometime Saturday, Sunday at the latest," I said. "That's my guess. We can prove we were in Boston together, and it's clearly a suicide. If we tell the truth, we'll be all right."

She didn't like it, but she agreed. And so the cops came and went, and then the undertaker came and went. By which time it was already full daylight. She fixed breakfast. Oddly, we were both hungry.

"I'm leaving," she said. "I'll get the movers to come later and pack everything up."

"What about the funeral?"

"I told the man I want him cremated."

"I've got to finish out the rest of the semester."

"I know," she said. "It won't look right if you don't. I'll be in touch as soon as I'm settled somewhere."

I just nodded.

"You got a garden hose that will reach down there?"

She pointed to the front yard. I went outside, hooked two sections of hose together, screwed on the nozzle, and then brought it down into the basement. Then went back up and turned the water on. Then back down again.

That's the last thing I ever did for you, Ray. Hose the remaining stains of you, and my vomit, too, off the wall and the floor and down the floor drain. It was clean and drying fast when I left.

There was no note. At least nobody ever found one.

That might have been better, after all. A crazy note. Or maybe a raging note. Or a self-pitying one. Even some heartbreaking and silly message. But you left it all to the imagination. You left each of us, separate and equal, to live with the blank cruelty of it always. Which may have been right and even just, but which was also unforgivable.

Well, I am ready to forgive you for that, Ray.

If St. Augustine is right (and it almost always turns out that he is), the dead have neither interest in nor concern for the living. The dead do not care anymore. Finally, they can be careless. Which means I don't have to ask your forgiveness too.

But, alive, I am able to forgive you. Not out of my own guilt. If I were ever to entertain guilt seriously, I would join you among the indifferent dead. Not from any guilt, but because forgiveness is the one free act of human love that is still possible for me. Not that people can ever really completely forgive each other. But in the ritual of wishing to and trying to forgive one another, in ceasing to judge one another and leaving Judgment to its proper Author, then for a brief moment we can find and feel the secret energy of divinity in us.

Forgiveness is a simple and glorious act of human freedom. Suicide and lunacy are not. Sartre and Camus were full of shit.

You think I'm too serious all of a sudden? Well, you're right, old buddy. Right about that, anyway.

Epilogue

NOISE
OF STRANGERS

Thou shalt bring down the noise of strangers,
as the heat in a dry place; even the heat
with the shadow of a cloud; the branch of
the terrible ones shall be brought low.

ISAIAH 25:5

NOISE OF STRANGERS

LARRY BERLIN is driving north on Route 27 when he spots the car. It is a new white Plymouth going too fast. No more than a dazed sudden smear of shine and chrome against the monotonous gray of the dawn. Any other time and he probably would let it go, let the car go by and on, to hell or safety for all he cares, rather than slowing down to stop and then turning around, which means having to doodlebug here with a ditch and dense pinewoods on both sides of the road and neither a trail nor a footpath to nose into.

It may be nothing more to him at this moment than a wince of surprise after long, slow, boring night hours, the surprise of now rounding a wide curve and coming almost face to face with a shimmering apparition of pure speed when he had every reason to look for only the yawn of the empty highway ahead of him. Or, maybe, it is something more. An abrupt, utterly thoughtless, visceral knowledge of danger. Danger and challenge. Whatever it is that warns and alerts him, he does not waste one second to make up his mind. He twists the wheel sharply to avoid the collision. He slows down and brakes. In two smooth motions, he doodlebugs his car, and now he is off in the other direction in pursuit, his foot jamming the gas pedal down to the floorboard. He can feel a slow easy grin begin to take command of his lips as he grips the steering wheel tight and leans forward. Like a jockey.

Whether he is now really gaining or it is only that the Plymouth has started to slow down after the first few tire-singing miles of the chase, he can't be sure. The car ahead grows in size, looms in the clear space of his windshield, and he knows for sure he is going to overtake and pass it in just a minute or so. It is then that he remembers to turn on the pulsing red light and touch the switch on the panel that sets his siren howling.

After that, the other car slows down in a hurry and pulls over to the side of the road. He noses in close past it, cutting sharp across and braking hard in a screech and a shallow surf of dust on the shoulder. He climbs out and now the driver of the other car is out, too, a big man in a dark suit shouting something at him and clawing inside his coat below his left shoulder with a frantic hand. Larry Berlin already walking toward him sees the sudden glint of gunmetal and without breaking stride he draws his own pistol from his holster, points, and fires. By the time his finger squeezes off a second round, the big man has staggered blindly, pitched, and fallen headlong on the highway as if struck down, smashed in a broken whimpering heap by the huge indifferent fist of a giant. Larry Berlin takes a few more steps and stands over the loose-jointed, crumpled form. The man is dead. He stands there, breathing deep, profoundly astonished, looking past the shiny tips of his own boots at the thick smear of blood slowly spreading on the road. He does not recall even hearing the sound of his pistol firing, so pure was his concentration. But now he does hear something—a sigh, a rustle of clothing, or a sudden intake of breath in that breathless moment. He whirls back toward the car, bent, both hands holding his pistol

Sheriff Jack Riddle is jolted out of sleep by the jangling of the phone. He knows, wide awake but with his eyes tight closed from the first ring, that it is not the alarm clock or the doorbell or any other of the irrelevant buzzings and ringings that mark and measure a man's time. Even so, he lets it ring and ring. In the hazy false dawn between sleeping and waking, he allows himself the immense luxury of simply ignoring it a little while, then speculating on what or who in the hell it might be at this hour before, exasperated, he finally rolls over heavy with a kind of a twitch and a flop like a catfish in the bottom of a rowboat. Grabs blind for the phone. Misses! It falls with a dull clatter. He wonders if he has broken it, but it rings again. Eyes still shut tight, he starts feeling for it, his right hand moving tip-fingered across a rough piece of rug and then on the slick floor until at last he blunders against the cold insistent shape.

He groans a little and lifts the receiver to his ear.

"Yeah?"

"Hello, Jack, this is Larry."

"Okay."

"I just had some trouble out on 27. I'm bringing in a prisoner. I think maybe you better be there."

"That's what you think, huh?" he says irritably. "Meet me at the office."

He leans far over the edge of the bed to hang up the phone. He leaves it on the floor. Then he lies back on his pillow, slowly and gently as if his head were fragile as a bird's egg, opens his eyes and looks with wonder and interest at the familiar spots and cracks in the ceiling.

His wife, Betty, has not stirred. She is sound asleep, her back turned to him, hugging her pillow like a teddy bear. He smiles. Then he eases out of bed, quiet and careful so as not to wake her, gropes on the bedside table where the phone had been, finds and lights a cigarette. He stumbles barefoot, stiff, huge and awkward as a bear, to the bathroom. Splashes cold water on his face and, dripping, takes a skeptical look at himself in the mirror.

He is a big man, big-boned and heavy, with a large, round, close-cropped head, cut so close to the scalp that the patches of gray are like a light stain. He likes it cut that way. Keeps him from having to think about it. When he was a boy, he was called Cannonball because of that head. His eyes are greenish in the light like a cat's and fringed with pale, sparse lashes. His nose is broad and flat and broken. He has a hard, sunburned face, cut with the fine deep lines of wind and open weather. But for all the intrinsic sculptured strength and brutality, it is a warm face. He is quick to smile and at ease with his power. He runs his fingers across his bristly cheek. He won't take the time to shave now. He will probably be back in plenty of time to shave and have breakfast with Betty.

Yesterday's khaki uniform is in a rumpled pile on a chair. He might as well wait until later to change his clothes too. He slips into the khakis, kneels to lace and tie his high-top shoes, and leaves the bedroom and the small frame house, pausing at the door to pick up his gray, battered, broad-brimmed hat. Pulls the front door to softly behind him. Squares his hat, hikes his britches, and steps over the rolled-up morning paper on the stoop, figuring he can save that for later too. Climbs in his car, easing his bulk behind the wheel, allows himself a long sigh, then starts the engine and backs out of the driveway.

The town of Fairview is small and old. It is the county seat. It offers for casual inspection a wide main street flanked by low brick buildings and running into and then out of a shady green park where the county courthouse stands and behind that, hidden from view, the squat two-storied shape of the county jail. The highway races headlong into Fairview from pinewoods and miles of bright, bare, flat fields, then snarls up and passes slowly for a few minutes through the dense, pleasant shade of the town, passes by the brick buildings, the brief glitter of storefronts and sidewalk, ducks under more shade trees, going by wide lawns now and white frame houses set back at a comfortable, old-fashioned distance from the street, houses grotesquely lively with the jigsawed scrolls and curlicues and latticework and the stained glass a generation of grandparents loved. Wide, airy front porches with railings and swings and potted plants. In the yards azalea, oleander, live oak, and the inevitable rich magnolia. And then the road is long gone again sprinting off breathless into the shadeless glare that leaps toward a vague horizon.

A traveler or tourist will remember Fairview, if at all, for its brief and unexpected blessing of shade and its couple of lazy traffic lights designed evidently to arrest the enormous and irresistible lunge of his progress elsewhere. He will recall it as a quiet place, a museum piece from the past, where he was forced to sit with foot-tapping impatience waiting for a light to turn from red to green.

Fairview is anachronistic, dying, but endures still as the center and hub of a sprawling, lightly populated county given over to small farming, ranching, and a few logging and turpentine camps. Before the turn of the century there was a short, deceptive period of prosperity, a fatness from the profits of naval stores. Most of the brick buildings and most of the big, fine houses were built on those profits. And, again, just before the Depression gripped this amazed nation in an iron fist, there was a time for a fantastic, gaudy daydream based upon a wildly inflated notion of the value of the raw land of the peninsula of Florida. But Fairview, inland, lacking everything to please the tourist except a mild climate, failed early in the Boom. Since then, there has been small reason for Fairview's existence, except as a place for people already there to age and die in, except as the legal and material heart of a poor rural county. Except as a place with a few commonplace memories and the dusty official archives. The town endures now without thriving and without really changing much, a preserved relic, it seems, of what at least from this anxious point in human history was an easier, gentler, more relaxed time to be alive. The only recent additions to the face of the town are the Bide-a-Wee Motel on the north edge, the Winn-Dixie Supermarket, and the glass and concrete of the hospital and medical center.

"At least we can die in a new building," the natives say.

The county jail was built well before the First World War. It is brick, too (there was a mayor in the brick business), and as solid as a fort or a blockhouse. It seems to have sagged at joint and sinew with age, to have hunched down on arthritic hams and settled into the earth. Or, perhaps, simply to have grown out of the earth like some monstrous plant. The long shadow of the stern, cupolaed courthouse falls across the lawn and reaches the front steps of the jail behind it. The upper story of the jail is for confinement, a row of small barred windows running completely around the building. Pass close by at certain times, like twilight, and you are likely to see fists on some of those bars, a tic-tac-toe of black and white hands against a graph of cold steel. And sometimes a lax palm waving or imploring. And sometimes music, whistling, a snatch of a song, a harmonica. And always some rude laughter escapes.

In the first clean washed light of a new day, bells ringing and the crowing of roosters echoing across the back fences of the town, the jail seems most shabby and forlorn. By the end of the day, light fading and one more day spent and smirched, it appears almost comfortable. This morning, as he drives up to leave his car in the parking lot behind it, it puts Sheriff Riddle in mind of an old hen, too old and too tough even for stewing, an old hen that has been roosting all night in a tree. Somewhere a tethered hound howls. Sheriff Riddle leaves his car and moves slowly across the crackling gravel and down a walk to the front door. He would not consider going in the back way.

Well, small and shabby as it is, it has always been enough, he thinks. *For drunks and bad driving and failure to pay fines and petty thievery and petty violence. About the last thing we need to waste good money on around here is a new jailhouse.*

Trapped odor of disinfectant greets him when he opens the front door. And the odor of dust, too, a ghostly compound and distillation subtly composed of the dust of all the years, the dust of public records and official forms, the dust of clothing and shoes going in and out of the building until the stone steps outside have been worn smooth and slick as a chewed bone. Dust that has eluded yesterday's sweeping and mopping details and will continue to escape somehow from all brushes, brooms, dust-rags, and wet mops from now on down to Judgment Day when he or whoever else is burdened with the office and responsibility of County Sheriff will be relieved once and for all of all authority. The dust escapes it all and lingers. Just as the faint, palpable odor of human sweat and tears and misery is somehow able to overcome any disinfectant and invariably triumphs over all the perfumes of the world.

He walks through the quiet empty hallway and through a door of frosted glass with his name and title painted on it. Flips on the overhead light switch, for it is still shadowy in the room with bits and pieces of the dying night. Snoring greets him. Deep, steady snoring. A small man, also wearing rumpled khaki, is curled up on an Army cot in the corner. A small, old, wizened man, the turnkey who is called Monk.

"Morning, Monk."

The snores stop. The little man sits up quickly, rubbing his eyes, and slips his feet into a pair of loafers.

"Morning, Sheriff. I was just resting my eyes a little."

The Sheriff snorts. "Your eyes are gonna need resting if you keep on looking at stuff like that."

Monk grins. Beneath the cot is a copy of *Playboy* opened to a pull-out page revealing a dazzling expanse of healthy nudity—a young blond girl casually and ineffectually clutching an expensive bath towel, her expression one of pouting astonishment, as though the privacy of her bath were being interrupted by the vast reading public.

"It ain't mine. It's Larry's."

"Yeah? Well, he's about the right age for it."

"Never too old to think about it, Sheriff."

Monk is up now, on his feet, smoothing out, then folding the blanket on the cot. Sheriff Riddle moves to his desk and glances at the stack of papers and an open notebook there.

"Anybody new last night?"

"Couple of drunk and disorderly," Monk says. "You're early this morning, ain't you?"

Sheriff Riddle does not answer him. He moves around behind the desk, sits down, and starts to straighten out the loose stack of papers. He hates to start the day with a messy desk, but his desk is always that way.

"Well, we had a real quiet night," Monk says, "peaceful and quiet."

The Sheriff bends over to read a letter. Reluctantly, he puts on his glasses. He gropes for a pencil and taps nervously as he reads.

"They brought in the Goatman."

The tapping ceases. The Sheriff shoves the letter aside, removes his glasses again, and looks up at Monk.

"Again?"

"I tell you, Sheriff, I just don't know what's the matter with that old fella. He goes out and he gets two drinks under his belt and then he's a holy terror."

"Hurt anybody?"

"Nobody but hisself. Fell down and busted his lip wide open."

"Do any damage?"

"He fell out before he had time to break anything."

"Poor sonofabitch," the Sheriff says.

"Seems like if you knew whiskey was your poison, you'd try and be a little bit careful."

The Sheriff stares at him. "How long you been working here?"

Monk smiles. His smile is a broad, weak, disastrous expression, an invitation to share in a small furtive lifetime. "Long time, Sheriff. I been locking 'em up and turning 'em loose for a long time."

Which is true. Nobody spends more than six months at the most as an involuntary guest of the county. Nobody except Monk, who has spent the better part of a lifetime here, so stained now with the indissoluble pallor of prisons, the hangdog, obsequious, foot-shuffling caricature of the perennial prisoner, that he might stand as the type for all of them. Doing life for all of them. Gentle, harmless, he is at home here and nowhere else.

"Send him down," the Sheriff says. "Have him bring me a pot of coffee."

The Sheriff listens to him go across the hall and slowly up the iron stairs to the second floor, hollering to the sleeping prisoners to rise and shine. Soon there will be coughing and curses, shuffling noises vaguely overhead as they all roll out and clean up to start a new day. And soon from the kitchen in the back, the smell of bacon and coffee.

Sheriff Riddle gets up from his cluttered desk and looks

around the small office. A few straight chairs, some filing cabinets, a radio set for contact with the cars—seldom used—a calendar on the wall, a heavy, old-fashioned typewriter resting for some reason on the floor in the corner. A cheap clothes hook where he hangs his hat. Bare with only the minimal necessary equipment to perform his duty. For anything extra, he must go elsewhere, to a more populous and prosperous county or to the State Police. He folds up the cot and the blanket and shoves them out of sight in a small closet already packed with cartons of old papers and documents. He opens the top file of the filing cabinet. He removes several coffee mugs and a paper sack of sugar. He gropes for some metal spoons. These things he arranges neatly on top of the filing cabinet. Seeing the magazine and shaking his head with a grin at the improbable young lady, he puts it in the top file. Then the phone is ringing.

"Sheriff Riddle, speaking."

"This is Larry."

"Where in the hell are you? I'm here."

"I'm out at the diner having breakfast."

"Where's your prisoner?"

"He's here with me. He's all right."

"Quit farting around and bring him in," the Sheriff says.

"I'll be right along. I just wanted you to know—"

"Listen, Larry, is it a nigger?"

"No."

"That's a blessing."

"Okay, I'll be along in a few minutes."

Sheriff Riddle hangs up. That boy, Larry, is something else! Stopping off somewhere to have breakfast. Don't let nothing ever interfere with a meal. If you got a prisoner with you, why you just handcuff him in the kitchen or to a post or something. Sometimes that boy don't act like he's got good sense. And one of these days, he is liable to wind up being sheriff of this county. If he's got the patience for it.

The door has opened so quietly that the Sheriff doesn't notice until he happens to look there that the man called the Goatman is standing just inside holding the handle of a big white coffee-

pot with both hands. He is a weather-beaten man in faded, ragged overalls, barefooted, dirty, unshaven, badly hung over. He
smiles at the Sheriff.

"Fresh coffee, Sheriff."

"Put it over there," the Sheriff says, gesturing toward the
filing cabinet. "And pour me a cup."

He picks up the letter he had been reading and puzzles over it.
It is from a farmer out in the county with some kind of a tax
problem. He complains bitterly about taxation in an almost il-
legible scrawl. There isn't anything the Sheriff can do about it
one way or the other, but they all write to the Sheriff because he
is authority; in his khaki uniform with his hat and badge the
government is tangible, real, solid, not some faceless, nameless
filing clerk whom they have never seen or voted for and for
whom they could be little more than names and numbers on a
list. "Tell the High Sheriff about it. He'll do something." As
much trouble as it is, it is not a practice that Sheriff Riddle
discourages.

"They gotta feel like they can blame somebody," he says.
Well, in a day or so, he'll check into it.

Looking up again, he sees that the Goatman has not moved.
"What you waiting on?"

"You know, Sheriff," he says, looking down at his bare feet (he
would be wiggling his toes in the dirt if there was any). "You
know, I'd be honored to pour you a cup of coffee. It's always an
honor to serve you in any way."

"What's wrong?"

"My hands."

"What about your hands?"

"They's too trembly."

"Lemme look at your hands," the Sheriff says. "Put that pot
down and hold out your hands so I can look at them."

Arms extended, palms down, the Goatman stands shyly exposing the uncontrollable twitch and tremble of his hands. He is
sweating. He tries to hide behind a bland smile.

"Just look at 'em shake!" the Sheriff says. "Ain't that something? How do you suppose they got that way?"

"I was drunk last night, Sheriff. I went out and got a little drunk."

"Did, huh? Went out and got a little drunk?"

Slowly, the Goatman has lowered his arms. Unhurried, he moves to hide his hands behind his back if he can.

"Keep 'em up where I can watch!"

Pity may be possible. Sheriff Riddle is known to be a good-hearted man. The Goatman, studying his adversary, wrinkles his brow and purses his lips.

"I feel terrible," he says. "I feel like I'm going to die."

The Sheriff is smiling at him now, a bland, untroubled, unbelieving smile. "Think you might?"

"I just might this time."

"Sit down, then. Don't just stand there and die on me."

The Goatman, immensely relieved, sits down primly on one of the straight-backed chairs. He manages to sit on his hands. He sits very straight on the edge of the chair with his knees close together and watches the Sheriff, who appears to have turned his attention to another paper on the desk.

"Might be the best thing if you did die," the Sheriff says, not looking at him. "Trouble is you're too old and tough and dirty to die."

The Goatman cackles at his cue to laugh, but he continues to watch the Sheriff, wary and apprehensive. The Sheriff looks at him again and they exchange a brief smile.

"You know what I'm going to do?" the Sheriff says. "I think I'm going to let you have a cup of coffee and a cigarette."

"I'd be much obliged, Sheriff."

"On one condition."

"What would that be?"

"It ain't too much."

Now the Sheriff picks up a pencil and writes something. The Goatman bides his time.

"What you want me to do?"

"Oh," the Sheriff says. "All you got to do is stand up straight and pour your own coffee and light your own cigarette."

"My hands is kinda trembly."

"And if you spill a drop, one little drop, so help me God, I'll make you wish you never saw my ugly face before!"

"Sheriff, my *hands!*"

"Get up," the Sheriff says. "Time's wasting."

He leans far back in his creaking swivel chair to observe this. The Goatman rises very slowly, freeing his hands, but still hiding them behind his back, a picture of study and concentration. Turning to the filing cabinet, he takes up the coffeepot and with great care manages to pour himself a cup, stopping well before the coffee reaches the rim. Setting the coffeepot down gently, he grasps the hot cup in both hands and gulps.

"One hand! One hand, goddamn it!"

The Goatman jumps at the sound of his voice and sets the cup down. The Sheriff stands up now and moves toward him, hulking over him. He shrinks and cringes without actually moving, but the Sheriff brushes past. He is only pouring himself a cup. He stirs it noisily with a spoon.

"How in the world are you going to smoke with both hands hanging on to the cup?"

The Goatman grins and shrugs eloquently as the Sheriff produces a pack of cigarettes and some matches. He sets them down on top of the filing cabinet.

"Light your own," he says. "One match is all you get."

Staring, almost cross-eyed with hypnotic concentration at the end of his cigarette, fumbling with his matches, striking three times before the match flames, the Goatman lifts the flame to the end of his cigarette. By gripping his wrist with his free hand, he is able to light it, just as the flame reaches his fingers. He drops the match. He puffs quickly, deeply. Then, triumphant, he turns to face the Sheriff.

"Well, you done it," the Sheriff says.

"Yes, sir."

"Now then, you pick up that cup with the other hand and sit down."

Again, straight-backed, chin high, eyes watery and bloodshot, tight-kneed at the edge of his chair, the Goatman sits waiting. The Sheriff sits easy on the edge of his own desk, sitting on top of loose papers. He sips his coffee and studies the Goatman with cold eyes. Then smiles at him.

"Damn if you don't look like somebody at a tea party," he says. "You ever been to a tea party?"

Now the Goatman can laugh. The first part of the old game between them is almost over. The worst part is behind them.

"You're a better man than you think you are," the Sheriff tells him.

"You're a good man, Sheriff," the Goatman says. "You talk rough and you act rough. But you're a good man."

Sheriff Riddle laughs at this. It is the common expressed opinion of him in the county. But his role, as he conceives of it, is beyond the simple boundaries of good and bad. Outside of those convenient fences, he is not even sure what these words mean anymore. But whatever, if anything, they may mean, he knows he is not "a good man."

"Much obliged for the coffee, Sheriff."

The Sheriff grunts and nods and then they sit there sipping their coffee and thinking.

The Goatman has been trouble for Sheriff Riddle for years. Not by violence, for the Goatman is seldom violent to anyone but himself. And not, really, for coming in and out of jail so regularly that he almost meets himself going in the opposite direction. But by his kind of letting go, his supreme disregard of himself as he lives in the eyes of others. Or is it, maybe, exactly the opposite? It's easy enough to imagine that he, too, like the Sheriff, has assumed a role which makes sense only in a borrowed light—the eyesight of his audience. Conscious of his own singular role, the quaintly formal gestures and attitudes rigorously required of him by the public office and trust he holds, Sheriff Jack Riddle has never been quite sure about the Goatman. And probably never will be. For the Goatman, too, lives outside neat ethical boundaries.

He guesses, without really caring to know, though somewhere it must be a matter of public record, that they are about the same age. He has heard the story that once in another part of the state the Goatman was a jeweler, a successful one. This is the kind of legend that a town like Fairview easily and invariably imposes on a familiar stranger in its midst. But it never fails to stir the Sheriff's imagination. It is possible to divest him of his overalls, give him a haircut and a shave and a white shirt with a necktie and to picture him seated at a jeweler's bench, squinting into the mysterious intricate jeweled hearts of watches through his eyepiece or using his long fingers gracefully to cut and to engrave letters on precious metals. Entirely possible. He has more than once declined the Sheriff's invitation to talk about it.

"That was a long time ago," is all he will say.

Now he lives on a piece of land that belongs to somebody else. He has built himself a tumbledown shack made of bits and pieces of old lumber, packing boxes, and crates. And he keeps a flock of goats. He sells goats' milk and cheese for the few things he needs, and he lives to himself like a hermit. Except for those times when he goes out to a roadside honky-tonk and drinks himself roaring and singing and staggering into an oblivion from which he is as likely as not to awaken in the county jail. He will keep coming back. In fact, Sheriff Riddle will be disappointed if, for some reason, the Goatman should suddenly bathe, shave, dress himself, and assume his rightful name and place. The Sheriff is, among other things, the chosen protector of his little world, the elected hero who must go forth to battle dragons and dark knights for them all while the townspeople live quiet and secure in the vague shine of the hidden treasure—respectability. He sees himself as a lone sentry protecting the chaste virtue of those fine houses along the main street. Within may be madness, despair, rage, and the seven deadly sins guarding a captive princess, but he is concerned only with the public world. The Goatman is a fool without cap and bells, who is somehow needed to question the value of disguise and appearances. He is respectability turned inside out. *I, too, am Man,* he says. *See for yourself.*

A trapped fly sings and buzzes against a windowpane in the office, and the Sheriff drinks his coffee and speculates about all these things.

"Who's looking after your goats this morning?" he asks.

"Nobody."

"Somebody's got to tend to them, don't they?"

"Yes, sir."

"You like them goats?"

"Yes, sir."

"Better than people?"

The Goatman has to laugh. "Better than some people."

Now it is not the hum of the fly they are hearing, but the sound of a siren, distant at first but growing louder as it screams toward them through the still streets. Sheriff Riddle jumps up and goes to the window.

"Damn that boy!" He says. "How many times do I have to tell him not to play with that thing?"

"Who is going to look after your goats while you're in here?"

"I don't know."

The siren has cut off. They have already heard the car braking in the parking lot, showering gravel. Then the slamming of the doors. Now they can hear quick heavy footsteps on the sidewalk.

"If I put you up in front of the Judge, he's liable to throw the book at you."

"Yes, sir."

Footsteps in the hall outside, then the door bangs and flies open and a man comes staggering violently into the room. He is handcuffed and his face is cut and bruised. He has been pushed hard from behind. He twists around, furious, to face the young deputy, Larry Berlin, who enters the office with a smile, carrying a sack and a guitar.

"Don't shove me again," the prisoner says. "Don't you touch me again."

Larry ignores him. He drops the guitar casually in the waste-basket and puts the sack on the Sheriff's desk. The prisoner stands there, a little hunched over, fury still written on his face, and looks around the room, squinting, puzzled. He is a fat man in a cheap old suit that does not fit him. He is not a young man, but it would be hard to guess his age. He is tanned and tired.

"I got a right to know what's going on around here," he says.

Sheriff Riddle looks him up and down contemptuously, as if aware of him now for the first time. "Why don't you take a seat over there and just keep quiet till I'm ready to talk to you?"

"I got a right!"

Larry Berlin shoves him toward a chair. The prisoner, off balance, staggers and almost falls again.

"Leave him alone," the Sheriff says. "He heard me."

The prisoner sits down, taking his time. The Goatman has not moved from his place, nor taken his eyes off the Sheriff. Larry goes to the filing cabinet, opens the top file, and finds his magazine. He leans back against the wall idly flipping the pages.

"What was I saying?"

"You were telling me all about what would happen if you was to haul me up in front of Judge Parker. He's a very religious man. He don't drink and he don't approve of those that do."

Listening to this, the prisoner begins to laugh. He hangs his head down between his knees and laughs softly and steadily. Larry glances over the top of his magazine first at the prisoner, then at the Sheriff; but the Sheriff evidently chooses to ignore the prisoner.

"You think you're still man enough to pull sixty days?"

"No, sir," the Goatman says. "The time was when I could do it standing on top of my head. But I just can't no more. It hurts my pride to admit it, but that's the God's truth."

The prisoner is still laughing to himself.

"Your pride?"

"Yes, sir."

Suddenly the Sheriff turns to the laughing prisoner. He moves quick and light-footed, slapping him hard across the face. The prisoner stops laughing. Then the Sheriff returns to the Goatman.

"Your pride? What kind of pride have you got?"

"Everybody's got some kind of pride, Sheriff."

"I guess you pretty nearly got shed of yours."

"Yes, sir."

Now Sheriff Riddle goes to his desk. He leans over it and begins writing something in the open notebook.

"What are you going to do with me, Sheriff?"

"I'm going to turn you loose," the Sheriff says. "I don't see why a lot of innocent goats has to suffer just because you're no damn good."

A slow, sly grin changes the Goatman's face completely. He no longer appears worn and defeated. Now he seems to have a wise face, a shrewd mask, the wary, agile wit of the long-suffering and the lowly.

"You going to let me go?"

"On one condition."

"Sir?"

"Next time they bring you in here drunk, next time I personally guarantee you a ninety-day haul. And that's going to be ninety days you'll never forget, if you live through it. I ain't going to let you mope around the jailhouse leaning on a broomstick. I'm going to put you out on the road with the young men, working from sun to dark. You'll sweat until you're as dry as an old gourd."

"Sheriff?" the Goatman says, standing now.

"Ain't you gone yet? You better get out of here before I change my mind."

"Sheriff, I ain't got a dime to my name. Not a dime."

Sheriff Riddle glares at him. The Goatman smiles and hangs his head. Then the Sheriff produces his wallet and gives the Goatman a folded bill.

"What in the hell do you think I am—the Community Chest?"

"Thank you, Sheriff. I'm much obliged."

"Get out!"

The Goatman scuttles out of the office like a pursued clown. Through the window they can see him run across the park waving both arms and helloing the world like a madman. Free again—

"You're making a mistake, Jack," Larry says. "He'll be right back here in a week or ten days."

"Maybe," the Sheriff says. "What's the story with this one?"

"I wasn't doing anything," the prisoner says, jumping to his feet.

"I'm not speaking to you yet," the Sheriff says.

"Listen, you big sonofabitch!"

Almost wearily the Sheriff moves close enough to hit him a lazy backhand blow across the face again. He staggers, sits back on the chair, and spits a little rope of blood on the floor.

"If I didn't have these handcuffs on—"

"Take 'em off him."

Larry Berlin tosses his magazine aside, produces a key, and removes the handcuffs. He steps back. The prisoner rubs his wrists and wiggles his fingers. He looks up at the Sheriff, shakes his head, and grins.

"It was a hot car," Larry begins.

"Put down that magazine."

"They was driving in a hot car."

"They?"

"The other one was doing the driving."

"Where is the other one?"

"He had a gun, Jack."

"He never had a chance," the prisoner says.

"He had a gun," the Sheriff says.

"That's right."

"He reached for a gun and you had to shoot him."

"That's right."

"He wasn't reaching for no gun," the prisoner says. "He was trying to get rid of it. The poor bastard was hollering *don't shoot me!*"

"Where is he now?"

"In the hospital."

"He's dead, Sheriff, dead!" the prisoner says, laughing again. "He was stone dead before he even hit the pavement."

"Yeah, Jack. They got him on ice over there."

Sheriff Jack Riddle whistles through his teeth. He stands with his hands on his hips looking at the young deputy. Larry is a big man, too, not so heavy yet, neat and crisp in his uniform, almost too neat and military for a policeman. He used to be in the MP's. The Sheriff notices his shiny belt buckle, the gleam of his boots and leather belt. In yesterday's khakis the Sheriff feels oddly ineffectual alongside Larry Berlin. Larry takes out his pistol, opens the chamber, and puts two empty shells on the desk.

"Two shots," he says.

"All right," the Sheriff says finally. "First thing you've got to do is get a death certificate from somebody at the hospital. Then you come on back here and make out your official report."

Larry Berlin nods.

"You got all the stuff?"

Larry Berlin dumps out the sack on the desk. It contains two wallets, a wristwatch, change, a key ring, papers and cards, a short-barreled .32 revolver, and a box of shells. Sheriff Riddle picks up the revolver, opens the cylinder, then sniffs the end of the barrel.

"Any luggage?"

"Got it in my car."

"How about the other car?"

"Wrecker came and got it. It's over to Gaston's Body Works."

"Got the registration and license?"

Larry pulls a pocket-size notebook out of his back pocket. Tears out a sheet of paper and gives it to the Sheriff.

"Well, you took care of everything. You collected it all and you wrote it all down. And then you stopped off at the diner and had yourself some breakfast."

"I was hungry. I been up all night."

"This fella give you any trouble?"

"He didn't get much of a chance. I shaped him up pretty quick."

"I can see," the Sheriff says. "Did you do it before or after you put the handcuffs on him?"

The young deputy flushes with quick anger. He bangs his fist in the palm of his other hand. "Goddamn it, Jack, if I was like you—"

"Yeah?"

The two men, heavyweights, stand almost toe to toe staring

into each other's eyes. The prisoner watches, incredulous. It is Larry Berlin who looks away, adjusting his hat on his head.

"I'd be dead, that's all. I could've been killed out there."

"Maybe."

"Maybe it don't matter to you. It matters to me."

"Everything matters. Everything that happens in this county matters to me," the Sheriff says softly. "If you get killed I want to be the first one to know."

Larry Berlin shrugs and crosses the room. At the door, his hand on the doorknob and the door half open, he turns back one more time. "I'll never figure you out, Jack," he says.

"That's the one thing you don't have to do," the Sheriff says, "as long as you are working for me."

Then he is gone. The Sheriff seems to slump a little, as if part of his straight, head-high posture were only a response to the challenge of Larry Berlin, the challenge of youth and strength and ignorance. He turns to look at the material Larry brought in.

Who would have thought a kid like Larry could kill somebody?

He looks around this crummy office with contempt. Wouldn't you know if he was to get busted it would be in a dump like this? Way out in the boonies. He has seen it all before in many places at other times. In his time he has been pushed and beaten and ignored in places where he was a stranger. And that's just about everywhere, buddy-bo, ain't it? He is not afraid anymore. When the young punk came out of his car shooting, he thought he was gone for sure. He scrunched down under the dashboard. He knew he was dead and gone and he could have pissed in his pants right there. But when he finally climbed out with his hands up, the young cop was so arrogant, cocky as a banty rooster, he stuffed his pistol back in the holster at the first sight of him. Daring him to make a move, just any quick move that would allow the cop to kill him right there. The young cop, the one called Larry, grinned at him, but the eyes were flat and vicious like the eyes of a mean dog crouched over a bone. It was not a bone he stood tall and proud next to, but the body of a man. He stepped slowly, one step at a time toward the cop, his hands still as high as he could get them, locked at the elbows, never once taking his eyes off the eyes of the cop.

"All right," the Deputy told him. "Stick 'em out here where I can put the cuffs on you."

He lowered his hands and held them straight out side by side like a sleepwalker. The handcuffs clicked tightly in place. Then he breathed easy again. Even when the Deputy, suddenly breathing hard through his mouth like he had just run a foot race or something, hit him in the face and knocked him down and kicked him savagely in the ribs. Through the pain he knew he was going to be all right. He wasn't going to die. And that is something to know. He expected it. After all, a man that's come close to dying and has just had to kill somebody else has got up a head of steam on him.

Now he sees his good guitar, the box he has been toting with him for almost twenty years and treating like a baby, jammed down in the wastebasket. That was unnecessary. But he knows, too, you give a young guy his initiation, let him have a little practice of his strength and power, and you can't cut it off like turning a faucet. It keeps leaking awhile. He keeps bleeding inside from the wound. The prisoner cuts his eyes away from the wastebasket and stares at the blank wall. If they ever get an idea you care about something they can hurt you. The only way you can be hurt is to have them take something you care about away from you. He doesn't trust any of them and never will, not even the big one here in the room, too, the Sheriff, who has on sloppy clothes like maybe he's slept in them. He hates them one and all, damn their eyes. And he will as long as he lives.

"You want some coffee, boy?" the Sheriff asks him.

"Don't try and sweet-talk me."

"If you want some, help yourself."

The Sheriff now sits down behind his desk, takes up the phone and dials. The prisoner looks past him to the wall, noticing the calendar and noticing that somebody forgot to turn the page last month. A month or two don't make no difference in a place like this. The colored photo on the calendar is of the Taj

Mahal. Now don't that just beat the whole world? The Sheriff probably thinks it's somewhere in Chicago.

He does not look at the Sheriff, but he listens carefully to the half of it he can hear.

"Hello, baby. . . . You okay? . . . Yeah, I'm down at the office . . . I didn't want to wake you up. . . . Larry got hisself in a scrape. . . . Oh, he's all right, but it's a damn mess. . . . I don't know. . . . Go ahead and have breakfast, I'll get something when I get home. . . . Okay, baby, I'll try to—'bye."

"What's the name of this here place?" He asks after a decent interval.

"Fairview, County of Coronado."

"I ain't never even been in Fairview before."

"What's your name?"

The prisoner laughs. "You'll find out soon enough."

The Sheriff paws over the wallets, papers, keys, and change. He studies the papers.

"This fella you were riding with, Tony De Angelo," he says, "what were you all up to?"

"Was that his name?"

"That's what it says here."

"Then what you gotta ask me for?"

"Just checking."

"I don't know much."

The Sheriff has picked up the revolver again. He opens the cylinder and empties the shells into his hands. He sniffs the muzzle again. "I know something. This pistol has been fired fairly recent."

"I don't know anything at all about that."

The prisoner grits his teeth now and sucks in a breath. What's the use? He speaks in a flat, soft, steady, outraged monotone:

"I was hitchhiking down the road, see? Fella stopped and picked me up maybe fifteen, twenty miles down the road from here, see? And we ain't had the time to do much more than exchange the weather and the bad news before your deputy came whaling up and run us clean off the road."

"You never saw him before?"

He laughs. Goddamn it to hell, he can't keep himself from laughing anymore since this morning. That's it, that's how come the young fella hit him. He must've started laughing right out there on the road. Well, it sure beats crying.

"It's a great big world, Sheriff. There's thousands and thousands of miles of it and all of it is outside of this crummy county."

The Sheriff's face doesn't change. He'll hit you when he has to, but he don't have to now. Big sonofabitch would probably make a hell of a poker player. You can't tell a thing he's thinking. Even that boy, Larry, he don't have a clue. He's liable to do most anything. He may be dumb and he may be smart, but one thing, you gotta pay something to look at his cards. He don't give nothing away until he's good and ready.

"You didn't have no idea it was a stolen car?"

"What do you think, Sheriff? Serious. He's going to pull up alongside me and say, 'Hop in, buddy-bo, if you don't mind taking a ride in a hot car'?"

"That's your story."

"It's the God's truth, Sheriff."

"Can you prove it?"

There it is again, the laughter again, bubbling up inside him like fizz water. Like he had to belch or something. Maybe it's like that, another kind of puking. The way a buzzard will puke on you. He coughs and clears his throat to stop it. Laughing ain't going to do nobody no good at all.

"You ought to be a detective, Sheriff. Like on the TV."

"Can you prove you didn't know the man?"

"What can I prove? Do I look like I could prove my right name?"

A pause. The Sheriff has got a bad habit of tapping on the desk with a pencil. Makes a man nervous. Just goes to show you the trouble you can get into if you take a country boy who ought to be following behind a plow or shoveling shit and make him go to school and learn how to read and write. He's liable to turn out to be a pencil tapper. Now he tries to listen to something else. He hears a fly bumping and buzzing against the window-

pane behind him. Somehow it's a sad sound for him like harmonica music or the cry of a far freight train in the middle of
the night.

"This fella tell you where he was going?"

"He said something about Daytona—Daytona Beach."

The Sheriff is writing it down on a piece of paper. He holds it
crudely. He holds on to the pencil tight like it was a carving
knife. Like he was going to carve Daytona Beach in the top of
his desk. He's writing it down so very careful. What's he gonna
do, preserve it for posterity?

"Where were you last night?"

"I don't have to tell you nothing."

"That's correct," the Sheriff says. "Were did you spend last
night?"

It's a funny thing about this fella. He's big and strong. He
don't have to like you. But he likes hisself enough so he ain't
going to bother to hate you. It's probably a fact this Sheriff
never hated anybody in his whole life. Oh, he can get mad. Mad
with righteous indignation. But he won't hate you. He's probably a religious man. Takes his wife or whoever else that "baby"
was, his wife, to church with him on Sunday and stands up
there in the choir and sings out with that voice filling the whole
church. A voice like that and he ought to sing.

"Nowhere," he says. "Nowhere with a name. The cold
ground was my bed last night."

That stops him up short. Whoa, boy! That raises his eyebrows. He is staring at the prisoner. See? He does listen to what
you have to say. Reacts to it sometimes. And that's a good thing
to know. And now the prisoner can feel the mood coming over
him, mastering him, getting away from him and running away.
He tries to fight it, but it's no use. What's the use? He throws
back his head, a kind of a high tilt of the chin with his eyes tight
closed and he opens his mouth and sings softly in a good clear
tenor voice:

> "Cold ground was my bed last night
> Just like the night before—"

Only a phrase from an old song, two lines from a kind of blues, white man's blues. But he feels better. Even the urge to laugh is gone. He leans forward, gripping his hands together, and looks the Sheriff in the eyes, intense.

"I been laughing, Sheriff. I couldn't help myself. I come in here laughing to keep from crying. A man don't get a whole lot of choice what he's going to do in this world. I come in laughing —I seen some things in my time, Sheriff, some terrible things, I swear to God. But in all of it I ain't never seen a man shot down right smack in front of me in the broad daylight. Like he was a mad dog—"

"Where are you coming from?"

The Sheriff, he ain't what you'd call happy, overjoyed about it neither. You can tell from the tone of his voice even if, as soon as he's talking at you, you gotta cut your eyes away and not be looking at him. You learn that the hard way. You've seen it in a dog, even a mean one, how you can stare him down. Don't let them treat you like a dog. Don't give them half a chance. And then you can still hold up your head when you walk out. If you had've seen the way his face looked, how he looked at that boy Larry when he come to find out there was a killing! But the young one's got a point too. If you was a cop, you wouldn't want to take no chances when you run a hot car off the road. Even if you didn't know it was hot then, not till you had done checked the license plates against the list. If you was a cop—God forbid *that*—you wouldn't want to take no chances at all. The big one though, Jack he's called, he don't carry a gun. At least he ain't got one on him now. No holster and no pistol belt. Probably don't believe in it. Probably fancies he don't have to. Big man like that, looks like he could yank a tree stump out the ground or pick up the back end of a automobile if you had to change a tire. Big sonofabitch and he ain't scared of a whole lot, surely nobody, at least nobody he's run into yet. And if you don't have a gun and everybody knows about it, then what kind of a man is going to work up the nerve to take a shot at you? It's like a spell or a charm. What if he don't kill you? What if he was to shoot and shoot and you just keep coming on like a movie

monster or something until you could get your big hands on
him and started to ripping the meat right off the bone? It ain't
all that brave, though, not as brave as it looks, though it takes a
brave man or a fool to try it in the first place. If you can get
away with it, you got the edge on an armed man. Make the man
with a weapon feel weak. The Sheriff, he ain't scared of a whole
lot. But one thing, he's scared of even thinking about that killing
out there on the highway. He don't even want to talk about it.
Right or wrong, he don't care. He don't like it even a little bit.

"Where are you coming from?" he asks again, not raising his
voice.

He's a patient man for a policeman. No wonder he can get
hisself elected.

"I was to hell and gone from here," the prisoner answers.
"Two days ago I was clear on the other side of Chattanooga,
Tennessee."

"Can you prove it?"

"You keep asking me that, Sheriff."

"I was hoping maybe you spent a night in jail or something. It
might help."

"What the hell do you care?"

And that's a fair question. A straight one. He's got no kind of
business caring. If he cares about a thing like that, wants it to be
so, it's a bad sign about him. He's gonna get hurt iffen he don't
wind up hurting somebody else first. Because, you know, a man
like that has got a tough job to do. It's a dirty job and if he starts
to caring one way or the other, look out everybody. Duck! Go
by the book, that's the only way. Because it just ain't true that
he can really care or should much about one car thief stretched
out dead that he ain't never even seen and another man sitting
in his office that he's only going to see this once in his lifetime.
You can't care that much. You can't hope for a stranger. The
Lord knows it's hard enough to give a shit about the people
you're supposed to love. And he knows that too. He's lived. He's
seen a few things naked in his life. What he must truly care
about, even though he may not know it yet, is that boy Larry.
That must really be hurting him. More than it ought to. Like he

had a stake in the boy. Like he is counting on him for something. Don't count on nothing, Sheriff, and you won't get disappointed. Couldn't you take one look in those eyes and see a killer? One look and see death? Why, sure. Surely you could. And he's been looking in them eyes a long time. *And he never even saw it!* And that's what it's all really about. What hurts the Sheriff is he has looked into the boy's eyes this morning for the first time and seen it and at the same time he seen it he knew it had been there all along, the whole time, and he had never even noticed it. He missed it until it was too late. You take a man's sense of his own judgment away from him, show him for the first time that he can guess so terribly wrong about somebody else, when his whole life depends on that strength, and it's like cutting the legs off a man. Why, the Sheriff must feel drunk now with his new knowledge! The whole world shifting and reeling around his head. Well, you was a virgin a long time, Sheriff. And ain't that a crying shame.

"Where are you headed for?"

"Where the spirit moves me and my feet can take me."

"Where's your home?"

"Where I hang my hat. If I had a hat—"

"What line of work are you in?"

He's tired, tired to death of it. He knows exactly where it is going, where it's all got to go. Which is nowhere.

"Why don't you just book me and print me and lock me up and forget about it?"

"I'm trying to make up my mind," the Sheriff says. "Maybe you did just happen to hitch a ride with a fella that just happened to be driving a hot car. Let's say that's so. If it is, I don't have a whole lot of business with you or time to waste on you. I'll personally drive you out in any direction as far out as the county line."

The sun is up good now. Coming in through the window behind his head. Has that old fly give up on it yet? Or is he just resting up a while, saving his strength so as he can buzz and beat his wings on the glass some more? Poor little old housefly, he ain't going nowhere. Ain't nobody going to personally drive him as far as the county line. It's getting real warm in the room. Gonna be a hot one. Sheriff is sweating already. You can see the dark half-moons of it spreading under his arms. You'd think they'd at least have a fan or something. Probably do, but it got busted and they ain't got around to fixing it yet. Or open a window maybe. He can hear the prisoners upstairs moving around and the banging of plates and cups and spoons. Maybe if he can just get out of this here sweatbox of an office, he can still get himself some hot breakfast and even stretch out a while on a mattress and take a nap before they make up their minds and run his fat ass out of the county.

"That's thoughtful of you, Sheriff," he is saying. "Considerate. I wouldn't have to lose no more time. And time is just about the only thing I got left to lose. The county here wouldn't have to waste no beans and bacon on me. And, naturally, I wouldn't be hanging around to testify at a inquest or anything like that."

That done it. Properly! The Sheriff looks mad now. Gone and got to him. See? Because he's got his pride, too, plenty of it. And he don't like to be in this fix. And he don't like to have to soft-talk and tell a lie. It isn't easy for him.

"Anything you might have to say wouldn't make any difference."

"I don't think so either," he says. "It just wouldn't all be so nice and neat if you know what I mean."

"Nobody would believe a word you said."

Now he's laughing out loud again and letting the words free. The words coming out in the room like a startled covey of flushed quail. Let 'em go:

"You right, Sheriff. Oh, you so right! I know exactly how a stranger and the word of a stranger would fare in a little old dried-up country town like this one here. Even if I was somebody, a lawyer or a banker, say, or a traveling salesman, even I was Our Lord and Savior Jesús Christ the Righteous, Who laid down His life even for the likes of me, and I come walking down the highway this morning preaching the Living Word of God!"

Now the Sheriff laughs, surprising him. "You some kind of a preacher or what?"

"Some folks might say so, but not the preachers," he says. "Lock me up. I'm all through talking."

The Sheriff, still grinning, shakes his head, truly amazed. Then he lifts the phone off the hook and, turning slightly in the swivel chair so that he doesn't have to look at the prisoner while he's talking and so that unless the prisoner is a very good, jail-house-trained listener, he won't hear what's being said, he dials and waits.

"Sheriff?"

"Huh?"

"What you waiting on?"

The Sheriff hangs up. He lights a cigarette. "Me? I'm just waiting for Larry to get back with that certificate."

"That might take a while."

"Maybe."

The Sheriff is dialing again.

"Sheriff?"

"Huh?" He's getting annoyed now. Messed him up in the middle of dialing and he's got to hang up and start over.

"You mind if I pick up my box out of the wastebasket?" Cutting his eyes toward the guitar and then away again quickly.

"Help yourself."

He can't help grinning to himself while the Sheriff dials again. The young one would probably bust it over his head right about now. The prisoner has been working at it, waiting to get his nervous hands on that box ever since he came in. You got to sneak up on something like that. Work all around it slow and easy. That old buzzard again circling up in the sky like a piece of burnt paper, biding his sweet time. Then the time comes and you pounce. Right time comes along and you can just ask right out and get a straight answer.

He slips out of his coat and hangs it on the back of the chair. Rolls up his sleeves over fat forearms to the elbows. Then moves to lift that box tenderly out of the wastebasket. Not a new scratch on it. Which is a blessing and a wonder, the way that boy was banging it around. Runs his hands up and down the neck and the body of it. Spanish-type guitar with a good woman shape. Real good Spanish guitar a long time ago to start out with. Bought it off a blind nigger in Galveston. Shipping out then in those days, working the Gulf. Been to many a place. Mexico, Panama, Cuba. Oh, lots of places. And that box was always good company. Only seen one just like it and that one a Cuban had in Ybor City down at Tampa and they stayed up all night playing and singing in a bar until the dawn come on and they walked back to the ship, playing and singing right down the street together and right up to the gangway and the last thing he seen was that Cuban standing all alone at the end of the wharf playing and singing while the ship pulled out. Ybor City, now that was a wild place in those days! You could see most everything. And boy you could eat there. All that good Spanish food, black beans and rice and chicken and all those things. Always did like Spanish people. Even Mexicans. Been through hell and high water, flood and fire, ever since then. Got tough old steel strings on it. Like to have nylon like the good guitar players do because it sounds better, though you got to learn to listen to it. Softer, but a whole lot better.

Tuning, he plucks one string very softly, with his ear right up next to the neck. He comes on down—E,B,G,D,A,E again. It's a way out of tune. He fiddles with it, till it's tuned as right as it will be. Then he plucks one string. The little sound thrills the drab room. He takes out his pick. ("What the hell is this?" the Deputy asked him when he searched him. "It's my pick. I use it to pick music on that 'ere box." "Well, that looks like all it's good for. You can't hurt nobody with it and you can't get nothing for it." "Can I keep it?" Magnanimous, positively *magnanimous:* "Why not?") Wishes he was good enough or anyway learned different so he didn't have to use it. That Cuban could play gypsy things and you could see the feet stamping down hard the skirts flaring out and the campfire burning and the bright eyes of the dark men in the night even if you had never even been there and never would get there either. Now he takes the guitar to him, hooking one heel over the rung of the chair, with the body of the guitar in his lap, his left hand on the frets and his right hand loosely held to pick or strum, bending his full-moon

face, a face as pocked and baggy-eyed and beat up as the man in
the moon, right up close to it, playing easy and soft, hardly more
than a little hum in the air and his voice so soft it might be
coming from a far distant place. The Cubans has got songs.
They all got music and songs. And so do we. All different, but
all saying the same things, saying the same big things anyway.
He plays along and sings a little country blues tune about not
owning anything and not being nobody, about being all alone
day after day on the open road and sleeping all alone on the cold
ground by night with the stars for your blanket and the hoot of
an owl or a distant freight train for your lullaby. It's a true song
for anybody, ain't it? Because we are all alone on that lonesome
road. And whether you sleep in a feather bed with a fine woman
beside you or you sleep on a hard mattress in a jail, it's all the
same, you sleep alone. You sleep alone and you die alone. Nobody knows where you come from or where you're going to.
And we're all strangers, the song says between the strict simple
lines, here on a tossed and whirling piece of rock lost in a black
sky. We're all strangers to each other and to ourselves. We don't
belong nowhere. And ain't that sad. And ain't that a crying
shame. But, wait a minute, don't go off blowing your nose and
feeling sorry for yourself. Because a sad tune makes you feel
happy. And you can think about all the good things, all the good
things around you that will be here long after you're gone and
was here too long before your daddy looked at your mama in a
certain way. You can think about trees and stars and stones and
cold water and sweet milk and the sun and the song of a bird.
You can't even call up all the good things there is. All you can
do, the sad tune is telling you, is rejoice, rejoice for the gift of
that little wink of light you call a lifetime. It'll be too late if you
wait till you're old and gray to find out. Sing a sad tune and
inside you something happy starts to happen like a bunch of
little children playing ring around the rosie right around the
broken rose of your heart. . . .

Even so, lost in his song and the exegesis of it, he's got one
trained ear cocked over to the Sheriff and his conversation, half
of it, with what seems to be a sergeant at the State Police Bar-

racks. Some people say you spoil things, doing two things at once. You don't have to. That's something about being a human being. You can do two, three, four, a dozen things at one time. Be here, yonder, and everywhere. Ybor City and the Taj Mahal in the moonlight and never even leave a room. Different from a machine that can do only one thing at a time. So he's playing and listening.

"Hello, Sergeant, this is Sheriff Jack Riddle down at Fairview. . . . Fine, thanks. How you? . . . Yeah, that's how it goes. . . . Listen, we picked up a hot car for you this morning. State plates Dog 71143. Registration Number 883620. Two people in it. Driver Anthony De Angelo, address Hotel Madison, Brooklyn, New York. Other one's a vagrant. Name of—Ike Toombs. . . . Yeah, double *o*. No address. . . . Yeah, we'll have prints and the rest of it for you later on this morning. Meantime give me a call if you get anything, huh? De Angelo's got eight hundred dollars in cash in his wallet and a gun. . . . Right!"

The Sheriff hangs up and swivels around again. As he does, Ike Toombs puts away his pick and strikes a loud, last, minor chord with his right hand. Puts the box down, leaning it against the wall.

"Looks like you already made up your mind."

"Just checking. Routine," the Sheriff says.

"You know something? I figured I'd be out of here by now."

"You may yet."

"You was asking me about my line of work."

"That's right."

"Well," he says with a fat, soft smile. "I don't do a whole lot of anything unless I have to. Work don't agree with me, see? I tried it once. Course when I need a little money—and everybody needs a little money now and then—I sing for it."

"Pass the hat?"

"I told you I don't own a hat. But that don't stop me. I strum on this little box and I sing songs. All kind of songs. Happy, sad, funny, every kind. Sheriff, I bet I know songs you never even heard of."

"They all sound about the same to me."

"Don't that go to show you! I picked you for a singing man yourself."

And now he picks up the guitar again and plays out loud and sings out with all his voice:

> "Some folks 'preciate a singing man.
> Some folks can't, but other folks can—"

Stops and his hands go slack on him and his fingers feel stiff. The song dies at birth as the sound of the siren screams up the driveway toward them. The Sheriff, angry as a hornet, is up off his chair and around the desk and over to the window, looking.

"Damn if that boy don't love the sound of that sireen," Ike Toombs says cheerfully.

Larry Berlin comes walking in the office wearing a great big grin, for some reason known exclusively to God and himself, waving a piece of paper. Which the Sheriff snatches out of his hand and ascertains to be the official death certificate dutifully signed, sealed, and delivered. That's how it all ends up—a piece of paper for the filing cabinet. And eventually for the closet. A piece of paper to yellow in silence and neglect and dust. Dust . . . It will outlast all of them unless the old place burns up or something. And even then, in all that confusion, somebody will probably risk his neck to save it.

"Sit down and type up your report," the Sheriff says, "before you forget what happened."

Larry Berlin shakes his handsome head to say *Jack Riddle, you're a case!* He goes around the desk and settles in the Sheriff's swivel chair. It's comfortable. He tests it, leaning back and twisting around while the Sheriff brings the typewriter from the corner and plunks it down in front of him. Larry Berlin looks at it and tests the keys, like a brand-new toy. The Sheriff fumbles around in the filing cabinet until he finds a stack of official forms he is looking for.

"What am I supposed to do with all these?" Larry asks, taking them.

"Six copies, boy. Everything serious comes in six copies. You know that."

Larry shrugs and ineptly tries to get the forms and the carbon paper lined up correctly in the typewriter.

"You want some help?"

"I got to learn sometime."

Finally gets everything in place, smiles, then rubs his hands and flexes his fingers like a concert pianist. Bending close to the machine, he begins by diffident hunt and peck to type out his report.

Ike Toombs has been watching all this with profoundly amused concentration. Kind of like watching a monkey play the piano or something. Worth seeing once. Now he is aware that the Sheriff has already asked him the question once and is repeating himself.

"You ever been busted? You ever done time?"

"I'm not denying it. You'll find out soon enough anyway."

"Maybe we could speed things up a little."

"What's the big hurry? Like I said, Sheriff, time is all I got plenty of."

The hesitant, stumbling noise of the typewriter, like a wounded insect rattling, stops. "Gimme five minutes with him, Jack."

"I'm still trying to make up my mind," the Sheriff says to Ike Toombs. Freed from the fortress of his desk, he paces restlessly up and down the small room, small for the length of his legs, pacing, idly picking up an object here and there, examining it without interest, without even really seeing what it may be that he has in his hands, but not looking at his prisoner directly. And speaking always in a soft, controlled voice. Like he was holding something back.

"I can't remember," Ike Toombs is saying. "I mean I been in jails and jails. All kinds of jails."

"How about the big ones?"

"Sheriff, I already told you I was all through talking."

Larry stops typing again. "Jack," he says, "you just walk outside and smoke a cigarette or something. Time you get back I'll have this smart mouth telling his whole life story."

"You finish up that report!"

"Lock me up! Lock me up!" Ike Toombs says. "I mean, I sure do enjoy you all's company, but I'm going be too late for a free breakfast."

At this moment the phone on the desk starts to ring. The sound fills the room, as shocking as a scream in the night. And for an instant all three men stop and stare at the small black instrument perched there smugly on the cluttered desk. They are tense, frozen. The sound of the phone seems to each of them and all together like a lewd interruption, a coarse fluttering tongue, a Bronx cheer offered in honor of them all.

It is Larry Berlin who picks it up. Listens: "Yeah, he's here—" Cupping his hand over the speaker, offering it to Sheriff Riddle, who comes to life himself now, grabbing for it. "It's for you, Jack. State Police—"

"Riddle, speaking."

And there is a long pause while he listens intently. His hard face has become impassive again, showing nothing, revealing no emotion or feeling, though he nods as though the speaker could see him and appreciate the gravity with which he is receiving the news. Ike Toombs and Larry Berlin sit still, watching him close for a sign of anything. The voice on the other end of the tense, strung line between here and somewhere else crackles in a steady, hurried rhythm.

"All right, I'll call you back," the Sheriff says. And hangs up. Gently, as if the phone were a delicate vase.

And then a curious thing happens. He stands bowed, staring at the cold, silent phone as if he expected it to come to life again, to rise up in the room like a wild bird and shriek at him. His face changes slowly as he stares, very slowly. He begins to smile. It is an expression Ike Toombs has not guessed the Sheriff is capable of. A slow, relieved softening of his puzzled, outraged features. All slowly softening like wax held too close to flame. As if now it all makes sense. Something has changed radically and something else has been restored to him. Something he thought he lost forever this morning has been returned to him by a single phone call from a stranger.

Ike Toombs grips the neck of his guitar. He feels a chill spreading over his flesh like a cold sweat. There is something about the Sheriff's smile that is like the smile of a man who has tasted something evil and found that it is sweet and good to eat. The Sheriff is a different man. Ike Toombs knows now, though he cannot let himself believe it yet, that he will not walk out of this office a free man. He won't walk away from this one with only a few little scratches and scars.

The Sheriff has turned away from both of them. He is pouring himself a cup of coffee. Carefully he takes two spoons of sugar and with that new smile fixed on his features, as if he now wore a stiff, painted, fierce mask, he is stirring and stirring. Finally he lifts it to his lips and takes a little sip, that's all, just a taste. He smacks his lips theatrically. He sets the cup down and lights a cigarette, inhaling deeply the first puff. Then he picks up Larry's magazine and unfolds the picture of the young blond lady with the towel. He stares at it, meditative, smoking.

Larry Berlin has long since shrugged and returned to his typing.

"Sheriff?" Ike Toombs says.

The Sheriff turns toward him and holds up the picture. "Ain't that something else?"

Ike Toombs blinks and looks at the picture. It means nothing at all and it means everything, too, if you think about it. Ike Toombs stares as if hypnotized. All the women he has ever known, in fact and in the rich harem of the imagination, are dancing before his eyes—whores and virgins, sluts and nuns, dark ones and light ones, skinny and fat, short and tall, without names and a few with names, and once, by God, even a wife with the name of Hyacinth, which is a name that sticks. Hotel rooms and boxcars, and once standing up in the men's room on a moving train, and barns, and the old green-grass hotel. And maybe he did and maybe he didn't because it all happened when he was young and strong and full of the juice of life which dries up just when you finally know how to use it. The old shuddering moment of *almost knowing* another human being, as close as you can come to knowledge. And the deprivation, the doing without until you learn it's one more thing you can do without, one less link on the chain you dangle from, that link by link he's pared down to where at last it's short enough now to tolerate. What is the Sheriff telling him? He's saying a lot of things at once like a song. But most of all he's telling him, Ike, we done got there. We got the thing stripped down pretty close to the naked truth. And he's saying something about life. There it is. Now you see it now you don't. Take a look because it may be your last one.

"I want to talk to you, Sheriff," he says. His voice sounds strange to him. He feels like he's a ventriloquist talking through a wooden dummy.

"I thought you were all through talking."

"A man is always willing to listen to reason."

The Sheriff throws the magazine away. It flies across the room in a flutter of pages and falls to the floor near the door. The girl's expression does not change. Now she's flat on her back looking at the ceiling.

"Well now, you just listen to this," the Sheriff says. If he had fangs, they would be showing now, Ike Toombs has come into the parlor of the spider, the lair of the wolf. "Seems like whoever it was in that car knocked over a little gas station in Ocala last night. And it seems like whoever it was had to go and shoot the kid that was working in the station. A high school kid. Seems like he is about to die on us."

Larry is banging the desk drawers, opening and closing them, rummaging irritably. "I can't find a freaking eraser."

"Seems like there may have been two men in that car," the Sheriff goes on evenly. "There's an eyewitness who says he is sure he saw two men in that car."

"Sheriff, I swear at the feet of God Almighty—!"

"Jack, do you know where an eraser is?"

"Ask Monk," the Sheriff snaps at him. "Maybe he's got one."

"You never can find anything around here when you need it."

Larry Berlin gets up and goes out. His heels click as he goes.

Ike Toombs is amazed. How come he didn't even notice that before? Taps on his boots, naturally. He would wear taps. But he never even noticed it until now. Where has he been—asleep? Has the shock numbed him out like a drug? The sound of those taps takes the heart out of him.

He rises to his feet slowly. His legs feel weak and rubbery. "You mind if I take you up on that coffee now?"

"It's cold."

"I don't care," Ike Toombs says with a little giggle. "Just as long as it's wet."

Sheriff Jack Riddle watches the man the way you might observe the undulant motions of a snake in a glass case. A fat and shabby shiftless bum with his guitar and the color and pallor of jailhouses around him like an invisible cloak. And the softness, the sag and jiggle of his belly, the soft, white, fish-belly hands, the loose jowls and the rings and rolls of it cropped up around his neck, the softness is disgusting. Probably got titties like a woman. And a little pecker like a cigarette. All the envy and pity he first felt for him has gone. Half an hour ago, ten minutes ago even, and he might just as well have turned the fella loose. Not just to save young Larry and the Sheriff's office from a bad name, though that was something to think about. But to set him on his way again. Because with all his smart mouth and the stain of toughness (which, soft or hard, is nothing more than the ability or the willingness to take a fair share of punishment) on him, he looked harmless. Just had the itch in his toes and on the soles of his feet to keep moving on across the dull, settled land. Never staying anywhere for long. Always a traveler. Always living in a world where everything was exactly what it seemed to be because that's all you ever had to know about any of it. Thus in a way childlike. Like a child for whom elves are as real as rocks on the ground.

This lack of the burden of sad knowledge is enviable to the Sheriff, who has spent most of his life in Fairview. Slowly, veil by veil, the truth has been revealed to him whether he has wanted it that way or not. Even though he has chosen to live by noble illusions. For what is Justice, he thinks, with all its elaborate machinery and ritual if not the strict preservation of the illusion of the possible freedom and rationality of man? And he has become, by custom and ceremony and long usage and experience, the protector of illusion, guardian of the secret nakedness. High priest of a veiled goddess. Obedient servant of the little, flimsy illusions of respectability and decency the townspeople live by and for. Without that, he is thinking, what do they have left to worship in a bad world? The world came through in a fast car. The world came into town in the morning paper and on the TV. Lying with a smile and killing with a kiss. The world had an Italian name and lived in a cheap hotel in Brooklyn, New York. The world passed overhead, so faint you couldn't see it, leaving a vapor trail behind. He stands between the world and them. Oh, he is all too familiar with their vices and stifled virtues. But he has remained the steadfast preserver of those secrets and their illusions. Because without them, he knows and believes, life would be unbearable.

He had envied, though, to the point of admiration, the lucky ignorance that allowed a man like this one, this Ike Toombs, if that is even his right name, the freedom of almost complete indifference. Innocence, ignorance, indifference, a few songs in his head like pennies in a purse. There was a kind of purity about it. That, too, was an illusion that seemed well worth preserving.

He has been wrong this time. In his own ignorance, the supreme ignorance of believing that after a certain time and a certain number of wounds and scars a man can faithfully trust his own judgment. He has failed even in his duty. He knows that he can say that much for Larry Berlin (about whom he has guessed wrong too), he may not have had a clue what he was doing when he did it; but when he drew his pistol and shot Anthony De Angelo, whoever he was or might have been, without a question, as reflexively as a trained watchdog attacks a prowler, he was right. He should have killed the both of them.

"You about made up your mind to answer some questions, huh?"

The prisoner, drinking his coffee, clears his throat and nods.

"All right, let's back up. How many times you been busted?"

"There's a lot of them. A lot of little ones."

"I can imagine," the Sheriff says. "Just give me the big ones. To the best of your recollection."

"Well, they got me one time, a long time ago, on assault with a deadly weapon. I was nothing but a fresh-faced kid then. Middle of the Depression. This guy was in plainclothes. He come running at me in the freight yard. I didn't know—"

Plainclothes, hell! He looked like a bum hisself. What would you do? He come running and hollering with a big stick in his hand. That was in Meridian, Mississippi. Which was a helluva tough town in those days.

"What else?"

"I didn't have no way of knowing he was a railroad bull," the prisoner says with sudden vehemence and complaint.

"What else?"

"Well now, the other one, the other big one. . . . It was what you'd call a kind of a rape, Sheriff. What I mean is, me and the lady in question, we had a little misunderstanding."

The memory of it tickles him. He can even laugh about that now.

"Is that all?"

"It's about enough, ain't it?"

Indignation is in that answer. You can take away a lot, but don't take away jail pride. He's done his time, walked in and walked out where many a man couldn't. Don't make light of his suffering and endurance. A man has little enough to comfort himself with.

"It's enough," the Sheriff says calmly. "Probably put you smack in the slammer for life on this felony murder."

"Oh Jesus—"

"You don't much like jail, do you?" the Sheriff says, that hard mask with the fixed smile on his face again. "A fella like you, a bum, a drifter, a singing man. You been in and out of plenty of jails. And you tough enough to take it too. But you never got to like it. You got to have your freedom."

"What are you trying to do, Sheriff. What do you want?"

The door flies open behind them and they whirl around to see Larry Berlin saunter in, smiling again, holding up for everyone to see the source of his smile, a small typewriter eraser.

"Got it."

"Jesus Christ," the prisoner says.

Ike Toombs is stunned. All his life he has been acting on the hopeful assumption that if you can just keep your hands more or less clean, if you never care too deeply or obviously about anything and therefore have nothing to be deprived of, you can lose only bits and pieces at a time. No more than time and the natural process of change and decay will deprive you of anyway, one way or the other and without asking your permission. It's the way of the world. He has philosophically learned to include injustice in the grand design and even learned to accept it. Like rain on your head. Like a stroke of bad luck. Freed in this way, freed from the fear of loss, he has been able to live and look after himself. A wily, wary life like a small scurrying rodent with sharp teeth. Alert, agile, dodging when he can and taking it when he has to. But total loss. Loss, the ultimate blind injustice of going all this way on his aimless pilgrimage only to find that something beyond belief was patiently waiting for him all the time, is hard to bear. He has propitiated. He has atoned to the greater and the lesser gods. He has lived poor and alone, offering up his unattractive body and all of the things valued in the world, in return for which he has claimed only the right to live out his time. But now, he thinks, there never was a bargain. His whole life has been the working out of an equation designed to prove that life itself is ridiculous.

This morning he has seen sudden death. Not for the first time in his life, but what a way to begin this day! He has seen himself able to cause a good man (for he has been convinced ever since he was first pushed blindly into the small room that the Sheriff is a good man and that that will be his salvation) to reveal pure and naked cruelty. Reveal a hidden hatred, hidden even from himself. He has been able to bring that out of the Sheriff like a dentist yanking a rotten tooth. He has been forced to be witness to the undeniable truth that the young deputy is neither cruel nor vicious, but merely possessed of a mindless, visceral brutality which might even be defined as innocence. It is an innocence which makes the young deputy, who just happened to be riding along the road at the same time, the exact and perfect instrument for the working out of Ike Toombs's fate.

He would curse and shake his fist in God's face now if he could. But who has ever seen the face of God?

Still, he is not defeated yet. They haven't tried, convicted, and locked him up forever. He still has chances and alternatives. He has the alternative of pleading for himself. A cry of mercy may be alms enough even to satisfy the good Sheriff. And it seems that the Sheriff may offer him this role.

"I'm still thinking to myself," the Sheriff says. "I can turn you loose. There's no reason in the world not to believe you. You ain't got nothing real to connect you with a holdup in Ocala."

"That's right. You didn't find nothing on me. No weapon, no money—"

"Or then again, I can do my duty and lock you up. Leave it to a jury to decide what to think about your story."

"You know what a jury will think."

"You never can tell."

Ike Toombs swallows hard. There is still the alternative of Job. Accepting even this and in so doing to be freed of the last humiliation. Or he can give the Sheriff what he wants, go on and say what he wants to hear. Acting on the unlikely supposition that the Sheriff hasn't already made up his mind, is not already confirmed in his will. Hoping that he can still be fooled and deluded. If he is right, he will save his life. And if he is wrong again, he will have paid out everything for nothing.

That's what it all adds up to, he thinks. *Nothing! Well now, you can't take nothing away from nothing. I went far enough in school to know that much.*

"You're kinda like God in this county, ain't you, Sheriff? You say, let this one go, he don't interest me. And you say, lock that one up cause I don't like his ugly face."

"I'll tell you the truth, I don't much like your looks."

"It don't matter, Sheriff. I never did want to be a movie star."

Larry Berlin laughs out loud. "You know something, Jack? He's pretty funny."

"You're lucky you're not dead," the Sheriff says. "You could just as well be laying there right alongside of your Brooklyn buddy in the icebox."

"I never even saw that fella before this morning," Ike Toombs says. "He had a nice friendly smile. That's all I remember."

He is remembering how it was now, coming out of the pine-woods where he slept under a kind of lean-to he rigged out of some branches, with soft, sweet-smelling pine needles for his bed. He slept good, woke once in the middle of the night because a mockingbird was singing his fool head off in the dark nearby, and fell back into a deep sleep. Woke stiff and came on out of the woods to the edge of the road while it was still night-time and the last stars were still out and the air was full of rich woodsy smells. Using a piece of old clothesline for a string, he slung his guitar across his back and set out walking slow and easy along the shoulder of the road. Walked along a good piece, feeling the stiffness coming out of his joints and legs as he moved, felt almost young again, as he often did with a good dawn and a great stretch of road in front of him. Walked along until that white car came and stopped for him.

He was a nice, smiley, soft-spoken fella. A big guy, but he talked soft. A Yankee, but most mannersable and polite for one. Probably a traveling salesman or something, either got up real early or been driving all night, and was lonesome for the sound of a human voice.

It don't take you too much time to make up your mind do you like somebody or not. You don't, you can't never know what a man you meet was like before, what kind of things he done in the past. And once he drops you out the car and leaves you by the side of the road and is gone for good, the future, his future, belongs only to him also. So what do you have to go by? He gives you a cigarette and you talk along a little bit about the weather and the road. He is sick of listening to the radio and turns it off to talk to you. He's got a real nice smile. Good teeth, and he's lucky for that. You know him for about half an hour maybe on the highway and the only things you got to know and judge by are good. And then here come a po-lice car running down on you from out of nowhere. And then the man is all of a sudden different. He's clean forgot about you. All he's thinking about is running for it, outrunning the cop. All the time that souped-up car is gaining. De Angelo has another little smile on his face. Maybe because he seen when it come close enough that there wasn't but one man in the car chasing them. He starts slowing down. And then just about that time Ike Toombs looks across and sees the pistol in the shoulder holster. Thinking, *Either, I hope to the Lord, he's a cop hisself, or else he's some kind of a gangster.* And there ain't a whole lot left to do but scrunch down real low in the seat and hope for nothing except that whatever happens neither one of them takes it in mind to shoot you, too, while they're at it. Or maybe just accidentally blow your head off.

"I don't care nothing about what kind of a smile he had," the Sheriff says.

"Yes, sir, you can sit here in this crummy office in the stinking jail and let somebody else, somebody like this young fella here, do your worrying and your dirty work for you. Let me tell you something, Sheriff. You might just as well have pulled that trigger your own self."

"People like you make me sick to my stomach."

Which is literally true. Sheriff Jack Riddle feels sick. He feels like throwing up in the wastebasket. He is thinking about the type of which this Ike Toombs is a single, miserable example. Without roots, without ties, without anything. They are worthless. Scum! Fungus on the tired face of the earth! They breed like maggots, feeding on dead things. Bounce aimless across the country landing one place and another like grasshoppers. A plague of grasshoppers! Might just as well have never been born.

"What about him?" the prisoner says.

"Who?"

"That old drunk you turned loose when we first come in."

"He can't help himself."

"You mean you can't help him," the prisoner says. "But it don't make no difference. He needs you and you need him around."

"I don't need you around."

"Turn me loose, then," the prisoner says, laughing. "Turn me loose!" Then he is serious again, but unable to resist faintly smiling at his enemy: "He's going to keep on coming back and you're going to keep on giving him his freedom. Because it makes you feel good. And, you know, the funny thing is a poor old fella like that, he's scared to death of his freedom."

Dirty scum spreading across the world! Corruption! You've got all the rest of it, but then you have to come here, even here, a quiet little old town trying to die slowly in peace. With nothing for you. Where you're not known or wanted. And you've got to bring trouble and violence and bad news with you. Like a sickness. A contagious disease. People like you ought to be purged off the face of the earth—

"Jack? You just going to stand around and listen to all that shit?"

"I ain't going to listen anymore," the Sheriff says.

He goes to the door, yanks it open, and shouts into the hall. "Monk! You, Monk!"

"You won't have to listen to me no more," the prisoner says. "Once I go out through that door, I'm gone."

"Monk! I'm calling you!"

"For something I never done."

"It's out of my hands."

Young Larry Berlin has finally finished up filling in all the required blanks on the form. The only thing he's got left to do is to fill up the blank space labeled "Remarks" where it says you are supposed to give the details of what happened in your own words. He is feeling pretty good. Lucky and glad to be alive. Before this morning he has never actually fired a weapon at anyone. But he feels no remorse. After all, it's what the county gives him an expensive pistol for. It's why he has to spend so much time over on the State Police Range learning how to use it. Why in the hell would they spend money on something, give it to you, teach you how to use it, spend all that time and money, and then, when the time came, expect that you wouldn't do anything? He wasn't wearing that pistol and keeping it all clean and everything just for decoration.

He took after that car because it was speeding, breaking the law. He didn't know it was a hot one until afterwards. He wasn't thinking about anything at all then except giving the driver of that car holy hell. Chewing him out for driving that fast and giving him a ticket. Even if it was just dawn and the road was empty. What if some farmer was to come out on the road in a tractor or a wagon? He wouldn't expect nothing to be coming at him that fast and he couldn't see good in that kind of light anyway. So he run the car down and got out. And here come the driver. Then it all happened just the way you practice for it, just like they teach you. Like on a cowboy show on the TV. Or something. The big guy is going for a gun and you don't even have to think (if he had to think he'd be pushing up daisies), you reach down and find the pistol in the holster right where it ought to be and it comes out and up in a smooth fast motion. He shot fast and well. And that was a good thing to know you could do, to count on if you ever needed it. Because if you goofed the first time, you wouldn't be around to try it twice.

It's just like hunting. Shooting a deer or a squirrel or a rabbit. And it don't make any more mess than that either. If you shoot a gun at an animal you better expect to look at some blood. And, anyway, he had seen a plenty of things on the highway, right after an accident, that looked a hell of a sight worse than that did. People call you a killer if you gun somebody, even just trying to protect yourself—and ain't that the first law of nature or something? But a man drunk behind the wheel of a car, he don't call himself a murderer just because he busts somebody open like an egg on the highway.

Maybe the old bum was telling the truth. Maybe the driver was just trying to get rid of that pistol. Throw it down on the road. Well, that was his lookout. He didn't have no business carrying it around with him in the first place. He doubts it, though. If he shot the kid over at Ocala, he wouldn't be so anxious to get rid of it.

Jack has sure bugged him this morning. Giving him a bad time about everything. Jack won't carry a gun and that's his business. He can take his chances if he wants to. This morning, though, without one on him his luck would have run out. Maybe he knows that now. Maybe it will put the fear of the Lord in his soul. You can sit on your ass around a place like Fairview and forget about a lot of things. Everybody knows who you are. You got a name and a reputation and you probably won't need a weapon. But then when somebody comes barreling in, driving a hot car and running for his life from a robbery you don't even know about yet, way down the road, he's going to cut you down without stopping to ask your name, rank, and serial number.

This won't hurt things for Larry around this county either. He's young and new at the job, but he can't stand in the shadow of Jack Riddle forever. And he isn't planning to. Now everybody will know he's his own man.

Jack is fit to be tied by the time Monk finally gets there. He's blinking his eyes. Probably been sacked out somewhere in an empty cell.

"Where in the hell have you been?"

Monk just grins and shrugs. One look at Jack's face and he knows better than to try and come up with some kind of excuse or story. Monk may be dumb, but he's smarter than that.

"Take this man upstairs and lock him up—solitary."

Monk nods, then tips his head for the prisoner to come along with him. The prisoner takes a step, then hesitates. He's a sly one, all right, but he ain't feeling so good now. He turns back to face Jack. Which is what you'd have to call a mistake.

"Can I keep my box with me?"

How dumb can you get? He could have walked right out the room with it and nothing would be said. Jack's so pissed off he wouldn't even notice. When you go out of your way to ask for trouble, the odds are pretty good you're going to get some.

"I don't want none of your music around here."

The stupid sonofabitch is begging him now. Honest to God. Tears in his eyes and everything.

"Lemme keep it," he says. "Please. I can't live without my music."

What do you think Jack does? Finally blows his top. Goes sky high, red in the face, foaming mad. You'd have to see it to believe it because it don't happen often. Monk's pop-eyed.

"Give him a comb, Monk," Larry says quickly. "Maybe he can blow some music on a comb."

You got to give it to the prisoner. Once it's gone, it's gone. He quits crying like you shut off the water valve and he slips on his coat that don't fit worth a damn and tries to suck in that belly and hold up his head. Ever see a big fat slob trying to look dignified?

"Let's go, fella," Monk says.

But the prisoner, he's waiting for something more from Jack. He shakes his head and stands there staring at Jack like Jack owed him something. Jack don't want to give him the time of day. He's all through being mad, but he's finished and done with the fella. He ain't going to stand there and let him stare at him, though.

"Anybody you want notified?"

Then the nutty old fool commences to laughing again. That laugh could bug you right out of your mind if you listened to it long enough.

"Answer me!"

"Nobody worth mentioning," he says.

And then Monk takes his arm and they go out with the prisoner holding his head up very high. Once they get outside the door he gets another laughing fit and you can hear the old fool laughing all the way up the stairs.

Jack is wandering all around the office looking at everything like he never saw it before. He stoops down and picks up the guitar and puts it in the wastebasket. He stops and looks at the calendar, cusses, and rips the page off because it's a month old. He picks up the magazine and starts to crumple that up too.

"Hey, Jack, that's my magazine."

"Take it," he says, throwing it. "Keep it out of sight. What do you leave a thing like that laying around for?"

He comes over and takes the phone and calls Betty. Won't be home right away, he says. Got a lot to do.

Larry Berlin is thinking maybe if he can finish this report Jack will let him go awhile. Paul is coming on duty any minute now. No reason why he should have to hang around all morning.

Jack is over there in the closet on his hands and knees fumbling around. After a while he kind of backs out. He stands up. Got a silly grin on his face. He's got something in his hands. A beat-up old leather belt with a holster on it. He puts it on. Goes to the filing case and pulls out a pistol, checks it to see is it loaded, and stuffs it in the holster. Can you beat that?

Then he walks over to the window. There's a fly over there buzzing against the pane. Jack cups his hand to catch him. He's quick, very quick hands for such a big man. Catches that fly and holds him in the cup of both his hands. Then he opens the window with one hand and leans out and lets the fly go.

The fresh air feels good. Takes some of the stink out of the room. It's not even the middle of the morning yet, so it's not too hot. They have the sprinklers on over by the Courthouse. Greenest grass in town except for the cemetery. Jack is still leaning out the window.

"Jesus, Lord in Heaven," he says.

"What's wrong, Jack?"

He turns around. "I feel so old and tired," he says.

Damn if he don't look wore out this morning.

"Aw, you got a lot of mileage left."

"We got work to do, boy. We got a lot of work to do on this thing."

"Yeah, I guess so."

"I feel like an old man."

He tucks in his shirt and hikes up his trousers. Puts on his hat.

Must be going home after all to clean up and have something to eat.

"Hey, Jack," Larry says. "How do you spell incident? One *n* or two?"

"How the hell would I know?" Jack yells at him. "Look it up in the freaking dictionary."

"All right, all right, all right. I was only asking."